Ganymede

a novel

Terrence Douglas

iUniverse, Inc.
Bloomington

Ganymede

Copyright © 2011 by Terrence Douglas

All rights reserved. No part of this book may be used or reproduced by any means, graphic, electronic, or mechanical, including photocopying, recording, taping or by any information storage retrieval system without the written permission of the publisher except in the case of brief quotations embodied in critical articles and reviews.

This is a work of fiction. All of the characters, names, incidents, organizations, and dialogue in this novel are either the products of the author's imagination or are used fictitiously.

iUniverse books may be ordered through booksellers or by contacting:

iUniverse
1663 Liberty Drive
Bloomington, IN 47403
www.iuniverse.com
1-800-Authors (1-800-288-4677)

Because of the dynamic nature of the Internet, any web addresses or links contained in this book may have changed since publication and may no longer be valid. The views expressed in this work are solely those of the author and do not necessarily reflect the views of the publisher, and the publisher hereby disclaims any responsibility for them.

Any people depicted in stock imagery provided by Thinkstock are models, and such images are being used for illustrative purposes only.

Certain stock imagery © Thinkstock.

ISBN: 978-1-4620-6208-9 (sc)
ISBN: 978-1-4620-6206-5 (e)
ISBN: 978-1-4620-6207-2 (dj)

Library of Congress Control Number: 2011919780

Printed in the United States of America

iUniverse rev. date: 11/8/2011

PROLOGUE

You who dwell in Lebanon,
Nested in the cedars,
How you will groan when pangs come upon you,
Pain like a woman in childbirth!

Jeremiah 22:23

    Colin usually woke before dawn, and today was no exception. He rolled out of the king-sized bed in the loft of his three-bedroom home, dressed in a pair of jeans, and within minutes was on his way to the beach on a frosty November morning. From his home, located only a couple of hundred yards from the ocean, he would greet the rosy-fingered dawn that Homer wrote of in his Odyssey in all the seasons of the year.

    Chris, his wife of fifty years, had passed away suddenly almost five years ago. Not long after her death, he relocated to the desolate region of the Outer Banks amidst wild ponies and sand roads that connected the few homes built among the dunes. Perhaps it was a sign of recovery from grief that he would say that he was not lonely—just alone. Those who knew him when he roamed the world pursuing terrorists or Soviets for intelligence might disagree.

He spent his days reading, writing, and reflecting upon life—some would say meditating. Few visited him because of his isolation, but he communicated with friends, his children, and his grandchildren through the Internet and phone calls. His time of driving ten hours without a break ended a few years ago when he found it difficult to endure the long road trips. The distance to the nearest airport served his self-imposed isolation as well.

He had gotten to relish the silence that surrounded him. It appeared to encourage his connection with an inner presence that he seemed to have misplaced years earlier. Chris used to say that he was a closet introvert who learned to lie on the psychological assessment exams so he could test as a fully engaged extrovert with strong interpersonal skills—basic personal characteristics for a spy.

He remembered the first time she shared this observation. They had just returned from a diplomatic reception in Warsaw where they mingled freely with the guests, snacked on the offerings, and drank Campari soda so as not to become inebriated for the reception to follow. Only she spotted an unease he so carefully disguised. Rather than object, he remembered laughing involuntarily, thus acknowledging the accuracy of her perception. She never revealed the secret to others because she wanted nothing to interfere with the world travel that took them throughout Europe, the Middle East, and Asia.

As a CIA officer, he was trained to troll the crowds to see if he could identify someone whose position suggested access to sensitive information and who appeared open to a more discreet contact. Colin would cultivate, if successful, recruit the individual to become an agent. Later it was his sacred duty to ensure the agent's security. The latter was a daunting challenge when the agent was operating in a hostile setting such as Beirut during its civil war.

On the beach the pink ribbon of dawn was just beginning to crease the horizon out across the flat sea. The moon was still over his shoulder in the west, as if to share in welcoming the sunrise.

There was no breeze. He was alone, standing in the sand, planning to catch that first glimpse of the hot lava brightness that would transform darkness into light.

And in those minutes that remained, his mind, or was it his heart, recalled his dear friend and agent, Hans, who once stood on the sand of the Mediterranean Sea in Beirut during the time of the civil war, forty years ago, awaiting execution. Though so much time had passed and he was standing six thousand miles from where Hans once stood, Colin felt a kinship with him as the past seemed to disintegrate into a present moment of time. With no resistance, he allowed himself to go back over the life-changing events that Hans—or Ganymede, as was his code name—represented to him even to this day.

*Ganymede is the cupbearer of the gods
and Zeus's beloved in Greek mythology.*

CHAPTER ONE

The scrape of the leather boots as they pushed aside the metal debris on the street could be heard in the stillness that precedes the dawn. Once a dark chocolate brown, they were now so deeply scuffed at the toes and along the sides that they had become a sandpaper tan. The original laces had been replaced with a garish red variety, since the boots had been pulled off the body of a soldier who had fallen in some nameless firefight in the middle of the city.

The young man wearing the boots was as anonymous as the battles in which he had fought. He was slight of build and gangly. His erect posture made him appear taller than his height. He was no more than sixteen years old. The dark hair above his lip and the occasional blemish of an adolescent were all that marred his smooth olive-complexioned face. His stride was even and purposeful. Yet one noticed that there was a weariness about him, or maybe it was caution in the almost indistinguishable pause as he brought forward one foot to replace the other.

Every fifteen steps or so he stopped in place and shifted his head slightly to gather in any sound around him—it was not light enough to detect much with his eyes. Still erect, he moved forward again, staying close to the pockmarked building line on his right. From time to time he brushed against the crushed concrete of a building front, creating a chalk-like smudge on his dull green fatigue jacket. It was zipped up against the early morning chill. The sleeves of an oversized gray sweatshirt were visible. He had pulled them down over his hands in place of gloves. He wore nothing on his head so as not to impair his hearing.

Slung over his left shoulder on a thick black leather strap was a rifle. It looked oversized for one so young. He had rescued it from a companion who was mortally wounded six months earlier. The weapon was a precision instrument that he had learned to care for as he once cared for a guitar in a more peaceful time. He recognized early that while the guitar promoted popularity with friends, the rifle gained respect from his elders.

Reaching the top of the hill, lined on either side by abandoned buildings, the young man paused again. With the suddenness and surprise of a mountain cat, he crouched and turned silently into the entrance of what was once a prosperous ten-story office building. The decorative wooden doors had long since been carted off for firewood. He walked up the marble steps into the lobby littered with pieces of furniture that had not survived the frenzied looters. He could not avoid the broken glass that crunched beneath each step. He proceeded directly to the stairwell on the right and began his ascent to the top floor. Gray light filtered through the window frames, shattered in rage by competing factions who alternately occupied the building.

He was not winded when he reached the top floor. Before he ascended further up the service staircase to the roof, he urinated against the wall. He then mounted the last twenty steps, dropping to his knees before he reached the top. The metal door had been pulled from its hinges long ago to allow easy access to the roof. He swung the rifle smoothly off his shoulder. The cold metal awakened his hands, which still bore stains from the cleaning oil. He removed the protective cloth from the sniper scope and snapped a single round into the firing chamber. On his stomach, knees, and elbows he crawled across the rooftop to a gargoyle decorating the edge of the parapet. He brought the rifle forward and into position in his left arm, and with his right hand he delicately released the safety. He spread his legs wide to allow as much comfort and stability as possible on the cold, hard surface of the roof.

The sun was beginning to inch above the horizon formed by the sea behind him. With the light, an expanse—the equivalent of six square city blocks—of shattered buildings stretched before and below him. All of this area was just across the Green Line in enemy territory. In an hour or so, the rising sun would bring warmth, but he would barely notice the difference. The gray of the false dawn slowly receded, and a clearer source of light crept over the rooftops and touched the crevasses of the city. He had selected at random an intersection below upon which to train his rifle that morning. Unhurriedly he moved the rifle into position and waited.

Three hours passed. In that time, the sun emerged, and with it a hazy blue sky became visible. The squawk of gulls could be heard faintly, the sound lifted as if it were on the strong breeze from the sea. A growl sounded in the distance as a generator started. Life was beginning to stir in the tortured terrain before him, though he yet perceived no movement. He waited. His right eye looked through the high-powered scope, which made it possible for him to select targets over a thousand yards downrange. From time to time he closed his eyes gently for a moment to avoid eyestrain. His shoulders and the rest of his body remained in position. Hours could and often did go by, yet he never experienced a muscle cramp or spasm.

In the fourth hour the furrows on his forehead deepened. Two dark-clad individuals negotiated their way cautiously through his preselected intersection. They were both dressed in long, loose-fitting overcoats. It was impossible to determine their age or gender. Without hesitation, he focused his sight on the individual trailing and squeezed the trigger purposely. The recoil jolted into his shoulder but did not interrupt his concentration or follow-through. The report from the rifle resounded in the cavern of cement and steel.

The intended victim fell. The second doubled back to assist and became a similarly inviting target, but the shooter on the roof was not greedy. Tomorrow was soon enough. He watched as the individual struck by the burst of metal was pulled out of the line of fire. At that moment he turned his eyes to the right, to that familiar, faded sign with the huge unintelligible letters painted on the side of the neighboring building.

Welcome to Beirut

CHAPTER TWO

It was late November as four elderly men sat huddled in the rear of the Bacchus Restaurant in East Beirut. They were there to share the grief of one of their number whose wife had been slain by a sniper three weeks earlier. Against his advice, Pierre Kettaneh, known as Kalenti, accompanied his wife to place flowers at the site on the Green Line where their son was slain in combat on that date the previous year. They were crossing a street in the abandoned section of the city when Kalenti heard the whine of the bullet. His worst fears were confirmed as he whirled around to see his wife of forty years drop to the pavement. Deep red blood poured through her overcoat from the gaping wound in her chest.

Anger and the desire for revenge permeated the silence that engulfed these old friends and comrades. But against whom would they strike? The assassin and his group, if he was not working independently, were as nameless as the victim to the person who pulled the trigger. No group had claimed responsibility—not that it mattered. This was the depth to which the barbarity had descended. No longer was the violence directed against one faction to right a real or imagined slight. Now, random acts of violence became evidence to the moral corruption and the disintegration of the society's fabric.

The murder of another unarmed civilian on the street—and this was by no means an isolated incident—kept constant the level of fear under which a whole generation of Lebanese citizens existed. These senseless killings sustained a feeling of despair within a population held hostage. They were unable to comprehend how their once-sophisticated society had descended into such depravity. The feeling was not unlike the sadness and helplessness one feels about victims of mob violence.

There in the Bacchus four old men sat—a confraternity of elders—in a conversation of silence while they witnessed the destruction of their cherished city. Prior to the outbreak of fighting on the streets, they used to meet each Thursday afternoon at the Café Suisse in West Beirut. There Lebanese bankers and financial traders from London, Geneva, New York, Tokyo, Dusseldorf, and Amsterdam nurtured their contacts. Those were the days when one could hear above the bustle of a late-afternoon meal the harmony of French, Arabic, and English acclaiming an appreciation of the good life.

Now, in the waning days of The Lebanon, few public dining rooms remained open, and then only when the fighting subsided for the litter to be cleared from the streets, produce delivered, and the owners emboldened sufficiently to return to their establishments. Before the war beautiful women were distinguished by haute couture; now in West Beirut they were subdued in purdah. Now the once-luxurious hotels and those of quiet elegance perched along and above the Mediterranean Sea—at least those that were still standing—provided shelter to impoverished Arab refugees.

In the Bacchus, its walls painted a garish yellow, the old men were safely ensconced in a Christian enclave. The smell of stale cooking oil from the kitchen lingered in the air. There they pondered the fate of their country, faith, and heritage. In a shared feeling of helplessness and despair, they discounted the present and lived in the past. During these desperate years, they had become like a chorus on stage, witnessing aloud the disintegration of their country.

"My brothers, without your presence and support I would be reduced to despair." Kalenti was the first to speak. He reached across the table and rested his hands on theirs.

"You were present as we greeted the birth of my son, as well as his burial, and now the murder of my wife, the mother of my son." Again, no words interrupted the deep emotions experienced. With all the sorrow of the last years, they had become skilled in the art of listening.

Kalenti was the informal leader of this group. His family had once been a prominent influence in the local business community and was equally well recognized among the Gulf State Arab sheikhs and members of the Saudi royal family who had once sought to invest their income from oil revenues. A patrician, Western-educated, Kalenti was greatly respected among the Lebanese Christians, both those who remained as well as those who fled the country following the outbreak of the civil war when brutal fighting erupted between Christian and Moslem factions. His family's home in the mountains was said to have been constructed over the foundation of their ancestral home, whose origin dated back to the time of the Crusades. They were equally respected for the influence the family held within the Maronite Catholic Church and the support provided even to the present time.

"Enough grieving." Kalenti released their hands.

"We go forward with our plan. There is no turning back. The torture of The Lebanon must cease."

"Are we agreed?" He looked around slowly, allowing his deep-set eyes to rest on each of his companions separately, deliberately, before moving to the next. They solemnly nodded their consent. The men were dressed in dark, European-cut suits that appeared worn and almost threadbare. Each man was protected by heavily armed bodyguards who sat in close proximity at a nearby table. Together they were the only occupants of the restaurant.

"We can no longer limit our response to retaliation and revenge. Such a strategy is leading nowhere except to impoverishment as we are besieged by illiterate infidels. They are sucking our lifeblood as each day passes, as they copulate within our borders." Kalenti breathed deeply before continuing. "We must expel them, and we need help if we are to achieve this goal. The life blood of our nation is being swept along as my wife's was on the city pavement."

In the next hour, Kalenti lowered his head and outlined in a whisper, so as not to be overheard, a strategy he had devised during his period of mourning. What distinguished the plan was its simplicity—the level of detail Kalenti had been able to develop. They were hesitant, even cautious at first, but as Kalenti spoke so did their confidence seem to grow. He recognized it in eyes that burned in intensity. Their shoulders, once stiff and rigid, loosened. When he concluded, he knew that he had won their allegiance.

"If you were alone on a parapet facing Saladin and his Moslem army, I would join you," Haddad spoke out. He was affectionately named Kuban for the years he spent as a youth attending university in Cuba during Batista's dictatorship prior to Castro's entrance onto the world scene. He smiled broadly and looked around the table at his comrades.

As Kalenti raised his glass of French Bordeaux, he was joined by the banker Shamir, as well as Zaquod, whose family name was Khoury and who had once served as a colonel in the Lebanese Red Beret paramilitary force.

"To our success and to that of our beloved Lebanon," Kalenti said through thin, icy lips that lingered at the edge of his wine glass. The glare from a naked light bulb reflected in his half-closed eyes. He placed the glass down softly on the once-elegant table cloth, recently patched to cover a cigarette burn. He pushed back the high-backed wooden chair to give himself room to stretch an arthritic leg, shifting his weight for comfort.

"Let me review our responsibilities. It is my job to get the team to the target. I'll be responsible on the ground."

"Zaquod …"

"Yes?" a deeply tanned, squat individual asked. He was bald

except for short clipped gray hair on the sides. His large, still-powerful hands were folded before him on the table and appeared to throb.

"Zaquod, you must find, recruit, and train the team. You will need at least twelve young ones for the attack abroad to succeed. I leave it to you to decide how many you will need for the operation here."

Zaquod reached into a silver-embossed case for another long black Turkish cigarette. He nodded his agreement as he lit the cigarette from the candle on the table, which he pulled toward him, careful to avoid the hot wax that had accumulated on the sides.

"Shamir—" Kalenti looked to his right at the small, frail man. His family name was Saad. He had a bluish, bulbous nose and thinning, dirty-gray hair. Shamir looked up from his hands and drew his lips together. His skin had a paste-like texture, and his eyes were clouded with cataracts.

"We need financing to support the operation. You must cover the travel expenses for our team. My brother, without you the operation would be doomed." Shamir acknowledged the praise with only a shift of his eyes.

"Kuban, my dear, you are to protect our gladiators. You must care for them. Do it well. We depend upon you."

Kalenti abruptly looked at his watch. The war had also affected this Christian redoubt in East Beirut. It was time to conclude the meeting so as to avoid being on the street after dusk. They rose simultaneously in their chairs, causing them to screech on the bare floor. Each of them followed his team of protectors out of the restaurant to their waiting vehicles.

☾*☾*☾

The next day, Saad, or Shamir, arranged the transfer of the equivalent of one million dollars to a numbered account in Switzerland. Shamir was a nickname given to him because in business he was as skilled as a Jew. He could always be depended upon to find a solution to any challenge that had proved insurmountable to his business partners. His energy was boundless and undiminished despite the passing years and his failing health. The enterprise that Kalenti described would receive his full attention.

That same day, Shamir confirmed that the account in Switzerland had been established. He recorded the information in a handwritten note, a copy of which he filed among his personal letters. He used this method to record his money-laundering activities over the course of his banking career. Each advance of funds was followed by a more exact accounting that was contained in a subsequent copy of a fictitious letter, since the original ostensibly was mailed to the intended recipient. True to his spirit of privacy and intrigue, only Shamir could break the code. He picked up what he had just penned and smiled.

November 12

Dear Pierre,
   It was nice to receive word that you will be traveling here next spring. I hope the fighting will have subsided by then.
   Thank you for your concern but my health remains strong, although not especially robust at 200 kilos. Only my eyes trouble me. I wish I did not need the daily dosage of eye medication, but that is the only relief I receive.
   Please write to me when you find time.

Affectionately,
Shamir

The date on the letter indicated when the transaction took place. The first paragraph provided a clue as to the purpose of the funds and whether the transaction was an advance or was to cover actual expenses. For Shamir, *traveling* connoted passports, the twelve that he had ordered; *next spring* signified that this was an advance. The second paragraph identified the amount of the transaction in thousands of dollars. Here the amount was two hundred thousand dollars. Shamir was proud of his accounting system. He placed the copy of the letter into his correspondence folder and destroyed the original.

"I did not learn this system in accounting class," he mused. He felt the pinch of the thick horn-rimmed glasses and shifted them lower on the bridge of his nose. Fifty years ago he had graduated from American University in Beirut with a degree in business administration. Since that time he had amassed enormous wealth and was not surprised when Kalenti turned to him to finance the enterprise.

Shamir was held in respect by the international banking community, from which he retired at the outbreak of the fighting. Only Kalenti knew that his last act before his departure was to plunder his bank of gold bars valued at over twenty million dollars. He had planned the operation in secret. Then he brought Kalenti into his confidence. The latter oversaw the operation when the internecine fighting had reached a crescendo of violence. Competing bands of Palestinians, Lebanese Moslems, and Christians swept through Beirut, bringing the commerce of the city to a standstill.

A heavily armed band of fighters in the employ of Kalenti executed a daring assault that forced the few security guards protecting the bank to flee. It was a time when anarchy reigned and the Lebanese government had no internal security forces to respond. The once-feared Red Berets of the Lebanese army had long since deserted the city for the Christian enclaves in the hills overlooking the Mediterranean. A hundred pounds of C4 explosive, a reel of detonator cord, and a handful of detonator caps were all that was needed to penetrate the underground vault where the gold bars were stored. Once the loot was in Shamir's control, he had the foresight to transfer and invest the wealth abroad. It proved to be a wise decision. At the time of the theft, three Lebanese pounds were still worth one US dollar. It would now take five hundred Lebanese pounds to purchase that same dollar.

After establishing the special account to handle the funding for this operation, Shamir removed his glasses and gently massaged his eyelids. He then walked to the kitchen and there prepared himself a cup of Turkish coffee, adding a tablespoon of sugar to the demitasse cup. The aroma of the coffee filled the room. He returned to his desk, put his glasses on, and found in his desk a particular address file. Under travel heading, he scanned the contact names and numbers listed. He realized that there was not much time to arrange the delivery of twelve false passports, especially when Zaquod still had to recruit and vet the team. He ran a thin index finger slowly down the names arranged in alphabetical order. He paused at the fourth on the list.

"No, he is too close to the Israelis," he said to himself. He continued. At the seventh, he smiled and picked up the phone.

"May I speak with Rashid?" After a short pause, he continued, "Oh, I am glad that I reached you so easily. This is Shamir. How do you fare?" Shamir had the gift of giving his full attention to an interlocutory, and he listened intently even as he stared at a fly seeking escape as it circulated around the window shade pulled halfway down.

"I am thankful you are well. May the fighting not reach your area. Pray that peace will shine upon us once again." He cleared his throat, which felt raspy.

"Rashid, I have an urgent, most urgent requirement." He paused and then continued, "For twelve passports." He listened intently to the response.

"Stolen or original—what is the difference?" There was another pause.

"Ah, I understand. I agree. No, we don't want INTERPOL to stumble upon …

"Yes, I agree, the numbers must be from a legitimate series already in circulation.

"No—not from this region. How about Europe, perhaps Canada?" He listened intently to Rashid.

"Yes, they will speak English—even French. We will take care of that.

"No, we have not yet selected those who will travel.

"Yes, I understand that you can do little without identifying data. At least begin the process—leaving it to insert later the biographic information and the photos.

"Good. How much for each?

"A king's ransom, my friend.

"I understand. Should I send the hundred and twenty thousand by courier?

"When can I expect him?

"The money will be waiting. In peace and victory." Shamir replaced the phone on the cradle. He wished they had more time.

He thought about the price but dismissed any concern. Excellence was assured, and for the same price accompanying documents in the form of international driving licenses, insurance certificates, and employment credentials would be provided. He trusted that Zaquod would be as efficient in recruiting the team. He needed personal information as quickly as possible to complete the transaction.

CHAPTER THREE

Kuban approached the challenge of securing a holding area and a safe house for the team in America with equal vigor. After all, the fate of The Lebanon hung in the balance. It had to be sufficiently close to the intended target that Kalenti identified—but not too close. They must not attract the attention of the authorities or inquisitive neighbors. Adding to the urgency was Kalenti's insistence that the team be ready to pounce on the assigned target within two months—not much time.

Kuban knew why Kalenti turned to him to assist here. Everyone at the table knew. His son, his only son, David, resided in the New York area where the operation was to be launched. After studying in the States, David had decided to remain there. He married an Irish girl he had met in New York. The marriage ceremony was not performed in the Maronite Church, and when the children were born his son failed to have the two children baptized according to the ancient Maronite tradition.

One week after meeting in the Bacchus restaurant, Kuban placed a call to David.

"My son, this is your father.

"Ah, you are surprised.

"I am well.

"Yes, it has been some time since we talked—three years?

So long. Yes, I remember, it was when I informed you that your grandmother died.

"Mother is in good health. She misses you and the children, and of course Katrina.

"Oh, I meant to say Kathleen. Are you all well?

"The reason for my call? I am coming to America on some business—soon.

"I arrive next week.

"I will explain when I get there.

"Yes, it would be wonderful if you met me.

"Yes, I look forward to staying with you.

"I'll let you know when I have my tickets."

༺ ∗ ༺ ∗ ༺

Kuban succeeded in obtaining an emergency visa from the American consulate. It had been over five years since his son had brought his family to Lebanon for a visit. Kuban was confident that his son would help him find shelter for Zaquod's team once Kuban had a chance to talk with the boy away from his American wife. Kuban believed that the survival of The Lebanon rested with the young man.

As he boarded the flight for New York, Kuban could not restrain his excitement. He was buoyed by the realization that they were finally striking out at the injustice Lebanon had endured for years—decades of frustration and grief as homeless Palestinian refugees invaded its borders. Success would lead to the resurgence of a united, Christian Lebanon. Kalenti was truly a genius.

༺ ∗ ༺ ∗ ༺

David was waiting in the front of the crowd gathered outside the customs area of the international terminal when Kuban exited carrying two bulky leather suitcases.

"Father, Father." He walked to Kuban, who seemed to have

aged noticeably since their last meeting. They embraced stiffly as Kuban handed the suitcases to his son.

"David, I am pleased to see you again." It was as if they had been together just days ago, so routine was the greeting. David could not think of a time when his relationship with his father was not strained. Growing up, he was never able to tell his father of his failures, anxieties, or even goals. His father only wanted to hear of successes, and those only when they fit into Kuban's preconceived notion as to what David should do in life.

In response to David's questions, his father would posture an image of strength, dedication, and certainty. He allowed no discussion. To David, he was someone who insisted that he was always right, and outside of a few close associates, the world around him was locked in a conspiracy against him. It was no surprise that there had never been an open display of affection between them. Early in adolescence, David pulled back from his father, and their conversations, limited as they were, became increasingly stilted and formal. It seemed to David that such a display by his father would be a sign of weakness, and David decided now that little had changed with his father's advancing years.

"How was the flight?"

"Tedious and long. It seems that the seats become narrower."

"Perhaps your size is expanding." David smiled.

Kuban ignored or did not hear his son's attempt at levity. The awkwardness of these first few moments demonstrated once again to David the futility of his expectations. Memories from his youth recalled that cold, hungry-like feeling that was once again echoing in his stomach.

David wondered if he should share some of the responsibility for this mutual inability to communicate. He admitted that the decision to remain in the States reduced the chances that the father-son relationship would ever mature.

Through the animated clusters of people greeting or bidding farewell to family and friends, father and son walked quietly, side by side, as if alone. Kuban's hands were drawn behind his back as he worked the worry beads through his fingers. They could have been mistaken for two monks returning to a monastery—and an orthodox one at that.

As David trudged along, he remembered telling Kathleen that if his relationship with her had been similar to that with his father their marriage would not have survived. She had been quick to point out that there would not have been a marriage in the first place.

Not another word spoken, David was so distracted that he forgot where he parked the car in the multistory parking garage. They walked around the extensive parking area for fifteen minutes until David remembered that his car was on another floor. His anxiety only increased as he imagined the critical judgments his father must have been forming but had not verbalized. In his growing panic, David found that he was walking faster and moving his head from side to side in his search. It was a relief that he finally discovered it.

They had little to say to each other on the ride to City Island, situated on Long Island Sound, just outside the city limits. Both seemed pensive—if only thoughts had voice. Though David was trying to give the impression that the New York traffic demanded his total attention, he was really searching desperately for the words to break through the barrier between him and his father. It was as if he had lost his place in the script and needed a cue from the prompter in the orchestra pit. Kuban, sitting silently at his son's side, seemed lost in thought.

Both seemed unaware that their communication, if it existed at all, occurred on an unconscious, nonverbal level. In years of trying to overcome the barriers that existed for personal exchange, they had both unknowingly come to accept each other's silence. This became an acknowledgment of the grudging respect each had for their differences. It was not much to boast about but was an achievement nonetheless in this modern age of openness.

"How was the weather, Father?"

"It was beautiful. Cool, brisk, clear. One could see the snow-capped mountains in the distance. I remember when we used to drive there to ski. I miss the chicken baked in peasant bread we used to eat in the roadside restaurant before returning home."

David nodded. It seemed a lifetime ago.

"The Mediterranean was a rare blue for this time of year. Few ships are visible. No cruise ships, no freighters, no naval escorts on port call. The fighting has stopped all that. If only the fighting …" He paused, caught in his reflections.

"If only the fighting would cease." He caught himself and started up again rapidly. "Grandpapa is well. He grows stronger, it seems." David listened attentively but did not reply.

It was late November, and the weather was gray and cold in New York. Winter had arrived with the temperature just above freezing. At they neared the exit for City Island, it began to rain. The collected droplets seemed to coagulate on the windshield. The older man looked through the passenger side window at the slick brown sticks of trees that lined the road.

David wanted to ask the reason for his father's visit or the length of his stay but decided that his father would tell him when he was ready. There were few cars on the road.

"And Katrina and the children?" Kuban's words sounded louder than he intended.

"Kathleen and the children are fine. Looking forward to your visit," David lied. "Will you be staying for the holidays?"

"Oh, I don't know. I have some business in New York that I hope to conduct quickly and be on my way."

"What kind of business? I thought you finally retired."

"It is some voluntary work." Kuban spoke in a controlled voice and immediately changed subjects. "Are you still working with computers?"

"Yes, Father." A bitter taste reached the back of his throat. He realized that his father had not read his last letter in which he explained with pride his recent promotion to senior computer analyst of the firm.

They crossed the short bridge onto City Island. The streets were deserted. In the summer season they would be locked in heavy traffic from visitors. In minutes they pulled into the driveway of a neat, wood-frame house. Kuban put his glasses on. As the car came to a halt, Kuban pulled his thick frame from the car and walked stiffly to the trunk to retrieve his suitcases.

✝*✝*✝

Of the assignments, Zaquod's was the most challenging. He had to screen and recruit two teams—one to undertake a difficult mission in Lebanon and the second to launch an impossible mission in the United States. Faced with a similar challenge, even the most resolute would waver, yet Zaquod lunged forward. The severe time constraints of his mission did not sway his conviction. The team had to leave for the United States within weeks. He must limit his search to volunteers who had already proved their dedication to the cause and had an advanced expertise in the use of weapons and the placement of explosives.

But if this were not enough, he had the added burden of selecting individuals not known in Christian and Moslem circles. They had to be experienced novices, Kalenti had explained. Nothing must put into jeopardy the plan to blame radical Moslems for both acts of terrorism. If his beloved Cedars of Lebanon were exposed as the guilty ones, Zaquod and the others were certain that The Lebanon would continue its precipitous decline into oblivion.

The Cedars was the armed cell of Christian fanatics whose followers distinguished themselves by the thick wooden crosses worn around their necks on thick brass chains. As an article of faith, they believed that the wood was cut from the "true cross" upon which Christ was crucified.

Zaquod sought candidates who could move about the United States without arousing suspicion. This meant at a minimum that they must be fluent in English. He did not know the location of the attack there. Kalenti had elected to keep the location to himself for the time being. An impossible challenge, he mused, but Zaquod trusted Kalenti.

The weapons and explosive refresher training was to take place at a military camp in the hills under the control of the Christian militia. The first batch of sixteen volunteers had one thing in common—they were all active members of the Cedars. One of them, Jacques Tawil, a dark handsome man of forty with bulging biceps, was famed as a survivor of the St. George Hotel siege—years earlier—when hundreds of Palestinians surrounded the hotel yet were unable to dislodge the small group of Christian defenders.

The Palestinians proved reluctant to storm the St. George and incur casualties. Instead, they put down a din of fire from protected positions—often firing blindly around corners with only the weapon exposed in the direction of the hotel. The actual siege lasted only thirty-six hours, but over time a listener to the Christian exploits would believe that they had endured for thirty-six days. When a cease-fire was negotiated, Jacques and the others emerged unscathed. The Palestinian attackers had suffered light casualties. Only the noncombatants—the women and children—suffered. Gathered on bread lines in the city, they were repeatedly cut down by mortar rounds fired and misfired again and again indiscriminately by both sides.

Zaquod's instructors received their training from the Israelis; actually, several traveled secretly to Israel for instruction. In addition to confirming each candidate's weapons skill, they were also taught the art of detecting concealed explosives. *Almost daily someone in East Beirut dies or is maimed by a car bomb or booby trap set by a Muslim fanatic,* Zaquod thought. In the past week, five bombs were detected and disarmed.

All the candidates excelled with a wide variety of weapons—automatic and semi-automatic—of both Western and Soviet-Bloc manufacture. It was evident by their skill level that all of them had spent the greater part of their lives under arms. The premier student in the firing portion of the instruction was Courtney Tannous. He was joined by a former American Special Forces soldier, Metro Asfour.

The explosive and weapons-effects training was conducted in the bombed-out interior of what was once the village's movie theater. The students received instruction in a wide variety of explosives, from those employed by military units and construction engineers to the homemade variety employed for earth-moving projects. The students quickly acquired an expertise in the employment of grenades, mines, and demolition and shape charges. In all they spent a week in the classroom. A diminutive young lady in her twenties, Michelle Nahas, attracted all with her beguiling, coquettish manner and the constant flow of technical questions she asked throughout the training.

After this phase of the training was completed, the recruits boarded an old school bus painted gray for a three-hour drive further into the hills. The ride was uncomfortable and perilous. The shock absorbers had long since given way on the deteriorating roads. Old canvas knapsacks served as cushions over the exposed seat springs. There was a thick layer of brown dust throughout the bus but especially on the inside windows, which the students wiped off with their sleeves or rags that littered the floor of the vehicle. The steering mechanism was so loose that the driver had to swirl the wheel constantly back and forth as he negotiated the tight curves; a high-pitched whining sound accompanied each revolution of the wheel.

It was a relief for all when they arrived at an abandoned Lebanese Army firing range. Two instructors had arrived the day before in the Land Rover beside which they now parked. The canvas tents and rations were unloaded from the truck that accompanied. The tents were set up in a clearing above an incline. When they finished, they paused to take in the spectacular view of the valley below. In the distance they could see the blue rim of the Mediterranean. They were silent as they allowed the sea breeze to dry the perspiration from their faces.

Once they reassembled, they climbed a steep neighboring hill and walked down into a large gully. A demonstration was being set up to expose them to the explosives with which they would become familiar in the next days. They followed one of the instructors through a series of abandoned structures bordering the firing range. He pointed out the position and characteristics of the various charges placed throughout the structures—yellow primer cord taped carefully along the ceiling and walls. Next, they followed the instructor along a line of rusting automobiles from which the engines had been removed. Here, too, various explosive devices had been attached.

Later, they took their places in a deteriorating cement bunker that served as the observation post. The students talked among themselves with rising excitement as they waited for the final preparations for the demonstration to be completed. What followed was a carefully timed display of the destructive force available to them. What they witnessed was not random destruction but the surgical application of minimum force to achieve a specific objective.

In the next days, they were issued their own material for building explosive devices under the direction of the instructor assigned to monitor their progress. They molded bars of C-4 into the liners of a variety of suitcases and observed at a safe distance the explosive affect when these and similar concealed devices were detonated.

Ramshackle sheds were constructed from wooden shipping containers and placed over the basements of army barracks destroyed during a Syrian artillery barrage in the past. The students set their charges to ensure that the destruction would be complete and simultaneous. The grade achieved was dependent upon whether any telltale evidence in the form of a detonator cap or a package of explosive material survived the explosion. The students gained confidence in working with the material and learned that they had nothing to fear if they handled the material carefully. The young beauty, Michelle, excelled in this class. She was joined by an enthusiastic young man, Danny Boutros, as the class leaders in the demolition portion of the instruction.

When the training was completed and the evaluations submitted, Zaquod made his selection. He then prepared his report to Kalenti—no small feat given the time allowed. He wondered if Kalenti would be able to assure the team access to the target, assuming that Kuban secured a safe haven in the States from which to operate, and finally, if Shamir had acquired false passports for the team members to travel.

Enough, no more worrying and hoping. I have done my job. That is sufficient, Zaquod thought as he tidied the papers on his desk and prepared to leave the room.

CHAPTER FOUR

"You're not still involved with those Christian fanatics, are you?" David inquired. They had just finished dinner.

"What are they called? The Wooden Crosses?" Minutes earlier Kathleen had left the table with the children to decorate a cake to celebrate David's birthday, but she could hear David's words.

"What do you mean 'fanatics'? Without the Cedars there would not be a Christian left in Beirut. We would all be cowering in caves, as shepherds during a sudden storm," Kuban replied.

For a week, Kuban's visit had been marked by an unusual gentleness father and son rarely displayed. Kathleen knew that it was only a matter of time before the impatience—or was it the repressed anger—erupted. Over dinner she observed the tension building like a barometer falling in anticipation of a storm front as the lines deepened around David's eyes. His face had developed a gray cast. Even though there was a chill in the air, David's forehead was moist with perspiration.

No one event caused the eruption. One week with father and son on their best behavior seemed to have fatigued them both. David lost his grip when Kuban became especially critical about America's failure to stem the tide of what he referred to as vagrant Moslems illegally entering The Lebanon. The discussion took a decided turn for the worse when David said that if Lebanon was to survive its leaders would have to accept the new realities.

"Accommodation and compromise are not signs of weakness but of confidence and strength," David lectured, his deep voice rising. From the kitchen, Kathleen was certain that David would regret his words as soon as he uttered them. His father did not respond. She was certain that David's comments only reinforced his view that his son had abandoned the land of his birth.

"Thank you, David, for your assessment." He sounded to Kathleen like someone determined to conceal his deep hurt, even anger.

"No doubt your academic credentials have contributed to your ability to be so objective in matters of heritage, heart, and homeland. Thank the Lord, Our Savior, for He has blessed the generation that remained with courage to resist the invaders." A chair was pushed back as the elder rose from the table.

"I am leaving tomorrow," Kuban said as he passed Kathleen on the way to his room. He did not look at her as she was entering the room with the two children. All three were holding the plate on which was balanced a birthday cake with white icing and blue candles. Her wide smile evaporated as she caught the crestfallen look on David's face. *What a pity,* she thought. *David had so looked forward to this visit.*

⁂

The next day, Kuban bid a calm farewell to the family. He was noncommittal about his plans except to say that after a few days in the city he intended to return to Beirut. He waved off his son's apology for his comments of the previous evening.

"I overreacted," Kuban offered. "I am an old man and unable to discuss Lebanon without becoming emotional and distraught. It is just as well I leave. It's been a good week." He handed his suitcases to the driver of the taxi cab.

"I will call you before I return home." He waved slowly from the rear seat. David and Kathleen watched the taxi depart. They returned to the house with his arm around her shoulders.

༺✦༻

Once in the midtown area of New York, Kuban dismissed the cab and made his way into lobby of the Waldorf Astoria hotel, located in the vicinity of Grand Central Station. From a telephone booth in the lobby, he placed a call to someone he was certain would be expecting to hear from him someday, Karekin Shalian. Karekin lived in Mt. Kisco, just north of the city.

"Karekin, it is me, Kuban. I am in New York. Can we meet?"

"My dear friend, where are you? I will leave immediately for you." Without hesitation Karekin added, "You will stay with me as long as you desire."

"No, allow me to take a train to your town and you can meet me at the station. I will let you know later when I am due to arrive, probably sometime tomorrow."

Karekin's offer of hospitality did not surprise Kuban. After all, it was Kuban who converted Karekin's devalued Lebanese pounds into US dollars.

"You are welcome to stay as long as you desire," Karekin repeated before he hung up the phone. Kuban smiled with relief.

The next day, Kuban caught the early morning express that lumbered along the Harlem River past Yankee Stadium and Grant's Tomb before it reached the Hudson River. There it gathered speed. Across the river the Palisades limestone hills filled the window of the rail car. Kuban sat on the left side in the train car, staring intently at the broad expanse of the Hudson River through the dirty window of the speeding train.

Although he had traveled in America previously, this time he felt a stranger. He longed for the simplicity of Lebanon, the connection with its natural elements. He missed the smells, the sounds, the sweep of the heavens, the mountain drafts, and the purity of the snow unblemished by the soot of civilization. The security of America could not compensate for the loneliness he felt. His mouth tasted bitter, as if his tongue had touched cold metal.

※

His friend—shorter than Kuban, slight of build, with stubby legs that were bowed from a childhood disease—was there to meet him at the station. They hugged each other warmly. Kuban's open display of affection convinced Karekin that he no longer blamed him for deserting Beirut for shelter in America. Still he could not overcome the guilt he felt, although at the end he could not control his fear of the violence on the streets. His decision to leave, which he characterized as abandonment, was necessary if he were to avoid going mad.

They drove along a narrow road lined on either side with thick, hundred-year-old trees. Picturesque estates remained hidden behind imposing fifteen-foot-high stone fences, not the primitive ones that Robert Frost had insisted made good neighbors.

Kuban asked Karekin to identify the names and logos of a few US multinational firms they drove past. Karekin did so, explaining that the corporations had purchased the estates from the tax-poor owners. As they headed up an incline, Kuban turned to his friend.

"I am reminded of the approach to the town of Zahle in Lebanon. Do you remember?"

"Only the azure of the vineyards is missing," Karekin replied.

Kuban agreed. He was optimistic that he would find Karekin's home a suitable haven for the team. The only question was whether he would be able to gain his friend's cooperation. He was running out of time before the team would be making their way to America; that is, if Kalenti's deadline was to be met.

Twenty minutes from the station, Karekin turned onto a secondary road. Two miles farther, he turned again, this time abruptly, up a long steep gravel driveway. There at the top and on the left stood a modest but large wood-frame house. They both left the car. Karekin insisted upon carrying both suitcases and led the way, the bags swaying forward and back. Kuban remembered Karekin's peculiar gait from the past as he swung open the door and insisted that Kuban enter first. Kuban looked around. He was in a spacious open kitchen with a table set with fresh fruit and a platter of cheeses and thin slices of meat. Within minutes the welcome ritual commenced—so ingrained in all who grew up around the Mediterranean.

Karekin boiled water on the gas stove, which he then poured it into an open copper pot that resembled an oversized butter warmer. Then he filled the small demitasse cups with thick Arabic coffee. The sweet aroma filled the room. Karekin sipped the coffee, his eyes closed to capture the moment. He then reached across the table for the bottle of Arak, reserved for this special occasion.

For the next three hours—to a sympathetic and interested audience—Kuban provided first-hand details of what life was in war-shattered Lebanon. He answered all of Karekin's questions about family members and friends remaining there. It was clear to Kuban that Karekin felt that he had abandoned the very country that had given refuge to him and other Armenians when they fled the Turkish genocide in the early twentieth century. It was Kuban's intention to stoke Karekin's feeling of remorse and guilt before he revealed his request. Kuban's assessment included a gloomy prognosis for Lebanon's future.

"I had thought that the Israelis would be sufficiently powerful to free our country from the Palestinians and the other troublemakers. But no; they just moved over for the Syrians and allowed the Iranian Hezbollah free access." Kuban helped himself to another thimble-sized glass of Arak.

"Syrians now control two-thirds of our country and have

stationed over twenty thousand troops within our borders." Karekin only nodded.

"Maybe the Israelis will return?" Karekin's inflection rose in a question, seeking an affirmative reply. A long silence followed.

"I had hoped so—but no. It is not politically acceptable for the Israeli condition."

In time, Kuban adroitly shifted the conversation to life in America. His friend appeared embarrassed to describe the prosperity and peacefulness that he had discovered there. He already employed two assistants to handle the business generated by a burgeoning population of young wealthy families who appreciated workmanship and did not question cost.

Karekin suggested that they take a walk so he could show Kuban his property, on which he grew a wide variety of apples. The old friends walked into the crisp, gray afternoon. Kuban clasped his hand behind his back, as was his custom, fingering his ever-present worry beads. When they reached the property line, they turned and returned slowly to the house. Once inside, Karekin refilled the glasses with Arak. It was time for Kuban to seek his friend's assistance.

"For the last year, my friend, I have devoted my time to finding temporary housing for young Lebanese men and women who seek resettlement in America far from the ravages of war that each experienced most personally," Kuban began.

"Oh, the war has changed you," Karekin interrupted. "This is not the Kuban I remember. That grizzled warrior." But he was quick to add, "Your compassion suits you."

"They have shed their blood," Kuban continued, brushing aside his friend's compliment, "in defense of our country, and they now need a respite—a time to recover, a place to earn money with which to return in the future."

Karekin only nodded his agreement and support. "My friend, I am relieved that you did not come here to coax me back. You must know that my home is open to anyone needing shelter."

Kuban was not surprised by the response and thought, *Kalenti will be pleased.*

"I must tell you," Kuban continued, "that some of these young people will not qualify for American visas."

"No matter, I stand ready to provide whatever you need. It was only six years ago that I was in the same situation when I declared to an American consular officer that the sole purpose of my trip to America was to visit a close relative and that I would return to Beirut and my family business of which I was president within six weeks. The consular officer was young enough to be my grandson. And I would do it again."

※ ※ ※

His mission a success, Kuban made himself comfortable in the room Karekin showed him. That afternoon, he would have Karekin drive him into town, where Kuban would place a long-distance call to Kalenti to report the good news. He was ready to receive the team. What a relief—so much pressure taken off his shoulders. He lay down on the bed to rest for an hour before he would ask Karekin to return him to the city. *If all goes as is planned, the young people will arrive within the next month.* The warm glow from the Arak had its affect; the events of the last days and emotional turmoil he experienced at David's drained him. He drifted off into a deep sleep.

※ ※ ※

A short, bulky man dressed in an oversized tweed overcoat buttoned tightly at the neck hurried along the street. He wore a blue knit cap stretched over a large head. His breath erupted rapidly into the cold dry December afternoon. It had snowed some days before, but in downtown Bad Godesberg there was no sign of it.

Horst Grobal threaded his way through the crowds of holiday shoppers on their way home. Queues formed at corner tram and bus stops along his route. Some of the shoppers delayed their return over dark coffee, warm pastry, and whipped cream in one of the several shops in the area. Many of the women were dressed in stylish furs, while the men were distinguished in tailored, conservative outerwear. The deep resonance of the bell atop the massive stone church intoned the third hour.

In apparent relief, he broke through the restraining crowd to a quieter side street. Alone, only his weight prevented him from making better time to the middle of the block where one of those ever-present Slavic restaurants was located. This one, the Balkan Grill, had soiled sheer curtains drawn across a large picture window. He entered the restaurant. It took a moment for his eyes to adjust to the dim interior light. He looked over the bare pine tables, each of which had a bright green and red plastic placemat on it along with a large orange ashtray. He searched the empty high-backed booths that lined both sides of the oversized room. He nodded when he spotted a gray-haired man about fifty years old with thick, round, horn-rimmed glasses facing him in one of the rear booths.

The man looked European except for his hair, which was closely cropped on the sides but sufficiently long on top to be similar in style to that of Robert Kennedy, the brother of assassinated president John Kennedy, who himself was later killed by a disgruntled Palestinian. The stranger was dressed in a nondescript, brown, textured suit, gray shirt, and red-and-gray striped tie. He watched Horst intently as he approached.

There was no expression of recognition in his eyes. Years of training and experience in the field had taught him to suppress such natural reactions. Nor did his face betray the impatience he had felt waiting for Horst. The man's clean-shaven face was dominated by a jagged nose. His eyes were hazel-green, clear, and alert. They were the eyes of a batter watching the delivery of a pitch or a combatant over a chess board.

Horst greeted the man as he took off the knit cap and wiped his forehead with the sleeve of his overcoat. He opened the top button of his coat and shuffled into the bench opposite. A relaxed but rehearsed smile creased the man's face. In front of him was an empty cup of coffee. A young dark Serbian waiter approached the table with a menu.

Horst ordered a half-liter glass of beer. He took a crushed pack of cigarettes and a box of matches from his coat pocket and immediately lit one with small, obese hands. The smoke enveloped and lingered over them both. He placed the pack before him.

"Well, my friend, it is good to see you," the stranger said softly in perfect but accented German.

"Yes, I too am pleased."

The waiter brought the glass of beer to the table.

"*Proust!*" Horst raised the glass with gusto. His companion started to do the same, but when he realized that his coffee cup was empty, he returned it feebly to the saucer. Horst took a deep gulp and placed the glass down. Momentarily refreshed—there was foam on his nose—he struggled to reach an inside pocket of his jacket. He opened a second button of his overcoat. With difficulty, he pulled out a postcard and presented it to the man opposite, whose hand was already across the table to receive it.

"I received it today." The stranger was silent as he read the card intently. He turned it over to inspect the winter scene of three trim skiers about to descend the slopes. The postcard was addressed to Horst at his local Bad Godesberg address. It was postmarked December 1 in Beirut. The message read:

Hi Lover,
I'll be in Athens for a few days from the 15th on. Any chance of slipping away from Momma? You owe it to yourself and ME.

Sabena

"I don't know how you do it." Horst barely disguised his envy between gulps of beer and another cigarette. The man remained in thought, looking up only when he was ready.

"You say you received the card today?"

"Yes, I called you right after the postman came. Is she French?'

"Who …? Or you mean Sabena. She's an old friend who does quite a lot of traveling. We've been close for years." A strained smile broke around his eyes.

"I just don't know how you to it," Horst said.

The man shrugged. He was distracted. He had to be on his way. He reached for a leather coin purse and placed enough deutsche marks on the table to cover the beer and coffee. He reached for the purse a second time to cover the cost of another beer for Horst, which gesture the latter noticed and appreciated. The man also gave Horst one hundred deutsche marks for delivering the postcard.

"I'm off, my friend. If I'm to see Sabena tomorrow, and I have much to arrange. We'll get together when I return."

"Thank you. You are generous. Auf wiedersehen."

The man rose slowly, deliberately. He seemed to be favoring his back. He carefully slipped on his dark overcoat, which was hanging by the booth, shook hands with Horst, and left the restaurant. He waited until he was on the street to put on his Austrian felt hat. He looked both ways before deciding to walk to the right, making his way unhurriedly to the public parking lot located beneath Wertheim's department store.

He found his two-door, battered red Volvo where he had left it. Someday, he hoped, it would not be there and he could put a claim in for it, realizing that the car was of little value now in this land of Mercedes. He drove off slowly. His mind was awhirl. There was so much to do and so little time to accomplish it. Mentally, he was planning his every action for when he reached the office. However, this preoccupation did not prevent him from glancing in the rearview mirror to see it anyone was following him. Again, years of experience had made this action second nature. He turned left and downshifted as he negotiated the winding hill to the Rhine, toward the Konigswinter ferry crossing, and finally to the complex of the American embassy, nestled alongside the river.

He turned left onto the service road that led to buildings that were constructed in the early 1950s, providing office space for the German housing and postal authorities in addition to the US embassy.

Colin Gramley Gordon followed the road to the front of the embassy, where a German security officer in a booth acknowledged his diplomatic tags and waved him on. He parked in the lot behind the embassy. An armored personnel carrier on wide, bouncy tires was just pulling out of the embassy area. It was a part of the routine protection provided by the German government to all diplomatic establishments to deter the terrorist outrages that erupted from time to time.

CHAPTER FIVE

Colin was an American Foreign Service officer, actually a Foreign Service reserve officer, assigned to the political section of the embassy. He held the diplomatic rank of second secretary. At least that was his official title and rank. In reality, he was with the Central Intelligence Agency, masquerading as a Foreign Service reserve officer or FSR. For the most part, Foreign Service officers remained in embassies reading, digesting, and later reporting to Washington the official foreign government position on a particular issue of interest. Over lunch, at diplomatic receptions, or during authorized visits to foreign embassies located in the capital city, they would trade background information on their respective governments' official positions. At least, that is how Colin would summarize their responsibilities—rather unkindly, he had to admit.

Colin and his CIA colleagues, on the other hand, were more difficult to spot. While the FSO was representing the official position of the US government and obtaining the positions from their respective foreign counterparts, the CIA case officer was conducting discreet and sometimes clandestine meetings at odd hours of the day and night in remote locations to obtain unofficial and unauthorized views of a similar sampling of foreign governments. Referred to as espionage, it was considered to be a legal activity by every intelligence service gathering such information intelligence and illegal by these same governments when confronted with the theft of secrets that could lead to the compromise of national security. As a profession, espionage bore striking similarities to investigative reporting.

Completing his second year in Bonn, Colin lived in embassy-provided housing outside Bad Godesberg with his wife, Chris. Their three children were grown and following separate careers in the States. This was not their first stay in Germany. In a career spanning twenty-five years, over fifteen years had been in German-speaking countries. Though eligible to retire, he could not imagine what he had to offer in his next career. Who wanted to hire a spy? His retirement check and his metabolism would require him a second career. Secretly, he was not even tempted to leave the CIA. He enjoyed the life and the intrigue with a passion that, if anything, intensified over the years.

The US Marine security guard in the protected enclosure recognized Gordon as he entered. He nodded and at the same time pressed the button on his control panel. The entry door in the vestibule opened abruptly and then closed automatically as Colin passed through. He proceeded to the bank of elevators to his left. The trip up on the aging elevator seemed interminable. He exited on the third floor, made a right turn, and stopped before the office on the left with the cipher lock. After entering the four-digit code, he waited for the buzzer and click before turning the handle and pushing the door open.

Maura looked up from her typing and smiled. Tall, brunette, her long dark hair combed back in the pageboy style he remembered his mother wore in the late 1940s, Maura LeBlanc was twenty-five years old, comely, dumpy, with simple tastes. Colin, however, had not worked with anyone more generous and dedicated. She was not at her best on the telephone—she became nervous or perhaps self-conscious—but she could type accurately and quickly the thickest intelligence report without a pause.

Colin remembered her sitting for hours typing a clean

document from an almost illegible copy of a top-secret document that an agent had photographed in a bathroom stall of an East European embassy. The ten-page copy when developed appeared fuzzy and almost impossible to read. It concerned impending Warsaw Pact cooperation in the Third World that directly challenged US national security interests. Had it not been that the subject matter was beyond Maura's understanding, he would have suspected that she had taken poetic license with the substance of the report.

What amazed Colin over the years was that she was able to devote full concentration to the task at hand while at the same time listening to the latest rock hit as she tapped her foot in time. Absolutely oblivious to her surroundings, she acted as if she were in an altered state. She was polite to all her co-workers, and no one was able to disturb her tranquility—not even Joan Farley, the spinster reports officer whose acid tongue everyone feared.

Joan heard Colin enter. "Well, what did he have?" Colin hung his coat and hat on the rack behind Maura's desk. His back was bothering him today. He worked his arms and shoulders in a circular motion. Maura looked up, smiling.

"A postcard from GANYMEDE in Beirut. He's calling for a meeting on the fifteenth—that's tomorrow in Athens."

"What's he doing in Beirut?"

"Not the foggiest."

"It sounds great. He may have hit on something." Joan was excited. "I'll pull together some questions for him. We don't have time to get much if anything from Washington."

"Maura, let me have the airline guide." He went into his office and pulled a folder labeled GANYMEDE, within which was the operational contact file. Opening the file, on the left side he saw a photo of Hans, under which was a manila envelope that contained copies of previous letters and postcards forwarded by him. On the right side were listed current meeting instructions. The parole was listed; that is, the words to be exchanged by Hans and a case officer unknown to him in the event that Colin was not available.

Colin thumbed carefully through the file. He was searching for the duress indicator—an innocuous signal that would indicate to the reader that Hans had been forced to write the message. The signal had to be sufficiently innocuous that it would not be spotted by someone examining the message before it was posted. All agents were issued such an indicator, but few appreciated its significance, and fewer still ever used one. Hans was one of those strange breeds who did not need a duress indicator but who followed his instructions on its use religiously. For him, if he capitalized the first letter in the second sentence of a message, it meant that he was being forced to write the message. If on the other hand, he was not under duress in writing the message, the first letter not capitalized would not draw the attention of anyone reviewing the message before it was sent.

Colin double checked the instructions issued to Hans and compared the postcard just received to those previously sent. Yes, indeed, Hans used the duress indicator—the first letter of the second sentence was capitalized. The question for Colin to decide was whether the use was inadvertent or not. Did Hans simply forget to add the signal in his haste to mail the postcard? Was he merely becoming lax like so many other agents, once the art of espionage became routine? It was impossible to say, but Colin would find out tomorrow. No cause for alarm now. Maura returned with the airline guide.

He ran his finger down the Koln-Bonn/Athens column. He wondered why anyone could have been so perverse to choose Bonn as the capital of post-War West Germany, or more appropriately retain the city as the capital once economic and political recovery had transformed the nation. Colin glanced at his watch. It was already four p.m. He would have to select his flights and make reservations quickly if he was to arrive on time for his meeting tomorrow. His glasses slipped further down his nose as he strained to read the small print, jotting notes at the same time on a pad of paper. He called to Maura.

"Please get me on the seven a.m. Lufthansa flight to Frankfurt and then on the eight fifteen a.m. Alitalia flight to Athens." It would be close, but if there were no fog and no delay landing at Frankfurt, he would be in Athens in time. *Big ifs,* he thought. *Fog at this time of year is thick and delays routine.* He composed an immediate-night-action precedence cable for the CIA stations in Athens and Beirut and CIA Headquarters in Langley, Virginia.

1. *Postcard calling for December meeting in Athens with GANYMEDE received from Beirut 14 December. Case officer Gordon plans to arrive Athens on Alitalia flight 271 at 1140 hours. Please meet.*
2. *Contact plan calls for case officer to be in lobby of Hilton Hotel at 16:00 hours—alternative Sheraton at 20:00 hours. Please rent room in each hotel for possible use as meeting site.*
3. *In event Gordon unavoidably delayed, request an Athens case officer plan to make meeting. GANYMEDE appears to be 45 years old, is six foot four inches tall, over two hundred pounds, wears gray Camelot-styled beard, blue eyes, and gray/white hair. He will be carrying a copy of "The Economist" in his left hand.*
4. *Parole for case officer is "Didn't we meet at opera in Berlin?" GANYMEDE's response: "No, I believe that it was in Hamburg."*
5. *Postcard postmarked Beirut, 1 December received by Horst Grobal on 14 December. GANYMEDE used, repeat used, duress indicator. While unusual in view of Ganymede's past performance, do not believe at this time that there is any cause for alarm. Will advise upon arrival in Athens.*
6. *We have no idea what prompted GANYMEDE to travel to Beirut.*

Colin reread the draft and looked up.

"Joan, do you have anything to add?"

Joan came back into the office carrying a sheet of yellow legal-sized in one hand and a Players Black Russian in the other. She scanned the draft and wrote a concluding paragraph.

> 7. *Please provide Athens directly for passage to case officer by immediate cable any additional requirements related to upcoming OPEC meeting in Tripoli. We already have sufficient background information related to ferreting out pricing strategy, Saudi initiatives moderating the price spiral.*

"Looks fine to me."

"Let it rip." Colin gave the draft to Maura, who would prepare it for transmission.

Colin extracted a locked cash box from the two-drawer safe in his office. The key for the box was in the top drawer of his desk. He counted out three thousand deutsche marks and half that amount in Greek drachmas. He placed two neat piles on his desk. He remembered doing the same in his youth when he counted out play money for Monopoly. He wrote the amount withdrawn on a slip of paper under the words "I owe the pot" and returned the box to the safe. Colin stuffed the money, passport, driver's license, and credit card into a worn, oversized leather billfold. *Someday I must buy a new wallet*, he thought.

From the top drawer of the safe, he pulled out a second file, labeled "Intelligence Requirements." Opening it he reviewed the list of questions that had been passed to Hans at their last meeting in Berlin.

> *Identify voting blocs within OPEC;*
> *What will be the impact of the Saudi initiative in resolving the Palestinian autonomy question?*

> *Any information related to Iraqi efforts to secure a cease-fire with Iran;*
> *Libyan interest in maintaining unity within OPEC while escalating the price of crude oil in a glutted world market;*
> *Saudi efforts to moderate and even reduce the price of oil;*
> *Mexican/US natural gas accord;*
> *Japan's dependence on OPEC oil and Western markets.*

"Oh, how dull," he muttered under his breath. He accepted his difficulty in stirring up interest in international economics. He simply was not an economist. What excited him was intelligence related to political unrest and upheaval. He envied colleagues who served in the hot spots around the globe, reporting on revolutions, coups, and insurgencies. In times of frustration, such as now, he wished he had the wherewithal to start a revolution or two. But such times occurred only when the bureaucracy of his profession got to him. The temptation passed quickly.

Despite his boredom in GANYMEDE's reporting, Colin had come to appreciate the information provided. He knew it would receive special scrutiny in Washington now that the Tripoli meeting was only a month away. For this reason—and this reason alone—Colin was satisfied. Case officers like Colin, unlike newspaper reporters with bylines, obtained their sense of identification, purpose, and gratification when their reporting was worthy enough to reach the senior policy makers in Washington. Unfortunately, this did not happen often enough to satisfy Colin.

While GANYMEDE's file was still on his desk, Colin reviewed the information that he had forwarded in the past to Washington. He found nothing spectacular. Hans was a knowledgeable economist and a talented geologist. He—like many other agents—reported what he had learned at closed-door meetings. Occasionally, he gained access to interesting documents that he had been trained to photograph covertly. Colin questioned whether the risk was worth the information, but pressure from Washington prevented him from discouraging Hans. No one, least of all Colin, expected him to develop unique and sustained access to sensitive intelligence.

To date, Hans's real value was in the relationships that he developed with individuals who held positions in foreign embassies of intelligence interest to the United States. He had written several personality assessments on OPEC functionaries whose life style seemed to make them vulnerable to compromising state secrets for financial incentives.

Among the personalities whom he encountered was Sulham Khalifa Ben Yousef, a man of increasing influence in Qadafi's inner circle. Ben Yousef was advertised as an oil expert, but he remained a mystery to the CIA. The experts could not decide why he had been assigned to the oil industry. There was no record on file that he had received any formal training or practical experience that justified the appointment. His attendance was noted at OPEC-related meetings and conferences abroad. However, his failure to contribute anything of substance at such events had drawn Washington's interest.

Colin made some cryptic notes from this file and slipped them into his billfold. Maura came in with Colin's reservations for the next day and confirmed that his cable had been sent.

"Tell the commo folks I'll be home if Athens or Washington tries to contact me this evening."

"Okay." She left the office on her very high heels. *How uncomfortable. She looks like she's on roller skates for the first time*, he thought.

⁕⁕⁕

Hans Weil, architect, engineer, geologist, and entrepreneur, was born in Breslau, Germany, now Wroclaw, Poland, in 1944. Two months after his birth, his mother and aunt bundled him and his older sister and rushed them off to Berlin in time to meet the onslaught of the Soviet armies. Hans's father was on the Russian or Eastern Front. After the war the family searched in vain for the repatriation of Lieutenant Weil. It was only in 1954 when Lieutenant Weil's comrade was released from a Soviet labor camp that they learned that his father had left the outskirts of Konigsburg on the Baltic Sea the day before the Soviet armies swept around them. He was in command of a ragtag engineering company whose instructions were to destroy a railway bridge that had survived previous attempts to destroy it. No one returned from that mission. Later, they learned that the bridge was still standing.

As a teenager, Hans tried to picture his father. He was told that he bore a striking resemblance to him. Hans wondered whether his father had experienced the uncertainties he felt as he found himself driving to achieve some elusive goal that translated in later years to recognition and success. Despite the wealth and prestige he accumulated by the time he turned forty, he still could not overcome an inexplicable dissatisfaction with his life. His marriage became a casualty to this restlessness.

Colin met Hans when he was attached to the US mission in Berlin. He had heard about this free-wheeling businessman with contacts throughout the international community. Colin arranged to meet Hans at a luncheon. He was surprised how much he enjoyed Hans's company from the outset. There was something expansive, generous, unorthodox, and bold about him. He was not what one considered a typical German. Later, he would flatter Hans by telling him that he was more Spanish than German.

Colin had realized Hans's potential early when he convinced him to host a small luncheon to which Hans invited an outspoken Eastern-European businessman who seemed to have extraordinary access to the political leaders of the Eastern Bloc. Colin wanted to assess for himself whether the individual was genuine in criticizing the communist system; what his family circumstances were; and most important of all, whether he had access to sensitive information. These were the type of questions necessary to complete a preliminary personality assessment. Colin was confident that as just another invited luncheon guest he could begin the assessment process.

Not long after meeting Hans, Colin was introduced to his wife at a German-American affair. She was tall and leggy and wore her long, light brown hair with a windswept casualness that reflected care and expense. Tastefully clothed, her natural beauty commanded attention. She spoke English slowly, haltingly, with a soft almost French accent. Colin was flattered with the responsiveness she showed him but quickly realized that each man she encountered received the same undivided attention.

Colin remembered the day that turned out to be a watershed in their personal and later professional relationship. He and Hans were at lunch. Hans seemed upset—even distraught. Colin had come to the meeting to ask Hans's assistance in brokering an introduction to a fellow German businessman who traveled regularly through sensitive areas in the Soviet Union. Colin never got the chance. Instead, Hans revealed what was tormenting him. His wife had just informed him that she had been having a long-standing affair with one of Hans's closest business associates. He was devastated.

Colin was never able to determine whether Hans was hurt more by the fear that others would find out of this deception or by the loss itself. In the weeks and months that followed the revelation, Colin became involved in what turned out to be a futile reconciliation attempt. With all the prestige and respect that Horst commanded in business circles, he was paralyzed to act. He was a troubled giant who could not embrace a formula for renewal and healing in his relationship. It was beyond his capacity to forgive. His pride, or perhaps it was the insecurity dating back to his youth, would not allow it. He could not forgive her, though he came to accept that her confession was a desperate attempt to salvage their relationship.

In the end, a man respected for his strong will proved unable to exercise it above his shattered emotions. For a time, he chose to live in opulent isolation with his wife. To all outward appearances, they represented an idyllic existence of wealth and success. In reality their lives were dreary and frozen; that is, until they agreed to terms for divorce.

Whatever the reason, that particular luncheon contributed to Hans's agreement to expand his assistance to Colin, which soon produced some peripheral intelligence related to East-West trade issues. Though it contained little he could not read in the newspaper, experience taught Colin that all agents had to begin somewhere.

From the outset, Hans made it clear that he would do nothing to compromise or jeopardize his far-flung business interests. Also, depriving the CIA of any kind of leverage, he refused to sign a secrecy agreement attesting to their clandestine relationship. Washington at first questioned whether Hans was worth pursuing with these caveats. However, when the OPEC cartel continued to strain Western economies and Hans was able to provide useful, if not valuable, information from some of his Middle East business contacts, the second-guessing about Hans's worth ceased.

As time passed, Hans seemed to enjoy the adventure associated with espionage, though he never altered his initial ground rules. When he received clandestine training, he was a focused student. He devoured the lessons in surveillance detection, covert document photography, intelligence reporting, and indirect personality assessment and elicitation. For Hans's safety, Colin moved what was once an open social relationship to more discreet contact. As Colin's tour in Berlin was coming to a close, he sought to prepare Hans for the time when Colin's replacement would be introduced into the operation, but each time Colin raised the subject, Hans brushed him off and seemed to apply himself toward developing personalities of intelligence interest.

During a business trip to Rome, Hans was introduced to Sulham Khalifa Ben Yousef, a senior Libyan official at an airline reception. The two spent most of the evening sharing stories and cocktails. When Hans returned to Berlin, he could not restrain his delight in reporting this success to Colin. Another time in Paris, Hans made the acquaintance of a Lebanese financier who was concerned about Soviet intrusions in the Middle East. There was nothing ideological in the Lebanese's desire to thwart the Soviets. Rather he feared for his real estate investments. Over time, this financier proved a valuable source of information on some of the Soviets' less-publicized activities, such as their liaison with prominent Palestinians implicated in vicious terrorist attacks. When the violence broke out on the streets of Beirut, this agent had less to report, since both the Americans and the Soviets curtailed significantly their activities in Lebanon.

Then the date for Colin's transfer from Berlin was set. As hard as he tried, he could not convince Hans to agree to meet his successor. It was a bitter disappointment and a professional embarrassment for Colin. Case officers could not allow an agent's attachment to interfere with a smooth turnover to one's successor. But it happened. Hans's decision was not entirely a surprise. On Colin's part, he did not want to admit his own personal commitment to Hans, which went beyond supporting someone who provided occasionally worthwhile intelligence. Nothing Colin said would convince Hans to change his mind. In the end Colin ran—in espionage parlance—Hans from Bonn, the site of his next assignment. Washington reluctantly agreed—it did not want the flow of intelligence on OPEC and the assessment data on the political and business leaders to be interrupted. Thus was born the GANYMEDE operation.

✢✢✢

In September of his second year in Bonn, Colin received a cable that was transmitted laterally to Berlin and the embassy in Warsaw. The message was terse:

1. *Sensitive intelligence source indicates that Libya developing dramatic proposal to be tabled at upcoming general OPEC meeting scheduled for mid-January in Tripoli. It was outline strategy for confrontation with West, specifically with US.*
2. *Request Bonn encourage GANYMEDE direct all his efforts on learning details of Libyan initiative soonest. Suggest GANYMEDE arrange to attend International Oil Users Symposium which Philips Oil Company sponsoring in Amsterdam on 14 and 15 November.*
3. *For Your Information Only: Sensitive source reported that GANYMEDE acquaintance, Sulham Khalifa Ben Yousef, involved in formulating this strategy. He has recently been noted traveling through Europe and Eastern Europe and is expected to attend symposium.*
4. *As you aware, Ben Yousef is undersecretary in Libyan oil ministry and a close confident of Qadafi.*
5. *Please advise if GANYMEDE willing to assist.*

Colin surmised that the information about Ben Yousef came from a foreign agent who learned it in the course of his official duties in an Eastern European capital. The agent was probably unaware of Washington's growing interest in Ben Yousef's travels. Colin placed a call to Hans in Berlin. He had the private number that rang on Hans's desk. He answered on the second ring.

"Hello, Colin. So very nice to hear from you."

"Same here. How goes life?" Colin asked.

"It goes with the same intensity. And some moments I long to disappear to an island with just a bathing suit."

"You say that, but I think three days of watching sunsets and you would return to the shadows."

"Three days? I wouldn't last two. Anything happening?"

"Washington wants you to attend the Phillip Symposium in Amsterdam."

"I knew you would call—my intuition is working overtime.

I'm just surprised you called so late. The good news is that I know the dates of the conference and freed up the time."

"Good show! See what you can do about renewing your budding relationship with Ben Yousef, who's supposed to be there."

"Yes, I will do my best. I have made plans to arrive in Amsterdam the day before the opening."

"I will meet you in Berlin a couple of days afterward. If you have to see me sooner, call."

"Of course. Cheers."

"Cheers too." Colin hung up the phone.

CHAPTER SIX

Colin's flight to Frankfurt arrived ten minutes late but in sufficient time for him to board the flight to Athens. He climbed over the young man on the aisle to reach the window seat. He pulled a magazine from his briefcase so as to discourage conversation. When the aircraft reached its cruising altitude, he put the magazine on his lap and closed his eyes. His mind throbbed from all the information he had absorbed prior to departure. Sleep was out of the question. Instead, he reviewed in his mind the arrangements for the upcoming meeting. He had not seen Hans for almost three months and expected that Hans would not be denied the opportunity to recount fully every single detail from start to finish. There would be no summaries or shortcuts in the retelling.

Hans's rudimentary knowledge of OPEC kept Colin's expectations in check despite Headquarters' urgent need. His limited social contact with Ben Yousef made it unlikely that—even if Ben Yousef attended the conference—he would confide in Hans. He expected that they would share Irish whiskey and discuss Hans's Mercedes and not touch on the sensitive information of interest to Washington.

Colin had to admit that he was surprised to receive a call from Hans just one day into the symposium, long after he and

Chris had retired for the night. The phone rattled on its cradle. He knew better that to answer it. Past experience reminded him to wait for her to reach the phone. Woken from a deep sleep, he could carry on an intelligible conversation, hang up, and not recall anything the next morning. This time he nudged her. Her voice was deep with sleep when she answered. She then pushed him into wakefulness.

From Hans's first words, it was obvious that he had been drinking. He had good news to report. Colin sat up in bed and reached for his glasses though the light was still off. Hans had succeeded in meeting Ben Yousef within an hour of arriving in Amsterdam. According to Hans, Ben Yousef was delighted to encounter him. They dined together that evening. After seven hours with Ben Yousef, he had just returned to his room.

Colin turned on the bedside lamp. He knew there would be no rushing Hans, and so he prepared himself to be a patient listener. Hearing Chris's deep, rhythmic breathing, he could tell she had fallen back asleep.

"The reunion went well," Hans reported, as if to indicate that he was referring to an academic event. "So well that I am off to Tripoli to pursue investment opportunities there."

Colin interpreted his comments to mean that the trip would result in the acquisition of worthwhile intelligence. "So good to hear of your evening," Colin encouraged. Even the description of the trip to Tripoli would be greeted by Headquarters. Anything else would be a bonanza. No longer would Colin have to endure the razing he received from colleagues who accused him of keeping Hans on the books to cover expenses for the good life in Berlin.

❧ ✻ ❧ ✻ ❧

"Please secure your seatbelts; we are on our approach to Athens International Airport."

Colin snapped alert with the announcement. When the wheels touched down, Colin checked his watch.

"On time!" he said aloud.

Sitting up front, he was one of the first passengers to deplane following the first-class passengers. Overnight bag in hand, he avoided the baggage claim area and proceeded directly passport control. Once he was cleared, he proceeded to a public telephone and called an unlisted embassy telephone as instructed in the cable from Athens.

"Hello, this is Mr. Bottomiller, calling for Mr. Frost. It is about tractors we are looking to market." The instructions he had received from Athens stated that he would be informed that Frost was out and was expected to return at a given time. This time plus one hour would be when Colin would be approached in a designated location in downtown Athens.

"This is Ted Frost," the person answering the phone responded.

"Ted, this is Mr. Bottomiller. It is about tractors we are looking to market." Colin thought that by repeating the message, Frost would recognize the reason for the call—even belatedly.

"Aaaaa … I mean …" Clearly Frost was confused. "Suppose we meet in an hour."

"See you then." *So much for the complex contact instructions.*

Colin walked outside the whitewashed terminal to a taxi stand. He intended to head for Constitution Square as directed in the original cable. He wondered why he had taken the trouble to copy verbatim Frost's instructions. He suspected that Frost was writing for a Headquarters readership that would conclude falsely that Frost understood what it takes to run a clandestine operation.

It's a pity someone from Headquarters does not have to act upon Frost's directions, he thought as he slipped into a taxi.

"You first time in Athens, mister?" the driver asked in halting English.

Colin ignored him. Instead he reviewed the intelligence requirements. He had to admit that requirements related to OPEC economic strategy did little to interest him. Constant repetition seemed to be the only way for him to retain the information and overcome his resistance to the subject. He reread the requirements, this time with the cryptic notes he made before departing Bonn.

The taxi lurched from lane to lane in the noonday traffic, and this jolted him from his concentration. The sounds of blasting horns and the shouting in the streets created a cacophony of riotous sound that convinced him that this was not the time or place for study. He leaned back in the seat. He closed his eyes when he caught the driver in the rearview mirror about to test his English again.

Colin still wondered if Hans had prepared the message under duress. The capitalization of the second sentence was perfect. If Hans was following instructions, indeed he was in trouble. Colin dismissed the possibility as too unpleasant to consider. Hans had simply made an inadvertent mistake—forgot the instructions. Next time, he would choose an indicator that required more attention to detail. When they met, he would give Hans a difficult time.

⁕⁕⁕

At exactly ten minutes to noon, Colin walked to the northwest corner of Constitution Square. He remembered being in the same area years ago when he spent an enjoyable afternoon watching the beautiful people pass—dark Greek beauties aloof to the attention of their countrymen and hazel-eyed, blond Swedish girls cultivating that pursuit. What stayed with him was the warmth of the sun, the glow of the ouzo as it threaded its way through him, and the pleasant aftertaste of the sweet thick coffee.

It was time. With his overnight bag in his left hand, a *Paris Tribune* in his right, and his briefcase tucked under his arm, Colin waited for Frost—wherever he was—to approach him. He felt conspicuous, like a high school student off for summer camp with all his treasured possessions in tow. Out of the corner of his eye, he noticed a man dressed in black slacks and a tight heavy wool sweater. The man had a dark complexion and appeared to be Colin's age. Several minutes passed as the stranger walked on the sidewalk adjacent to Colin. Finally, he approached. Colin became tense. The man looked Greek. What had he done to attract the attention of the authorities? When the stranger spoke, Colin was relieved. There was no cause for alarm.

"What am I supposed to say?" the stranger asked in a pseudo-English accent, catching Colin with his mouth agape.

"What are you supposed to say? What are you supposed to say? After sending the most complex and detailed contact instructions, you now ask me, 'What am I to say?'" Putting his suitcase down, Colin reached inside his jacket pocket and pulled out the index cards on which he had transferred Frost's instructions.

"You were to say, 'Is this where the American Express bus leaves for Corinth?' My reply was to be, 'I do not know. I have just arrived from Skiathos.'" Frost grinned sheepishly and led Colin without another word to his car, which was parked on a side street.

"Why couldn't I just take a taxi to the embassy? I'm on a diplomatic passport."

"There's a terrorist alert in effect. The marine security detail has been beefed up with marines from all over Europe. We were afraid that you would attract attention at the gate."

Colin had heard from case officers in Bonn that Frost was an Arabist who had served most of his tours in the sand piles of the Middle East, as they were called. Athens was his reward. Surely he did not want to do anything that would curtail his tour in Greece and what it offered compared to the hot sun, sand, and incestuous Western communities of the Arab oil nations, or more importantly jeopardize his chances of being assigned to Rome his next tour.

In the Arab Emirates the most sensitive intelligence activity for Frost was to meet local officials under the guise of a diplomat—hardly worth the US taxpayer's investment. At least that was how Colin judged the contribution from an admittedly biased perspective. After many years abroad, Colin expected that Frost was skilled in the art of etiquette but needed a crash course in the art of espionage. *Terrorist alert! Hmph! Even training wouldn't help Frost now; he would continue to bluff until he was out-ed.*

It was a ten-minute drive to the embassy in the noon traffic. The car Frost drove did not have diplomatic tags; thus it would not attract attention parked on a street near the embassy. A vehicle with diplomatic tags had recently become the target of incendiary attacks. There were those who still held the United States responsible for Greece's continuing inability to wrest control of Cyprus back from Turkey. Though US military forces in Greece continued to face harassment from time to time, American and Western tourists were welcomed for the hard currency they brought to the country.

Clutching his personal items, Colin followed Frost to the embassy gate. Greek uniformed police in an ill-defined perimeter surrounded the embassy. The two men flashed their US passports and were allowed to proceed to the next loose collection of husky young men—bulky in newly acquired suits. If there was any doubt of the mission or nationality of this contingent, it was dismissed when Colin observed the uniformity of the civilian dress.

More intent on screening visitors than their Greek counterparts, Colin expected to have his passport scrutinized closely. He was surprised when one of marines, whom he recognized as being assigned to Bonn, approached Colin with a greeting and led him without fanfare inside the embassy. Frost was delayed as his credentials were confirmed. Colin could not restrain a smile at the irony of the situation.

※ ※ ※

"How do you take your coffee?"

"Just black," Colin responded. Frost wandered out of his windowless office. He returned ten minutes later with two small bone-china cups, half-filled with Greek coffee. Under Frost's arm was a manila folder. Colin burned the tip of his tongue on the first sip of the aromatic brew.

"I had to come this morning at three thirty to review this night-action cable from Headquarters." Frost pulled the cable from the folder and gave it to Colin.

Colin read the cable carefully. He was self-conscious about his slow reading speed. With Frost looking over his shoulder, he would read even slower. Sometimes he regretted not taking a speed-reading course in his youth.

"Well, I do not see anything new here, except maybe the request for anything that implicates Ben Yousef with Libya's terrorist network. And that seems pretty obvious when you are dealing with rag-heads, don't you think?"

Frost flinched at the term rag-head. "Actually," he retorted in a clipped British accent, "I don't know why all the fuss. Hans is incapable of gathering or reporting coherently complex petroleum data. As far as I'm concerned, he has no competence in the terrorist field unless related to some Neo-Nazi group. It's inconceivable to me that he could develop a meaningful relationship with any Arab, much less one as sophisticated as Ben Yousef. Arabs, you see, do not as a rule take rich Germans into their tents or confidence."

"Touché," Colin muttered as a half-hearted apology. He was suddenly on the defensive. Next time he would be better prepared.

"Have arrangements been made for the hotel room in the Hilton, with the Sheraton as backup?" Colin asked as he looked at his watch. It was three fifteen.

"Yes. Your room in the Hilton is 605. It has been reserved under the name Kenneth Blake." Frost gave him the key.

"If Hans doesn't show, we'll reserve a room in the Sheraton and get the key to you."

"That should not be necessary. How can I reach you?"

"My wife and I are hosting a sit-down dinner this evening for several members of the diplomatic community. We will be home." Frost looked away.

"I do hope that he is prompt for the Hilton rendezvous. It would be awkward to extricate myself from the reception."

"How can I reach you?" Colin asked again.

"My number is 62-43-76."

Colin jotted the number on a piece of paper that he slipped into his wallet, refastening it with a thick rubber band. He looked at his watch—he had just enough time to review the material from Headquarters.

"We have so much yet to arrange for the dinner party," Frost said, stressing what for him was his priority. Before he left, he introduced Colin to Stacy, a young analyst who just entered the room.

"When you're finished with the file, I will return it to the safe," she said as Frost hurried from the office, assuming the air of someone trying to disguise the fact that he was leaving work before quitting time.

Colin decided that the reaction was caused by a perceived violation of some Protestant work ethic and the guilt engendered. Frost departed with his head raised high on a mission to buy flowers.

CHAPTER SEVEN

Colin remained in the embassy until four thirty that afternoon. He returned the folder to the young lady who patiently sat in the next office. He had already forgotten her name. Once outside, he decided to walk from the embassy to the Hilton. The air was brisk. He tucked his scarf loosely around his neck. The sun was beginning to dip behind the buildings. *The sunset through the scattered clouds should be spectacular,* he thought. The Greek security detail was still positioned around the embassy, as were the marines—though he did not see his acquaintance among the.

He walked on the embassy side of the street, down the sloping hill past the museum toward the hotel. He remembered years ago boarding a helicopter with Chris and the children about this same time of day—though it was summer—for the thirty-minute flight to Skiathos Island, located northeast of Athens. It was to be for them an idyllic stay in a villa perched high above the Aegean Sea.

He snapped himself from his memories back into the present. To keep his focus, he reviewed again the questions for Hans. Colin knew from experience that his success depended upon the planning that preceded his agent meetings. Preparation and repetition—there could never be enough even if the subject matter didn't sound very exciting. Perhaps that was why little was written about such traits in the books about espionage. Who would buy a book that unmasked the routine and boredom that accompanied the occasional adrenaline rush? It was, however, the rush that kept him in the business. He felt an excitement rising within as he anticipated seeing Hans after over a month since their last meeting and learning what intelligence he was able to acquire. It was like deep sea fishing, and he was about to reel in the line after the sharp tug on the line. He hoped he was not raising unnecessarily expectations. He still did not understand why Hans had decided to be so dramatic and trigger the meeting with the postcard. Up until the receipt, he had expected to receive a routine call from him requesting a meeting once Hans returned to Berlin.

The backfire of truck that had just passed, coasting downhill, caused Colin to flinch and look around. His gaze caught a man walking on the other side of the wide avenue. The man was dressed in a leather jacket and was wearing a dark cap. He did not seem Greek—maybe because he was carrying a large plastic grocery bag in his arms. It was the woman's role to buy groceries—at least in Greece. He smiled as he thought how Chris would respond to his comment.

Colin decided to cross the street at the light as the shortest way to the hotel. When he reached the other side, the man whom he spotted earlier was no longer in sight—not that he was looking for him. He must have entered any one of the three-story buildings that lined the avenue. Five minutes later, the hotel loomed before him. He looked at his watch. He should have remained in the embassy longer. There was still an hour before Hans was due.

He walked around the hotel and noticed a small coffee shop on a side street. He decided to pass the hour there. His movement seemed to surprise a man dressed in a woolen sweater with a camera slung over his shoulder. He was intent on crossing the street before him. However, when Colin paused, the man did likewise. *Strange*, thought Colin. There was something about the man that reminded him of the fellow carrying the sack just minutes earlier. Colin took note of his brown crepe-sole shoes—

one of the shoes had a stain on the side—as the man moved out of sight down the street. Maybe he had been seeing too many spy movies. In the coffee shop he asked for a double cup of the thick, black coffee, prepared Greek style in Athens and Turkish style in Beirut or Cairo. It was not as good as the coffee that Frost prepared earlier, but he preferred the atmosphere here.

He settled down to what all case officers—at least good ones—learn early in their careers. They become quite accomplished in the art of wasting time. Colin had an hour to pass. He focused on the upcoming meeting. He had to admit that he was putting more emphasis on its success than was his custom—at least with an agent like Hans.

His thoughts turned to the past, when he had to spend more time waiting for an agent and when there was real doubt as to whether he would appear. In such instances, Colin had learned patience in public places like restaurants, train stations, and hotel lobbies. Though idle for sometimes hours, he became a master at discerning the relationships between people who populated these venues. He remembered as a boy how much he loved to spend an afternoon at an airport terminal observing the rush and press of the crowds. Certainly this had been fine training for the profession he would later choose. He attributed his childhood experiences to the keen intuitive sense he cultivated, especially in detecting surveillance or sensing something that was not quite right—out of the ordinary.

When he was not observing the people around him, he would jot down thoughts on a napkin if that was all that was available. On his own, he learned to sketch and would apply himself to a building or the outline of a tree visible through a window shade. He sometimes thought that his career was largely spent waiting for phone calls or watching the minute hand move into position before he walked off to exchange a package with an agent.

As a young case officer, he remembered hearing a white-haired, diminutive, senior official say, "Where else could you get paid for having so much fun?" With the attention this fellow commanded he had emphasized the infrequent but exciting, even thrilling, moments of being a spy. He half expected that he would give a similar assessment to doting young officers, but he hoped he wouldn't.

Colin looked at his watch again. *Time to go.* He left some change on the table and walked directly across the street into the Hilton. It was too early for the coffee and ice cream crowd, but in the lobby there was a swirl of motion as several holiday parties were underway simultaneously. Military uniforms from Western nations were accompanying women in elegant cocktail dresses. He knew from experience that for the next three weeks a night would not pass without the participation of the international military and diplomatic community at some event. He noticed the formal uniform of a British officer walking in his direction. His partner, a stunning brunette in a shattering red dress, complemented the élan of the Green Jacket—the regiment to which he was assigned.

Colin continued through the lobby into the bar, looking for Hans with a feigned casualness. He did not expect Hans to approach, but one never knew what to expect. Although he had to admit that Hans usually responded well to his instruction, sending the postcard still puzzled Colin. Perhaps it was his way of tantalizing Colin with a promise of important intelligence.

As he turned the corner to the gift shop, he bumped into a gentleman who was staring intently at an empty newspaper rack. Colin excused himself, but the man said nothing and looked away. There was something familiar about him. He wore a tweed sports coat and brown shoes with thick crepe soles. On the side of the left shoe was a grease stain. It was the man he had noticed earlier. Could this be a Greek surveillance team positioned outside of the embassy? The package the man had been carrying probably contained a change of outer garments. Only shoes were difficult to change on the move. Colin had been trained to notice shoes. From his experience he knew that surveillants would do anything to avoid eye contact with their target. Colin's senses jolted awake.

Ganymede

What had he done to attract surveillance? As he moved through the gift shop and back into the lobby, he reviewed his actions since he had arrived in Athens. Nothing seemed out of the ordinary until he was halfway between the embassy and the hotel. Maybe the man in the crepe shoes belonged to a police surveillance team, assigned to cover visitors to the embassy. If so, bad luck. Why had Frost not seen fit to warn him of the possibility? Frost should have never brought him to the embassy in the first place. He decided that his identity had been confirmed when he presented his passport to the uniformed Greek police around the embassy. He speculated that someone, or a surveillance team, was dispatched to follow him to learn what he was doing in Athens. Bad luck again.

If Hans was in the area, Colin hoped that he would not approach now. So what if the police confirmed Hans's association with an American diplomat? Colin still decided that it was prudent to leave the hotel. He must lose the surveillance before implementing the alternate meeting arrangements. First he had to contact Frost—once he was satisfied that he was clean.

Oh, will Frost be pleased to hear me, he thought. *They're probably just sitting down to their intimate dinner.* Colin looked forward to describing his difficulties—difficulties that could have been avoided if Frost had been professional. He would have Frost drive by the Sheraton first to see if he spotted anything in the area—that is, if Frost was up to the task. Colin left the Hilton by a service door near the men's room. Whatever confidence Colin could muster regarding Frost's professionalism was quickly diminishing.

⁘ * ⁘ * ⁘

They met at a tavern in Kifissia, a suburb of Athens to the north. Colin entered only after he was satisfied that he had not been followed. What would have been a thirty-minute drive by taxi had turned into an odyssey of an hour and a half in three taxis. *No one had ever said that the spy business was efficient.* Frost was already seated at a table. It was seven thirty.

"When I left, our first guests had not yet arrived." Colin did not know whether to interpret that as good or bad news. Actually, he did not care.

"So?"

"You know that I have better things to do with my time than spend it with you this evening." Frost was equally irritated.

"Let me say something to you once. Your diplomat friends will have to wait. I have been under surveillance—had to scrap the primary meeting for the secondary, and now we must prepare for the second. All this could have been avoided if I knew about the coverage on the embassy."

"What coverage?" Frost's voice was rising. "Let me say emphatically that the Greeks are not following American diplomats. If that were the case, don't you think I would have mentioned it? From time to time we have received some vehicular coverage, but not now—not during the holiday season."

"Well, who was following me?"

"Are you sure you were being followed?"

"I'm sure, and I want you to make sure that I am not under surveillance for the next meeting." Colin was visibly impatient, even dismissive of Frost.

"Have you ever conducted counter-surveillance?"

"Of course, but do you really think that's necessary? I have twelve guests about to descend on my home for dinner. If you were to have your way, I would be playing games on the street through dessert."

"Not on the street. Pick a place in the vicinity of the Sheraton where you will be able to observe me and anyone following me as I pass by." Colin's anger was resurfacing. "I then want you to proceed to a second location, perhaps in the lobby, where you will do the same, but this time, give me a signal that I am clean. Hold your scarf in your hand. Do you understand?"

"Is this really necessary?" Frost looked forlorn and resigned.

Such demands had not been placed upon him when stationed in Doha—a desolate outpost surrounded by sand and oil.

"I'll be seated in the window of the tavern located just across the street from the hotel. I forget its name, but you will see it," Frost said, resigned.

Frost stayed behind to pay the check.

⁂

It was nine thirty and time for Colin to move from the darkened corner where he had been standing since he was dropped off by a taxi some minutes earlier. He was satisfied that he had not been followed from Kifissia into the area. Frost should be in position, seated at the window of the tavern. From that vantage point he could detect whether or not Colin was still attracting attention. The walk-by would occur about five minutes before Colin was to enter the hotel lobby.

Colin felt a twinge in his lower back. He had been experiencing the pain intermittently lately. He guessed it was caused by the extra twenty pounds he was carrying. The tension he had experienced in the last few days had not helped. Failure to follow the stretching regimen recommended by his doctor only compounded the problem. Now he found himself favoring his back and sacrificing some agility in the process. He resigned himself to more of the same as he approached his fifty-third birthday. He had to admit that he was not as philosophical when his hair began to turn gray twenty years ago.

The route he selected to pass before the tavern was circuitous, winding through quiet streets in the vicinity. It was an ideal route because it would channel undetected surveillance into one narrow street. No matter how large the team behind him, someone would have to commit and pass the taverna and thus be spotted by Frost. Colin still believed that the Greek police were responsible—Frost's insistence aside. He was thirty feet from the taverna when he noticed Frost rushing down the street in his direction and then darting inside.

"Damn," Colin muttered, "why is he so late?"

Colin continued walking toward the window where Frost was to be; however, the seat was occupied. He could not see Frost as he passed.

From there Frost was to proceed to the bar inside the hotel. From any one of several tables in the lounge, he would be able to determine again whether Colin was being followed. If all was clear, he should be holding his scarf in his hand. He decided to give Frost an extra five minutes to find his position in the hotel before he reversed directions and walked toward the hotel entrance.

He began to feel the same icy excitement he remembered so vividly from his days just before a race. He was the stroke for his college eight-oared racing shell. He loved the joy, excitement, uncertainty, anxiety, and hunger for victory that gripped him in those seconds before the start of a race. He especially relished racing in Canada at the Royal Canadian Henley where shotguns were fired to start the races.

"Are you ready?" The words were spoken by the starter and followed almost immediately with "Row!" An ear-shattering blast followed from the shotgun held aloft. He could still recall so many years later the clatter of oarlocks as each crew strived to achieve an early lead with an unmerciful beat of forty-five strokes per minute. Most teams settled down within the first quarter of a mile to a beat of thirty strokes and maintained that pace for most of the race—though not Colin's team, which kept the stroke at the higher beat for most of the two thousand meter race to compensate for their relative light weight of their team. Five minutes of excitement crowned hundreds of miles of practice at dawn and dusk for months. His back was stronger then.

Was it worth it? Yes, indeed. Perhaps it was because his back was stronger then and his mind was still developing. *So here are my five minutes of excitement*, he thought as he pushed the revolving door into the hotel lobby.

"As far as I'm concerned you're clean." Frost had walked casually up to him as he entered the lobby.

"You dumb son-of-a-bitch!" Colin hissed under his breath. "I'll see you back in Kifissia." He walked into the lobby as calmly as possible, ignoring Frost. His heart was pounding with anger. He purchased a *Paris Tribune* at the newsstand and took a seat in the corner of the lobby where he could see Hans when he entered. For some reason, the Sheraton was quieter than the Hilton. He then realized that at nine in the evening it was still too early to attract the restaurant patrons of Athens.

At 10:20, Colin decided to leave. He was not concerned that Hans had not appeared. He probably had not grasped sufficiently the alternate meeting instructions. It was a pity, because this was the first time that Hans had requested a meeting on his own. Just as well. There was no reason to take any chances with Frost's demonstrated ineptitude. The information Hans had could wait.

⁑⁎⁑

Back in Kifissia, Colin tried to temper his criticism of Frost.

"Next time, see what you can do about getting into place on time."

"Please, Colin, you were not meeting with the prime minister," Frost said, attempting to deflect the criticism.

Colin felt the hair on the back of his neck bristle and a flash of anger burst in his chest. Only with the greatest effort did he avoid losing his temper. After a pause, in a low, almost guttural tone, he spoke.

"I didn't ask that you be assigned back-up. In fact, you'd be the last person I would have chosen. All these years masquerading as an operations officer when in fact you are not much more than a liaison puke."

Colin paused as the waiter served a copper carafe of retsina wine. Frost's eyes were locked in hatred, or fear—Colin could not decide. The year-round tan was drained from his complexion. A slight flicker in his left eye betrayed an inner turmoil.

Before Colin could continue, Frost enjoined in an outwardly calm, measured voice, "I suspect that you have been under considerable emotional strain. I trust it is limited to some professional anxiety and that there is no personal tragedy that prompted this unreasonable outburst."

"Jesus Christ!" Colin reached across the table and grabbed Frost's wrist. "What the fuck is wrong with you? Do you realize you're a professional disaster?"

Colin released Frost immediately. Frost had a grim smile on his face. In this profession one must never lose control. Colin felt his anger drain.

"I'd better get to my hotel. We can discuss this when I have had a night's sleep." He tossed some bills on the table, rose, and walked quickly out of the restaurant.

Rather than wait for a taxi to appear, he turned down the street. He had gone a block before he realized that he was proceeding away from the busy thoroughfare that offered him the best chance of hailing a taxi at this time of night. He abruptly reversed direction, crossing to the other side of the street to minimize the chances of Frost observing his disorientation.

⁂

Back in the small room of the pensione, Colin regained his composure. As he reviewed the day's events, he could not point to one positive outcome. He cringed at the thought of returning to Frost's office the next day. Apologies came hard. He reluctantly concluded that he owed Frost one.

His experience over the years was that it was difficult to become comfortable sleeping alone in a double bed. He was not sure whether he missed the warmth—the presence—of Chris more or his pillow. He tossed and turned, first tucking the foam rubber pillow in the crook of his arm, attempting to sleep on his side. It was not long before his back began to throb. Finally, he rose on one elbow and turned on the bedside lamp to view the clock. He had been in bed two hours. He resigned himself to a sleepless night and decided to lie still so that at least some portion of his body would be resting—if not his mind. He dozed off just before sunrise.

CHAPTER EIGHT

A shrill noise provided the background sound to Colin's dream. He was running across a field in ankle-deep mud, trying to reach the safety of the trees, but he could not seem to put any distance between himself and his pursuers. His breathing, even in sleep, became heavy with exertion and fear. The sound pulsated at regular intervals, increasing his drive to reach the trees and safety, his arms pumping.

He opened his eyes and wiped the perspiration from his brow. The dash across the field vanished from his consciousness, except that the anxiety lingered and the shrill sound continued. Colin could not decide at first where he was. The darkness was total. He reasoned that the sound was not the alarm clock—he would have recognized that. Finally, he realized that it was the telephone. He swung his feet out from under the blankets and onto the floor. As a blind man he reached for the phone, twisting his ankle on a shoe.

"Hello?" he managed, clearing his throat.

"Colin, this is Ted."

"Who?"

"Ted Frost. Are you awake yet?"

Colin snapped alert. "I'm sorry. I am now. What time is it?"

"Seven thirty. I'm calling from the embassy. I must meet you as soon as possible, but I don't want you to come here."

"Why?'

"I'll tell you when we meet." He gave him the address of a restaurant within walking distance.

By the time I return to Bonn, Colin thought, *I will have quite a collection of sites for the German tourists.* "Why couldn't I just come to the embassy?"

"Sorry. When can you be ready?"

"I will see you there at eight." Colin sensed tension in Frost's voice. *That makes two of us,* he said to himself after he hung up and rushed to the bathroom to get ready. He was dressed and on his way a few minutes before eight.

Frost was already there, watching Colin. As he approached, Frost glanced down at his coffee cup.

"Well?"

Frost continued to avoid Colin's gaze.

"I was called into the embassy again this morning to read a cable. It was from Bonn. It seems that the evening papers carried the story of a Horst Grobal, who was killed by an unknown assailant yesterday as he was walking his dog. He had been shot in the head three times at close range. Police say that he was facing his murderer as his right hand was pierced by one of the rounds—he tried to ward off the attack."

Colin felt as if someone had punched him in the solar plexus. *Horst? Why Horst—a lonely man who received mail for me and was paid a modest sum for his service? He gained as much enjoyment from the occasional beer we shared as from the monthly stipend.*

"Are they sure it was my Horst?"

"Yes, they are. And though it's too early to speculate on the motive, as a precautionary step, we're moving you into a safe house in Glyfada, near the airport." Frost paid the bill, and they left immediately for Glyfada.

⁜✳⁜

At the apartment, Colin took the time to write the events of last evening while Frost waited—soliciting at the same time guidance from Headquarters. He began by reporting as fact that he was under surveillance on his way to the primary meeting site. For this reason he aborted the meeting in favor of the alternate meeting arrangements. He omitted any reference to Frost's indiscretions. He wrote that Frost conducted countersurveillance and that they were both satisfied that Colin was no longer under surveillance. He concluded his report by writing that Hans failed to show for either the primary or alternate meeting, though he waited twenty minutes before departing. The last lines of the draft cable read:

Case officer believes that GANYMEDE's failure to appear is result of confusion on his part regarding meeting arrangements. Until GANYMEDE surfaces, case officer can only surmise that Grobal was innocent victim of urban crime. See no reason at this time to associate death with message sent to his address from GANYMEDE.

Colin passed the draft to Frost, who read it silently and added a last line.

However, we are taking all necessary precautions in the interim.

Colin read the addition and agreed. Frost departed, promising to call with any news. Until then, Colin was confined to the sparsely furnished apartment with nothing but a few dated English-language Greek newspapers to read and an apple and a piece of cheese in the refrigerator to consume. It was clear that this safe house was reserved for the occasional meeting and was not occupied full-time by a safe-house keeper.

In his career, this was not the first time that his movement was curtailed. He recalled when he was locked up for days in a New York hotel waiting for a Polish agent who at the last moment was assigned as a replacement to accompany an official delegation to a UN meeting. Colin only had time to give the agent an alias under which he would rent a room in one of the larger New York hotels.

At that time, he was thankful that the hotel had vacancies. Three days of nervous anticipation began until the agent called—though he learned in advance from the FBI where the delegation was staying. He could not initiate contact for fear of jeopardizing this sensitive agent. When he did call, they met and the agent provided intelligence that justified the waiting and the concern.

The situation was different now. What could Hans ever produce that would be worth Horst's murder—if in fact the murder was somehow linked to his cooperation with the CIA. Colin could not avoid recreating Horst's last walk in the park. Though not stated, Colin was certain that he had been attacked along the same bicycle path that wound along the Rhine River between Bonn and Bad Godesberg. Horst loved the smell of the open sea, and short of visiting the Baltic, he had gained a similar exhilaration from the passing barges plying their way in the center channel of the river. In his younger days Horst fled the postwar deprivation of West Germany and joined the crew of a Danish freighter hauling chemical fertilizer between South Africa and Europe.

Later in life, Horst won a position in the fledgling German civil service. Only three years ago he became eligible for retirement. Colin's chance meeting with him occurred a year later in Bad Godesberg. Horst valued the friendship with Colin. Colin's interest was in using Horst as a low-level support agent who allowed agents to communicate with Colin indirectly and securely through the open mail. Horst did not hesitate to accept the proposal and never asked any questions.

For Colin the conclusion was inescapable. If—however remote—Horst's murder was related to the mail that Hans posted, then Hans was in danger and Colin had no way to warn him. Colin took relief in the conviction that Hans was no longer in

Athens but was on his way back to Berlin. There was nothing for Colin to do but wait patiently until Hans called and hope that his rising concern for Hans was without basis. Perhaps Frost would receive a message from Berlin reporting that Hans had arrived.

To occupy himself, Colin wrote down his estimate of the damage done by losing Horst's support as an accommodation address. Horst's address had been registered in Washington. As far as he could recall, aside from Hans, the address had only been issued to a Soviet official who traveled infrequently to the West. The Soviet was supposed to use the address to arrange a personal meeting with his case officer who was stationed in Europe. If Horst's death was caused by his association with Colin, he discounted the possibility that the Soviets were responsible. They simply did not bother with people like Horst—at least not any longer.

He wondered how Horst's death could affect Hans's business activity—especially if the assailant had not been identified. Hans would not take kindly to precautions that Colin sought to impose earlier, especially if they curtailed his business or social interests. Colin dreaded the thought of informing Hans that there had been a problem and that his life might be in danger. He caught himself. *You're being too dramatic.* He flicked on the Greek morning television station.

⁂

Frost called in the afternoon. Colin answered the phone on the first ring. He had forsaken the television for an adventure novel he had purchased before boarding the plane in Cologne two days earlier.

"Nothing to report. Bonn states that the police have no suspects. He was shot by a forty-five, and there is no trace of the weapon. The murder took place at seven forty-five in the evening just below the Konigswinter ferry landing, not far from the embassy."

"Do they have any suspects?"

"The answer is no. They believe it might have been a robbery attempt that was foiled when someone ran to assist minutes after the attack. No money had been taken. If he was killed by a terrorist group—which no one believes—no group has claimed responsibility. The only comment made by the police official in liaison with the embassy was that it seemed to be the work of someone familiar with weapons."

"Why is that?"

"Because his aim was steady, deliberate, and effective. A very tight pattern on the victim."

"Were there any witnesses? Who found Horst?"

"The shots were heard by a man who had passed Horst five minutes earlier. The man ran back and found Horst crumpled dead on the grass. He noticed no one in the area when he returned to render assistance."

Brave man, Colin thought. *The killer or killers were probably still lurking among the trees.*

✝ ✱ ✝ ✱ ✝

Hans estimated that it was an hour before dawn. In the next room he could hear loud guttural Arabic being exchanged with a newcomer and the two guards. The handcuff that secured him to the metal side of the cot cut into his right wrist. He had not slept. His cheek throbbed from the blow he received last night with a pistol handle.

Is this is all so unnecessary? he thought. *I have answered all their questions. What more do they want?*

Suddenly, a short, angry-looking Arab burst into the room. Blotches of red marred his unshaven face. He was out of breath and sweating profusely. His light blue shirt was stained around the armpits and stretched over his extended stomach. The two guards accompanied the intruder into the bare room. They carried automatic rifles loosely. Hans did not know the model or make.

He could not even tell if they were loaded. Guns were not his specialty, and he had no intention of challenging their authority.

One of the guards reached into his jeans for a key ring fastened on a leather thong. He searched until he found the one for which he was looking. Leaning his rifle against the wall, he opened the handcuffs. He pulled Hans to his feet and swiftly pinioned his arms from behind. The handcuffs closed rapidly on his wrists, catching the skin in the metal clasp. Hans offered no resistance. He stood still—even cooperative—as leg irons were attached to his ankles. They felt cold, as did the terrazzo floor under his bare feet. They pushed him through the door and out into the dark.

Finally, freedom from these bleak surroundings, he thought as they parted the heavily curtained door to the street and he breathed deeply. The cold air hurt his lungs momentarily. A white Peugeot was waiting, parked at the curb, its motor vibrating visibly. *Must be difficult to arrange a regular tune up,* he concluded, trying not to focus on his current predicament. The driver looked vacantly at Hans as the guards nudged him from behind and shoved him into the rear seat, forcing his head down as he was squeezed into the narrow space. When he looked up, he saw a guard on either side. The short Arab joined the driver in the front seat.

Hans was cramped. His long legs were doubled in pain, and he longed to stretch out—to be free. He no longer felt the pain on his cheek. Fear had tranquilized him. The driver leaned forward and moved his foot several times up and down on the gas pedal. The car responded with a roar. He could feel the gears slip momentarily and hear a clanking sound from the motor. *Soon they will have to confiscate a vehicle to replace this one,* he concluded, resting his head on the back of the seat.

The Arabs were shouting at each other. He could not tell if they were angry with each other. Perhaps they were simply conversing. It was jabber to him. All these years traveling in the Middle East and he still could not understand a word of the language. The car careened without lights through the narrow, darkened streets of Beirut. He recognized the Corniche as they turned onto the avenue that bordered the Mediterranean, which he could barely make out in the gloom. He heard a muffled explosion not far from the shore. He looked and noticed the light from a lantern about thirty yards distant. It probably hung above a motor launch, but he could only detect the mist-like rainbow glow. *A couple of impatient fishermen in all likelihood using a grenade to stun the fish just below the surface. It's a wonder that any fish survived, especially lacking a native intelligence that would teach them to avoid this shoreline. But more importantly, why did I return to Beirut?*

There was no movement on the street—just the Peugeot driving with purpose and speed. After about fifteen minutes the car stopped abruptly. Before them stood five Arabs, all heavily armed, huddled around a fire in a spent fuel barrel. Army-issue woolen ski hats were pulled down over their ears. He did not notice the cold as they pulled him roughly from the car. Perhaps fear was warming him. His mind was occupied trying to determine what he found strange about the ride. Then he knew. He had not been blindfolded. *Aren't they concerned that I will be able to identify them?*

As in a dream he was pushed toward the sea. The sand felt wet on his feet, but he knew it was just the cold. He winced as his toe struck a rock and folded under, but he continued on at a half run. He could hear the sand rough between his toes, and the noise was like the waves on the Baltic coast when he was young. He reached the edge of the water. No one was between him and the sea. They were all behind him. He took a deep breath, imagining that he could smell the fullness of the sea; it seemed saltier than he knew it was. Facing the east, he could detect the first hints of gray, which foretold another sunrise. The night always seemed the longest for him.

He turned to see an Arab approaching him. It was his interrogator—the young fellow who spoke such refined French and passable German. Before the glare of his flashlight blinded him, he could see his wide familiar smile, white teeth against the olive-amber complexion, and the light fisherman sweater.

Without warning, he heard an unidentified shock blast in his ears and then the screeching sound of a high-pitched flute. Too late, he realized as he fell to the sand that the flute had been his cry in death.

⁑⁑⁑

That evening in Athens, Colin walked slowly into the den after an exquisite French dinner, prepared under the watchful eye of Frost's wife, Asher.

"I'll have a Drambuie on the rocks, thanks." Colin took his seat on the thick sofa. Frost fixed the drink at the rosewood sideboard. Asher joined them. Frost poured a brandy for her.

Colin looked around. Floor-to-ceiling bookshelves lined two of the walls. Expensive leather volumes filled the shelves, interspersed with museum-quality miniature sculpture pieces. It was obvious that the Frosts were living beyond any government salary and that there was some family money involved, and he decided that it was on Asher's side. *How could one be poor and named Asher?* He was not envious even when he estimated that he could not afford to pay the shipping charges for such extravagance without considering the value of these treasures. Anything Chris and he had acquired during their years abroad fit well within the weight allowance assigned them.

Frost had telephoned Colin in the early afternoon to say that there had been no news. He invited him to their home for dinner that evening. Colin accepted. Sitting around the safe house was tedious. Frost lived in an elegantly appointed white stucco home in the diplomatic enclave of Kifissia. The table had been stylishly set. Baccarat crystal and a baroque silver service complemented an intricate Wedgewood pattern. Chris would have turned a plate over, if she were there, to identify the pattern. The Frosts' servant, a native of one of the former British colonies, served the meal. She had been with the Frosts for several tours—commencing in Jeddah some years ago.

The conversation at dinner had been stilted. For his part, Colin was distracted by the events of the last days. But that was not the reason for a tension that lingered in the air. Asher's coldness was probably the result of Frost describing their encounter the previous evening. Yet they invited him to dinner. *It must be upbringing*, he decided. *One was expected to entertain out-of-town visitors, or maybe they wanted to learn more about him as competition*, he thought less kindly. Several times at the table, Asher steered the conversation to a description of Frost's former successes and the perquisites these outstanding performances had won for them both.

"In Dubai, where Ted served as chief of station, we were able to choose our favorite china for our extensive entertaining," Asher interjected during an interminable lull in the conversation.

Colin nodded, and his mind drifted and probably contributed to the lulls. He missed Chris's easy companionship and friendship. Even the quiet of his safe house apartment was beginning to be appealing to him. *Why did I accept the invitation? It must be upbringing*, he surmised with a smile. The telephone rang at about the time that Colin was thinking of excusing himself, and Frost answered it.

"Yes?" He listened for a few seconds before responding. "I'll be right down."

"Well, there's another cable for me to read. I don't know what it concerns."

"Perhaps I'll accompany you and you can drop me off." Colin was relieved that the call provided him the necessary excuse to take his leave.

Frost and his wife seemed equally relieved. He accepted Asher's outstretched hand in farewell.

"Thanks for a delightful meal." Colin wondered what she would do if he grabbed her and gave her a hearty hug. He didn't have the courage. It was only in his dreams that he acted so boldly.

The ride to the embassy in the evening traffic took fifteen minutes. Frost loosened up along the way—describing his college days in New England and how he was looking forward to his thirtieth reunion that spring. Anticipating another message to read seemed to restore his confidence. Colin could identify with the feeling—at least the expectation side of it when called in to the embassy after hours. In his experience, too often the cable contained nothing that could not have waiting until morning. It was usually sent by someone who did not appreciate the time difference between continents. Once he remembered receiving orders transferring him to another post in the middle of the night, though he was not due to leave for weeks, and even those orders were countermanded when he was assigned elsewhere.

Who knew, maybe this cable would announce Frost's reassignment to Rome, which they sought, a promotion, or recognition for valor from duty at his previous post—though the latter possibility seemed quite remote. Colin hastily corrected his lack of charity. For him, he hoped that the message announced Hans's safe return to Berlin. If that was the case, Colin would depart Athens on the earliest available flight tomorrow. Frost rattled on about the upcoming reunion, though Colin heard only half of what was said. Instead, his mind rested on the thought that he might be returning home very soon. In a sense they were both like children, Colin concluded, each searching a Cracker Jack box for a prize. He never understood why the prize always seemed to be at the bottom of the narrow box.

The gate to the embassy had been secured for the evening. They had to wait until the marine guard had identified them both and returned to open the iron gate, swinging it closed after they entered. Once in the embassy, they proceeded to the third floor and waited behind a vaulted door for the communicator on duty to produce a copy of the cable. In the interval between summoning Frost and their arrival, three more cables had come in for Frost to read. The communicator was busy processing them. When he finished, he appeared with the four cables, arranged in chronological order.

Frost took them and read them, beginning with the first to

arrive. They both remained standing. Colin wished that Frost would finish, assuming that they concerned him as well. He finally passed the first cable to Colin. From Frost's expression, the message was not good news. It was from Beirut and addressed to Athens, Washington, Bonn, and Berlin. The text was terse and laconic.

1. *GANYMEDE's body discovered this afternoon. It had been tossed outside embassy from nondescript pick-up truck. GANYMEDE identified after matching photograph in West German passport found on body with photograph in operational folder.*
2. *Remains turned over to German ambassador who is making arrangements to have them flown home to his family in Germany.*
3. *We are concerned that body dropped at the US embassy rather than at German embassy. Cannot avoid conclusion that those responsible determined to signal they know of GANYMEDE's intelligence affiliation with US.*
4. *Will advise developments.*

Colin felt a sharp pain in his eyes as they lost focus behind his glasses. *First Horst. Now Hans.* What began as a routine operational trip had turned into a nightmare—like an endless spill into oblivion. *What is happening?* Hans, the successful industrialist, agrees to become a bit player in the theater of espionage. Death was not a factor, nor should it have been. It did not happen in real life—only in adventure novels. Aside from his friendship, espionage had appealed to Hans, at least at first, because it served to distract him from the pain he suffered as a cuckolded husband. But the therapy, if that is what espionage served, should not have led to his death. Without a word, Colin reached out for the next cable, this one from Berlin, and like the first it too was brief, requesting Washington's guidance as to what compensation if any Berlin should be prepared to send Hans's family.

"Dumb shits! Didn't they read the file?" Colin erupted. "He is and was separated from his wife, who was shacking up with his buddy. The question is not about compensation but rather about warning his survivors." Colin placed the cable behind the first and read the third. It was sent by Washington to the same addresses but inexplicably included Sophia, Bulgaria, on the address line.

1. *Distressed to learn of GANYMEDE's death. Please convey our regret to case officer. Also, ask Gordon to suggest manner in which we can convey same, if appropriate, to GANYMEDE's children, who file reflects live in Hamburg.*
2. *While there is insufficient information to link murders of Horst and GANYMEDE at this writing, it certainly should not be discounted. Not knowing motives or identities of perpetrators, request Bonn do everything possible to protect case officer Gordon's wife. As interim measure, direct that Bonn move her to safe haven pending decision as to whether situation serious enough to warrant her return to US.*
3. *For Athens: Suggest Gordon return to Bonn ASAP to prepare recommendations regarding steps to be pursued to discover who is behind these deaths.*
4. *For Sophia: We are forwarding relevant cable traffic and summary of GANYMEDE's operation for background information and to assist in debriefing ICARUS.*

"Who the hell is ICARUS?" Colin asked. Frost shrugged. He then picked up the fourth and final cable from Bonn. It had been sent prior to the receipt of Washington's cable yet had correctly anticipated Washington's guidance.

1. *Gordon's wife has been moved to a safe location in Bonn. Twenty-four-hour protection arranged with cooperation of German authorities.*

2. *While German intelligence suspect that Hans worked for us, we are satisfied that they will provide all information acquired in pursuit of this investigation.*
3. *For Athens: Please advise Gordon's ETA. Will meet.*

Colin had received his wish. He would be returning to Bonn tomorrow on the first available flight. How he hoped now it would have been under different circumstances. Frost returned the cables to the communicator on duty. Before leaving the embassy, Colin checked the flight schedule in Frost's office. He jotted down the relevant flight numbers. They walked in silence along the corridors of the darkened embassy. It was almost midnight.

"I will make arrangements"—Colin was the first to speak—"when I get back to the apartment and will be on my way on the first available flight."

"Not a chance. I will drive you."

"Ted, I insist. You have enough to do. Please."

"Okay," Frost reluctantly agreed. "I'm terribly sorry for what has happened."

"Thanks, Ted." He bid farewell as they pulled up to the apartment house after traveling in silence for thirty minutes.

Colin wearily mounted the steps to the entrance. He was getting too old for this. Why did he get so attached to his agents? Once he thought it was because he felt guilty working from the security of the embassy. With the violence directed at US embassies and personnel, he no longer questioned that premise. Whatever the motivation, he regretted not having prepared both agents for the threat that ultimately led to their murders. He felt deep grief for their loss as he put the key into the lock of his door. Two fine people dead in as many days.

After making reservations for the flight the next day, Colin climbed into bed. He felt sapped of energy and anticipated another fitful night. Contributing to his exhaustion was the numbing pain in his neck and shoulders. He drifted off into a semi-conscious sleep. When he woke the next morning, it was with a taste of stale oysters in his mouth. In his younger days, that taste would have indicated an evening of beer drinking with friends. Now his internal system revealed the mounting strain and anxiety under which he was operating.

CHAPTER NINE

"Good afternoon. St. Moritz on the Park. May I help you?" The voice of the young lady glistened through the telephone.

"Yes, do you have Mr. Haddad staying there?"

"One minute, sir; let me connect you to registration."

On the third ring, another equally vibrant voice invited attention. "Yes."

"I am trying to determine whether my father, Mr. Joseph Haddad, is staying in your hotel."

"One minute, sir." David was put on hold. This was the eleventh hotel he had contacted in midtown New York. His father had departed two weeks ago with the promise to call before he boarded a flight back to Beirut. Not hearing from his father, David had resorted to using the Yellow Pages in his search.

"I'm sorry, sir, but we have no Mr. Arthur staying with us."

"Not Arthur. Haddad, H-A-D-D-A-D."

"You say he is your father? When was Mr. Haddad supposed to arrive?"

David hung up the phone, his finger already selecting the next hotel to call.

"Any luck?" Kathleen asked. She had just put the children to bed.

"I wonder where he is. If he wants to behave like a child—let him!" he said. It was her idea for David to try to locate his father by going down the list of hotels in the Yellow Pages. She now regretted the suggestion.

"Do you think he's back in Lebanon?" David asked.

"I think he took the car from here to the airport and never made it to the city," she responded.

"Why would he do that?"

"Simple—he didn't want to face a farewell with his only son that at his age might be his last." Kathleen spoke with sympathy in her voice. "He realized that we would be more disturbed if he said he was returning immediately. I guess he was afraid we would blame ourselves for the disastrous visit."

"What are you talking about? I'm certain he's here. How could I feel worse for causing this rupture?" David began dialing the next hotel on the list.

"Have you called him in Beirut?"

"Of course! Why do you think I'm certain he is in New York? The housekeeper confirmed that he was still in America."

The receptionist answered, and after a few minutes of conversation, David slammed the receiver onto the cradle. He crossed out the name of the hotel so roughly that he ripped a hole in the page.

⁂

While David was searching for his father in New York City, Kuban was north of the city in Larchmont, concluding the purchase of a Volkswagen van. He had spotted the advertisement in the local newspaper. The middle-aged couple selling the vehicle had seen the last of their children leave for college. They no longer were obliged to travel between various extracurricular activities throughout the county. It was with some regret they decided to part with this once-reliable companion.

For Kuban it was roomy enough for the team. During his brief test drive, he realized that it lacked power and was barely able to maintain fifty miles per hour on the highway. But he did not view this as a drawback. The operation was planned so as there would be no high-speed chases. This box-like model was still common on the road and would not attract attention as did some of the more modern and radically designed foreign products. He also believed that minor modifications in the way of a hand-painted sign on the side panel would serve to disguise the team as employees of a private maintenance company.

Kuban paid for the vehicle in cash. The asking price was a pittance, well within the amount allocated by Shamir. However, he could not resist bargaining with the family as he would have done in Lebanon. As far as they were concerned, the vehicle was for his son who was involved in a food-distribution program for the disadvantaged. In addition to reducing the price slightly, they also allowed him to retain the license plates so that the food deliveries would not be interrupted.

⁋ ∗ ⁋ ∗⁋

The flight to Cologne/Bonn airport was on time. Colin remembered little of the journey, so caught up was he in the events of the last days. Only when the stewardess announced that they were in the final approach and he refastened his seatbelt did he turn his thoughts to the present and to Chris.

He was one of the first passengers off the plane onto the ramp that led to the modern terminal. He recognized one of the embassy security officers standing in the arrival section waiting discreetly for him to clear customs. The officer led the way to the embassy car, which was double-parked in front of the exit. Colin looked around. He half expected that Chris would be waiting for him. Just as he ducked his head to climb into the passenger side of the large American sedan, he spotted the senior embassy security officer sitting in what he presumed to be the follow-on vehicle. He was a bear of a man, more akin to a Polar bear—white crew cut and thick hair reaching down the back of his neck and emerging as coarse white wool-like matting on the back of huge hands. The scars his hands bore he earned as a lineman in professional football. He still maintained his physical condition with a vigorous, daily exercise regimen.

Colin was impressed with the precautions. It was so unlike the embassy, or for that matter the State Department. With few exceptions, the Foreign Service viewed security as an unwarranted restriction upon its ability to conduct foreign policy. He wondered if in this case they were overreacting.

"What pensione were you staying at in Athens?" his driver asked.

"I was in a safe house last night," Colin responded absently, forgetting for the moment that he was talking to an embassy officer and not a CIA colleague. The security officer ignored mention of a safe house.

"No, I mean the night before."

"The Telemachus. Why?"

"Do you remember the room number?"

"Two-Zero-One," Colin's curiosity piqued.

"I just wanted to confirm what Athens reported. It seems that a chambermaid was killed in an explosion yesterday afternoon when she opened the door to that room."

Colin leaned back in the seat. He let the air leave his lungs slowly and closed his eyes.

Thirty minutes later, the two-car convoy pulled up in front of the embassy entrance. He had never made the trip in faster time, though he considered himself something of an expert in the last-minute dashes to and from the airport. After two decades of international travel, he took perverse delight in seeing how close he could shave his arrival at the airport with the departure of the plane from the gate. What a change from the person who in his early years would arrive hours before a flight was scheduled to depart. He wondered if his guides were not demonstrating some opposition to his frequent trips by encouraging frantic dashes.

"Hi. What have you been up to?" Joan asked as she placed

her cigarette in an ashtray. Colin smiled weakly. It felt like he had been away for weeks.

"I'm afraid this is one time you have all the answers." He placed his leather briefcase on his desk.

"Do you have a number where I can reach Chris?" Colin asked. Maura looked up from her typing for the first time.

"I knew that would be his first question, didn't I, Joan? Welcome home."

Chris was relieved to hear Colin's voice. She had learned about the bombing at the pensione when additional security was assigned to her temporary residence.

"As soon as I review some things with Joan, I'll join you. Maybe we can take a nap." He laughed. "Nap" was their code word for the hours they would reserve for lovemaking. If anything, their physical relationship had intensified with the years; that is, unless his memory had failed him. Memory, they say, is the first thing to go.

"You're all talk." He knew she was smiling. "But I'd be ready, just in case." Colin swallowed hard and hung up the phone. He loved the way she was able to stimulate his baser instincts almost on command.

"I've reviewed the files we have on both Horst and GANYMEDE, and for the life of me I can't understand why any group would be so determined to kill them," Joan interrupted.

"I could make an argument that GANYMEDE was just unlucky enough to fall into the hands of Hezbollah during a visit to Beirut." Joan hardly paused for breath. "But the question is what was he doing in Beirut in the first place? And if he was there under the protection of Ben Yousef, how could this have happened? And furthermore," she continued, out of breath again, "if Hezbollah was responsible, why would they dispatch someone to eliminate Horst? And …"

Colin hoped she would slow down. He was still thinking about his conversation with Chris.

"Since when did Hezbollah have an operational capability in Europe? It just doesn't add up," she concluded.

"On the other hand, what if the Libyans discovered on their own GANYMEDE's cooperation with us?" Colin added.

"Look, Colin, GANYMEDE was looking for information on oil strategy in a glutted market. Horst's only action was to receive an occasional postcard or letter. Big deal! Even the Libyans don't kill over that. There has to be more at stake." She lit another Black Russian.

"You seem to think that a group is involved. What kind of group?"

"You continue to deny that the murders are linked. I don't care what you wrote from Athens, but you're crazy if you believe it." Joan looked intently at Colin until he nodded.

"Next, consider if you were running the operation what you would need in the way of support to synchronize the murders of two individuals within twenty-four hours in two different countries."

"I don't run assassination operations." Joan ignored the quip. "Incidentally, did you hear about the bomb going off in the pensione? Was that your place?"

"The answer is 'Yes, yes, and yes I heard, and yes that was my pensione.'" He was pleased to find his sarcasm emerging under Joan's questioning. "If not Hezbollah, you could argue that the Libyans or Syrians have the organization in Europe to accomplish the assassination in Bonn, mount surveillance in Athens, later rig a room with a bomb there, and kill someone in Beirut. But I am still plagued by the question, 'Why?'" Colin seemed exhausted.

"We won't discover the reason for their deaths soon enough to prevent Washington from recalling you in the interest of your safety—and that would be a pity, because I would miss you."

"Me, too!" Maura joined in, momentarily breaking the rhythm of her typing.

"I think that you're both being a bit premature. Maura, call security. I need a ride home." Colin had to get away. He gave them both a smile and left the office.

⁂

In the embassy car, a follow-on car with two armed guards behind, Colin recalled an incident years ago. Chris had met him at an airport after he had been away for three months. He assumed that they were on their way home to be with the children. Instead Chris made a slight detour. He thought nothing of it until they pulled into a hotel parking lot. With a sparkle in her gray eyes she informed him that the key in her hand was to a room she rented for the evening.

He remembered waiting impatiently for the elevator to reach their floor. Chris wore a dark brown skirt that outlined her thighs and a light tan silk blouse that dared him to unbutton it. Once in the room, he suggested that they undress and get under the covers. She laughed. He was surprised when she, her eyes twinkling, pulled him down on the bed and began to open his belt. He reached down to lift her and discovered as he staggered onto the bed that she was bare under her skirt.

"You must be tired." It was the embassy driver.

"Oh, not really," he lied. "How much further?"

"Two minutes."

They pulled up in front of a substantial prewar residence located on a quiet, tree-lined street. He recognized the uniforms of two German policemen as belonging to GSG-9, the elite anti-terrorist unit. No one was taking any chances.

"Not bad." He opened the car door and retrieved his bag from the trunk.

CHAPTER TEN

"Tell me again. Why did you come to the embassy?" The question was posed by a CIA case officer assigned to the consular section of the embassy in Sofia, Bulgaria. When a Spanish national had requested to see an American, he was directed to this consular officer.

"I'm tired of running. I have already exceeded the life expectancy of someone in my profession. It's time to settle down. I need money—protection. I know you can provide both."

Jamie Casasnovas, or ICARUS—the cryptonym assigned by Washington with traces requested by Sofia—entered the consulate on Friday, two days previously, on the pretext of visiting the library maintained by the US Information Service. His companion was a slim attractive blond in her late thirties. What was at first taken to be two Europeans on vacation turned out to be a couple for whom arrest warrants had been issued by several Western governments. He and, to a lesser extent, his lady friend were bona fide international terrorists.

From the three lengthy debriefing sessions, the American had learned that ICARUS was thirty-two years old and a native of Mallorca, Spain. For the last five years he had served as a foot soldier with the Red Army Faction, a West German anarchist group noted for its violent, well-planned operations. He had been involved primarily as a courier transporting arms and explosives from the Middle East to Germany.

His modus operandi was to steal a vehicle in Western Europe, preferably a Mercedes, and drive to a designated country in the Middle East. There he would wait while the car was modified and the arms and explosives were expertly concealed. Mercedes were the preferred choice because of their power and because the door panels and fenders were ideal for concealing weapons and explosives. Usually he had to wait two weeks for the concealment to be completed. He would then return to Western Europe along a scenic route—popular with the tourists—on a second set of false travel documents procured by the RAF in the event that he had aroused interest from the border authorities earlier.

Upon return to Western Europe, he would drive to a predesignated town and call a telephone number he had been issued for specific delivery instructions to take place within an hour to minimize the chances that ICARUS would double cross his patrons. In this business no one trusted anyone. Usually he was directed to a public parking areas, often near a train station, where he parked and locked the vehicle. Following delivery, he returned to Santa Ponza, Mallorca, where a money-order payment would be wired to his account. The amount he received ranged from five to twenty thousand dollars depending upon the complexity of the assignment and the amount of contraband arms and explosives he transported. All this he told the American, who took detailed notes and recorded the debriefing as well.

"What do you want from us?"

"I want asylum for Brigid and me in your country—a pardon from prosecution and protection from those who would pursue us."

"And in return …?"

"What I'm doing now. I will tell you everything I know."

The American continued to probe ICARUS using the requirements he received from Washington. He knew very little about terrorism and in fact avoided the subject to the extent that he could. He judged terrorism to be corrupting and of short-term interest and duration, and definitely not career enhancing.

Washington's participation in providing timely questions for the case officer and analysis was critical in vetting the potential agent and determining his or her worth. To date, the debriefing revealed that ICARUS had not been in contact with any prominent terrorists. His value would be more toward identifying lower-level foot soldiers who manned the supporting infrastructure of terrorist organizations—no small contribution given the paucity of intelligence collected.

"How long is your visa to Bulgaria valid?" He was running out of time before the Bulgarians would show interest in ICARUS. He was puzzled as to why Washington had yet to accept, or reject, his offer to cooperate. Though traces had been provided, he had yet to receive any indication of interest in him or of Headquarters' willingness to meet his preconditions. He wanted to dismiss this volunteer, or walk-in, as soon as possible, assuming that he possessed information of only minimal intelligence value.

"We still have two days."

"Good—come by tomorrow at noon. Mix in with the crowd entering to see America Today."

As soon as ICARUS left, the American drafted a message to Washington:

1. *Please provide guidance as requested.*
2. *ICARUS insists that he has not had contact with individuals cited by Washington. He has not traveled to Libya, nor can he recall any contact with Libyan nationals. We will focus future debriefings on his knowledge of terrorist infrastructure in Europe and Middle East, with which he seems well versed.*
3. *Subject and his companion must depart Bulgaria tomorrow when their visas expire. If interested in reestablishing contact with them in West, provide*

contact instructions by opening of business (local time) 19 December.

That should prompt some response. He was pleased that he had exaggerated the time constraints by one day—anything to speed their departure.

Sofia's first cable reporting ICARUS's offer of assistance arrived in Washington on Friday, two days before GANYMEDE's body was discovered. It was the responsibility of the Near East desk within the CIA's Counterterrorist Center to prepare a coordinated response to Sofia—this despite the fact that someone could have argued that the European desk in the same Center should have the action. After all, ICARUS appeared to have possible access to information related to an active Arab support network and the Red Army Faction seemed to be in a dormant state.

Once the action had been assigned to the Near East desk, Kay O'Neil became the point of contact for generating and responding to all cables concerning the GANYMEDE operation, including those related to Horst's murder—a definite bureaucratic infringement on the European desk's authority that would not go unchallenged. In fact, had the European desk chief learned what was happening in his absence he would have returned to the office promptly—thus forfeiting the end-of-year leave his wife had insisted that he take—so much for the priorities of bureaucrats!

Kay O'Neil managed the Near East desk. She was a tiny, white-haired, thin ghost of a woman who traced her intelligence lineage to OSS and World War II. It was not difficult to imagine her in caricature parachuting into occupied France—her oversized angular face drifting above her seeming empty fatigues. Before landing she would surely have had to adjust her half-frame reading glasses with one hand and clutched a cigarette with the second. No one tried to estimate her age, but one young clerk commented wryly that his grandmother had more contemporaries living than Kay. His grandmother was seventy-one years old.

Kay took in stride the fact that she was swamped with high-priority cables—all demanding immediate responses. Stacy, her young research assistant, arrived in Kay's cubicle of gray room dividers. Stacy carried the stack of files that Kay had requested. Among them was a thick file that contained information on the GANYMEDE operation. A second was devoted to Sulham Khalifa Ben Yousef, the Libyan oil advisor, better known for his suspected ties to Libya's terrorist network.

Over the years, Kay had gained a reputation for her intuitive, almost uncanny, operational sense. She was convinced at the outset that Horst's and GANYMEDE's murders were connected. News of the bombing of Colin's pensione reinforced her view and confirmed the respect with which she was held. She was also certain that these crimes were perpetrated for motives more serious than a possible bungled attempt by GANYMEDE to gather information on OPEC strategy.

On her own authority she sent copies of the relevant cables to Sofia. She was formulating some role for ICARUS in this case, even though the idea had not yet crystallized. Before she pursued it further, she wanted to have the station in Sofia establish ICARUS's bona fides beyond a reasonable doubt. That is, the case officer had to test rigorously the potential agent's access to intelligence and, to the extent possible, his truthfulness. Only then could she begin to estimate his potential value to Washington. At a minimum, she wanted to know if he had ever come into contact with Ben Yousef or any other Libyans or Syrians with suspected terrorist connections.

The second cable from Sofia that morning disappointed her. If ICARUS was telling the truth, it seemed that he would not be much help. His contact with individuals of interest was yet to be established. She also did not like the tone of the cable. It angered her, in fact.

"Wait till that rascal draws a Washington tour." She turned to Stacy. "I'll remember him. Where does he get the nerve to give me an ultimatum? The silly soul, if only he read his first message where he reported that this chap must leave Bulgaria—and it wasn't tomorrow." She gave her full attention to Stacy. "Well, what have you found, dearie?"

Stacy handed over the stack of files. Kay began to examine them immediately. She pulled Hans's file first. Beginning with the page at the bottom—that is, the earliest entry—she studied the personality profile that Colin had prepared early in his relationship with Hans. This was the period of time when Colin was delving into Hans's private life to determine whether he was suited to the double life of espionage. She was impressed by the care Colin took in assessing Hans's personality. He went beyond the superficial comments made by so many case officers in their haste. This case officer sought to discover Hans's true motivation, his life goals, and his primary interests. The level of detail contained was impressive and well written.

"They're not all that good," she said without taking her eyes off the report. Stacy looked up before she realized that once again Kay was not addressing her. Rather, Kay was totally oblivious to those around her now as she was now so focused. From time to time she interrupted her study to jot notes on the index cards at her side. Later in the afternoon, she would meet with a collection of senior operations officers. But before she did she wanted to draw her own picture of Hans and the operation, which he supported.

Three hours passed. Kay had not stirred from her seat other than to light one cigarette after another. Her eyes burned either from the smoke or from the intense reading. It was time for her to review the index cards that were filled and scattered on the desk. She underlined Hans's attraction to high-technology gadgets to the extent that he installed a flight simulator in his living room and an elaborate electronic exercise machine alongside the outdoor pool. He always had a pocket recorder in his pocket to capture insights and ideas that popped into his head in the course of a day. One of several cellular telephones was always within his grasp.

Hans had a keen attraction to foreign cultures and travel—even though his languages had been limited to fluent but accented English and his native German. He traveled extensively throughout

Europe and in the United States and had taken several business and vacation trips to Lebanon before the violence erupted. He seemed to favor Spain—thus joining thousands of his countrymen who annually fled the drabness and order of northern Europe for the warmth, disorder, and women of southern Europe.

Under education, Kay noted that Hans had turned a basic education in engineering—receiving the equivalent of a junior college education—into a multimillion dollar corporation that built printed circuit boards, primarily for Siemens' huge computer-hardware manufacturing division. His five hundred employees faced no more complex task than soldering under a microscope or checking Siemens' computer flat packages for imperfections. The initial 80 percent rejection rate created another lucrative business line, which Hans had the foresight to exploit by correcting the flaws in the existing flat packages.

Hans's personal life suffered while his flair for business flourished. He outgrew the bride of his youth. *She probably outgrew him*, Kay thought as she read Colin's male-biased assessment. Hans's estranged wife still resided in Berlin in the apartment of his disenfranchised business associate. His two grown children lived in Hamburg. Kay noted that Hans seemed unable to accept responsibility for the state of his personal affairs and leaned heavily on the advice of his case officer.

"Thank God, I am alone. Books have more feeling." At Kay's audible comments, Stacy looked up again but returned to what she was doing when she realized that Kay was not talking to her. Kay remembered long ago reading the typewritten text of a note from an American official's wife who had committed suicide abroad.

Living with you is like living with a stone.

The word *is* was crossed out roughly in pencil and the words *has been* inserted above as the woman projected her demise.

She turned next to Hans's hobbies. He had a consuming interest in powerful automobiles, airplanes, and the collection of religious icons. What a combination! He intrigued her.

He owned a Rolls Royce and a Porsche. To satisfy his interest in flying, he earned a license to fly the Lear Jet he had purchased the year before. Kay felt no envy. She still drove her 1952 Pontiac sedan to and from work, and she was deathly afraid of flying. Where possible, she still traveled by train or bus. On her infrequent trips abroad, she took a horse-sized pill, prescribed by her doctor before boarding the aircraft. Over the years, she suspected from its aftertaste that the pill was probably not a sedative but an over-the-counter placebo—though she never raised the subject with her doctor.

Hans's interest in icons was unusual. On the surface he appeared uncultured—nouveau riche. However, the image emerging now was a man who had developed a sophisticated appreciation of art. His wealth allowed him to amass a priceless art collection. In quieter days, he roamed the streets of Beirut, seeking Russian icons from any number of reputable dealers with supply networks into the Soviet Union and Eastern Europe. According to Colin, the walls of one room in his home were lined with the finest acquisitions. She made a mental note to ask Colin someday what had prompted his interest in icons. Kay also had a modest collection, but hers consisted of modern reproductions for which she would have to wait five hundred years to pass before their value would go beyond the fifty dollars she paid for each.

Whatever group was responsible for his murder, it was ruthless, determined, and capable. It was no mean feat to mount and sustain terrorist operations in Europe, where the penalty once apprehended was becoming ever more severe. Unable to reason what prompted the killing, she uttered again aloud, "Did he stumble into something?"

"What did you say?" Stacy asked.

"Oh, nothing." Kay took up Ben Yousef's folder.

⁑∗⁑∗⁑

Later that afternoon, Kay timed her entry into the small,

sparsely furnished conference room one minute before David Brody, the director of the Counter-Terrorism Center, arrived. Already present were six operations officers who filled various senior positions. They were handpicked by Brody for their compatible approach toward operations. Kay summed this approach as risk-avoidance. The purpose of the meeting was to discuss follow-up action, if any, in response to Hans's murder. Kay was not impressed by her younger colleagues. She had seen them all enter the agency decades before—fresh out of college and graduates of the agency's specialized intelligence and paramilitary training.

Like clockwork, Brody's appearance took place in a whisper as he flowed into the room and took his seat at the table. He never occupied the same seat twice. There was always some shuffling about as the others followed, seeking to conceal their uneasiness. The confusion resembled a game of musical chairs. It would be humorous if Brody were not deadly earnest in keeping people off-balance with the seating arrangements, but also with his intentions. Kay had little respect for Brody's folly and the reaction of his underlings. She slipped into the seat in front of which she had been standing.

"Who called this meeting?" he asked—always asked.

Kay, who had left too much work on her desk to wait for one of the unlikely heroes present to respond, said, "You did—to discuss the GANYMEDE case."

"Fine—where are we?" In the uneasy silence, Kay scanned the faces of those around the table. They never had anything to say. As usual, they were waiting for someone else to speak up.

"Have you read the pertinent cables that I sent to you late yesterday afternoon?" Brody nodded affirmatively to Kay's question.

"Well, the question before us is what do we do with the case officer. There are three options as I see it—one, reassign Gordon to the States and pursue the matter no further; two, turn over what we have to the Germans and provide backup support from our station in Bonn; three, retrace Hans's path and try to discover why he paid the price he did—without, of course, losing anyone else."

Kay paused and stared at Brody. A lively discussion ensued about the relative merits of each option. Brody was not one to appear cautious in front of his staff. He saved that for his decision meeting, usually with one individual. After what seemed like an endless discussion, he interrupted with a question addressed to Kay.

"How would we begin to retrace Hans's steps?"

Kay sighed audibly. The decision had been made, at least until he returned to his office. He would allow Kay to pursue Hans's murderers. She knew from previous exchanges with him that she would have to stimulate enough activity and generate sufficient reporting so that a self-sustained momentum would be reached—and soon. Brody would then be unable to quash the operation without obvious effort—something he would be reluctant to do. He was no risk taker, but even more, he was concerned about preserving the carefully cultivated image of himself as a master strategist.

CHAPTER ELEVEN

In Bonn, Chris spent the day discussing their impending return to Washington with the embassy's shipping and travel offices. She was glad that the children were grown and living in the States. She did not have to concern herself about withdrawing them early from school, nor did she have to worry about transporting pets as they did when the children were young. Colin was the one who always became spastic during a move. He was especially sensitive to the attention that their menagerie of pets caused at an airport. He could handle twice the number of children—they had five in their early tours abroad—if only the pets would disappear during departures and arrivals. Yes, indeed, this pack-out would be a lot less stressful.

❧*❧*❧

While she was orchestrating the move, Colin was in the process of turning over his responsibilities to the other case officers in the station. He expected to receive travel orders any day. It was impossible for him to do what he was paid and trained to do—that is, run clandestine operations—with the German police stationed outside his door ready to protect him. And he did not expect the coverage to be withdrawn soon.

As he relinquished responsibilities, he thought about Hans

but made no progress in solving the riddle of his murder. German liaison provided the embassy the report from the medical examiner. It also contained a list of what he had on his person when he was found. Colin read the list—trying to distance himself from the pain he experienced.

1. *Pair white poplin trousers*
2. *Short-sleeve white shirt*
3. *White cotton undershorts*
4. *St. Christopher's medal and sterling silver chain*
5. *350 Lebanese pounds*
6. *Sewing kit needle*

He did not leave much behind. At current inflationary rates, the Lebanese pounds amounted to less than one US dollar—incredible, when compared to the fortune he had amassed in his fifty years. Colin could not avoid a sense of guilt for somehow sharing responsibility in his demise—thinking to himself *if only*. In consolation, he remembered the fellow from Georgia with whom he occasionally played poker. Whenever anyone voiced regret for throwing in cards early and then seeing the winning card that would have been dealt him had he remained in the game, Tom would announce, "If a frog had wings, it would fly."

The autopsy report was direct. Hans died from the trauma that followed the entry of a chunk of lead from a 9 mm Remington fired close range into his heart. His body bore numerous bruises that had been applied systematically by a professional interrogator. His left cheek had been broken. A photograph was attached, which reminded Colin eerily of a death mask. For a man whom he remembered as always having an anxious look in his eyes, in death he seemed peaceful—at rest.

Colin glanced up from his desk. There was little else to do but wait for travel orders. He dreaded the move back to Washington. It would be expensive for them, and he knew the work would lack the pace and excitement of the field. He had no interest in transferring his operational skills to the byzantine bureaucracy that awaited him—despite the past friendly warning, or was it advice, he had received from colleagues. A tour in Washington, so they said, would give him a crack at commanding his own station the next time he was assigned abroad. It would be good for his career, he was told. How often had he heard the same words accompany an assignment that was unappealing?

He decided to shake off his gloomy disposition by going home for lunch. Chris returned at the same time from her bout with the haughty embassy employees. They both decided that lunch could wait. With no preliminaries, they moved up the staircase, focusing their attention on what bedroom they would select for their noontime tryst. Their abandon and base appetites rivaled that of an illicit affair.

He lingered so long entwined in Chris's legs and arms that by the time he returned to the office two hours had elapsed. He expected some comment from Joan or Maura. He was not disappointed. He entered the office still perspiring. Maura was alone in the office.

"Have you started jogging?" Her eyes sparkled with recognition. Any doubt was erased as Colin fumbled for words of explanation. Before he could extricate himself, she changed the subject.

"We just received an immediate cable from Washington. It's on your desk."

Colin walked quickly into the next room. He bumped his knee on the edge of the metal desk, sending a shiver up his spine. The pain did not dampen his excitement. He expected the cable to announce his reassignment. Who knows, they might find themselves in a remote safe place outside the United States; if he was to be in Washington, maybe he'd receive one of the few mind-expanding assignments available. He picked up the cable and read that it was addressed to Bonn, Athens, and Sofia.

1. *Washington desires to pursue further motive for murders of Horst and GANYMEDE. Consensus here*

Ganymede

is GANYMEDE uncovered intelligence of value and was eliminated because of it. His association with US intelligence was at most ancillary factor.

2. Must assume that before he died, GANYMEDE revealed full extent of cooperation with us and identity of his case officer. Recognizing this danger, we still ask Gordon to consider remaining involved in the operation, at least during initial stages. Our goal is to ferret out strategy which Libya uses on surface, doing everything to protect.

3. If agreeable, desire Gordon to travel to Athens within week and meet with ICARUS, who is on his way there from Sofia. Latter has indicated willingness to assist in return for asylum in US for him and female companion—read common-law wife. Gordon is designated ICARUS's primary case officer.

4. Our goal is to have ICARUS attempt to penetrate Ben Yousef's circle by offering himself directly to Libyans. We believe that there is a good chance that Libyans will find him attractive. He has demonstrated ability to travel throughout Europe in support of RAF terrorist objectives. Also, he would attract far less attention than Arab national working at their behest.

5. Defer to Athens, but believe that there may be some merit in having ICARUS approach Libyan embassy in Athens for visa. Confident that Libyans on their own would soon confirm ICARUS's identify and it is possible that they would invite him into inner sanctum.

6. Bonn: Please advise of Gordon's decision.

Colin read the cable a second time. He felt clear, surging, pulsing elation. Was it the excitement of the chase the cable outlined? Maybe it was his own Walter Mitty dream of participating in the kind of daring action that he would have shied away from in his youth. He could feel the adrenaline course through his veins to the tips of his fingers that actually throbbed. He was grinning uncontrollably. Why was he so happy? Was it because he was needed? His answer was an unequivocal *yes*. At least for now, he was able to put aside the thought of Washington. He had escaped momentarily the paper wars of the bureaucracy in favor of what was for him combat. He could remain in field operations for just a while longer. He heard deep inside a kind of archetypal assent to battle. If only his back did not ache. He stretched his hands above his head in elation, hoping Maura did not enter and see the foolish grin he could not erase from his face.

Years ago, his back was strong when he answered a similar call, or was it challenge? Then he had to overcome what he and all of his colleagues acknowledged—raw, natural fear. He was about to make his first night parachute jump. He was sitting tensely in a C-47—the eerie red glow of the interior lights on them. He, along with thirty others, was sitting on one of several metal benches within the aircraft. Suddenly the hoarse command of the jump master sounded over the engine noise. In measured intervals Colin would recall until his death, "Stand up! Hook up! Turn to the door! Move to the door!"

He could still hear the shuffle of the booted, fatigue-clad troops in the steel cavern of the aircraft as they advanced to the open door and recall that instant when he paused in the door, wind hissing around his face, one thousand feet above the ground, in total darkness. Then the jump master tapped his shoulder and shouted in his ear, "Jump!"

He was free in that instant from the fear of anticipation, as he was free from the security of the plane. He was totally dependent—dependent upon the equipment and those who packed the chutes, upon the skill of the pilot who had determined the flight path to the jump zone, and upon those on the ground who were supposed to meet them. An eternity of three seconds passed as he crossed another threshold of life with the billowing of his chute. Thrilling!

It was with the same anticipation that Colin greeted the

receipt of this cable. So what if the idea of inserting ICARUS—whoever he was—into a terrorist network seemed whimsical? It provided him with the escape that he desired—the rejuvenation his back and years demanded. He picked up a pencil. He would later explain to Chris that he did not know what he was doing by accepting—but he did. In fact, he had not even thought about her or anyone else or what accepting this assignment would mean for them. Washington needed him. Of course he would accept the offer. He drafted his response.

1. *Gordon welcomes challenge.*
2. *Plan to arrive Athens by end of week. Will advise exact itinerary. Also, forwarding to Athens pertinent operational files maintained here.*
3. *Please provide contact instructions.*

He gave the cable to Maura. She began to type it. Her only words were "Now what have you done?" He smiled. He could not wait to share his decision with Chris.

⁑⁂⁑

"You did what?" Chris delivered the question in a voice a bit shriller than Maura's query but implied a similar diagnosis—namely, that Colin had lost his mind.

"Oh, no, you just don't understand. It's only until things get started."

"Do you expect me to return to the States alone and open our home while you go traipsing off to Greece on some wild goose chase? Not on your life."

"But Chris …"

"Don't give me 'But Chris.' When are you going to stop fantasizing about them chiseling a gold star in the lobby at Langley in your honor? Don't you realize that only dead heroes are so honored?"

Colin was speechless. If he had tried to speak, he would have stuttered, such was his confusion. His childlike enthusiasm for adventure had come up against Chris's stark, sober reality. He had greeted Washington's cable with relief. He would have volunteered for anything to remain in the field. Indeed, he was vulnerable. More seriously, in a flash he realized that for him, surviving and succeeding in Washington might have been the greater challenge. He would not be able to prove that point now. It would have to wait until this temporary assignment was completed. His elation of minutes ago vanished. There was nothing for him—for the both of them—to do. He had sent his acceptance. He could not withdraw it. Chris was equally subdued. She, too, knew that it was too late to alter the course of events.

⁑∗⁑

There he was on the *CBS Evening News*, Sulham Khalifa Ben Yousef, reading from a prepared text. It was the opening of the OPEC plenary session in Tripoli. Kay was surprised to see him surface so soon and so prominently. She was viewing a tape of yesterday's broadcast in one of the monitoring studios at CIA Headquarters in Langley, Virginia. Ben Yousef did not look like someone who had just directed the execution of a couple of American agents, but then she wondered how a murderer was supposed to look.

He had a dark complexion, enormous hooked nose, and a black beard flecked with gray. Most striking of all—his eyes were blue. As the camera zoomed in for a close up, Kay noticed black coarse hair stood on the back of the hands that held the text of his talk in a brown leather cover. His oversized shoulders gave him a powerful appearance. He offered a striking comparison to the frail, puffy, and tailored OPEC delegates of all nations seated in the audience. Kay estimated his age to be mid-forties. She noted how animated he was and how easily he moved behind the podium. His knowledge of the oil industry was impressive.

Pretty good for someone who is probably as facile with an Uzi, she thought.

Present in the studio was one of the operations officers present at Brody's planning meeting two days earlier and three analysts from the Intelligence Directorate responsible for writing the National Estimate for Middle East Oil Production. Kay had reviewed a draft of the document yesterday. If she were to become involved in this case, she needed the background.

Ben Yousef spoke Arabic in quick, abrupt phrases—though he allowed time for his message to be translated simultaneously into Oxford English. His message was one of accommodation and reconciliation. Perhaps, Qadafi fears another bombing from the U.S. Navy. She found it incredulous that Libya was satisfied with the current level of production and that they would be willing to retain current production schedules in return for industrial concessions from the West.

"He must be joking," she said aloud attracting the glances of the others in the room. "Perhaps, Qadafi wants to sign a friendship treaty with us." More glances.

"Those duplicitous bastards!" Astonishment registered on those around Kay.

When the clip ended, Kay was on her feet before the lights turned on, and the first one into the corridor on her way back to her office.

She had no better sense of Ben Yousef than prior to the broadcast. Clearly, he was well-educated. By birth she remembered reading that he was a Palestinian—raised in a UN sponsored refugee camp in Jordan, and, if the information was accurate, attended American University in Beirut on a UN scholarship. After college he entered Qadafi's civil service. His fervor and devoted loyalty was recognized early. Ironic that as a Palestinian he was a Qadafi loyalist, while thousands of his fellow nationalists were in the employ of the Kingdom of Saudi Arabia—the most conservative Arab regime in the Persian Gulf region. Whatever his background, Ben Yousef was a success story and her goal was to identify his link, if any, to Qadafi's terrorist conspiracy.

CHAPTER TWELVE

Jamie and Brigid departed Bulgaria for Greece by train on Friday evening, December 22. They obtained the last two seats in a second-class coach after he passed the conductor a bribe that was the equivalent of the man's monthly salary. Travel by train did not expose their passports to the scrutiny they would receive at an airport. There the authorities had direct access to Interpol's database. They reached the Greek border after two a.m. on the twenty-third.

Immediately, the train screeched to a halt as Greek officials boarded and proceeded to check the passports of the sleepy travelers, awakened from their slumber. As expected, the examination was so cursory that the official failed to place entry stamps for the four passengers in the compartment. The train started up again with a lurch. Brigid smiled at Jamie, and they both dozed off again.

It was almost four hours before they reached their destination. The engineer sounded the whistle announcing their arrival to the town that Jamie had selected. It was still dark. They gathered their possessions—one cheap valise and two canvas bags—and climbed down onto the step the conductor had placed to accommodate Brigid. They decided to wait on the thin wooden benches in the cold, damp waiting room for dawn. Back-to-back they provided each other some warmth. Ten minutes after the train departed, their heads were already nodding in fatigue—this despite the rising crescendo of conversation around them as the locals gathered for the next express train to Athens.

It was nine a.m. before they forced themselves into consciousness. They rose. Brigid stretched her arms above her head as she did when called upon to exercise in elementary school.

"Good morning. Another day closer to …" She did not continue, not wishing to jinx their decision.

He grunted a greeting as he gathered up their possessions. He was not yet quite awake. They located a coffee shop five minutes away by retracing the steps of those heading toward the station. On their walk they did not escape the glances of the pedestrians. This tiny village with its white-washed one-story dwellings did not attract tourists until the heat of summer. The clop of a donkey's hooves pulling a produce wagon could be heard ahead of them. The melodious ring and echo of the Orthodox Church bell sounded from a hilltop in the distance.

"Yes, please …" Jamie pointed to the hard cheese and bread behind the glass cabinet.

"Yes, coffee." He held up two fingers, pointing to the cups before two other patrons.

The proprietor, sensing their need for accommodations, left to return with a local driver who would take them to a friend who rented out beds. She gave a note to the driver, and he led them to his old Mercedes parked in the town's only taxi stand. They drove along a dusty road lined with mature olive trees to a secluded area on the outskirts of the town. They did not speak on the drive but looked out the window. Both were thinking of how they both needed the peacefulness that surrounded them.

They were welcomed by an elderly woman dressed in a floor-length skirt and a black blouse buttoned below her wrist. On her head she wore a black bandana that held her hair neatly tucked beneath. She looked like she had been awake for hours, working around her house—and she had. After reading the note and smiling to them both, without a word she led them along a dirt path to a small one-room stone cottage located one hundred yards behind the main house. The cottage overlooked an olive grove. Higher up on the hill behind the cottage were the stone remains of a monastery that now provided shelter to a herdsman and his flock of scraggly goats. The old lady opened the unlocked door.

"You are welcome," she said with a wide smile, exhausting the extent of her English. With rudimentary sign language, she indicated that it had just been renovated. He took out his billfold and paid her more than she expected in dollars, which she gladly accepted, the smile never leaving her face. They moved their bags into the room, and the old lady returned to her house.

"I don't know why I can't go with you."

"It's too early to trust the Americans. Words are cheap. I will get back as soon as I can."

He had already worked out a plan in his head as to how to deal with the Americans without submitting totally to their desires. The first piece of that plan was for Brigid to be settled in a safe place about which the Americans knew nothing.

"Look," he continued, "they don't expect to see me until after Christmas, so we have that time to play without looking over our shoulder to see if we have been found out. Let's enjoy this time."

They both were, or had become, quiet people. The time together before he must depart was distinguished by pleasant periods of silence as both indulged themselves in private thoughts, reflections, and dreams. He found his mind wandering back to the time of his childhood on the rocky northern coast of Mallorca.

He lived with his family in a huge old house that had been in the family for over a hundred years. On the outside, the building looked like a large, solid square. But from within, one experienced in the center a spacious court with a huge, thick tree in the middle whose branches touched some of the windows. He remembered how sad it was when the house was lost to bankruptcy. Investment management was not the family's forte—but who could expect more of a family known for its genteel artists, robust children, and an occasional priest?

Brigid seemed equally absorbed. He feared that she was thinking about a time with a lover who might have satisfied her more than he. Just when he had gathered the courage to ask, she looked at him. Obviously, she had misinterpreted his glance and moved toward him with an affection leading to great passion. Before long each abandoned cares, thoughts, and dreams to the reality of the present moment.

Their lovemaking was marked by its abandonment into a totally physical dimension. There were no words now—just an exchange of visual and sensuous excitement. They became two souls grasping desperately for a level of communication that is too rarely achieved. Later, his confidence in their relationship restored, his concerns erased and jealousies exposed, he experienced a calm he rarely knew before Brigid. With the pleasant afterglow enveloping them both, discovering her innermost thoughts seemed no longer so urgent.

¤*¤*¤

A week later, just as quickly as they entered the village, he departed it. Brigid had remained in bed, nodding to him as he looked toward her once before opening the door in the predawn light. No tearful good-byes—although the significance of his undertaking was not lost on either of them. They were determined to upset the forces arrayed against them. The first step had been taken. After deciding to break with the RAF, they had made contact with the Americans. They would soon learn how reliable their newfound protectors could be. With the Americans' assistance, they might just be able to begin life anew. They had reviewed their options and the future that awaited them long into the night.

The morning of his departure, he was anxious to be underway. He had a goal, and it was a worthy one. He left behind all the remaining money minus the cost for the train ticket to Athens and some food along the way. If he could not contact the Americans, he would not worry. If necessary, he'd walk back to the village. It would not be the first time that he had to use his wits to survive. He took his seat in the third-class compartment.

⁂

Jamie felt comfortable in Athens. It was a frequent transit point on his journeys to and from the Middle East. At the main station, he proceeded to the central market area, which was filled with people as he arrived at noon. He then made his way toward the area of the national museum—selected by the Americans for the initial contact. He still had some time to waste, so he decided on a lunch of grilled fish in a large covered shopping area, taking a seat at a long table where several laborers were already seated. He drank mineral water with the meal. When he had finished, he pulled the crumpled schoolbook with lined paper from his coat pocket. Before he departed Sofia, he had scrawled in it the contact instructions. He was conscious of the weight of the .22 caliber pistol in the holster above his left ankle. Carrying a concealed weapon was another reason he chose to travel by train. Before he left the restaurant, he removed his Greek knitted sweater and zippered rain jacket.

⁂

At the same time that Jamie's train was pulling into Athens, Colin's plane was touching down. He also enjoyed those last moments with Chris as Jamie had with Brigid. Now he regretted that he was so hasty in accepting the assignment—though pleased that Washington gave him a reprieve until after Christmas to be introduced to ICARUS. Now he was anxious to complete the business and return home. Both Colin and ICARUS were committed to success; only ICARUS's had to be total if he was to achieve the goals both he and Brigid sought—political and protective asylum and a chance for a new beginning.

✸✸✸

For his part, Frost tried to take credit for rescheduling the initial meeting to win Asher's approval. When he learned of the delay, imposed by Washington, he told Asher that he had taken the initiative in requesting the same from Washington. He neglected to say tell her that the same cable had announced that Colin would remain the primary case officer.

She wanted to believe that his professional star was on the rise—finally. But try as she might, she could not avoid thinking that Frost was the same lackluster individual whom she had married after college. She suspected that he was telling her what he thought she wanted to hear. Pity she did not see through his posturing before they married. She concluded that, pampered as he had been as a youth, he was unable to change. Her assessment of Frost lacked the same insightfulness found in the process of probing her own shortcomings. She might have discovered that both of them shared a uniquely similar trait. They both spent an uncommon amount of time finding the apparent flaw in the other.

✸✸✸

It was cold and dismal as Colin made his way from the terminal to the taxi stand. He expected rain and regretted not bring an umbrella—though his rain slicker fitted in better with the rest of the pedestrians. The upcoming meeting was like so many he had prepared over the years. He relaxed in the taxi and felt rejuvenated and eager to follow this operation to its conclusion. In the last days, he was surprised that reassignment to Washington no longer posed the threat it did earlier. At least that's what he told Chris before he departed. She just smiled.

He had the taxi drive him directly to the small hotel not far from the airport, which the Athens station had suggested. He would call Frost from the hotel. The taxi moved through the heavy traffic, and he wondered why Washington had retained

Frost in the operation. The taxi pulled in front of the hotel with a jolt as the driver inadvertently jumped the curb. Colin paid the fare, looking at his watch as he did so. Two hours remained before his first encounter with ICARUS.

Before leaving Bonn, Colin had received the contact instructions for his meeting. He loved the cryptonym for the Spaniard—ICARUS. He was sorry that DAEDALUS was not assigned to Hans. Perhaps the little ladies in tennis shoes who assigned cryptonyms before the age of random computer selection would have accepted Colin's suggestion—though he doubted it. The little old ladies had long since disappeared.

From his room on the third floor of the modest hotel, he called Frost to announce his arrival. He then reviewed the information forwarded to him in Bonn about ICARUS. He still had not received the photograph of ICARUS, though it had been sent over a week ago from Sofia. The holidays were probably responsible for the delay. He read Frost's contact instructions, which were much improved from what he provided for their initial meeting. The review complete, there was nothing more to do but wait—a precious verb shared by anyone involved in clandestine operations—until he hit the street, as one old mentor described it.

The plan was for Frost to observe as ICARUS climbed the staircase leading to the national museum. If everything appeared normal, Frost would hold a rolled-up magazine in his left hand. Colin would exchange recognition signals with ICARUS and give him the meeting time—two hours later—and the room number of the hotel.

Frost and Colin would then proceed separately to the hotel. The adjoining room had been reserved by Frost so that they could meet to discuss last-minute developments. It was a tight schedule, but Colin believed that keeping Frost to it lessened the chances of error. Once he established direct contact with ICARUS, Colin intended to keep Frost's involvement to a minimum.

In the park, everything went smoothly. It almost worried Colin. Frost was in place and correctly gave the safety signal from a park bench in Constitution Square as Colin passed. Thank God it was not raining. Frost would have looked odd sitting with a soggy magazine in hand. He spotted ICARUS at the top of the staircase. He looked older than his thirty-five years. His blond hair was distinctive, especially in December when there were few tourists visiting. From a distance he looked Scandinavian, not Spanish, or rather Mallorcean. Colin began the walk up the hundred or so granite steps.

He felt his breathing increase as he climbed higher. As he did so he tried to recall when control of Mallorca had been finally wrested from the occupying Moors. Halfway up, Colin tripped without warning and fell to his knees. His glasses clattered five steps down. A young high-school-age student ran to his assistance. *So much for a discreet approach*, he thought as he waved off the student, retrieved his glasses, and resumed the climb. His left knee stung where it had struck the edge of the step.

"Where can I get some retsina?" Colin asked of ICARUS. He was by now out of breath. He passed him the meeting information on a rolled-up piece of paper. He was certain that Frost had remained in the area and had spotted his awkwardness. *Damn*, he uttered to himself.

"Central Park is located in Manhattan," ICARUS responded with a smirk—a look of disdain on his face. He then continued down the steps into the square.

A casual observer would not have noticed the encounter. Colin hoped he didn't attract anyone other than the schoolboy. He swung open the large brass door of the museum and entered. His first impression of ICARUS was that he was every bit the professional one would expect from a courier experienced in supporting terrorist cells and eluding the detection of counterterrorist forces.

Colin was relieved. Their success and survival would depend upon it.

⁌*⁌*⁌

Thirty minutes later, Colin knocked at the hotel room and Frost opened the door.

"How did everything go?"

Colin could not be sure if Frost was being sarcastic. He knew that Frost was irritated that Washington had denied him the lead role in the operation. From Frost's expression, it was clear that he was not overjoyed to be working with Colin—as he probably sensed Colin's continued low esteem for him professionally. Further, though he could not admit it, Colin was convinced that Frost was not comfortable in counterterrorist operations. *But who was?* Frost's demeanor was of envy and thwarted personal ambition.

Colin was surprised to see that Frost was armed. Surely it had been years since either of them had fired a weapon. It was almost surreal to see Frost with a revolver. It was as if two boys had reunited after so many years to play guns. Frost caught the look and placed the weapon on the coffee table between them. Colin reached down and pointed it away from both of them.

"I will remain here for the meeting," Frost announced.

"What will you do if something doesn't seem right?" Colin looked at the large suction cups affixed to the common wall and the wires leading to a compact briefcase receiver with earphones.

"Uh … I will come in to back you up."

"This is almost farcical," Colin said, looking at the wall and the wires. "What are they supposed to do?"

"The techs say that I will be able to hear everything happening in your meeting without pressing my ear to the keyhole." Colin's experience with techs was such that he would have chosen the keyhole.

"Just be careful. We don't want to get hurt. That means

me and you. Don't burst in prematurely. He will be armed and probably fires at lot more than we do." Frost seemed relieved at the lecture.

"Let's go over the plan." Colin referred to his notes. "We want him to apply for a Libyan visa in Athens. I can't understand why I can't tell him about GANYMEDE."

"That's the way they want it, I guess." Frost reached into his briefcase for an envelope.

"Better count the five hundred dollars for him and sign the receipt. Here's the South African passport issued to Horst Torrez."

Colin signed the receipt and flipped open the passport to see ICARUS's photo affixed and the valid Greek visa on the following page.

"Fast work."

"Headquarters also deposited ten thousand dollars into his Swiss bank account. Tell him the money is a bonus for agreeing to this operation." Frost was reading from the notes that he had taken. "Tell him that an additional two thousand dollars will be deposited for each month he is involved."

"Damn! There they go offering outlandish sums before he has proved himself," Colin objected. "Where's my leverage?"

Colin was not looking for Frost to reply. He managed a sage nod of his head. He looked up in time to catch Colin looking away in disgust. Abruptly, Colin got up and walked out to the connecting room to wait for ICARUS. Frost closed the door behind him.

CHAPTER THIRTEEN

Promptly at seven thirty there was a knock at Colin's door. He crossed the room in three strides. Jamie Casasnovas entered without a word. He was shorter than he had appeared on the museum steps. Slight beads of perspiration had formed on his forehead, and his glasses were fogged. As if he had not slept well, his face appeared puffy. Colin thought that perhaps the strain of the last few days had taken its toll. Jamie carried a black leather men's pocketbook that still retained some popularity with Europeans. If he was armed, Colin believed that the weapon was in the purse. Colin was wrong.

"Good to see you." Colin extended his hand.

"Yes," Jamie managed.

Colin poured fruit juice from the mini-bar for each of them, approaching this first meeting with the need to keep a clear mind. He did the same when he used to play chess with Eastern Europeans. Jamie seemed tense.

"Where is Brigid?" Colin handed him a glass.

"In Greece. Safe."

"Don't you think we should know in case we need to contact her?"

"No," he replied firmly.

"Suppose she needs something?"

"She knows where the embassy is." He would not be moved.

Jesus, Colin wondered to himself, *I must work with his prick. If only we had agreed upon a signal for Frost to burst in and shoot this asshole.* He smiled, thinking that with his luck Frost would either shoot himself or Colin.

"Here's your passport." Colin was sitting and going through his notes and the items on the coffee table between them. Jamie examined it carefully—more carefully than any other agent who received false documentation from him in the past. Colin refilled their glasses.

"Looks good," Jamie said at last. Colin could not explain why he felt such relief.

"We want you to go to the local Libyan consulate and apply for a visa with this passport. If they clear you for travel, the chances are good that they know your true identify and might invite you into the periphery of their terrorist network."

"I'm not so confident," he spoke.

"We'll see." Colin moved to the next topic on his agenda. "State as your purpose that you are seeking work in the oil fields. Once in Tripoli, if you are not contacted earlier, make your way to this location." Colin showed him a map of an area outside of Tripoli and handed him a card with an address.

"What's this?"

"It's a camp for what we call foreign malcontents." Colin looked directly at Jamie, who was writing cryptic notes in his pad.

"You would fit in as a member of the RAF, don't you think?"

"Suppose so, since no one knows about my desire to sever ties. My last courier mission was six weeks ago," he said proudly. "And I must say it was successful."

Colin recalled reading the description of his last mission as told to the case officer in Sofia. Colin hoped that they were successful in neutralizing the operation lest the police come in with the sole purpose of arresting all concerned and not at all interested in protecting the source of the intelligence.

Colin then outlined the intelligence requirements relating to Libyan oil strategy and upcoming meetings. Though he rewrote them so that Jamie would readily understand them and could make similarly innocuous notes, he didn't expect Jamie to have much success.

Listed as a secondary objective by Headquarters, but considered primary by Colin, were questions to be addressed if Jamie succeeded in reaching Beirut. Headquarters wanted to know Libya's interest in Beirut and whether that interest relate to satisfying their terrorist objectives.

Next, Colin gave him a post office box in Hamburg for use in reestablishing contact if something prevented him from making regularly scheduled meetings. He also gave him a phone number in Athens with which to reschedule on short notice an emergency meeting.

"What name should I use?"

"Henry Crystal," Colin responded.

"What do I call you?"

"That's for you to decide," Colin said abruptly.

"How about Yossarian?" Jamie said with a tight smile.

"Fine." *The smart son-of-a-bitch reads*, Colin thought, recalling that Yossarian was one of the main characters in *Catch 22*.

"Now let's talk about finances." Colin again referred to his notes. Jamie leaned forward in his chair. "This is to confirm that we already gave you a thousand dollars in drachmas as an advance for expenses." He put a receipt in front of him to sign.

"When do I receive information about the Swiss bank account?"

"How about right now?" Colin pulled out a bank document that showed the amount of ten thousand dollars deposited in a newly opened account to Jamie Casasnovas.

"Two thousand dollars will be deposited into this account for every month you participate in this operation."

"What about when Brigid and I are sent to the States? What do we receive then?"

"I think it's premature to talk about …" Colin began.

"I disagree," Jamie responded. His thick glasses seemed to fog up. "The American in Sofia informed me of our value. He said we were one of a kind. 'One of a kind' translates into dollars, Mr. Intelligence Officer."

Colin bit his lip to suppress his irritation. *First I have to deal with Frost, now this idiot.* He forced a smile.

"Give me some time," Colin managed. "You will see that we are generous."

"Okay." Jamie leaned back in his chair.

Colin was beginning to feel like an administrative assistant, but it wasn't the first time. It seemed to come with the job of handling agents who had an inflated opinion of their value. "Look, I think we covered what I wanted to cover. Let's meet in two days."

"Where?"

"Be ready to leave Zorba's Grill in the central district at six thirty in the evening," Colin said in a businesslike fashion. "As I am entering the double doors, you leave. I will pass you the time and address of the next meeting. If you want to meet earlier, call."

They both sat back in the chairs. Colin still wondered whether or not Jamie was armed. When he placed his leather pouch on the side table, he was relieved.

"Can I have a match?" Jamie asked before getting to his feet.

Colin thought he was reaching for a pack of cigarettes in his sock. Before he could answer, Jamie pulled a small revolver from an ankle holster and pointed it at the stunned American.

"In this business you can't assume anything," Jamie said with a mischievous smile. "See you in two days." He put the gun back in its place and departed.

↧*↧*↧

The next morning at nine thirty, Colin stood in a thunderstorm on the corner specified by Frost. He pressed against the building to avoid as best he could the torrential downpour that started without warning soon after leaving the hotel for his five-block walk. He would have returned for his raincoat, but he was running late. His clothes were drenched. His tweed jacket, more accustomed to a northern clime, had a musky odor. He looked down at his flannel trousers—now more like formless work-out pants, not the creased ones as they were when he took them from the closet that morning. Water dripped off his glasses onto his nose and chin. A chill formed in his lower back and quickly spread through the rest of his body. Frost was to meet him at the corner and then drive him to the embassy. *Where was he?* Colin wiped the moisture from his watch. It was almost nine forty-five.

At ten, Colin saw Frost appear from the opposite direction. He passed Colin, made a U-turn, and stopped. Frost leaned over to unlock the passenger side of his white Audi. Colin hopped in. He could hear the sponge-like squeeze of the water on the seat. He placed his arms straight out on his parted knees in a futile attempt to restore the crease in his trousers and to control the dripping of the cold liquid down his arms and legs.

"What kept you?"

"Oh, I'm sorry. I have been at the wrong intersection for a half hour," Frost explained.

Colin said nothing. His lips tightened for an instant. *What other excuse could he expect from this incompetent?* He wiped his forehead and his hair with his handkerchief. He was sorry now that he had not gone back for his raincoat. They both remained silent.

The morning traffic was heavier than Frost expected. Colin had not appreciated until now how chaotic the Athens traffic could be. The rain only made it worse. Reduced visibility in no way deterred the aggressive drivers and the daring pedestrians. He was glad that he was not driving. If nothing else, Frost seemed to know his way around the city. This was no time, however, for Colin to daydream. Just when Colin would have put his foot to the brake, Frost invariably accelerated. *Is this what it takes to survive here, or is Frost displaying a combativeness missing in his professional life?* Twenty minutes later, they drove into the embassy parking lot.

"Where are the marines?" Colin asked as he looked around. The marines who had circled the building during his earlier visit were no longer present.

"They are standing down," Frost announced. "The threat alert has been lifted."

How ironic—just when things were heating up, the danger is viewed as having subsided. He followed Frost through the lobby, up the stairs, and finally into his windowless office. Stacked on Frost's desk was a neat stack of files that Colin had forwarded to Athens before his departure. Frost left the office and returned walking slowly as he balanced two cups of coffee.

"Thanks," Colin said, though he had not forgotten being stranded in the rain. He shivered involuntarily, recalling the incident. He kept his lips on the edge of the cup before sipping as he breathed in the aroma.

"Begin with GANYMEDE—the background file," Colin suggested before he pulled a legal-sized pad from the top draw of the desk and took up one of the several sharpened pencils sticking out of a tall antique leather cup on the desk. Frost took a seat and before long was immersed in the file.

When Colin sought to isolate his observations or focus his concentration or even reach an important decision, he would jot down his thoughts on paper. For decision making, he drew two columns; labeled one "pro" and the other "con." The technique helped him reduce—or at least identify—the conflicting emotional factors that were unknowingly or unconsciously influencing and sometimes complicating the decision process. He was ever amazed at how nonthreatening a previously important consideration appeared once it was captured on paper.

He was first introduced to the process during his early years in the Jesuit seminary at St. Andrews-on-the-Hudson—now ironically the home of CIA—the Culinary Institute of America. He was obliged then to observe a vow of silence. Without the opportunity to verbalize adequately his innermost thoughts, writing assisted him in exploring regions of his heart. Years later, he came to understand that he joined the Jesuits to restore the tranquility of his youth. The quiet of a mountain retreat overlooking a verdant valley, the rush of a stream, meditation in a candle-lit chapel, a bell echoing long after being struck—all served to lure him to the seminary and to what he thought would be a contemplative life. It was the vow of celibacy that powered his resignation from the order. He never regretted the decision to leave. Later, the CIA's Clandestine Service satisfied in him a desire to be with another close-knit fraternity.

Colin recorded on the pad his initial thoughts about this case. His purpose was to resolve the various inconsistencies that haunted him. He wrote confidently in a bold script, but he felt far from assured in his observations to date. The tip of the pencil broke off, reminding him not to be too rash in his conclusions.

- *Murders of GANYMEDE and Horst are linked*
- *Same group is responsible for both*
- *GANYMEDE was murdered for sensitive information he uncovered and for information he had in his possession*
- *Horst was murdered for his connection to GANYMEDE*
- *Ben Yousef and Libyans appear to be responsible*
- *Surveillance and attempt on my life meant to keep information from me or prevent me from revealing information I have or had*
- *GANYMEDE was tortured and before he died provided complete details of his cooperation*

- *Tossing GANYMEDE's body on steps of US embassy meant to signal us they knew about his work with Americans*
- *Those responsible probably have headquarters in Libya, although able to operate in Lebanon, Greece, Germany, and elsewhere in Europe*
- *Group has sufficient resources and knows how to accomplish its mission*
- *Group is not hesitant to act boldly and decisively*

As he underlined that last observation, a chill went up his spine and he became aware again of his damp clothing. He momentarily squeezed his eyes closed as he imagined Horst's murder along the Rhine and GANYMEDE's cruel torture. Colin looked over to Frost, who was deeply engrossed in the file. Colin turned the page and began to write on a clean sheet of paper some preliminary questions to which he needed answers.

- *What is the sensitive information for which both GANYMEDE and Horst were murdered and an attempt on my life made?*
- *How can we bring the Libyans to justice and thwart future acts of violence?*

Colin wondered if the pursuit was worth the effort. No US law was broken. *But what about our resolve?* The threatening words uttered by Reagan aside, he was convinced that the government would continue to vacillate. The Germans and the Greeks would do nothing to threaten the flow of oil. As for the Lebanese authorities, they were helpless. Even if Colin had in hand a signed confession from Hans's murderers, they would remain free as anarchy reigned in Lebanon. Colin felt drained emotionally and weary—though the pursuit had just begun.

Where was that enthusiasm of a week ago, or better—years ago? Chris made more sense than he gave her credit. Her cynicism—so much healthier than his search for adventure—stung him. Could he do no more than acknowledge her wisdom? Though his desire for the chase had waned, he hoped this feeling of helplessness would pass.

"Are you a philatelist?" Frost's question jolted Colin from his revelry.

"A what?"

"Philatelist," Frost repeated.

"Oh, no. Why?"

"This is quite a nice Lebanese stamp. Mind if snatch it?" Frost showed the postcard to Colin.

"If you really want it, be my guest." Colin had been caught off guard. He could think of no way to refuse Frost short of being curt. One simply did not walk off with items from an operational file, especially one that represented the death of two agents—the sender and recipient of the postcard. If there was ever any doubt—and there was none—that Frost needed some remedial training, it vanished with this request. But Colin had to do something to salvage a working relationship with him if there was any chance of solving the puzzling developments of this case.

The stamp was commemorative and symbolized the resiliency of Lebanon. An expressionist rendering of the famous cedars of Lebanon filled the stamp rectangle with greens, browns, and yellows. Once covering the expanse of Lebanon, the cedars were now limited to the hundred or so that had survived the woodmen's greed and the artillery shells exchanged between warring factions.

"This is how you do it," Frost explained as he held the stamp side down over a kettle of boiling water he had brought from the kitchen. Carefully, he pulled the stamp—only partially affixed—from the postcard. If Frost was indeed a collector, he was surprised that he paid little heed to the postmark. But then he noticed that the war-weary Lebanese postal worker had missed the stamp entirely with his cancellation stamp.

"Let me see it." Colin picked up the postcard and fingered it absentmindedly as he reread the last message from Hans. It seemed so frivolous on the surface, yet the import proved to be fatal. He remembered when he had received the card from Horst—another scene in a separate act. He so regretted not lingering with Horst that final afternoon, so distracted he had been by what he would have to accomplish before departing for Athens.

Without thinking, Colin allowed his thumb to pass over the area to which the stamp had been affixed—across an inexplicable rough pattern. Just then Frost's secretary came in with a cable from Washington. Without thinking more about patterns, Colin tossed the postcard and his notes into the folder.

"Thanks," Frost said as he received the message, reading it quickly before passing it to Colin.

"So the OEC meeting is disintegrating into an internal squabble," Frost summarized, "with Libya aligned with the Saudis, Venezuelans, and the Nigerian producers on a pricing strategy—more in keeping with US and Western consumer interests." Colin read slowly, mouthing the words to keep his focus.

"I've not witnessed a more unlikely alliance," Colin offered.

"Agreed!" Frost voiced.

"There really doesn't seem much here." Colin spoke. "Unless I'm mistaken, it seems we won't see much come out of this session other than the usual aggressive anti-industrial policy statement."

"Who knows—maybe GANYMEDE frightened them off from implementing a more disruptive game plan." It was Frost speaking.

They got no further in their analysis. The phone rang for Frost.

"Yes Asher?" Frost responded. After a pause, as he listened, he cupped the phone and turned to Colin. "Care to join us for a sandwich downstairs?"

"Sure." Colin regretted his reflex acceptance as soon as the word left his lips. *What else could I have done?* Another encounter with Asher waits. He put the GANYMEDE folder back into the stack they had just received from Bonn and followed Frost out of the office.

CHAPTER FOURTEEN

A brilliant morning sun glared off the tin sign about the entrance of the grocery store further up the hill. Jamie was on his way to the Libyan consulate located in a residential section of Athens. He favored the winter season in Greece without the sun-bleached tourists arrayed on every street corner.

The three-story building of the consulate stood before him—the Libyan seal above the wooden door. He rang the bell and pushed against it when the buzzer sounded. A small vestibule served as the reception area. Once it had served as the waiting room for a prominent Greek physician. He admired the dark cherry wood floors. From the smell of the paraffin in the air, he figured they had been waxed that morning. Behind a low counter sat an emaciated man in his fifties reading an Arabic magazine. A full minute passed before the man looked up. His eyes were blank and his face expressionless.

"I am here to get a visa. I want to work in the oil fields." Jamie spoke though no question had been asked of him. The clerk continued to stare at him. He wondered if he understood English. He decided to wait him out, maintaining direct eye contact.

"Passport!" Without warning, the clerk reached a thin, bony arm over the counter.

Jamie retrieved the South African passport from his purse

Ganymede

and gave it to him. Turning to the page where the Greek visa was stamped and his photo pasted, the clerk looked from Jamie to the passport and back again. Without a word he left the area through the curtained French doors behind him.

Jamie took a seat on an imitation Scandinavian couch with unyielding pillows—an Eastern European creation no doubt. On the wall hung a photograph of Qadafi in a field marshal's uniform—alongside which was an Arabic calendar printed by a Libyan farming commune. The reception room was more appropriate for an impoverished African nation than one that boasted such huge oil and natural gas reserves. Within ten minutes the clerk returned with an application and Jamie's passport.

"I regret … qqq … ota … full. Fill out papers." He spoke in halting English. "When possible, you will—allowed travel."

Jamie was not disappointed. He expected the Libyans to be cautious. He took out his pen and filled out the detailed application. Although not required, he included a photograph taken the day before at a corner kiosk—anything to help the Libyans to identify him. He also included a one hundred drachma note with the application. The clerk looked away, but not before he slipped the bill swiftly into the pocket of his soiled white trousers.

Once outside the consulate, Jamie decided to return to the city on foot. He wanted to be sure that the Libyans did not put surveillance on him. There was a possibility that the Greeks had staked out the consulate. If so, it was conceivable, though not probable, that they would seek to identify visitors to the office.

Surveillance did not trouble him. He knew how to lose even the most determined team. But before he could do anything, he had to be sure, and being on foot offered him the best possibility. The morning sun warmed him, as did a young Greek woman who passed, but not before she flashed her dark eyes toward him with a smile. The almost balletic swirl of the policeman directing traffic at the intersection reflected the rhythm of Jamie's mood. His blood was pumping. He was alive.

☩∗☩∗☩

Colin prepared for his meeting with Jamie. Frost offered no resistance when Colin said that the preferred to handle the meeting later in the afternoon alone.

"The safe house is located in the central district. Here is the key and directions." Frost clearly had other plans.

"Are you sure that it will be empty?"

"Yes, I called. The safe-house keeper won't return until tomorrow," Frost assured him and departed.

☩∗☩∗☩

Jamie was standing on the commuter train platform as directed when Colin suddenly rushed from an arriving train. Before Jamie realized what had happened, Colin had slipped him a piece of paper and departed. It wasn't until he was sitting on the train that Jamie opened the slip of paper to find the address, apartment number, time of the meeting, and directions to exit the train at the next stop.

Not bad, Jamie thought as the lights dimmed and the train lurched into a sharp turn. In a couple of minutes it entered the next station. Just before the doors closed, he jumped quickly to his feet and exited the train. *Good. No one else exited*, he thought, trusting his peripheral vision.

Jamie did not notice the dark-complexioned individual who had left the train as soon as the doors opened. He lingered in the shadows at the north end of the station as Jamie mounted the steps to the street. Before taking the steps himself, the stranger pulled from his belt a small transmitter the size of a cigarette pack. He looked around and then uttered a short phrase before continuing.

Meanwhile, Jamie walked slowly along the shops and five-story office buildings. He was not hungry, but even if he had been it was too early to have dinner. He liked being out in the cool December evening. If he appeared to be someone just wasting time, he was. He had no destination in mind. In fact, he was unfamiliar with this section of the city. After thirty minutes or so, he developed an uneasy feeling. He could not identify what prompted it. Something did not seem right. He felt constricted, like he was in a box and could not get out or there were weights on his ankles. He had come to trust his instincts—they had proven reliable in the past. If something did not appear right, experience had taught him that it was not.

Yet he was puzzled by the tension he felt. He was going to a routine meeting with someone from the CIA in a friendly area and not about to cross an international boundary on a false passport with smuggled arms. Perhaps he was becoming paranoid. There had been no way for him to attract attention, and he was certain that no one left the train after he exited. But still the feeling persisted. He trusted his senses. He had survived before with such trust.

There were too many people on the street for him to detect surveillance. He had to isolate himself from any uninvited companions. He turned onto a quiet street, determined to silence or confirm his suspicions. If there was someone there, he would have to commit and follow him down the lane he was now walking. Whoever was there—if indeed there was someone—he could not allow him to make contact without being observed.

Thirty paces onto the quiet street and he had not heard another set of footsteps behind him. Thirty steps further and still nothing. Unable to restrain his curiosity further, he did the unthinkable. He turned back as he crossed the street. No one was there. *I must be imagining things,* he thought, disappointed that he had committed the cardinal infraction of looking back. If he had been under observation, he would have confirmed to those stalking him that he was surveillance conscious. Those concerned about being followed usually had something to be concerned about.

⁂

The apartment in which they would meet was leased in the name of a retired American schoolteacher. Each six months she received a six-month advance payment from Frost's assistant. The station paid for everything—including utilities and telephone—for the privilege of holding a meeting with a select agent. It was a small price to pay when one considered the problems created by keeping an apartment unattended. There had been too many instances where the local police had stumbled upon a safe house—when in actuality they were looking for a terrorist hideout—because the water usage was well below the profile of an occupied apartment. About twice a month the retired schoolteacher received a call directing her to leave the apartment for several hours. When she received the call, she stayed with friends in Athens.

Promptly at eight fifteen, Colin heard a quiet tap on the door. He had been sitting close and opened the door quickly, inviting Jamie in with a gesture. They shook hands without a word. Colin didn't trust him and had to assume that the gun he had pulled during their last meeting was now hidden in a different place. *It's probably in his crotch,* he thought rather unkindly. Jamie looked around the apartment confidently.

"A glass of wine?" Colin asked, going to the refrigerator for a bottle of red domestica. Colin chilled everything—red wine, beer, even an after-dinner drink—but he kept the latter quirk from everyone but Chris.

"No, I prefer juice."

"Did you have any trouble finding this place?" Colin poured the drinks—annoyed that his feeble attempt at establishing rapport with this agent over a glass of wine had been rejected.

"No trouble." Jamie answered. "I applied for a visa at the Libyan consulate. They told me that the quota was filled; however, the clerk took my visa application and the drachmas I lent him to speed the process. I also gave them a spare photo."

"They'll use it to identify who you really are. Hopefully, they'll figure the RAF connection," Colin added.

"I know," Jamie responded.

"Let's not give them much time. Go back to the consulate on Saturday. It will show some urgency on your part, and after all Saturday is a work day for the Arabs. We must push things along." Colin said as he paused for a sip of wine. If you were seeking refuge from the authorities," Colin continued, "patient endurance would not be among your virtues," Colin said, trying to keep the conversation alive.

They spent the next half hour reviewing the intelligence requirements for the next meeting to be held in two days. Colin reviewed the re-contact instructions in the unlikely event they were unable to meet before Jamie anticipated travel to Libya.

"That is, if you receive the visa."

"I'll get one," Jamie said confidently. "What do I do for expenses? I've used what you already gave me."

Colin took from his wallet the drachmas he had to cover just such a contingency and passed it to Jamie.

Jamie counted the money carefully and signed in alias the receipt placed before him. Their business concluded and clearly nothing more to discuss, Colin bid him farewell at the door.

Colin remained to straighten the apartment. He put the remaining half bottle of wine in the refrigerator. Ten minutes passed before he was satisfied that the apartment looked as it did when he entered. He turned out the lights and entered the darkened hallway on his way to the elevator.

The hall light seemed to have burned out—forcing Colin to guide his way down the hall by running his finger lightly along the rough stucco wall.

He heard the metal click and flinched just before a figure lunged at him in the darkness. A strong hand gripped his throat and pushed him against the opposite wall. Colin twisted his body in attempt to get free—feeling the strain on his lower back. He heard the dull sound against the wall as to what must be the long blade of a knife. He was overwhelmed by the strength of his opponent, who only grunted between deep breaths of air.

Colin was helpless. He felt that he was losing consciousness in the unrelenting grip on his throat. The pain in his back and shoulders was excruciating. His hands felt numb as he tried to hold off his attacker. Yet all he could hear was a deep, barely audible growl from his foe and his own pounding heart.

Then, there was a pop sound—similar to the sound a child makes snapping gum. He was certain that his assailant had broken his neck. He waited for paralysis to immobilize him, wondering if he would experience a gradual loss of feeling to his extremities. Instead, he felt the grip on his throat loosen and finally fall away as his assailant seemed to ease gently to the floor.

"Help me carry him to the room," a voice whispered.

"Jamie?"

"Yes, help me."

Colin now realized who was responsible freeing him.

Colin proved to be of little assistance. He had difficulty finding the key to the apartment; his hands were shaking so that he feared he would go into convulsions. Once in the room, Colin turned on the desk lamp in time to see Jamie pull an inert figure through the entrance face down. The man was dress in a dark leather jacket. Colin noticed a neat round hole burned in the back level with the man's shoulder blades.

"What's going on?" Colin was whispering.

Jamie did not reply. He turned the man over to check his pulse. He was dead. Jamie searched his pockets. He found a 9 mm pistol.

"He carried no identification," Jamie muttered in frustration. Then he smiled when he pulled a small box from the back trouser pocket.

"Look at this—miniaturized transmitter and receiver, and head set," he said, moving the items from hand to hand.

Colin looked at the dead man. He was in his thirties—solidly built, black curly hair, dark complexion. Before Jamie turned him over again, Colin noticed his brown suede shoes and the grease stain across the left shoe—last seen in the lobby of the Hilton two weeks ago.

"We'd better get out of here. His friends will be waiting to hear from him," Jamie said. He was acting like a professional rescue worker called to the scene of a devastating accident instead of being the one responsible for causing a fatal injury.

"What will we do with the body?" Colin asked.

"If we value our lives, we leave it. Is there another way out of here?"

"I don't know," Colin responded.

"Fine. Let's find out." Jamie covered the body with a blanket from the next room and led the way out of the apartment. Colin turned to extinguish the desk lamp.

"Leave it," Jamie cautioned. "Somebody might be waiting for him or us on the street."

Colin followed Jamie in the darkness. They turned to the left away from the elevator. Colin's eyes were not yet accustomed to the dark, and he found himself pinching Jamie's jacket so he did not lose him. Despite the close distance separating them, the step-down caught Colin by surprise, and he nearly plunged into Jamie, who was moving steadily down the stairs. Colin counted four flights and had thought there would be no more. Yet there was another to the basement and an exit door—leading out the backside of the building. It was evident that Jamie had checked out the building prior to the meeting.

They were in a courtyard now, making their way in unison, wordlessly, along a dirt path that wound through dry bramble bushes. In less than five minutes, they reached the street that ran parallel to the one on which the building entrance was located. They turned left and continued quickly out of the area.

"I'm starving," Jamie said after fifteen minutes of almost jogging with no let-up. He sounded light-hearted, as if he were really enjoying himself. The last thing Colin could think of was food.

"I need a drink." Colin's hands were still shaking. His back felt like it had been twisted in a tight knot. *Thank God Jamie was there to help.* He had never been as afraid for his life as he had this time.

Jamie signaled a passing taxi. He used his map of Athens to direct the driver to an area where they would find a restaurant where foreigners would not be out of place. It was ten o'clock.

When the taxi pulled up in front of his selection, Jamie was out the door in an instant, leaving Colin to pay the fare. *That cheap bastard*, Colin thought, though not unkindly.

⁘ ⁘ ⁘

"Why did you return?" Colin spoke first after he finished the double Metaxa—the premier Greek brandy—on ice.

"I never left. When I entered the darkened hallway—and it was lit an hour earlier—I sensed that something was wrong. I knew where the stairway was since I used it to get to the apartment. I simply walked down a flight and returned quietly waiting for you to leave."

He did not say that it was his intention to follow Colin and discover his identity. Such information could be useful if the Americans decide to renege on their promises. He also wanted to see how good Colin was operationally. Would he detect that he was being followed?

"About the time you moved toward the door," he continued, "I heard a rustle in the hall. I figured correctly that someone was waiting for you, and he just didn't want your autograph."

They were silent when the waiter served Jamie psito—slices of lamb, heavily seasoned in garlic, and served in natural juices, a salad of tomatoes, feta cheese, and anchovies, and a side order of pasta.

"I don't know how you can eat at a time like this. My stomach is still in turmoil." Colin declined a second brandy and instead settled for a glass of red wine from the decanter the waiter served.

"How did you know where the stairway was?"

"I just told you—I used it coming up. You have to get in shape," Jamie mentioned casually as Colin stretched his arm to the side in an attempt to relieve his aching back.

Jamie did not say anything about his experience that afternoon at the train station. This was no time to tell Colin everything. In fact, there would never be a time when he would tell anyone everything—and that included his newfound American friends.

⁂

"Shall we have some dessert?" Jamie asked after he finished the platters of food that were placed before him. "Some Greek coffee?" Colin motioned for the waiter and ordered coffee and dessert.

The coffee was thick and half sweet. The baklava was dripping with thick deep brown honey and served on a paper doily.

"I probably should have ordered some food. My appetite seems to be returning." Colin consumed the dessert quickly. As he drank the coffee, he lazily ran his finger over the paper doily, tracing the pattern slowly.

"What does this remind me of?" Colin asked before he tossed it on the table. Jamie looked up and then returned to the baklava.

"Well, what's next?" Jamie asked.

"What do you mean?"

"For starters, what happens when the body is discovered in the apartment?"

"Oh, shit! I've got to call the office." Colin roused himself, got to his feet slowly, and hurried off to the rear of the restaurant and the telephone, searching his pockets for change as he walked. He returned fifteen minutes later. By then the waiter had cleared the table and Jamie obviously had no objection drinking wine as he had already poured the last of the wine into his glass.

"We want you to proceed to Milan as soon as possible. You can't remain here. Use the money I gave you to purchase a ticket tomorrow for Rome."

"What do I do when I get to Rome?"

"I want you to take a train to Milan," Colin instructed. "Go directly to the Libyan People's Bureau and reapply for a visa. Tell them that your application is pending in Athens."

"What's my reason for not waiting here?"

"Simply say that you overstayed your welcome. They'll understand." Colin sounded reassuring.

"Okay."

"I'll meet you on the thirtieth at seven thirty in front of the La Scala Opera House. Do you know where it is?" Colin asked.

"I'll find it." Jamie was distracted about the money he would need. Colin must have read his thoughts.

"I'll have more money for you in Milan. If for some reason, we don't make it at seven thirty, let's return at nine thirty to the same place. Call the Athens number if we still don't get together. If you are in another town, just give the time and date and I'll meet you in the lobby of the first hotel that appears in the town's phone book."

"Very clever." Jamie smiled. If things did not work out with the Americans, maybe he would suggest the technique with his old employers, but he checked himself. *Never again!*

Jamie was determined to break his ties with his terrorist sponsors once and for all. The only chance he and Brigid had was with the Americans. Time was indeed running out for them. As he thought about the evening's activities, he wondered how safe he was with the Americans. He was glad that he had not informed them about Brigid's location. Although he had not realized that Colin's assailant had followed Jamie to the apartment, he would have gained little solace to learn that a second individual had trailed Colin and had been outside waiting for his companion while Colin and he fled through the basement.

Colin seemed oblivious to the significance of Jamie's smile. Colin prepared to leave while Jamie remained behind and finished the wine.

CHAPTER FIFTEEN

Just after midnight a black four-door sedan drove slowly past the building from which Jamie and Colin had made their hasty escape. At the end of the street the vehicle made a U-turn and returned to park in a fire zone across the street from the entrance to the building. First the headlights were extinguished, and then the ignition was cut. The passenger and driver doors opened simultaneously. Two heavyset individuals got out and crossed the street—but not before each locked his respective door.

The sound of the car doors closing served to pierce the silence of the night. The only other sound was the faint whining of a dog locked in an apartment in a neighboring building. The owners had probably left the dog overnight and it was getting impatient for them to return. The two men looked up and down the street before making their way to the entrance of the building. Both wore dark, formless raincoats. One of them shifted a large revolver from a holster on his hip to the raincoat pocket. It was a snug fit. They both disappeared into the building.

They were the off-duty police inspectors who received, unbeknownst to their superiors, a monthly retainer from an American attached to the embassy to run traces on individuals and license plates of interest. While they never asked, they knew that their American contact was a CIA officer. They had run their own traces once they established his true name—different from the one provided. From routine tasks over time, the assignments became more intricate, and for these they received payment in addition to the monthly stipend. The pay had always been good for special assignments. This time they knew it would be especially rewarding.

Fifteen minutes later they emerged from the building entrance. Again, they looked both ways before crossing to their car. Barely visible between them hung a figure, which they supported easily in their tight grasp. The figure appeared unconscious. His feet did not touch the ground. One of them reached to open the car door with the keys that he held in his clenched fist. His companion propped the figure against the side of the vehicle. With the door open, they shoved the individual into the back seat unceremoniously and swung the door shut in one motion. The driver started the car by the time the second had reached the passenger door. They drove off slowly, waiting until the end of the block before putting on the headlights.

⁑ ∗ ⁑ ∗ ⁑

In front of the same building the next morning, a small moving van pulled to a stop. The driver was joined by two muscular laborers. They had been difficult to locate on such short notice during the holiday season. People wanted to be with family and friends. It was no different with those who abandoned the parched treeless regions of Greece in search of work.

The three standing before the building were planning to return to their village for the holidays, but not before they completed this task at triple the wages. They would work quickly to complete the job. The owner did not care how long the job took. Once in the building, they rode the elevator to the fourth floor. Referring to a crumpled piece of paper, the driver found the door he was looking for and entered using the single key on a tattered shoe lace he pulled from his pocket.

Everything was as it had been left after Colin departed hurriedly the previous evening. That is, everything but the corpse, which had been removed by the police inspectors. The occupant of the apartment was not present. Molly Tauler, the CIA officer assigned to manage safe houses, had intercepted her in the morning and informed her that it would be best if she did not return to her apartment. Before she had a chance to protest, Molly gave the former grade school teacher sufficient funds to rent a small villa on the island of Skiathos—her favorite island in the Aegean. She was to remain in splendid exile until Molly contacted her. Molly also promised to arrange the safe storage of her furniture and belongings. The inconvenience and suddenness of the move were offset by her fond memories of Skiathos, its solitude, and of course, the generous compensation she received.

One of the movers returned to the truck for cardboard boxes, packing material, and tape, while the others surveyed the task before them. They worked methodically, efficiently, and quickly. Even the half bottle of red wine was taken from the refrigerator, its cork secured, before they wrapped it for storage. Within three hours the furniture and the larger items were wrapped in padded blankets and other items in boxes for the ride back to the warehouse. As the driver maneuvered the van into the traffic, he thought of the money they had earned and how in just hours they would be with family for the holidays.

⁂

"What's going on out there?" Brody did not direct the question to anyone in particular among those gathered in the staff conference room in the waning days of December. No one broke the silence that followed.

"We have Athens, Beirut, Bonn, and Berlin all tripping over themselves, and we still have no idea why those Germans were killed and a couple of earnest attempts have been made on our case officer's life." The collar of the white shirt seemed to pinch him noticeably as he stared down at those gathered around the table.

"What am I to say up front? When they ask me, who am I to say is responsible? Can it be the Libyans who appear almost docile after the OPEC strategy meeting?" No one present yet responded.

"I want the case officer in Bonn—what's his name?" Brody seemed to be having difficulty focusing.

"It's Colin Gordon," Kay spoke up.

"I want him here to explain in person."

"We can't do that yet." It was Kay again—to Brody's consternation.

"What do you mean—we can't do that?" Brody was losing his patience even with Kay.

"He can't do it because he is with ICARUS and must remain with him until we find out whether the Libyans will issue ICARUS a visa. After that he can come home for a quick visit, if you wish." Kay's voice was conciliatory.

"Good. We'll wait." Brody did not want to risk tangling with Kay. If she gained the advantage in the discussion, it could lead to others challenging him as well. He rose with a flourish like a pouting prince, turned on his heels, and left the room with a distant, almost vacant, look—only this time like a prince who was considering a career change.

⁑ * ⁑ * ⁑

It was before dawn in the Greek village that Brigid now called home. A solitary figure stole through the streets at a quick pace. Only his white pants flickered in the moonlight as he left the village for the path leading to Brigid's cottage. In twenty minutes, he was at the door. He tried the metal latch carefully so as not to make a noise. The door was unlocked. The figure disappeared within, closing the door as softly as he had opened it.

"What are you doing?" she murmured from a deep sleep. He

had slipped quietly into her bed and under the down comforter. He began to run his hands over her bare breasts and across and below her thighs.

"The question should be, 'Who are you?'" he said in a deep whisper as he stroked her more deliberately. She responded by moving her lips to his nipple and then following her hands, which were already active on and below his waist.

Later, their skin moist from lovemaking and legs still entwined, she said, "You haven't been that good in months."

"I haven't felt as worthwhile in months." His head was cradled in her left arm. He ran his right hand playfully down her arm and back across her exposed breast.

"How is it going with the Americans?" She held his hand on her breast.

"Fine."

"Do you want to talk about it?" she asked.

"No. I haven't told them where you are."

"Why?"

"I don't trust them. Also, they're not that good." She held his hand from pulling away.

In the twilight of dawn, they discussed quietly their plans and dreams for the future. They spoke in whispers lest someone overhear and sabotage their search for peace and happiness. Optimism and confidence grew in this intimate sharing, encouraged, perhaps, by the soft gray dawn emerging through the slats from the bedroom shutters. The village was still quiet except for an occasional rooster announcing the day or the footsteps of someone heading toward the village on the path beyond their window.

"I hope to arrange our travel to the States by next month." He did not reveal his cause for optimism—he was counting on being in and out of Libya by that time.

"When do you think our German friends will see what we've done?" She posed the question calmly, but he recognized a certain anxiety in her eyes.

It was his turn to keep her hand on his, and at the same time he moved his other hand between her thighs. He knew that she was as determined as he to start afresh. But they were both realists. It was only a matter of time before their treachery was revealed and some effort was made to punish them—a brutal reminder to discourage others from taking a similar path.

"If they don't learn directly from the Americans, we may have two or three months." His assessment was more positive than it deserved to be. Neither said anything for some minutes, though they seemed to communicate through the continued gentle stroking each enjoyed.

"I won't see you for a while—I've got to travel," he said, breaking a long silence. He had been searching for words to soften the impact of this impending separation.

"You have money, and I'll send more. If something should happen," he said, as casually as possible, "call Colin Gordon at the American embassy in Athens." He reached across and pulled a slip of paper from his wallet.

"Here's the telephone number. If he's not there, he'll be at the embassy in Bonn. And here's that number."

"How did you manage this?"

"I went to the Marine House. It's where the American guards live. I had a couple of beers with a fellow who said he was in charge of the detachment. Have you ever heard the rank 'gunnery sergeant'?" She had not. He continued.

"I learned that someone who fit the description of the American was Colin Gordon. I could reach him by calling the political section of the embassy, but I had to call soon because he was only a temporary employee due to return to Bonn soon." He smiled at Brigid.

"Not bad for an evening's entertainment."

⁑⁕⁑

"So explain what happened." The speaker was a man in his early fifties. He was deeply tanned, with smooth, almost oily skin.

His face had the features of someone in the slick Italian movie magazines. He was seated in a deep easy chair, upholstered in expensive raw silk with a subtle floral pattern. His fingers were long and thin, nails carefully manicured. Black and white hairs circled his wrists and were visible below the sleeves of a black evening robe. He moved a set of worry beads through the fingers of his left hand. They were made of amethyst stones attached to an antique silver chain.

"I waited for the young one to appear." The second man was powerfully built with huge biceps pressing against a dark pullover sweater. "First the light went off in the apartment, and then it went back on. I waited."

"So?" the older of the two asked.

"Nothing happened. I tried to call him on our radio, but he didn't answer. I figured he couldn't speak."

"You were right—he was dead!" The older man was losing his patience.

"After two hours, a car pulled up in front of the building. Two men got out. I am certain that they were policemen—there was an insolence about them."

"They left their car and leisurely walked across the street toward the building entrance. As they did, one of them checked his weapon. They entered as if called to the building." He paused. "I was tempted to go in and help, but I feared more police were on the way."

"You feared," the older man hissed.

"In ten minutes they reappeared holding him between them. He was limp as if drugged— but believe me he was dead. The car drove off, and I called you as soon as I could."

"What happened to the American and his friend?"

"I don't know. I didn't see anyone leave the apartment."

"Is there a back exit?" the questioner continued.

"I thought you'd ask. Yes, I checked it out. You have to take the stairs down to the basement. There is a door that leads into the courtyard and from there onto a path to the street opposite."

"What you are saying is that the young one could have been alive for the two hours before he was carted off dead—if he was dead?"

There was no reply. The older man dismissed him with a wave of his hand.

When he was alone, he placed a telephone call to Beirut. The international connection was poor—a crackling noise provided constant background noise. "What could one expect during war?" he muttered. *The phone is at least more reliable than the water supply, which has long since been contaminated.*

"Hello? Hello? Kalenti, this is Athens," he shouted. He recalled his days in the army when life was simpler and war was a series of maneuvers and exercises.

"Yes, I hear you," Kalenti said. There was a pause. "You believe our man was killed," he repeated where they had left off earlier before the line had been interrupted.

"But can you be sure?" Another pause filled the static similar to the sound of the surf.

"You must confirm," Kalenti said as his voice again faded.

"You must find out if he talked. Do you hear me? You must find out. We will take precautions here," Kalenti said as the line went dead.

✣ ✣ ✣

Unidentified Male Found on a Dock in Piraeus

It was the headline to a brief item that appeared on the back page of the English language Athens newspaper. The article continued,

> *The victim who appeared to be in his thirties had been shot in the back at close range. He was dressed in a dark leather jacket with the label from a once fashionable shop in Beirut, brown slacks, and suede shoes. Police request*

that anyone with information call the local Piraeus office conducting the investigation at 52-63-73.

Frost read the article twice. Both he and Colin were in the airport terminal awaiting the departure of Colin's flight for Rome, where he would catch a connecting flight to Milan. Colin gazed absently at the people in the immediate vicinity; some were looking around frantically for their departure gate.

"Let me read this to you." Frost interrupted Colin's thoughts. "It must be him." Frost read the item aloud quietly.

The annual exodus from Athens was underway for those who could afford a vacation in Europe, skiing in the Alps, or shopping in London. Not many Greeks were included in this elite property class, but those who were flaunted their status and hoped that their presence in the departure lounge would not go unnoticed. Their absence from the capital made room for tourists from the north who would scour the shops and sites of Greece for a memory or artifact to speed the passage of winter.

Mental and physical fatigue had taken its toll on Colin. He was exhausted. He had not slept in almost forty hours. His back throbbed from the strain of his hallway encounter. He had taped himself around the shoulders and chest that morning. When he looked at himself in the mirror, he noticed how uneven the bandage was wrapped. He understood why Chris never allowed him to wrap Christmas presents. To make matters worse, the tape did not offer the support he sought. He winced when he thought of the sound the tape would make and the pain it would cause when he pulled it from his chest and back hair.

His neck bore several nasty bruises. That morning he also administered a foul-smelling Greek ointment he purchased from a local pharmacy to the affected areas. Some of the bruises were large enough that he half seriously believed a forensic expert could recover fingerprints from them. Thank God for the cold weather. The scarf around his neck hid the bruises—something he could not have worn in summer.

Colin's flight was called over the airport intercom. He rose and picked up his carry-on, having already checked one suitcase. On the way to the gate, Colin requested that Frost review the files again to see if they could have overlooked some piece of information that might explain the fervor of his pursuers. As almost an afterthought, he asked Frost to look at GANYMEDE's postcard again.

"Maybe there's something there that we missed." Colin handed the boarding pass to the attractive Olympic Airlines stewardess and walked slowly up the ramp to the aircraft. He could not tell whether his shoes or the rubberized mat was responsible for cushioning his deliberate footsteps.

↕*↕*↕

The Greek newspaper reporting the discovery of the body in Piraeus was also read by the man—Lebanese by birth—who had reported the disappearance of one of their own to Kalenti in Beirut. He had first come to Athens fifteen years ago on what was to be a two-year assignment as the senior marketing official for Middle East Airlines. As the situation in Beirut deteriorated and then never bounced back, he continued to represent MEA, even when there were no MEA planes flying and the airport in Beirut was closed. He paused on the last page and picked up the phone to dial a local number. A woman answered. Her voice sounded old and tired.

"Momma, read the article on the last page of today's *Athenian*. Find out if the man is ours."

He hung up the phone without waiting for acknowledgment just as a young Greek maid dressed in a white uniform served him a late morning breakfast of Israeli melon, yogurt with mountain honey, and black Arabic coffee.

CHAPTER SIXTEEN

After bidding Colin farewell, Frost went directly to the embassy. He had promised to meet Molly so she could recount the details of that morning. He would have preferred to go home. Asher was being obstreperous about the amount of time he was devoting to what she considered Colin's operation. She envisioned no professional advantage accruing to him. In fact, she had advised that the less support he rendered to Colin the sooner those at Headquarters would recognize Frost's worth.

Frost was also reluctant to become more involved in this case, but for a different reason. Though he told himself that terrorism was not his bag, he really had to admit that he lacked the drive—ambition—to succeed. Simply stated, he confessed to himself that he was lazy. In this rare moment of introspection, he could not recall any goal that he set for himself for which he was ready to make the necessary sacrifice to achieve—an assessment he could not share with Asher. The experiences of these last weeks had uncovered deep professional insecurities that even he could not ignore. And so he must distance himself—do everything possible to avoid a Headquarters assignment—at least until the upcoming promotion list was announced.

Frost was momentarily startled when he reached for the knob to his office door and Molly swung it open. She had heard him walking down the corridor. Before he had taken a seat, she began a minute-by-minute description of her activities since he had called her to the embassy. He feigned interest in Molly's briefing. She was exuberant, with enthusiasm gushing forth. She reported that the schoolteacher offered no objection to a respite on Skiathos—in fact, she welcomed it.

As for the movers, they performed as she had expected. And though discouraged from entering the apartment herself, she confessed that she checked the apartment after they left. Frost just listened. He wanted to get home as soon as possible before Asher became unmanageable—as if he ever managed her. He also had a deep aversion to being in the office on Saturday.

"If you have time, Molly, look over the files from Bonn so you acquire a more comprehensive understanding of the operation.

"Also," he said, recalling Colin's words at departure, "see if the message from GANYMEDE has an additional meaning—beyond scheduling the Athens meeting—that we might have missed."

"Great!" Molly was appreciative. She immediately went to the safe and pulled a stack of files from the opened drawer and went into the next room, humming happily to herself. Before she took her seat, she made a pot of coffee.

☩⁕☩⁕☩

Two hours later, Molly's emotions were soaring. She had just called Frost at his home, asking him to return to the office. Here she was the junior officer, calling the old timer to return to the office.

Twenty minutes later, Frost arrived. Long delayed by her research, she had just finished her cucumber-and-tomato sandwich. He didn't look good. She could not tell the cause. *Maybe it was something he ate, or it was that bitch to whom he was married?* Molly corrected herself. Frost was no catch. She might even feel sorry for the lady.

Had she known that Frost had endured caustic criticism from

Asher for allowing a junior officer to call him back to the office; she might have withdrawn her sympathy. Asher could simply not understand what could be so important that he sacrifice his professional image to the impulses of a junior officer.

⁜

"Look what I found." She was clutching the postcard in her hand. "There's something here. I don't know what, but there's something there," she repeated as she handed it to him.

Frost ran his thumb across the surface as indicated by Molly. He felt a pattern in the space where the stamp had been.

"See?" she asked impatiently. Frost held the card before the light but was unable to get the light to glance across the pattern.

"I just called the camera tech away from a picnic. Let's see what he finds."

"Well, I'm not sure that was necessary." Frost was painfully aware that the idea had not occurred to him. He also was trying to estimate how long before the tech arrived—he could not remember his name. He was sure that he lived in the American residential area near the air force base—some distance from where they were. More precious minutes he would have to account for with Asher.

Frost's comment to Molly was brusque. They waited in separate occupied silences. He spent the time catching up on his accounting while she reorganized the file drawer of the safe.

"I hope I didn't overstep my authority," she asked.

"No, it's all right, Molly."

⁜

The technician arrived almost an hour later. He took the postcard and disappeared into his laboratory. Molly's self-doubt persisted until the technician returned with a copy of the pattern that he had succeeded in identifying—almost like lifting fingerprints from a letter. What was before them was a collection of pinpricks formed into a definitive tight grouping.

>   *
>   ***
>   ****
>   *

"What do you make of it?" Molly asked.

"I don't know." Frost was reluctant to grant Molly a *well done*. "It looks like a Christmas tree."

"Yeah, I guessed so." She was examining the card closely again to see if she could feel any other irregularities. The tech assured them both that he had examined the entire surface on both sides. There was nothing else on the card.

"I'll bet GANYMEDE applied the pinpricks with the needle found on his body," Molly suggested.

"With the what?" Frost had no idea what she meant.

"With the needle." She retrieved the relevant folder and turned to a clipped page on which was printed the inventory of items taken from GANYMEDE's body.

"Item number six," she read, "one sewing kit needle. Do you think that they knew what he was doing?"

"Who knows," Frost offered in as matter-of-fact a manner as he could muster. He had a perverse desire to smother her satisfaction. He slid a pad of paper before him and began to compose a cable to Headquarters, Bonn, and Rome for passage to Colin. It reported that "the station" had discovered the pattern on the postcard. He did not give singular credit to Molly as was warranted, nor did he show the draft to her as he walked off to the communications center to have the message transmitted.

Molly had glanced at the draft as he read it and looked with pity at Frost. She returned to finish the second half of the sandwich and the last cup of coffee from the pot before returning to her apartment.

In Milan that day, a young Libyan visa assistant examined Jamie's passport and sought to confirm his status by checking the name under which he was travelling in the database to which the consulate had access.

"You already applied for a visa in Athens," he said officiously. "Why didn't you wait in Athens?"

"I couldn't; it was time to move," he responded.

"Well, you're in luck. I have permission to issue you a visa, but you must leave today on the Alitalia flight."

"That's fine. I need work."

Jamie was on the street minutes later with a newly stamped Libyan visa in his South African passport. He went to the nearest central post office and placed a call to Athens, leaving a message on the voice recorder.

"I cannot meet Yossarian." He was tempted to use Colin's name, which he obtained from the gunnery sergeant, but his knowledge was too valuable to squander. "I have a visa and leave today."

He walked to the central bus depot, where he found that transportation to the airport was about to leave. The ride to the airport took over an hour in the moderate traffic. He found the Alitalia counter with no difficulty and purchased a ticket for the flight to Tripoli. He converted his remaining lire into deutsch marks and slipped them into an envelope that he addressed to Brigid. He wrote no note and wrapped the bills in two clean sheets of stationary that he purchased at a newspaper kiosk. He hoped the envelope would reach Brigid intact. She would know it was from him.

He had not realized that the flight to Tripoli was almost three hours, and he had no funds left to purchase some wine to go with the veal scaloppini that was served on the flight. He relished every morsel of the meal—realizing only then that this was for him the first meal of the day. He hoped that the Libyan authorities were alerted to his arrival. He did not want to play poor any longer. He leaned back in his seat and dozed off into a fitful sleep.

He woke as the wheels of the plane touched down in Tripoli. The landing was smooth, as if the plane had used extra-sized balloon tires to cushion the impact. He waited patiently in his window seat until the last of the passengers passed him in the aisle before making his way to the exit door. He was the last to debark. It was bright and sunny and about twenty degrees warmer than in Milan. As he reached the last step, a customs official dressed in a loose-fitting blue uniform approached him.

"Monsieur, we have been waiting for you." They shook hands. Without another word, he led him to a waiting ancient American sedan. Jamie deciphered through the grit that the car was a Plymouth. Everything seemed to be going according to his plan, however hasty it had been in the formulation.

The drive south was along a narrow macadam road that ran straight through a barren desert region. After more than two hours, the driver turned off the main road at a wooden sign whose red and white paint had blistered in the sun. The road was bumpier, made of hard-pressed sand over a base of crushed rock. The suspension system of the Plymouth was being tested. After an additional forty minutes, he saw in the distance—just off the secondary road—a complex of Quonset huts and a butler-type hangar, painted white.

As they drove closer, he spotted two fifteen-foot barbed wire fences that appeared to surround the compound. At the far end was a soccer field. He thought that the squat wooden structure to the left served as a control tower for the arrival and departure of small aircraft, ferrying people to and from this site. A high sand wall had been built, and from behind it he could hear the firing of automatic weapons. He had arrived at a military camp, but it was not the installation that the American had described in such detail. He wondered how a nation so powerful could be so misinformed. *No wonder they are paying me handsomely.*

☩*☩*☩

Ganymede

As soon as ICARUS's message was retrieved from the recorder, it was cabled to the American consulate in Milan in hopes of catching Colin before he departed for the opera house—where they were to meet. Unfortunately, Colin had not checked the consulate for messages. He had deliberately avoided the consulate, given his experience attracting surveillance in Athens. After waiting fifteen minutes at La Scala, he called the consulate and learned of the message. He was relieved. He had feared when ICARUS did not show that something similar had happened to him as with Hans.

⁂

Athens also relayed ICARUS's message to Headquarters. There it was reviewed with some anxiety. No one had focused on what to do if ICARUS received his visa. Most—led by Brody—assumed that he would be stalled indefinitely from entering the country. As worried as Brody was about the implications of having an agent in the enemy camp, he was terrified about what criminal act or acts ICARUS—now in the employ of the CIA and the US government—would have to perform to remain there. Past attempts to infiltrate terrorist networks foundered when the agent was required to take part in a particularly vicious act to demonstrate loyalty to the terrorist cause. Brody now regretted that he had not followed more closely the reporting received on the debriefing of ICARUS at the station in Sofia. *If something goes wrong, it could be my career*, he ruminated.

Following ICARUS's apparent success in penetrating the Libyan infrastructure, Brody was hounded by the legal counsel's office that had learned of the case only that morning. Representatives of that office began every sentence with "What if ICARUS ..." The last thing that the US government and Brody's career needed was a revelation in the press that an accused terrorist was in the CIA's employ.

For the lawyers, now joined by the peripatetic Brody, ICARUS represented a looming bureaucratic time bomb. Brody was only concerned about the political fallout this case could cause him. The possibility that the operation could yield valuable intelligence was remote, and he would not defend too vigorously the handling of the case by the field case officers. Already he considered the speed with which ICARUS was launched as a demonstration of the overzealousness of the officers involved and their failure to exhibit professional caution. Press exposure and congressional oversight could cause Brody many sleepless nights.

If this were twenty years ago, Brody would have little to worry about with regard to Congress or even press exposure. Careful cultivation of selected members of Congress and a quiescent American public had given the CIA license to undertake a plethora of covert schemes with little or no accountability, and with goals that were chimerical at best. With an active—some would say aggressive—congressional oversight, an operation like this would not go unchallenged. Some applauded the changes; Brody did not.

※ ※ ※

Over the next days there arose a flurry of bureaucratic, treadmill-like activities, documented by streams of cables between Headquarters, Athens, Bonn, and Milan. Kay was unmoved by Brody's churlishness. She understood him and others of similar ambition. Before everything got out of hand, Kay decided that Colin for his own protection should be brought back to Headquarters for consultation. She wrote a cable to that effect and hand-carried it to Brody for his signature. He read it studiously and looked up at Kay.

"It says here that I drafted the cable." He smiled nervously.

"I decided that before you and your staff surrender Colin to the Justice Department lawyers, you should have him here to give his assessment of ICARUS and an overall evaluation of the operation's future."

"Thank you." He signed the cable.

CHAPTER SEVENTEEN

The room was lit by a naked low-watt bulb attached to the end of a black cord—crusty with grime. A young medical student entered pushing a gurney through the double doors. One of the wheels seemed permanently stuck and squeaked shrilly as he steered the conveyance to the center of the room below the light. The young man was the duty agent for the police medical examiner's office that Sunday. He usually worked after hours and on Sunday for his medical school tuition. As he moved to the side of the room, a man and an old woman moved alongside the long, narrow gurney and the prone figure wrapped tightly in a white sheet.

Hours earlier, the old woman had walked into a local police station. In her hand was the news article that reported the discovery of the body in Piraeus. She was short and stocky and had to be at least seventy years old. Her loose black dress reached to her mid-calf, revealing thick black stockings. She wore a black cloth coat; her collar was turned upward to ward off the chill in the air. Her hair was a dirty gray and held in a tight bun with two huge hairpins.

The police officer who interviewed her learned that she was a refugee from Lebanon. In halting Greek and some French, she explained that she feared that the man found in Piraeus was her son. She had last seen him years ago as he boarded a motor launch in Darmour—just south of Beirut. Her husband had died hours later in Darmour in a massacre carried out by the advancing Palestinians. Though the coincidence was great, she feared that the dead man was her son and wanted to determine for herself whether or not it was so. The police officer made the necessary arrangements with the morgue.

"Old lady, are you sure you want to see the boy?" the police official asked. She nodded affirmatively.

The medical student moved out of the shadows quietly and pulled the sheet from the cadaver. She looked at it with intensity that belied her years. After three minutes during which the only sound was of an electrical switch malfunctioning, she gave no sign of recognition. She motioned for the attendant.

"Turn over, please," she asked—motioning what she wanted done with her hands.

He responded quickly by extricating the edge of the sheet tucked tightly around the rest of the body. Suddenly, the police official rushed to the table—his glasses clattering onto the cement floor—in time to catch the chilled corpse before it fell. In an effort to accede to the old lady's request, the young man had pulled too vigorously on the sheet.

The glare in the policeman's eyes conveyed a message not lost on the medical student. With his free hand, the policeman reached to retrieve his glasses. But he said nothing to indicate his irritation out of courtesy for the old lady.

She looked over the length of the body. "Please turn over again."

This time the police office did not wait for another mishap to occur. He remained on the opposite side of the gurney—still breathing heavily from the exertion of minutes ago—while the attendant rolled the stiff body onto his stomach. The police officer's patience was being tested as they looked to the old lady—awaiting her response.

"Not my son." Without another word, she turned on her heels abruptly. The two men were left to rewrap the body.

※ ※ ※

Later that day, after the old lady made her report, another call was placed to Kalenti in Beirut.

"Hello, this is Athens." Again there was only static at the other end.

"Are you there? This is Athens," he repeated. Telephone service to Beirut had not improved.

"Yes, yes, what is it?" Kalenti sounded as if he was in a tunnel.

"We confirmed that the young one was killed. Was killed," he repeated. "Do you hear?"

"Yes. By whom?" Kalenti asked.

"We don't know for certain, but we think the American was responsible. We are searching for him."

"We must presume that he talked?" Kalenti's voice rose in a question.

"We don't think so. There were no signs of torture on his body. He was shot once in the back."

"Good, I hope you are right. We go ahead then with our plan. You will be hearing from …" The connection was broken.

※ ※ ※

On the day after New Year's Day Frost returned to the office. He had not been there for three days. He had been tempted to see if there had been any cables logged in during the time. However, when he raised his intention with Asher, she derided him and questioned whether he was simply trying to avoid responsibility at home preparing for the New Year's Day reception she had planned. It was best that he forgo the office.

"Happy New Year!" Molly greeted him in the hallway outside of the office. There was an air of independence in her demeanor.

She informed him that a cable had come in from Milan, and as they entered the office together; she retrieved it from her desk and placed it on his. Frost checked his watch and noticed that it was almost nine. Molly had been in the office for over an hour.

Frost took his seat behind the metal desk. He had tried to have it exchanged for the more prestigious wooden variety that his CIA rank allowed but with no success. An ever-vigilant embassy employee, a Greek national who had been with the embassy staff for over twenty years—and was not a fan of Frost—observed that Frost's rank in the Foreign Service did not entitle him to a wooden desk. The employee was technically correct, and no embassy employee would attempt to overrule the decision. It seemed that Frost had unwittingly insulted the Greek when he tried—again unsuccessfully—to circumvent the Greek employee's authority in clearing his furniture on his own through Greek customs. And so Frost was left with a metal desk whose drawers echoed whenever he open them.

The cable was from Colin in Milan, dated January 1. Frost was surprised that Colin had not sent it night-action, as that would have required the communications officer on duty to call Frost. Instead, the cable had remained in the incoming traffic to be deciphered routinely.

1. *Request Bonn attempt to learn where the needle was found. Interested in confirming view held here that it was hidden in GANYMEDE's clothing and that pattern was meant by him as a sign that may have gone undetected by his captors.*
2. *Agree with Athens that its outline appears to resemble a tree. Request Athens pouch postcard to Washington for further examination.*
3. *Consider this potentially important clue to determine motive for GANYMEDE's subsequent murder.*

Frost frowned. Here he had a chance to grab the initiative,

Ganymede

and he failed to do so. Instead of wrestling with the significance of what appeared to be the outline of a tree and the needle found on GANYMEDE, Frost had merely reported the discovery of the pattern and then spent his time preparing hors d'oeuvres. It had simply not occurred to him to go further. Colin was gathering momentum. He decided that Colin had deliberately sought to squeeze him from the operation. He felt a sense of nausea sweep over him.

⁂

Colin was already on his way back to Headquarters. He reacted immediately as soon as he received the cable summoning him home. He considered ICARUS's success in reaching Tripoli an achievement beyond anyone's wildest expectations. It was so sudden that Colin did not feel sufficiently prepared. He looked forward to discussions at Headquarters. He presumed that that was the reason for the summons. However, his enthusiasm was dashed when Kay informed him in a private back channel message of the mood there and of Brody's concerns and those of the government lawyers. He was truly a novice to the intrigues of Washington—he spent so little time there. If it was as Kay described, he would do everything possible to remain abroad. *To hell with all the advice about a Headquarters' assignment serving my career.*

⁂

Kay and Colin were the first to arrive for the Friday-morning meeting. They took their seats at the conference table, which seemed to fill the room with its size. The carpenters who built the table clearly had envisioned it for a larger space. Stacy joined them shortly after their arrival, carrying under her arm three operational files. One of the folders contained all the appropriate information on GANYMEDE, the second addressed Libyan support to international terrorism, and the third—the thinnest of the three—was the ICARUS file. Two operational analysts joined the group minutes later. One of them was an expert on international terrorism, and the other worked for the Lebanese desk chief.

Kay was not surprised to see a representative from the Inspector General's Office office enter the conference room and take a seat. *ICARUS in Libya has them worried*, Kay thought. She could not remember his name. *There were just too many from the Inspector General's office roaming the halls and attending meetings to remember them all.* She had first met him when he was a young recruit—fresh from a two-year study program abroad financed by the government. Health problems, she recalled, prevented him from achieving any fame overseas. He was respected as an analyst and he could be counted upon to provide sound advice—that was the extent of what she remembered. And she still could not recall his name. She nodded to him when he looked her way.

"Let's begin," Kay began.

"This is Colin Gordon. If he looks sleepy—he is. He just got in from Milan last night." She turned to Colin.

"Why don't you review what has happened since you received the postcard from GANYMEDE in Bonn?" Kay turned to Colin, as she reached for a cigarette.

I*I*I

Colin coughed to clear his throat. He felt a momentary nervousness. With the exception of Kay, he did not know anyone in the room. All eyes turned toward him. When he began, he forgot his nerves. He spoke about the meeting with Horst, receiving the card, the dash to Athens, attracting surveillance, GANYMEDE not appearing at either the primary or alternate meeting sites, learning that Horst had been slain, then GANYMEDE, and finally on his meetings with ICARUS—including the attempt on his life in the hallway.

He spoke for twenty minutes without notes. It was an impressive performance. One of the analysts marveled to her neighbor at the quality of the information conveyed—a far cry from the Cecil B. de Mille productions at the Pentagon where they relied upon the color of the graphics to titillate and assuage an audience—even though the thirst for information was not satisfied.

"Before I open for questions, let me summarize," Colin was in full command of the session.

"GANYMEDE discovered something that someone thought was worth taking his life. We have not found out what that was—even though attempts upon my life indicate that someone thinks we are close."

"What was GANYMEDE doing in Lebanon?" The question came from the chief of the Lebanese desk. Embarrassed silence followed as Colin considered a response.

"I have no idea what he was doing in Beirut. I thought he was in Tripoli." Colin paused before continuing.

"I was not concerned when I did not hear from him. He was not what you would call an especially controlled agent. For those of you who have reviewed the file, GANYMEDE's far-ranging business interests made him difficult to track."

Colin paused. It was obvious to all present that GANYMEDE's demise had taken its toll upon him.

"As you appreciate, before his contact with Ben Yousef, he was of little or no intelligence interest," Colin resumed.

"During my relationship with him, we shared a close friendship."

Colin's voice cracked ever so slightly when he mentioned his friendship with Hans. He looked vacantly at a reproduction of a Matisse painting on the wall. Some at the table avoided direct eye contact with him.

"From his postcard message," Colin began again, "I assume that he accompanied Ben Yousef to Beirut. Even when he departed Tripoli I didn't expect much. Sure, he had been briefed on our OPEC intelligence requirements, but quite frankly *The*

Washington Post's coverage of OPEC equals or surpasses what we have been able to gather."

Some of the intelligence analysts squirmed with Colin's candor, but no one refuted the observation. The chief of the Libyan desk asked the next question.

"What's the significance of the dots on the postcard that GANYMEDE sent?"

"I don't know." Colin shrugged his shoulders.

"We received a report from the Germans that a sewing needle was found tucked in the inside collar of his shirt on the right side. I don't know if that's an important detail, but I think it is. You see, Hans was left-handed and it would have been easier for to hide the needle from his captors on the right side where it was later found." He paused. "But who knows?"

"What do you expect to accomplish with ICARUS?" It was the first question from the representative of the Inspector General's office. He was a pipe smoker and spent most of the session constantly trying to keep the pipe lit. Several discarded matches in the ashtray in front of him attested to his diligence, or incompetence.

"I must admit that we may be shot-gunning here. It may even be whimsical," Colin began.

Kay looked sharply at Colin. He caught her glance.

"Out of frustration and a conviction that the Libyans are responsible, we dispatched ICARUS into the lion's den to have a look." For the second time in minutes he ended his thought with "Who knows?"

If only there was more of a science to clandestine intelligence operations, Kay thought.

"What sort of controls do you have on ICARUS?"

It was same questioner. He put his pipe down before him on the table.

"Not many," Colin admitted. "He has a way to contact us through the Athens number we issued to him, but we have no way to get a message to him."

"What about his lady friend?"

The question was from a well-clothed effete official who once roamed Africa and South Asia on intelligence assignments. Now he covered international terrorism from Headquarters to allow his liver time to recover from the relentless abuse it received during constant drinking bouts abroad. The fellow was years younger than he appeared and belonged to a diminishing breed of Ivy League graduates who once chose service in CIA over Wall Street.

Lady friend! Kay did not like the fellow who had asked the question. *He should be so lucky to lay such a lady from the description received from Sofia.* She colored visibly—what prompted her to think up such imagery? At her age she was supposed to be beyond that. She laughed inwardly; her emaciated frame and unisex look was supposed to keep her isolated from such thoughts. They didn't.

"We know, or we think we know," Colin offered, "that she is in Greece. But where, we don't know. ICARUS wouldn't tell me. He doesn't trust us." He paused. "Of course, if he's interested in money and resettlement in the States—which he was promised—we'll learn soon enough."

"What training has he received?" David Brody had slipped into the room unnoticed.

Colin looked up at Brody, displaying no emotion.

"He definitely needed no training in self-defense, as I can attest." A murmur of agreement followed this comment.

"He did receive some training in document copying. I also reviewed some tradecraft principles with him, like preparing innocent text messages to conceal hidden meaning. I instructed him on telephone security—what to say and not to say on an open telephone line. We discussed what could be done to a telephone so that it transmitted conversations taking place close by, even though the instrument was on the cradle. Please remember that the instruction was—in my opinion—a review of what he had already learned working with the RAF. ICARUS is a survivor who doesn't need much formal instruction."

"How confident are you that he was honest about his past involvement in terrorist operations?" It was a second question from Brody.

"I'm not."

Brody blanched slightly. He turned to an analyst from the Counter Terrorism Center.

"Has any additional information on ICARUS surfaced?"

"No, sir. As far as we know, his activity was limited to impersonal courier activities in support of the Red Army Faction."

The meeting came to a close soon thereafter, and those in attendance, including Brody, dispersed to their offices.

"You did fine," Kay said as he followed her back to the office. Once inside, Colin wondered aloud whether he should have dispatched ICARUS to Libya.

"Please, no second thoughts—we will see what unfolds," Kay consoled. "Our challenge is to discover why GANYMEDE was killed."

"Well, what do we do now?" he asked.

"Nothing. We wait. When do you plan to return to Athens?"

"Wednesday. I leave here on Monday and fly to Bonn for two days."

"Any plans for the weekend?"

"Nothing special. I plan on expanding my knowledge of Lebanon by attending a Lebanese folk festival near Walter Reed Hospital in Washington."

CHAPTER EIGHTEEN

Upon arrival at the military camp, Jamie understood the rush to fly that same day. He was the last student enrolled, and they were waiting for him. The *they* were the camp administrator—a figurehead Libyan bureaucrat who had been injured in the US Navy raid on Qadafi's compound—a Palestinian refugee from Jaffa, and two East German weapons and explosives experts. These Germans were assigned to Qadafi, as the British Special Air Service experts are seconded to the sultan of Oman.

Jamie's credentials had been accepted as legitimate. He had proved his support for revolutionary movements by his countless courier missions. His expressed desire to become more actively involved was accepted by the camp administrator, who was responding to higher authority in Tripoli.

He learned that the course of instruction would last a minimum of two weeks—depending upon his proficiency and that of the other students. The first week was devoted to small-arms refresher training and passed quickly. He was one of twelve students and was on the firing range by eight in the morning. They did not conclude until well after eleven in the night.

Jamie was by far the most qualified of the students—a few of whom had never fired a weapon previously. A Sikh from India, a Malayan of Chinese stock, a French woman, and Jamie were the only non-Arabs in the class. Before the week would end most of the Arab students had been pulled off for additional training—so lacking in experience and basic skills were they in firing the range of weapons to which they were being exposed. On the other hand, all the foreigners, of whom Jamie was considered one, demonstrated weapons familiarity that came from actual operational experience.

He was looking forward to the end of the week when they would participate in practical shooting exercises instead of confining their time to the firing line. The following week he would begin the explosives training and detonation portion of the instruction. They would receive, he was told, instruction in surveying a structure for destruction. As part of the lesson, they would be divided into teams and be evaluated on their ability to identify key structural elements for attack with an economy package of twenty-four pounds of explosive charge—the amount that could be stuffed into a light-weight knapsack. Although in his operational life he had smuggled hundreds of pounds of explosives through Western border control points, he had never so much as handled primer cord. *After this I will be qualified*, he thought, *but for what?*

Jamie had still no indication of what they planned for him once he completed his training. He had succeeded in penetrating a training center for aspiring terrorists, but he was not sure of the significance of this accomplishment. He could not answer whether there was any connection to the network that so interested the Americans. If it was the network responsible for the attempted murder in Athens, he hoped that there was no one present who would recognize him as the person responsible for killing one of their compatriots in the darkened hallway.

He wondered why the American had made such a point of having him read the questions related to Libyan oil policy. The people whom he had met to date did not seem interested in economics or oil strategy. He decided to be patient—as if he could control his desire for answers. Instead, in the quiet afternoon following a light meal of a curry substance served over rice, he returned to his bunk for a nap.

⁕ * ⁕ * ⁕

Colin drove alone along Beach Drive in Rock Creek Park that Sunday morning. He passed a picnic area in a clearing along the creek and recalled vividly a picnic scene with Chris thirty years earlier. Their oldest daughter was less than two years old. He remembered the excitement Chris created in their relationship and was pleased that her company was every bit as stimulating now—this despite the realization that their physical, emotional, and intellectual needs had grown over the years. At least these needs had not grown old.

He glanced at the morning sun filtering through the dense patch of trees. It was unseasonably warm, and there was the occasional jogger and cyclist leaning into the long hill toward the Calvert Street exit. Out of the park, he continued north on Sixteenth Street, past Walter Reed Hospital. He turned right on Alaska Avenue and stopped halfway up the block in front of a two-story red-brick residence. The drive was easier than anticipated. He was early for the Sunday service that would be followed by a festival, attracting Lebanese from the surrounding suburbs. Before him was a wooden sign that identified the building as the Maronite Seminary. He got out of the rental car, locked it, and walked toward the building from which a priest was just exiting.

"Welcome. I'm Father David." The priest extended his hand.

"I'm Colin Gordon. I've always wanted to attend a Maronite service."

"Come with me. We have time, and I will give you some background." Colin followed him to the rectory. Inside Father David showed him to the study and then excused himself for a moment. Colin took his seat on the deeply stuffed couch but rose immediately to investigate the books contained in the floor-to-ceiling shelves that lined the room. The priest returned with two tiny cups and a pot of Arabic coffee.

"I have always been interested in Lebanon. I'm in the Foreign Service and had hoped someday to be posted there—the Paris of the Middle East—until the troubles."

"Do you know that I have never been to Lebanon?" Father David said.

"Now how is that possible?"

"My family settled in southern Utah, and that is where I was born." The priest smiled at the surprise registered on Colin's face. "Yes, they fled the Turkish massacres and found temporary refuge in France before arranging passage to America. They had intended to settle in California, but the mountains of Utah reminded them of the Chouf Mountains in Lebanon, and they went no further."

Colin and the priest exchanged light conversation and sipped the coffee until it was time for the service to begin.

Father David led Colin to the chapel that was built alongside the seminary. Colin found a seat in the back on a metal folding chair. During the service he was mesmerized by the incense rising in a thick cloud and the melodic chanting of the liturgy in Syriac.

Father David had mentioned earlier that Syriac was an ancient language related to Aramaic—the language spoken by Christ. The Maronites traced their spiritual lineage to the first patriarchy established by Saint Peter in Antioch. The priest chided him gently that Rome was the second patriarchy and surpassed Antioch only when Peter was martyred in Rome. Colin was not certain where Antioch was now, but he decided that it was in Turkey. *Good thing Rome was an early choice too,* Colin concluded.

After the service, Colin decided to attend the Lebanese celebration scheduled to be held when the chairs could be moved to the sides. In the interim he walked around the outside. In front of the building he looked to the right of the seminary entrance along the walkway to the house. He froze and did not notice

Father David approaching him. Colin was totally absorbed by the Maronite cross.

"Is this the first time you noticed it?" Father David asked after looking over his shoulder to see what held Colin's attention.

"Yes, until now I never appreciated how much its outline resembles a tree …"

"Yes, a Lebanese cedar," the priest replied.

"I must go, Reverend." Colin excused himself.

"I thought you'd stay for our feast." The priest appeared disappointed.

"I'm sorry. I just remembered. I have another appointment—someone to meet. Thank you for your hospitality. We'll meet again." Colin extended his hand and walked to his car, looking behind once to wave and to glance at the cross one more time. He drove directly back to his hotel.

☩∗☩∗☩

"Hello, Kay, this is Colin. I think I solved the mystery of Hans's dots." Colin was out of breath. He had dialed her number as soon as the door to his room closed.

"Yes …?"

"It's a cross."

"A what?"

"Kay, it's a cross, a Maronite cross."

"I'm afraid you've got me. What does it look like?"

"Draw a vertical line. In the upper half draw three horizontal lines of varying lengths to conform to the pattern of a Christmas tree. That's it, a Maronite cross," he said, unable to contain his excitement. "We had taken the pattern left by Hans to be a tree when in fact he was trying to describe a Maronite cross."

"And what does it mean?" Kay asked.

"I don't know …" Colin hesitated. "Yet." He paused again. "But let's assume or explore that whatever Hans discovered it somehow is connected to the Maronite Church or its followers."

"No, you don't really think so?"

"Kay, I just don't know." He was already having some second thoughts about his premise.

⁂

At their regular Monday morning meeting in Jerusalem, the American Intelligence liaison officer received an intelligence report concerning Lebanon from his Israeli counterpart. According to the report, an order for several false passports had been placed by a single but yet-to-be-identified client.

"What does this mean?" the American asked.

"We don't yet know what it means, but note that the order was placed for the passports to be manufactured rather than altered stolen passports," the Israeli responded. Noting the dwindling interest of the American, he began a short tutorial on the significance of this information.

"You see, my friend, and you probably know this already, it is considerably less expensive to locate stolen passports that you then change to fit the profile of the person who receives it." There was hardly a glimmer of recognition from the American. "And you do understand that such passports are also obtained with little difficulty from a friendly, tolerant, or corrupt Middle Eastern country?" he continued.

"Our interest was piqued by the order for several passports in one package." The Israeli wished he was still on the street involved in operations rather than required to deal with this dull American masquerading as an intelligence operative. It really didn't matter that he was not taking notes; the Israeli had prepared a report on this information that the American would have to forward to his headquarters.

"We also learned that the passports were to be delivered before a certain date, indicating—so our analysts conclude—that they will be issued to one group. Additionally, passports from a Middle East country were not acceptable." Still no reaction from the

American, though his eyes were still open. The Israeli was not to be deterred.

"We interpret this to mean that those traveling had to possess better language skills and that their physical appearance had to pass for European. If our informant is accurate, it could be an early indicator that a trained and sophisticated terrorist group is being sent to the West," the Israeli paused for dramatic effect, "or even to America."

The Israeli, who was visibly excited by the report, noted that the American finally stirred and took some notes out of politeness. But it was only out of politeness. When it came to terrorism, the Israeli judged that the American believed that Israeli simply overreacted, despite the fact that this was the third report he had passed to the Americans in as many weeks regarding the use of false documentation by suspected terrorists.

As with the others, CIA Headquarters had not been able to corroborate the contents from its own agents or from its huge communications intercept capability managed by the National Security Agency. The view held at Headquarters was that the Israelis were becoming unjustifiably edgy. If anything, what concerned Headquarters and what was conveyed to CIA's station in Tel Aviv was that the Israelis were laying the groundwork for another incursion into Lebanon by leaking information to gullible allies.

"Before moving to the next topic on the agenda, the emigration of Jews from the Soviet Union, we ask urgently for any information that would help to identify the group in need of passports and, of course, the intended targets."

Earlier in the day at his meeting with his British liaison officer, the Israeli had asked for similar assistance. Tomorrow, he would meet with his French counterpart and convey the same sense of urgency. The Israelis treated all such reports seriously because the odds were that Israeli territory or interests were the ultimate target. It is for this reason that all Israeli crossing points had been notified and placed on high alert status. Northern Command, responsible for the buffer zone between Israel and Lebanon, initiated aggressive tank and lightning strikes along the border as a form of deterrence.

⁘

The American returned to the station exhausted following the three-hour meeting. He could not understand how the Israelis could manufacture so much information in a week's time. If he found the meetings difficult, he found the writing of the after-action report as equally challenging. There was so much to do administratively. He was annoyed that Headquarters had yet to fill the administrative assistant position. He feared that it would never be filled as Headquarters wrestled with budget and staff cutbacks demanded by Congress.

He picked up a pencil and drafted a routine cable that summarized the information obtained. He would pouch directly the report the Israeli passed to him on the false passport issue. Whoever provided the information, by the time the Israelis distributed the information to the allies in contact with them, he thought, the agent's life would be in danger.

⁘

Something was afoot. That was Kay's thought as she sat at her desk reviewing the cables coming in from Europe and the Middle East. The situation in Lebanon was becoming anarchic, yet the Christians seemed unusually quiet and even passive. By their inaction, they seemed to be inviting destruction from the Moslem Shiites. They appeared content to increase efforts to reach émigré communities in the West and plead their desperate case for assistance as the onslaught of the Moslem fundamentalism descended upon them. All the intelligence indicators pointed to a Christian leadership eschewing any activity that could incite their Moslem adversaries. *Most unusual,* Kay thought. In refraining from launching an offensive they seemed determined not to alienate would-be supporters in the West.

Terrorist groups like the Popular Front for the Liberation of Palestine and similar radical groups that traditionally touted Libyan propaganda themes in return for material support also appeared quiescent. For over six months, no terrorist incident could be traced to them, nor did any of them claim responsibility for the handful of bombings that had taken place in France, an isolated incident in Greece, or another in Belgium. Yet, during that time, Kay could see a determined struggle emerging between US intelligence operatives abroad and an unidentified terrorist organization with ties to the Libyans.

Then there was the tantalizing report that had just come in from Tel Aviv, indicating that a sophisticated terrorist operation could be in the final planning stage. Kay considered it final because the Israeli report mentioned an approximate number of passports and the kind of passports, excluding at the same time certain countries of origin in the Middle East. It was clear that sufficient funding was available and a target must have been selected, and it appeared that the target was not located on the usual battlegrounds of Europe and the Middle East.

Could there be a connection between this and Colin's operations? Call it intuition, and that was exactly why Kay was so respected among her colleagues. She saw relationships between incidents and events before most. This is not to say that the circumstances around the murder of Ganymede did not continue to puzzle her—even frustrate her. Also, they had still not received any communication from ICARUS. He must still be in Libya. Pity he only had a telephone number in Athens to call.

She was glad that Colin was back in Europe. Perhaps he would uncover some clue to identify those responsible for murdering Hans and Horst and for the attempt on his life. Whoever was responsible for the attempt on Colin's life seemed to have backed away from further confrontation after the assassin was killed. Could he have been acting on his own?

What about those pinpricks under the stamp? She concluded that GANYMEDE made them, and it was only when the card was posted that he was forced to reveal what he had done. Colin's interpretation that it represented the outline of a Lebanese cedar or the lines of a Maronite cross, while intriguing, left her unconvinced.

Kay rubbed her hand over her left eyebrow to relieve the stinging sensation she felt. Whenever she puzzled over a problem, the hair on her eyebrow bristled, causing the sensation. "What was GANYMEDE trying to say?" she asked herself in a whisper. If his sign was a Lebanese cedar, was he trying to say the Lebanese were responsible for his imprisonment? That would appear to have been obvious, since the postcard was mailed from Beirut and pictured a scene in Lebanon. If, on the other hand, the signal represented a Maronite cross, was he trying to say that the church there had imprisoned him? Unlikely, but maybe not the official church but someone aligned or affiliated with it.

Maybe, Kay surmised, all GANYMEDE was trying to say was, "Hey, this isn't as it appears." But she was still at a loss to describe how it appeared—much less speculate on what was real. Suppose the group that held and later murdered him was the same group that had ordered the batch of false passports? Did the cedar or cross hold any special significance then?

Perhaps GANYMEDE was warning that we must be careful before assigning guilt. This time we could not, on reflex, blame the radical Palestinians but would have to look further afield—perhaps among the Christian groups. It sounded ludicrous when Kay said the words. Yet there was a ring of reasonableness in the analysis that surprised her. In the end she still had not answered the question—*was the outline that of a tree, a cross, or something else?*

She jumped ahead to Horst's murder. Why did he have to be killed? What did his murderer gain? Revenge? It simply made no sense. After further interrogation or possibly through some act of bravado on GANYMEDE's part, his captors learned that the signal had been sent to the West. That could explain the promptness with which they moved against Horst and attempted the same with Colin. *It may even explain the decision to murder GANYMEDE*, Kay thought.

The intense mental activity had stimulated her to such a pitch that she realized it was time to put it aside. Her head was throbbing. She pushed the files aside and lit a cigarette, breathing in deeply the iron taste of the nicotine. She felt a cough emerging from the depths of her chest and reached for her cup of cold coffee to suppress it. It was time to pack up and go home.

CHAPTER NINETEEN

Graduation day! Jamie had completed the training but still had no indication whether he had attracted the attention of those who directed Libya's terrorist network. Several students were scheduled to remain behind for additional training. He was not to be among them. The Sikh did not appear for class the last three days. Jamie assumed that he had departed Libya for India and a Sikh separatist group operating in Rajasthan. Or perhaps he was destined to work against Indian government or commercial interests abroad.

Jamie had second thoughts now about his decision to advertise his ties to the Red Army Faction. He feared that the Libyans might have allowed him to enroll in order to demonstrate their solidarity with their German brothers but had never intended to include him in their ranks.

But what else could he have done to obtain a visa so quickly? He was scheduled to depart for Rome the next morning with a continuation flight to Athens that same afternoon. Anticipating his next meeting with the American, he decided that the stub from his free airline ticket would convince them that he succeeded in reaching Libya and that his ties to the RAF had been accepted by the Libyans.

He wondered if he would still be considered of value to the

Americans. He translated value to mean whether the Americans would continue to deposit money into his Swiss account for the nest egg Brigid and he would need for their new start.

Changing loyalty from the RAF to the Americans was not a difficult decision to make. In fact, it was long overdue—a sensible decision. What he was discovering—much to his surprise—was that he missed the adrenal rush of working with the RAF. He sorely hoped that he would not be relegated to the sidelines by his new sponsors. His decision to turn on the RAF was as much influenced by the promise of excitement as it was for resettlement, and it was definitely not tied to some moral code or the ethics of the Americans. In the final analysis, at this moment, he was frustrated at the lack of progress made in elbowing his way into a terrorist apparatus as directed.

He was ready to acknowledge failure—at least according to the severe criteria he applied to himself—when a knock on his door interrupted further introspection. It was the Arab who had arrived in the camp only days previously. His name was Sulham Khalifa Ben Yousef—though he was introduced to the students as Abu Tarif. Jamie recognized him as the well-publicized oil expert in Qadafi's entourage. Dressed in dark winter robes for this desert region, he entered the sparsely furnished room.

"My friend, it is good to finally meet you privately. You have done quite well in the training."

"Yes, I enjoyed myself." Jamie was surprised that he spoke to him in fluent, though accented, Spanish. He was almost six feet tall, and his dark hair and complexion highlighted his deep blue eyes.

"Tell me about your time with the Red Army Faction," he said as he sat on the chair next to the desk. Jamie took a seat on the edge of the single bed. For the next thirty minutes Jamie recounted his courier work—the countries through which he traveled—but he did not share operational details that could have compromised him or the RAF. He could not determine whether he was being tested or if Ben Yousef was probing for new information.

"I see you have packed." Ben Yousef observed Jamie's bag in the open closet. "What are your plans?"

"Return to Greece. I'll rejoin my friend's supply business." Ben Yousef nodded to indicate that he understood Jamie's meaning. "Why do you ask?"

"Oh, I just wondered." Ben Yousef paused before continuing. "It's a pity, what with all the training you have received."

"What do you have in mind?" It was Jamie's chance to question.

Ben Yousef smiled. "My young friend, I have a proposal for you."

In the next hour and a half, Ben Yousef described an offer for what he termed *limited employment*. Limited in the sense that Ben Yousef estimated that Jamie could complete the task in one month or so, and for his troubles would be paid twenty thousand dollars.

"Tell me more."

"You would travel directly to Lebanon—which we would arrange. Once there you would infiltrate Christian circles in East Beirut," Ben Yousef outlined.

"Lebanon. Christians. What's this all about?"

"We have reason to believe that the Christians are planning a major operation. The fear, I repeat fear, is that Libya will be the target of a Christian plot in league with the Americans. Our supreme leader wants no repeat of the consternation caused by the surprise American bombing of our land."

"And what can I do? Just get to know those Christian troublemakers?"

Ben Yousef smiled. "Will you accept the assignment?" He adjusted the thick gold chain that hung around his neck.

"Yes," Jamie answered, hoping he didn't sound too eager.

"I must tell you that another friend went to Beirut for us, but we have not heard from him. You must be careful. I have arranged that wherever you find yourself, report to the nearest official Libyan establishment and show your passport. Someone will meet you as soon as your identity is confirmed."

Jamie marveled at the plan's simplicity. He did not have to memorize any international numbers or complex meeting instructions—as with the Americans. Just knock on the door of the nearest Libyan office. He wondered why he had not worked for them sooner.

Ben Yousef bid Jamie farewell.

Alone again, he completed his packing and was on his way to the airport within an hour. He departed Tripoli on a direct flight to Damascus. Though the aircraft made no stops, the flight time was four hours, as it flew in a circuitous route over the Mediterranean to avoid the range of Egyptian and Israeli fighter aircraft. The Libyans had no desire to tempt their enemies to disrupt such sensitive unscheduled flights.

It was already dark when Jamie landed in Damascus. He was met on the tarmac by a civilian who greeted him and accompanied him to a white Mercedes. The car was distinguishable by the dent on its right fender, caused no doubt by a stray or deliberately fired fifty-caliber round.

Within two hours, his driver reached the Syrian-Lebanese border. After showing some documentation to a uniformed infantryman assigned to the border post, the driver was allowed to maneuver his vehicle into the middle of a Syrian army relief convoy that was about to depart for Beirut. During the wait the driver pulled out a package of cigarettes. From the odor, Jamie knew that Latikiya—that strong, pungent Turkish tobacco—formed the basis of the mix. The driver offered one to Jamie without a word being spoken. He accepted, realizing that his companion only spoke Arabic—a language that he had never been able to utter more than *en shallah*.

The column of twenty Russian five-ton trucks, three scout vehicles, and a Russian tank leading and following departed two hours late. The delay was caused by the first truck in the convoy, which had developed engine trouble. Since the truck was assigned to carry the contraband items for sale in the bazaars, the decision was made to delay the convoy until it was repaired.

When they were finally underway, the vehicles stayed close. No one wanted to stray from the highway where they would become attractive targets for one of the self-styled regional militias that controlled areas along the highway. The column averaged twenty miles an hour and did not reach the outskirts of Beirut until after two in the morning. There the vehicles parked in a large open field surrounded by barbed wire. The slovenly clad Syrian sentries did not realize that the enclosure had been occupied until the second tank roared inside. So much for Syrian security, Jamie thought as he drifted back to sleep.

⁜

Colin was alerted on Sunday afternoon in Bonn that ICARUS had called the Athens number from Beirut. Chris was preparing dinner when he told her that he would have to go into the office. She said nothing. He had no idea how long it would be at the office. Before he departed, he called Joan at home and asked her to join him.

The transcript of the message that ICARUS had left on the voice mail read:

> Halo, I am here in Beirut. I have work which will interest you. The pay is good. Meet me in the bar of the Hotel Riviera tonight any time after nine, or I'll see you when I return to Europe.

"What do we do now?" Colin passed the cable to Joan, who had already read it. She lived closer to the embassy than Colin did. He was still housed in the quarters provided and protected by the German government.

"I don't know whether it's a good idea for you to meet him in Beirut, especially in West Beirut. I checked. That is where the

Riviera is located. Remember what happened to GANYMEDE and almost happened to you in Athens. Wait for him to get to Europe."

"Let's see what Headquarters says. I'm sure they'll want to get involved," Colin said.

⟊∗⟊∗⟊

At Headquarters, Kay—given the time change—went directly to the twenty-four-hour-watch center to view the message. A Styrofoam cup of black coffee in her hand and a long cigarette handing dangerously from her mouth, she was waiting for the clerk on duty to retrieve a copy of the night-action cable. It was five in the morning.

Kay had the same sentiments as Joan. She feared that they, whoever they were, might try to snatch Colin. She sipped the hot coffee loudly against the cup's lid before placing it on top of a file cabinet so she could light another cigarette. She reread the message.

"I'm returning the cable," she said, deciding that any action could wait for the opening of business. She caught the clerk's attention before he reentered the communications area, which was protected by a special shielded enclosure. Kay was at the elevator on her way home when the clerk popped his head out the door.

"I have another one for you."

This cable was from Athens station and referred to the previous Athens message. It was addressed to the stations in Bonn and Beirut as well as Headquarters.

1. *Believe it critical that meeting with ICARUS in Beirut take place. See no way for Gordon to attend. First, flight connections would not get him there until Monday; second, if it is trap, Gordon has been previously identified as GANYMEDE's case officer.*
2. *As alternative, propose that Frost travel to Beirut this*

afternoon using false passport on file here in name of John Afionyan. His knowledge of Arabic makes possible for case officer to move easily in West Beirut. Confident that Frost will be able to establish contact with ICARUS securely.
3. Any objections? Please advise soonest. There is much to be done.

Kay held the cable loosely and reread it. It was clear that Frost had read the transcript hours earlier than either Colin or Kay and that he had more time to mull over this response. How many times in her career had she observed the phenomenon of courage emerging from individuals not noted for taking risks? What caused it? Was it frustration with a life advertised to the outside world as daring but known to insiders as cautious routine, interrupted by isolated moments of unbounded excitement? Had Frost embraced one of those moments? She could not argue with Frost's logic, and if the station in East Beirut had no objections, she planned to support Frost's recommendation with Brody.

Colin's reaction to Frost's cable was quite different. He was angry and envious—envious of this bold proposal. Colin had wanted to be the one to meet ICARUS. GANYMEDE was his agent. It was his responsibility to identify the killers. He picked up a pen and drafted his response.

1. Strongly object to Athens's suggestion. Prepared to leave immediately on Syrian Airline flight 203 for Damascus and travel by road to Beirut in time to make evening meeting with ICARUS.
2. If approved, will call embassy in Beirut upon arrival. Please advise.

Kay had just reached the uniformed guard at the front gate when he waved to her to halt. He told her that a third message had been received for her to review. She returned to read the latest cable. She asked for the two previous ones and with them walked to her office. She decided that any chance of returning home had vanished with the latest missive.

"Men!" she uttered aloud. "Such children."

At her desk, she drafted Brody's reply. She would have to be careful. It was bad enough losing an agent. Brody would fear survival in the bureaucracy if he lost a case officer. It would shatter his career goals—already on the ascendancy—in an instant. At least that is how Kay figured Brody would assess the situation.

1. *For Bonn: Headquarters does not, repeat not, approve Gordon's travel to Beirut at this time. Instead, provide insights and thoughts for meeting with ICARUS to Beirut by immediate precedence.*
2. *For Athens: Frost authorized to travel to Beirut but must confirm approval to meet with ICARUS upon arrival.*
3. *For Beirut: Please provide contact instructions for Frost ASAP.*
4. *Potential high-level intelligence justifies obvious risk; however, we insist case officer keep us advised of his every move.*

Kay lit her eighth cigarette of the early morning and wondered if she would ever be able to kick the habit. Her hand shook as she gave the cable to the clerk for transmission. She also was drinking too much coffee.

CHAPTER TWENTY

In retrospect, Frost did not understand why he had acted so precipitously in volunteering to meet ICARUS in West Beirut. It had something to do with envy—envy of Colin and activists like him, and the professional success they seemed to attract. The difference between a fourteen, Frost's civil service grade, and Colin's rank of fifteen was the difference between a light and a bird colonel. It only amounted to a few thousand dollars in salary per year and offered no special perquisites. Yet Frost found himself tormented alternately by the thought that he was a failure or that the promotion system was unjust.

When he rose that Sunday morning, he felt listless. He was not one to jump out of bed, but this morning he felt particularly sluggish. He was bored with himself more than was usual. He had never found himself particularly good company—at least for many years this was so. He could not endure the customary Sunday noonday breakfast with Asher. She would lecture him on his need to be more ambitious. Sunday seemed to stimulate such thoughts in her. If only she could vary the lecture, or at least shorten it.

He dressed and was surprised to find himself in the car heading for the office before ten. Asher had not even stirred in the bed next to him. He had no work to do. He never did. He would spend his time leisurely hanging an art acquisition in his office—already filled with priceless items. *Thank God for the marines,* he thought as he was admitted to the embassy compound. This contingent of twenty marines provided twenty-four-hour protection for his possessions.

Frost concluded that his inertia was in part caused by the reluctant admission that in his career he only served in sinecure positions. It was not easy for him now to return to the paper shuffling that usually filled his days. He felt like he was in the middle of a leaden pond. The only difference now was that he was aware of it. He could no longer disguise his lack of professional ambition made clear to him working alongside Colin. Soon after arriving at the embassy that Sunday, the technician responsible for servicing the recording devices connecting several telephone lines tracked him down to tell him of the message that ICARUS had left on one of the devices.

Frost read the transcript of the conversation several times. He assumed that Colin would be anxious to make the meeting in Beirut. Frost also knew that he would have the advantage in responding, since Colin would not have received the transcript yet. Motivated by a desire to show Colin that he was as much the professional that Colin purported to be, he drafted the preemptive cable to make the meeting.

In a quick call to Asher, he informed her that he would have to leave town on business. She sounded encouraging, believing that her attempts to influence Frost were finally beginning to show some results. He could have dashed to the airport and attempted to catch a Cyprus airline flight that stopped in Larnaca and continued on to Beirut, but he decided to book a more leisurely direct Middle East Airlines flight. There had been too many warnings issued about the vulnerability of Cypriot Airlines flights to hijacking.

He took a taxi to the airport and was there in plenty of time before the scheduled three thirty departure. Only at five thirty did he have second thoughts about the wisdom of taking the second flight, as he glanced out the terminal window at the MEA aircraft undergoing repairs on the runway. Already two hours behind schedule, Frost felt an acid hiss in his stomach. He now would have done anything to have been on the late-morning flight.

Ringing in his ears was the criticism he would receive from everyone if he were late for the meeting with ICARUS. Whoever *everyone* was, he was not sure. *Everyone* always changed, but everyone was no less critical. He moved abruptly from the window and began pacing another circle around the terminal—trying to control his mounting anxiety. He wondered why he was so unlucky.

He should call the office and inform them of the delay, but he was afraid that if he checked in, a cable might be waiting that cancelled the trip. He had something to prove, although he was having difficulty understanding what it was. When he was at the far end of the terminal, the announcement of the flight's departure penetrated the fog of his gloom. He turned on his heels and walked hurriedly to the departure gate.

He felt the penetrating look of the MEA ground staff to whom he handed his false Canadian passport. He wondered if the passport passed inspection. Within seconds the document was back in his hands and he was on his way to the aircraft. He took his seat by the window and immediately buried himself in the ancient Armenian tale, *David of Sassoun*. It was appropriate that an Afionyan—his alias for this trip—would be familiar with the tale. Someone could question whether he was prudent in carrying this valuable volume into rapacious Beirut, something that had not occurred to him, along with any concern for his personal safety. Perhaps bravery nurtures such innocence.

❦ ❦ ❦

Jamie used his prior knowledge of West Beirut to good purpose. He searched out a building where he had once stayed for a couple of months several years prior. He noticed that a wrought iron fence had been installed across what had once been a fashionable marble foyer and lobby. The bell for the concierge was beyond his reach through the fence. He rattled the fence to gain someone's attention. The door to an apartment directly in front of him was open. Through the dim light of its interior he caught the shape of a rifle pointing at him. He stopped shaking the fence and kept his hands in view.

"Monsieur, it is your friend, Mr. Jamie; I stayed here once. I need a room for a couple of weeks."

A prone figure stood—weapon in hand. He smiled when he recognized Jamie, though he did not understand him as he spoke only Arabic. Immediately, he approached the fence and opened the door, inviting him to enter with a warm gesture and bow. He locked the fence after Jamie entered.

The concierge was a Palestinian who was elevated from maintenance man to concierge—actually, he filled both positions—when the fighting broke out on the streets. Tall, gaunt, his broad smile widened over an unshaven face and framed the ragged edge of front teeth that had once suffered an encounter with an immovable force.

Language was no barrier to their communication. He led Jamie up the flight of stairs—the elevator was not in service—to the two-room apartment that he had once occupied. It had once been an elegant suite on the tenth floor overlooking the Mediterranean. During the siege of the city, a stray Syrian artillery shell had destroyed the upper portion of the building's façade and reduced the size of the apartment to its present configuration.

"See, see," the concierge said as he gestured with his arms wide—one still holding the AK-47—to the sea, "Bene, bene!"

"Yes, bene," Jamie agreed. There was still something that violence could not destroy.

He paid the concierge a month's rent in advance, though he expected to be on his way sooner, and a generous gratuity for remembering him. The good will of this grizzled warrior was worth the extravagance.

✟∗✟∗✟

It was eight thirty when Frost finally landed in Beirut—long past sunset. Every seat in the airport lounge, including the floor space next to the wall, was occupied by passengers scheduled to depart the next morning or by those who had arrived earlier. They shared a common fear of getting caught on the road between the airport and the city during the hours of darkness. The inconvenience of spending the night on a soiled or damaged lounge chair in the terminal was small compared to the risk of violence on the road.

If Frost had any sense, he would have taken note and remained at the airport as well. But this option never occurred to him. In truth, he had not even noticed the people in the chairs and propped along the wall. If he had, he probably would not have understood their reason for remaining in the terminal.

Instead, he hired a private taxi that was parked outside the exit door. He paid the driver in advance an exorbitant fare, even though he realized that there was little likelihood of reaching the Riviera Hotel on time for the scheduled meeting. He still considered it worth a try. During the first five minutes of the bumpy ride filled with potholes—once the premier road connecting the airport to the city—his only goal was to reach the hotel before ICARUS departed. After the taxi was forced to the side of the road at the first traffic circle, basic personal survival was his only objective, superseding concerns about meetings and career.

A Mercedes bursting with seven heavily armed Arabs careened from its concealment alongside the road. With no warning, it pulled alongside the slower-moving taxi—scraping the side of both vehicles in the process. Those on the side facing the taxi waved their automatic weapons menacingly at the terrified driver, who tried to ignore the intrusion by gripping the wheel tighter and staring straight ahead. Finally, seeing out the corner of his eye the weapons aimed at him, he brought the car to a screeching halt, but not before it hit the side of the Mercedes as it skidded momentarily out of control. The driver of the Mercedes was the first to reach the taxi. He pulled the driver from the taxi violently. In seconds, they were all around the driver inspecting his identity card, which listed him as a Kurd.

They then came for Frost, who had remained in the rear seat of the taxi, shaking. Had he not opened the door, they would have pulled him through the window. As with the Kurd, they scrutinized Frost's Canadian false passport under the glare of the taxi's headlights. They yanked Frost by the hair so that his face was in the beam of the headlights and they could compare him to the photo in the passport. They stripped Frost, on his knees by this time, of his wallet and wedding band.

It all happened so fast that Frost tried to convince himself that he had dozed off watching a film on an aircraft. The chilling reality of the scene caught him when the taxi driver, moaning softly, tears flooding his face and mixing with the perspiration of fear, was hauled off into the bushes. A short burst from an automatic weapon silenced his pleas for mercy. The blood lust of his abductors satisfied, they returned to Frost. They inspected again his Canadian passport and slapped him a couple of times in the face, drawing blood around his lips and nose. Then, inexplicably, they released him and he fell to the ground upon the small rocks that littered the road. The intruders rushed back to their car laughing as they observed Frost seemingly paralyzed in the dirt. The last of the doors slammed when the car was already thirty feet down the road, gathering speed.

Frost was alone in the darkness surrounded by the outline of the foreboding trees. The silence was complete except for the sound of the Mercedes fading in the distance. A full moon in a star-filled sky shed the only light on the scene. He felt a desperate urge to scream into the blackness for help. He restrained himself by imagining the contempt his colleagues would hold him if they learned that he broke under the pressure of the moment. He stumbled on uncertain feet to the abandoned taxi. The keys were not in the ignition. He knew that the next logical place for them was in the pants pocket of the driver. Frost did not know how he could summon the courage to search the corpse. He wanted no reminder of the fate he came so close to sharing.

Instead, he skipped to the next most logical place for the keys—somewhere between the taxi and the bushes. He was hoping that the driver had dropped them as his killers were hauling him into the woods. He reached into the taxi and pulled a knob for the lights; instead the windshield wiper whined across the window. He pulled a second knob, and a soft glow of light reached across the road, indicating that the car battery would soon need replacing.

In an ever-widening arc, Frost searched. He did not know what he was looking for. Was it a single key? A ring? Would they be in a leather case and not visible in the light? He reached down once assured that he had found them—only to cut his finger in his haste on a piece of glass. On reflex he put the finger in his mouth to stem the bleeding, only to wince with the taste of blood mixed with grains of dirt and oil grime from the road. After a moment, he resumed his search.

He exhaled audibly when he spotted a glint in the weeds at the edge of the road. A brass ring holding several keys lay on the dirt path along which the driver had been dragged minutes previously.

He rushed back to the car in the long unsteady stride of someone who had been drinking. After several tries, he finally succeeded in fitting the key into the ignition—all the while pumping the accelerator. When he tried to start the engine, the smell of gasoline overwhelmed him. He had flooded the carburetor. He turned off the headlights and waited for what seemed an eternity to try again. The motor clattered into action. The sound released in Frost a second wave of terror and fear—almost nausea. He released the brake and then the clutch, accelerating so forcefully that the sound of the gravel against the side of the car drowned out for a second the clanking of the motor.

Frost knew the airport road from past travel to and from

Beirut. He kept the windows open and drove as fast as he could and still control the car. The headlights remained extinguished. He decided to rely on moonlight—anything to reduce the chances of encountering another ambush. There was no one on the road, nor did he pass another vehicle during the twenty-minute drive. When he reached the vicinity of the Riviera, he pulled to a stop and parked behind the shell of a car that had been destroyed in some previous firefight. Using a book of matches he found on the frayed seat of the taxi, he saw that it was ten o'clock.

Before he got out of the car, he stayed silently in place with the windows open, trying to detect any movement in the immediate vicinity. Satisfied that there was none, he opened the door carefully, making as little noise as possible. He pulled his suitcase from the trunk, where it nestled among a car jack and oily rags. *Strange that they didn't steal the bag*, he thought. He walked quickly toward the hotel—four blocks away. The palms of his hands were cold and clammy to the touch. His feet were swollen, and his shoes felt tight. As he neared the hotel, his pace increased to the point that he twisted his ankle on a rock, which he had not noticed in the path.

Wet with perspiration, he approached the entrance of the hotel on the Corniche. He noticed four armed men observing him. They were leaning against the wall of the hotel in the shadows. Not many guests arrived at this hour with a suitcase in hand. Frost must have passed inspection as he continued toward the entrance uninterrupted.

"Excuse me," Frost said, standing before the elderly clerk in repose. His throat felt dry. These were the first words he had spoken since he had given the taxi driver the name of the hotel. The man opened his eyes without moving his head from its resting position against the top of the chair. Deciding that there was nothing to fear from the haggard stranger, he smiled.

"Yes, monsieur."

"I have reservations. My name is Afionyan." Frost displayed the open page of his passport. The clerked leaned forward and peered through squinted eyes at the photograph and identifying data on the opposite page. Satisfied, he rocked himself to his feet—his once-powerful arms providing the final thrust to his aging frame. The cushion of the chair inhaled to its previous shape in triumph. The clerk limped behind the counter. Frost could not tell if the man's legs were infirm or if one or both legs had fallen asleep.

"Who are those chaps outside?" Frost asked.

"Our Druze guards. You know that this is a Druze neighborhood?" He checked the registry and the reservation book and passed Frost the necessary forms to complete, including a currency declaration, a duplicate of what Frost had filled out at the airport. It amazed Frost that the bureaucracy survived the anarchy and chaos. He began to fill out the form, but the clerk waved his hand as he handed him the room key.

"Tomorrow, s'il vous plait; bring the papers back." It was clear that the clerk wanted to return to his chair and the better days envisioned in his dreams. Frost was relieved that he had not been asked to present his American Express Card, which was stolen along with his wallet.

"Can I get a drink?" Frost asked.

"I'm sorry, monsieur. The bar closed an hour ago, but I will allow you to pour a nightcap to take to your room."

"Have you seen a man about thirty, blond hair, earlier in the bar?" Frost asked as he poured himself a paper cup full of scotch whiskey. He didn't recognize the brand.

"Yes, monsieur, there was such a man. He is not a guest in the hotel. When he finished his drink he left—maybe two hours ago."

With the room key attached to a heavy brass ball, Frost held his suitcase in one hand and the paper cup in the other and entered the elevator. He looked down at the paper cup as the singular success of the evening. At the room, he placed the cup carefully on the frayed green rug and turned the key in the lock. A dank, musty smell greeted him upon entry. He placed his bag down and returned for the cup. Once he bolted the door closed, he tossed his jacket on the bed, took a seat in one of two straight-back chairs, and slipped off his shoes from the heels without untying the laces. He pulled the second chair closer to rest his legs and took a sip of the harsh dark scotch. It made his eyes tear.

What an evening, he thought—nearly lost his life, witnessed a brutal killing, wallet stolen, and missed meeting ICARUS. What more could happen? He took a second, deeper sip and placed the cup on the floor. Still fully clothed, he lay on the bed to relax and woke five hours later. In the dark, he removed his trousers and shirt and crawled between the covers.

CHAPTER TWENTY-ONE

At ten the next morning, Frost called the front desk after no one answered from room service.

"Hello, is there someone who can bring me some coffee and croissants?"

"Oui, monsieur. I will be just there."

While he was waiting for his breakfast, he called his contact at the American embassy in East Beirut and summarized his experience of the previous evening as well as that he had missed the meeting with ICARUS. The person at the other end appeared sympathetic to his plight.

Frost was glad that Colin was not with him in the room. Surely he would have become apoplectic with Frost's lack of security in discussing sensitive information on an open telephone line. But he had no choice since he was instructed not to travel between the western and eastern districts of the city.

"I need an alternate meeting site and time for the chap I was supposed to meet." There was silence at the other end. "Are you there?" Frost asked.

"Yes, I was taking some notes. I will get back to you," he said finally.

"Oh, there is another matter," Frost paused. "My wallet was stolen. I need funds."

"We'll do what we can. Unfortunately, I am not authorized to travel to West Beirut; however, I will do my best to arrange a delivery."

"Also, please cable Athens so that they can alert my friend here."

"Will do." The American sounded impatient and signed off.

After hanging up, Frost went to the window and noticed that the joggers were out now in pairs or alone. Their path was a brown ribbon of sand between the winding road and the aquamarine sea. With no exceptions, they were dressed in colorful sweat suits, looted no doubt from shipping containers or the upscale shops that once lined Hamra Street.

There was no better indicator that it was safe to leave the hotel. People outside meant that the internecine warfare had ceased for this Monday—or at least it so appeared. After twelve, the embassy contact called back to describe where the funds and key to an alternate meeting site would be left in a dead drop for him. Just a short walk from the hotel, he was to unload the drop after four in the afternoon.

He spent the afternoon in the room, going down once to eat a lunch of humus and pita bread, accompanied by a glass of bitter French white table wine.

At three forty-five he checked to see if pedestrians were still strolling outside—they were. It was time to leave. Once outside he headed north up the Corniche to the campus of the American University of Beirut. The grounds once resembled a lush garden—luxuriant thick grass manicured to golf course perfection, mature palm trees providing shade, and rock grottos from which to view the ships transiting the port. Now, deep tire tracks marred the once popular quarter-mile track and dead tree limbs littered the walking paths. Plants that in a former day would have been moved during winter to the indoor botanical garden maintained by the university now stood yellow-brown in death.

Once inside the iron entrance gate, Frost looked for a cavity somewhere in the fifteen-foot rock wall. He was not informed whether it would be at the level of his feet or above his head, nor did he know how far down the wall to search. For someone with so little experience in the servicing of dead drops, Frost regretted now not asking some questions. In fact, this was the first dead drop he was to unload since his days of training—over twenty years earlier. Finally, he found the cavity in the wall. It was two feet up on the wall in a cavity. The package was wrapped in an oilskin wrapper. Inside was the cash he had requested plus the key and directions to the safe house. *Now that was not so difficult*, he thought, walking off, triumphant.

⁜

Jamie had not been surprised when no one appeared at the hotel. He decided that they didn't have sufficient time to dispatch someone. Perhaps they had already withdrawn their people as the fighting escalated. Why had he suggested the Riviera? At the time, he did not realize how isolated each section of the city had become from another. He decided to make his way to East Beirut and the restaurant that Ben Yousef described as a haunt for prominent Christian leaders, especially Antoine Saad, whom Ben Yousef suspected was the aging but leading strategist for the infidels. According to the Libyan, this same Saad maintained a brisk trade in rare icons with European clients despite the ravages of war. Jamie hoped to convince Saad of his own interest in icons—thus satisfying the requirement to develop the contacts for which the Libyans were paying him. But before he did anything, he had to call Athens.

⁜

"Please hold" were the words repeated to him by the young woman who became increasingly nervous when ICARUS explained the reason for the call.

He waited patiently in the post office booth from which he

placed the call. After a pause of almost five minutes, the voice of the young woman returned.

"We are pleased to hear from you. Is everything all right?" she asked, obviously reading from a hastily prepared script.

"Yes, except there was no one at the hotel," ICARUS responded.

"Sorry, our man had trouble reaching Beirut on time. He is there now and eager to meet you." She was inexperienced in speaking with non-English speakers. Her articulation was sloppy, and she had a tendency to rush her words. The static-filled phone line only made her more nervous.

"Good. Where and when?"

"Proceed to 15 Katab Street. It is located behind the old Phoenicia Hotel. Go to apartment number forty-two. The time for the meeting is three in the afternoon, tomorrow, January 16. The alternate is next day at four, or any day thereafter, same time, until contact is established."

"Is that all?" Jamie waited. "Who will meet me?"

"Do not worry. Your contact will be in the apartment waiting for you. Do you have anything more to report?"

"No." Jamie was sorry that they had not shifted the meeting site to East Beirut since he would be traveling there anyway. He did not like the idea of crossing the Green Line too often. He hung up and paid the charges to the postal employee. Since it was too early to find the target at the restaurant, he decided to locate the address of the meeting location he had just been given. It would take fifteen minutes to reach the area.

↕*↕*↕

The hulking remains of the once-flourishing Holiday Inn formed a haunting backdrop to the building for which he searched. The Holiday Inn had lured the free-spending European tourists from the more fashionable St. George or more European Phoenicia Hotel—that is, until it was rendered uninhabitable within just a few years of its formal opening. Since then, the hotel's exterior had absorbed thousands of rounds of machine, mortar, and artillery fire. Its interior suffered equally as Christian and Moslem combatants became locked in mortal combat. The hotel was deserted now. The original furnishings—selected by the hotel's opulent Saudi Arabian investors—had long since been looted and now adorned the homes of the remaining or surviving Christian and Moslem antagonists.

Without pausing, Jamie walked past the building where he would meet the American later. It was six stories high. From what he could see there was only one entrance to the building, and if his memory served him, the old French embassy was located behind and down the hill. From the street he could not tell whether the apartment fronted on the main street. He would learn that soon enough, but it was an important question to answer. Experience and his survival had taught him always to find an alternate entrance or exit. The affair in Athens could have turned out differently had ICARUS not taken the time to reconnoiter the escape route through the basement.

He turned the corner, still concentrating on the building he had just passed. A boy of no more than thirteen years old startled him. The boy blocked his path. In his hand he brandished a forty-five caliber pistol. In the other, he held a stack of papers. The weapon was pointed at Jamie's head.

"Please, you wish to buy a copy of *Arab Liberation?*"

A novel marketing scheme, Jamie thought as he reached into his pocket with his left hand and at the same time viciously struck the boy in the face with his right hand before he could react. The boy collapsed on impact, blood and teeth soiling his face. Jamie picked up the weapon from where it had landed. The newspapers were scattered over the prone figure. He walked from the area not wanting to attract the attention of an elderly couple who were about to enter a building across the street with their shopping. He slowed his pace once he had cleared the hill and was on level ground again. He was pleased to be armed again. It was time to head for the Bacchus Restaurant.

⁑⁂⁑

After crossing the Green Line, he found the restaurant with no difficulty. He opened the door into the dimly lit interior. There were only two tables occupied. He stood for a few minutes waiting to be seated. The manager, if there was one, did not appear. His presence had caused one of the patrons to look up briefly. No one was in a rush to accommodate him. He took his seat at a table near the rear of the large room away from the two that were occupied. His back to the wall, he could observe the entrance as well as the door leading to what he assumed was the kitchen. He waited for someone to serve him. Finally, a young waitress came through the swinging door. She came up to his table and flipped a menu before him and was about to leave.

"Please, a bottle of red wine."

She returned with the wine and proceeded to open it without going through the ritual of showing him the nondescript label.

"I am looking for some icons for a client in Spain."

She looked at him as if she did not comprehend. At the same time she turned the corkscrew. She was unnerving. He did not think it was possible—until now—to open a bottle of wine sensuously. His eyes roamed over the supple arms of the young woman. In the rush of events these last weeks, he had forgotten how much he missed a woman's touch. Her light brown skin roused him. He decided that she was from the Seychelle Islands. In more peaceful times, many of the Seychelle young ladies came to Beirut as au pairs to Western families assigned there. There they earned their dowries before returning home. Others did not return to their dreamy island paradise in the Indian Ocean. They became enmeshed in the sweet corruption of Beirut and ultimately victims to the opulence and vice that always existed just below the surface of this once fashionable, civilized, and cultured city.

The girl still held Jamie's attention. He could not decide if it was her smooth skin or high angular check bones. He was mesmerized. Sensing the hold on him, she smiled provocatively, stretching her lips over glistening white teeth. Her slight build seemed designed for the jeans she wore, or perhaps her hips were designed for the jeans. She wore a dark knit sweater with a zipper sufficiently low to reveal a hint of her small, well-formed breasts.

"What do you do when you're not waiting on tables?"

Although she had still not answered his first question, he wanted to keep her from leaving. She said nothing but continued to look at him as if she did not hear him or understand his overture. He was not sure whether he should pursue her further. He needed no further entanglements. Life was already sufficiently complex.

"Beirut has icons, but the war has interrupted such trade," she said in perfect but accented French, convincing him that she understood his second inquiry as well.

The energy flowing from her glance teased and unnerved him. The bulge under her sweater seemed inches away. He was tempted to bite her. He laughed out loud. If he was not careful he would forget why he was sitting in the Bacchus. What excited him was that the girl understood her impact on him. He was about to say something—anything—to keep her at the table in close proximity, to breathe in her fresh lime-like odor. But before he could, she turned away gracefully and approached another table where two older gentlemen were sitting alone. She took their order and returned to the kitchen.

"You want icons, monsieur?" Jamie had finished his meal and was staring into space, still wondering if pursuing a liaison with the waitress was smart.

"You want icons?" an elderly but well-preserved gentleman repeated. Jamie recognized him as one of the two men sitting with a companion.

"Yes, she must have told you." He looked up at the old man.

"What kind of icons?"

"Sixteenth-century originals from the monastery of St. Gregory in Thessaloniki."

"How much are you prepared to pay?" The old man smiled, perhaps appreciating Jamie's apparent knowledge of the art.

"For top quality—top price." He sounded casual.

"I am Pierre Kettaneh at your gracious service. My friends call me Kalenti." He extended his hand.

"I am Jamie Casasnovas—prepared to prolong your good life."

"Come join my partner." He smiled and gestured to the table that he had left.

Jamie rose and noticed that the men sitting at the second table had suddenly stopped eating and were staring at him intently. The bulges in their jacket pockets and the hands of the one closest gripping something under the table convinced him of their bodyguard role. The man with a day's growth on his face with thinning hair was probably not gripping his knees, or something else, under the table but a weapon that was trained on Jamie.

"Shamir, as he is known." Kalenti gestured.

Shamir extended a quivering frail hand in Jamie's direction. He thought at first that the old man was blind but then noticed the shifting eyes behind the dark glasses.

"I understand that icons find favor with you?" Shamir asked in a raspy voice.

"Not with me—I can't afford them—but with my clients."

"You must know something about them?" Again, Shamir spoke.

"Yes, indeed. I have traded icons for several years now, as I have traveled between the Middle East and Europe."

"I don't recall seeing you here in Beirut before," Kalenti said.

"Are you the lord mayor?" Jamie asked with a smile.

"Not the lord mayor, but he is informed and current on the flow of icons from Eastern Europe and the former Byzantine

Empire to Phoenicia, to Europe, and beyond," Shamir stated with a note of irritation in his voice.

"Phoenicia, I haven't heard Lebanon described as such." Jamie was unyielding. "Then you must remember that I was through here four years ago and spent a few weeks waiting for some parts before my car could be repaired. I examined hundreds of offerings at that time and purchased three priceless specimens from an Armenian who had a shop between the Phoenicia and the American embassy on the Corniche. If I recall, his name was Roger Choukasyan."

"Poor Roger was killed two years ago when his car drove over a land mine left over from the Israeli occupation," Kalenti offered.

Jamie looked up and noticed that the mahogany-shaded waitress was observing him. She smiled deliberately at him before attending to a table of new arrivals.

"How long will you be here?" Shamir asked.

"For one week at most."

"That is sufficient time. Suppose we arrange a private showing tomorrow? What would be a convenient time? We will pick you up." Kalenti asked.

"Excellent—tomorrow morning at ten?" Jamie wanted to keep the afternoon open in the event that the American did not appear today.

"So early?" Kalenti asked. "Okay, we will arrange."

"You know that if you find something that you like, we will expect payment in hard currency," Shamir interrupted.

"I remember when Lebanese pounds were considered hard currency." Both men flashed at his remark.

"Someday—soon—that will again be the case in The Lebanon," Kalenti said with fervor.

The remark reminded Jamie of the Libyan's interest in him meeting these men. Perhaps he was on to something.

"I will have George drive you to where you are staying," Kalenti said.

"You may not when I tell you that I am in West Beirut."

"You are brave, young man," Shamir interjected.

"Our boys are prepared for anything," Kalenti said as he motioned to the man holding something beneath the table. He rose quickly with a duffel bag gripped tightly in his hand. A second man from the table accompanied Jamie outside. On the way out, he tried to catch the attention of the sprite, but she ignored him.

"Do not concern yourself; you are our guest," Kalenti said as Jamie was reaching for his wallet. He also caught the direction of Jamie's gaze.

"Thank you, until tomorrow." On his way out Jamie looked again over his shoulder, but she was not to be seen.

⁜*⁜*⁜

Jamie took his seat in the back of the new-model, charcoal black Mercedes. George, who was holding the duffel bag, took his seat on the front passenger side. He opened the bag and placed it between his legs while his hawk-nosed companion took the wheel. Jamie explained where he was staying. The driver started the vehicle and with a squeal of tires made a U-turn and sped down toward the Green Line.

⁜*⁜*⁜

Back in the apartment, Jamie made himself comfortable on the balcony overlooking the Mediterranean. He decided to disassemble the weapon that he had lifted from the young extortionist—cleaning and oiling each part. He examined the weapon afterward, praising his work. It had not been cleaned in months.

At two thirty he left the apartment by the back entrance. He made his way on the quiet streets, trusting that his earlier altercation with the young thief had not attracted the attention of someone who could identify him when he returned to the area. He was confident that the young boy would not. *Too bad for him*, he thought. He was satisfied that he would not be roaming about—at least not that afternoon.

CHAPTER TWENTY-TWO

Zaquod's ancestral home was located in a valley deep within the Christian stronghold, surrounded by the mountains of central Lebanon. Each of the peaks that lined the valley was a veritable fortress. There the Christians were entrenched. Their confidence in repelling any invader was based on the extensive military training they conducted and the surfeit of equipment accumulated—first from the French before the troubles of 1975 and then from the Israelis who sought to secure their northern boundary following the bombing of the US Marine Corps barracks and the withdrawal of the Americans, who had once played a pivotal role for the Christian strategy.

It was late afternoon when Zaquod entered the spacious reception room of his estate house. Preceded by his two bodyguards—constant companions in these days of strife—he was casually dressed in slacks, a heavy ski sweater, and boots. He had just returned from a day of skiing.

Already seated in the great room were seven individuals—five men and two women. All of them were dressed comfortably and warmly. There was a chill in the room except for those closest to the large stone fireplace in the center of one of the walls. At first glance, the gathering appeared social. However, no one was drinking and there was no food in sight, nor was there an exchange of light conversation. At Zaquod's entry, each in the room stood and greeted him.

This was the first time the team had been brought together. Zaquod was proud that he had been able to meet Kalenti's deadline. All in the room had successfully completed the training. Now it was necessary to inform them of their mission. Up until this time, anyone selected for the advanced training was told that they were needed for the defense of their country. These seven represented the finalists, despite Zaquod's efforts to enlist twelve. In the time allowed, it was virtually impossible to find more than this number with the advanced weapons skills required. The severe security constraints of the operation also hindered the recruitment process. Each was selected only after Zaquod was personally satisfied with his or her commitment to the cause.

"Welcome, welcome," he said softly as he moved among them, reaching out to touch them as a cleric entering a room of believers. Arrayed throughout the room were priceless antiques, and rich canvases lined the wood-paneled walls. Though the gathering was being held in what could be considered a formal setting, there was an air of informality in his caring manner. He took his seat on an original Louis XVI chair. With a motion of his wrist, he dismissed his bodyguards. The seven pulled up chairs—sturdy representatives of a past culture and craftsmanship—in a semicircle.

"Well, here you all are," he continued. "Not many of you. Does anyone know why I stopped at seven?" He looked over them. Each continued to look at him in silence. No one ventured a response, nor did anyone appear uneasy with the silence. *A confident lot*, he thought.

"Well, seven represents perfection, and that's why you are here," he lied.

"Thank you. I would have thought that the number was more influenced by the fact that you could only find seven to qualify for the honor."

Zaquod looked at the speaker—Marc the sniper. Marc

preferred to be called by the name a girl in Ireland gave him—Courtney. Brown hair, smooth skin, unusually light beard—he looked younger than his twenty-eight years. His quick tongue demonstrated a caustic wit or quick intelligence—or both. His innocent face belied the forty-three kills to his credit atop the buildings of Beirut or high above the city along the mountain paths. There he would wait for hours until an unsuspecting Palestinian, Syrian, or any other follower of Muhammad moved into his line of fire.

Courtney shared with the others a lust for revenge that was the common bond they all shared. Each had experienced personal tragedy during the communal fighting from which Lebanon seemed unable to recover. Courtney's innocence was shattered with a mortar round that landed next to his mother. He had been in line to buy bread during what he and others thought was a lull in the fighting. He was only eleven years old at the time. His mother sent him to recover her purse, which she had inadvertently left at the grocer's. Perhaps she had a premonition. When he returned, he found her motionless on the pavement. Others were sitting on the curb stunned while rescue workers administered bandages. Women and children were the only casualties. So much for Arab bravery, he would say.

"We're both right." Zaquod addressed him. "Seven is a sign of perfection, and I couldn't find more of you in time." He said nothing about the fact that another group, equally qualified in weapons and explosives but less gifted in foreign languages and experience, was assigned to undertake a critical, supporting operation soon.

"When will we learn our mission?"

Zaquod turned to the questioner, Jacques, one of his two gunners. Jacques had been a member of the Red Berets, a paramilitary organization of the Lebanese army. He and the rest of his colleagues had joined Christian fighting units when public order disintegrated during the civil war. A bear of a man in his late forties, he still divided his day between bodybuilding and firing automatic weapons on the range. There was not much else for him to do after his two sons were killed in a firefight with the Palestinians.

"I can tell you that most will be leaving for America within ten days." He looked around and caught surprise in their eyes. That was all—surprise not shock.

"Well," he asked, waiting for one of them to speak up. He was not disappointed.

"America? Who's in America?" Metro, the second gunner, asked.

No one knew where the name *Metro* originated, and Metro was silent about its origin. Looking more than his forty years, he wore thick round glasses; he had light thinning brown hair, pale skin, blue eyes, and a thick handlebar moustache. He would shave the moustache before departing Beirut—it was too distinguishable.

Metro had been raised by relatives in the United States, where he had been sent as a youth. America was his home. He enlisted in the army and served with distinction in the Special Forces during Vietnam. With the defeat of South Vietnam and with no job prospects, he returned to Lebanon. He would say that he wanted to recapture his heritage. In truth, he enjoyed his profession, especially if he could justify killing with a noble cause. If it had not been Lebanon, he would have joined a mercenary group let loose in Africa. His shooting skills and experience were easily documented, though Zaquod came close to rejecting him because he did not have the level of dedication that flows from an uncompromising hatred of the Moslems and what they were doing to destroy The Lebanon.

"In time you will know, and more importantly, you will come to understand. But let me add that one of you will be departing tomorrow." He smiled at Karina, who was in charge of logistics in America.

Karina was in her early thirties. A tall, vivacious girl with brilliant eyes, she was consumed with anger. She was Shamir's granddaughter and had lost both parents in the shelling of her village. Later, her grandmother died from a sniper's bullet fired from one of those tall buildings in Beirut. Karina considered their deaths accidental in that the Syrian artillerymen did not know her parents and the Palestinian who shot her grandmother only fired at a vehicle moving slowly along the coast on a beautiful Sunday morning.

Of the team members, no one was more trusted that Karina. It was her responsibility to inspect the quality and quantity of the ammunition, weapons, and explosives available to them in America. A protégé of her grandfather in various international trading ventures, she had gained extensive contacts with arms merchants and had especially cultivated those who could provide anything for a price—especially weaponry and explosives of Eastern European manufacture.

Karina was also responsible for the travel documents that would speed the team out of America and back to Lebanon. She controlled the three hundred thousand dollars that Shamir had transferred to a bank in America. However, she, like the rest of the team, was unaware yet of the intended target.

"Good, I am ready." Karina nodded, and no emotion showed on her face.

"I knew you would be. Kuban will be at the airport to meet you." He walked over to a wall safe, opened it quickly, and retrieved a sealed bulky envelope.

"Here is your passport and tickets." He presented her with the package.

"Who is Kuban? How will we know him?" It was Danny, one of the two bombers. Danny had lost his older brother to a Shiite band that ambushed the car in which he and two other teenagers were returning home after curfew. A rocket-propelled grenade was fired against the side of the vehicle. It struck the gas tank, causing the car to explode in flames—charring the young boys alive. A Christian rampage the next day resulted in the killing of over two hundred Moslems. Most of the victims were pulled from cars within the city limits and killed once the identity cards were checked to confirm their Moslem heritage. The bloodletting did nothing to ease the hatred that boiled inside as Danny watched his parents grow old in their grief.

"Our close colleague has arranged everything for you in America," Zaquod answered. "Don't worry how you will recognize him—he knows each of you."

"What kind of passports will we be using?" asked Michelle, the second bomber.

Michelle was an accomplished artist of assassination. Her grandparents and parents were slaughtered by the Palestinians who invaded the Christian enclave in Darmour. Trained by the Israelis, she used to good purpose her diminutive build and shy demeanor to place bombs into seemingly impenetrable areas. Among her accomplishments was the infiltration of one hundred pounds of explosive into a neighborhood controlled by Arafat's Al Fatah. She pushed a grocery wagon past the watchful eyes of the Arabs assigned to secure the area. At one point, two of the guards helped push the wagon up a slight incline. Later, she watched the television coverage of the car in which Abu Salah, Arafat's closest advisor, was killed by the explosion that she detonated remotely as his car made its way through the congested area past her grocery cart.

"Your own Lebanese passports, of course," Zaquod replied, pleased that someone had asked that question. "What do the authorities have to fear from the travel of Christian Lebanese to America?" He paused. "Why make things complicated?"

Before the next question, he informed them, "Afterward, each of you will return to your country on a different passport by a different path." He raised his chin in pride at this particular twist.

"I'm going to need a license, if you want me doing any driving." The request came from Jon. He had been selected to be in charge of the team's vehicle—a position complicated by the fact that he would be required to steal a succession of vehicles and adequately disguise them to ensure that the team's execution of the operation would be flawless. His skills in operating on the streets in and around Beirut had brought him to Zaquod's attention. The fact that Jon had worked years previously in New York as a taxicab driver while attending New York University secured him a position on the team.

"It has already been taken care of," Zaquod responded. He was pleased with his team. He had found the children of the strife that he had sought and upon whose shoulders the success of this operation relied. The group was committed to an independent Christian Lebanon in the Chouf Mountains and was formed to avenge what each had suffered at the hands of the invaders—the heathens.

All of them shared in the agony that reflected Zaquod's own—his wife, son, daughter-in-law, and three grandchildren were killed by Moslem fanatics. A car bomb exploded in front of their three-story private residence, causing the top two floors to tumble down onto his family, which had gathered around the dining room table to celebrate his grandson's birthday. Zaquod could still recall returning home that day and seeing the rubble. He was in time to hear the fading cries for help that ceased by the time the rescue workers had cleared away the debris.

He looked up to see the team members observing him. They had allowed him this moment without interruption to revisit the hurt within. The injury never seemed to heal. Perhaps he did not want it healed. He was spurred, even invigorated, by revenge for the lives lost, for the nation endangered, for the church besieged. He bowed politely to his audience and with a motion of his long sculptured hand invited them to the dining room and an elegantly served meal.

☦ ☦ ☦

Kay was alone in her office reading a report that Brussels Station had just received from the Belgian intelligence service and forwarded to Headquarters.

> There has been a delivery of high-quality forged passports to a group operating from Lebanon. Each passport contains the necessary visa for unimpeded travel on the Continent.
>
> The source is reliable. He gathered the information in the course of providing an unidentified individual with current policies and procedures for travel in Europe.

That was it; no more. Kay did not like the first words of the report—*There has been a delivery*. She had so many questions. Experience told her that most would go unanswered. She was lucky to get that much and was certain that the unidentified individual of the report would remain so—even if the Belgians knew who he was. They could not take a chance that some self-serving American bureaucrat or politico would leak the individual's name to the US press. If the Belgians knew the timing of the intended travel, how many passports were involved, or if there was any inkling of travel to the United States, that information would have been contained in the report.

Kay recalled the recent information they had received from the Israelis that passports were being prepared by a forgery expert in Tripoli. Perhaps they were the same passports. It was time to tickle the Israelis for any additional information. She felt like an ingrate because she suspected that the Israelis had not received any information in return for the initial report. Liaison with the Israelis was often reduced to weight of the pages exchanged. That was the reason the Israelis were never empty-handed when it came to passing intelligence to the Americans.

Intelligence analysis was wrestling in the mud of maybes and what ifs. How could she blame the higher-ups for not basing policy on intelligence assumptions? It's too risky, she remembered Brody telling her once.

⁂

Frost arrived at the safe house at three thirty that afternoon.

He had no difficulty locating the building. His confidence had waned only once when he realized that he was the only one on the street. Not a good sign. Heavy fighting could break out at any time. He was thankful that he only had to subdue his rising panic a bit longer.

The apartment consisted of a sitting room, a kitchen, and one bedroom. In Beirut's halcyon days, it probably served as some aspiring Francophile's pied a terre to meet his young mistress. Now the apartment had the same musty smell as his hotel room. He pulled back a curtain that faced the rear of the building. In the distance, he noticed a French flag flying over the enclosed compound of the French embassy. He wondered if the French still operated from there or if they had like the Americans moved to the eastern sector of the city.

He took his seat in the rocking chair behind the dark oak-paneled entry door to wait for ICARUS. The rocker squeaked—its left blade was in need of repair. A half hour later, at the time Frost expected him to appear, he flinched involuntarily as a heavy exchange of automatic gunfire broke out on the street below. He immediately slipped off the chair onto the floor, the back of his head grazing the edge of the seat. He feared that a spray of automatic fire might cut through the curtained front window. He felt perspiration form on his upper lip.

After the initial burst, it was silent again. No windows opened or closed—just silence. He waited on his stomach for about fifteen minutes before he ventured to the door and looked through the peephole. Everything on the other side of the door was distorted as if he were looking through a Christmas ornament. He half expected to see ICARUS clutching his side from which blood gushed. There was nothing to see but the elongated tile in the hallway. Whether accurate or not—he could not say—his sense of hearing was magnified to the point where he could hear, or thought he could hear, someone walking in the entryway three floors below.

He rushed to the back window, the one overlooking the

French embassy. If he needed an escape route, this had to be it. There was a metal water drain hanging from the roof down the corner of the building to the ground. He wondered if it would hold his weight—assuming that he had the strength to hold the drain as he lowered himself. He would be forced to try, if anyone tried to storm the door. He had no idea who *they* were.

Why had it seemed so important to upstage Colin in the first place? he wondered.

At the knock on the door he froze. The knock was repeated. Softly, slowly, he made his way along the wall to the door. Carefully, he positioned himself behind the peephole, not wanting to give away his position for fear that someone was poised on the other side with an automatic weapon. By the time he looked through the hole, he caught the back of an old lady walking slowly away; her oversized leather slippers flopped on the marble floor. He opened the door.

"Yes?" he called.

"Oh, monsieur," she turned back and said, "I am the concierge's wife. I saw you come up. Everything is all right now. I did not want you to worry."

"Thank you very much. I knew everything would be fine." He sounded like a seasoned veteran—though he still felt the cold perspiration on his forehead. The accumulated moisture on his lip tasted like tears as his tongue reached up.

"Oui, monsieur. There is something else. Two month's rent is due. Seven hundred dollars."

Frost reached into his wallet—his hand was still shaking. How was he to know that the woman was only a tenant herself and had decided to exploit the confusion of war? Frost paid her, not even asking for a receipt. He had less than two hundred dollars remaining. He would have to contact the station again for money. The old lady counted the money, thanked him, and ambled down the corridor.

⁑ ⁑ ⁑

Jamie was in the vicinity of the apartment when the gunfire erupted. He moved quickly into a hallway and checked his own weapon. He waited in silence for about fifteen minutes, satisfied that whatever caused the disturbance had been resolved. He smiled—some dumb Arab was probably clearing his weapon or was firing into the air in honor of a comrade who died. He recalled how someone once suggested that the Israelis encouraged the practice so they would waste ammunition. Before looking outside again, he decided that maybe someone was telling him that it was not safe to continue to the meeting. His instincts commanded his attention. He decided he didn't need the Americans at the moment—they could only endanger him. He reversed directions.

It was after six in the evening when he reached the grillwork entry to his building. He rattled it again. Armed with a pistol in his belt, the concierge appeared and opened the gate. He smiled and motioned with his hands upward. He was trying to convey a message, but ICARUS was fatigued and could not catch his drift. There were some nationalities that had great difficulty comprehending that their language or culture was not universally understood. The concierge belonged to that group.

Jamie thought he heard some rustling in the apartment as he approached the door. Weapon in hand, he burst inside to find the waitress from the restaurant sitting on the couch reading a French-language newspaper.

"Hello." The word came out in an unintentional whisper. He cleared his throat and repeated, "Hello."

"Bonjour, monsieur." Her white teeth released a sparkling smile. She was dressed in the same pair of designer jeans, but her top was a French-style oversized pullover. He could not decide if it was supposed to be large on her or whether it was the only size available on the black market. In either case, she looked exquisite, and the pullover seemed inviting enough to slip off. She had not stirred. He realized that he was still brandishing the gun. He put the gun back into his jacket pocket and closed the door. He did not and could not take his eyes off her. Her feet were tucked beneath her. Fur-lined half boots were on the floor at her feet.

"You have not eaten?"

"No, I have not." *Something is not right*, he thought.

"Bon, I have something for you."

She surprised him with her quick movement off the couch and into his arms, snuggling her mouth below his ear, pressing the length of her body against him. She pushed her pelvis with particular insistence. He responded mechanically and gathered her closer. She slipped out of his grasp and darted into the kitchen.

"First, we eat. Later, who knows?" She produced a canvas bag from which she pulled an assortment of dry cured meats, special cheeses, a large loaf of bread, and two bottles of French red Bordeaux. "Voila!"

He was mesmerized by what was unfolding. He hesitated to become an active participant and checked his heavy breathing as he was trying to sort out what was happening. He did not like the idea of being manipulated. Also, for the first time in his life, he wondered what Brigid would say or do if he told her about this scene.

He was troubled by the thought that she was waiting for him in a quiet Greek village hundreds of miles away. He reminded himself that she would never find out about this dalliance, if he did not choose to tell her. Yet, fidelity, trust, and commitment were intruding on his otherwise secure psyche. Or was he troubled by this apparent good luck? He was tenaciously suspicious. Phantoms urged him to take this poor, less-than-innocent, sweet female to bed. But he resisted. He tried to dismiss the notion of breaking Brigid's trust by considering her infidelity to him before they met. Before they met? He was convinced that he was losing his mind.

The girl was standing in front of him, still holding a bottle of wine aloft. She seemed puzzled. He was convinced that he was acting as if he was some sort of a pervert, or perhaps gay. He smiled lamely at his indecision. His mind was being bombarded with observations from his interior monitor—flashing a warning message. For someone who relied upon his instincts, he wondered if he could selectively choose the areas for which advice was sought. If so, he preferred to dismiss warnings related to sexual excursions. He hoped it wasn't too late, or if all this time with Arabs had changed his sexual orientation.

His conscience ducked the blow with the realization that he was just as physically aroused by this young sprite as he was with Brigid and those that preceded her. No change in him. What he found confusing was that she too noticed his healthy manifestation, but he still seemed paralyzed to act.

"Are you all right?" She asked. The moment had passed—even if it seemed to him like an eternity.

"I am fine. You see …" He did not know what to say. This was definitely a situation where actions would have spoken louder than words.

"I must go," she said cautiously, still uncertain of his stability. She was relieved that he did not obstruct her way to the door.

Jamie was equally uncertain as he heard the door close softly behind her. If virtue was its own reward, he did not feel virtuous. He chided himself and decided to enjoy what was left of the day. He opened a bottle of wine, broke apart the bread, and with the cheese and meat, proceeded to the balcony and the single hardback chair—still bundled in his jacket.

CHAPTER TWENTY-THREE

C. Jennings Hollingsworth had arrived in Beirut as the American ambassador six months previously, and he still had not traveled outside of East Beirut. He was tall and portly, with premature white hair and a studied Princeton accent. Above all else, Hollingsworth was known to be ambitious. He was excited—not visibly, of course—when he arose that morning. It was a clear sunny day and the fifteenth day of no widespread or sustained violence—this meant he would visit Byblos, an ancient Crusader village located an hour's drive north of Beirut. His security chief had agreed to accommodate the ambassador's long-standing request if a respite in the fighting lasted for that period of time. Finally, he would be able to get out into the countryside and be visible to the local populace.

"Good morning. I trust you slept well." He was calling his head of security. "As you see, another day of calm—that makes more than two weeks, as we agreed.

"Yes, I do wish to drive to Byblos this morning. I will not consider another delay, so get your team together and pick me up as soon as you are ready. See you then."

He hung up the phone and prepared for the trip, seeing himself in the back of the factory-fresh Cadillac sedan—plush leather seats, his ambassadorial flag flying off to the side of the right fender.

⁜

Within the hour his security team arrived—the sedan with a follow-on vehicle to which two team members were assigned.

"Well, sir, are you ready?" the chief of security asked.

"I was ready two weeks ago," he responded churlishly.

"Before we leave, I want to tell you something about the vehicle and its protection."

"Please, can't we do that while we're underway?" His impatience was showing.

"It's your show," the security officer sounded resigned to doing what the ambassador wanted. Once in the vehicle as they headed out of Beirut the security chief tried again. "Sir, this vehicle has been armored at great expense and will withstand a projectile fired directly at it by either an AK-47 or an M-16."

"Sounds great. Do you think I really care? Let's concentrate on the scenery."

As they moved along, Hollingsworth thought about his ex-wife. If only she could see him now, she would regret leaving.

"Did you know that I served here ten years ago?"

"Yes, sir. You were here at a dicey time as well," the security officer acknowledged.

"Ah, so perhaps you understand why I consider that I know my way around." A smile of confidence expanded across his face. "Only then I drove around on my own in a beat-up Volkswagen Beetle and, do you know—I survived it all, including several trips to Byblos."

"Yes, sir, I do understand. Excuse me, sir." He picked up his radio connected him to the follow-on car.

"Tiger Two, do you read me?"

"That's affirmative," responded the team driving behind in a Chevrolet armored to Level II, half the level of the Cadillac's protection. This meant that most sidearms fired at close range would not penetrate the vehicle's interior—though the glass would be shattered.

"Maintain no more than ten feet distance from us on the open road."

"That's affirmative." He turned to the driver, who speeded up. Lebanese nationals were at the wheel of both cars.

The ride out of Beirut was without incident. There was little traffic, which in itself should have cautioned the security officer to reconsider the trip.

"I'm surprised there is so little traffic on the road, sir."

"To me that's a good sign. We'll make good time and return before dark." The ambassador was not to be discouraged.

They had just left a village beyond Beirut and were moving at about forty miles an hour when the road gradually arched to the left and then to the right into a gentle curve. The sun was high in the sky and created a glare on the surface of the road. The driver slowed the car to about twenty-five miles per hour.

"As soon as you round this curve, I want you to increase your speed."

"Yes, monsieur," the driver responded, looking intently forward. Suddenly he pressed his foot firmly on the brake and came to an abrupt halt in time to avoid disrupting a Maronite priest leading a funeral procession down the middle of the road. The priest held his miter high in the air. He could have been taken for a drum major during a half-time show in a football stadium. Following the priest were the mourners carrying an unvarnished coffin aloft. The tension caused by the quick stop eased when the occupants of both cars realized the solemnity of the occasion.

"Can't they use the side of the road?" the ambassador asked impatiently.

"Mr. Ambassador, I guess the priest is reminding us not to rush too fast to our end."

The priest looked up and seemed annoyed that the cars had disturbed the procession. He was not to be deterred. Not missing a step, he walked straight ahead toward the vehicles, passing along the right side of the ambassador's Cadillac and continuing toward the Chevrolet. No one paid particular attention to the fact that there were no women among the mourners—just two rows of men, about twenty in number. One row moved up the left side of the cars. The drivers of both cars seemed disinterested in the procession of mourners; one row now passed, with the priest on the right side of the vehicles.

At exactly the time that one of the mourners, who was wearing a red piece of cloth tied to his left sleeve, reached the fender of the follow-on vehicle, another individual, also with a red cloth tied to his sleeve, reached the fender of the Cadillac. In unison, although in separate cars, both drivers hit the override control of the door locks, unlocking both with a snap.

In an instant the doors were yanked open by the erstwhile mourners, armed with assault rifles with silencers attached. The surprise was complete. The security chief lunged to protect the ambassador and was gunned down. No resistance was offered, nor was any possible, in the follow-on vehicle. The ambassador was removed immediately from the line of fire, while those in the back-up car were gunned down without mercy in their seats.

"Please, not me," the driver of the ambassador's car screamed when he saw that he was next to be eliminated. "I have sworn allegiance to the cause. I have family … I …" To no avail—he died in a volley of fire clutching the wheel of an armored vehicle that stood silent and violated, its four doors flung open.

The ambassador had not uttered a sound. His vocal chords were paralyzed with fear. His ruddy complexion was now ashen; his formerly slicked-down white hair was askew and marked by a spurt of blood from his American bodyguard. Holding a weapon on the ambassador, one of the assailants roughly drew him forward.

"Remove your belt!" When the ambassador seemed to hesitate, he was slapped across the face. Awakened, he removed his belt as if he were undressing in the dark after a night of drinking.

"Now your shoes. Quickly!" The ambassador leaned against the vehicle, blood flowing from the corpses within, and pulled off one shoe at a time without untying them. One of the assailants examined both the shoes and belt.

"Here it is!" he shouted, holding up the transmitter that indicated the location of the ambassador under all circumstances. He rushed off to the shore, where he tossed it as far as he could into the water.

With no warning a member of the party approached Hollingsworth and plunged a hypodermic needle into his arm, causing the diplomat to let out a shriek, his first sound. In seconds, he lost consciousness. He was shoved unceremoniously into the oversized empty casket and carried swiftly off the road along a path leading into the foothills. The last action taken by the men at the scene was to scatter the inflammatory literature of the Hezbollah.

As it had been planned and exercised many times, four of the group ran at full speed two hundred yards to the beach. There they hauled a launch, large enough to accommodate ten people, into the water. One of them started the motor while another checked the rope affixed to the steering wheel so that the boat would maintain its westerly direction—pointed as it was toward Cyprus. Satisfied that all was in order, the man at the steering wheel put the motor into gear, stayed with it for twenty yards, and then went over the side into the water so as not to disturb the craft's direction. He stared at the departing boat and then turned to run in the waist-deep water toward his companions. They all ran north up the coast, remaining in the water to eliminate their footprints. They splashed at each other as they ran. In another time or place, their laughter might have been commonplace, but not now in Lebanon.

Later, a telephone call would be placed in Europe to the office of a major Western newspaper asserting Hezbollah's responsibility in the kidnapping of the American ambassador and insisting that the United States, Great Britain, France, and Italy close their embassies in Lebanon within forty-eight hours. If their demands were not met, Ambassador Hollingsworth would be executed for crimes against the people.

⁂

Kalenti was reading *The History of The Fourth Crusade* by T. Powers when Shamir and Zaquod arrived that evening. He rose, keeping his place in the book with the fingers of his left hand.

"Friends, I am so pleased to see you both." Kalenti put a slip of paper in the book before closing it. He returned it to the shelf above the liquor cabinet. He did not ask their preference. After all these years, he knew that Shamir would enjoy a cognac and Zaquod a fine wine. For himself, he preferred Arak on ice, a modest drink for the son of a fisherman who once plied the waters between Lebanon and Cyprus.

"We heard the news on the BBC," Shamir exclaimed as soon as the door was closed. "Congratulations. Our first decisive step appears successful."

"Hezbollah is being blamed," Zaquod added. "The American Sixth Fleet is moving toward our coast. The American president is calling his cabinet into an emergency session. Wonderful!"

"Now we turn to phase two." Kalenti spoke.

"Is everything set in America? What is the word from Kuban?" Shamir asked.

"He called from New York yesterday," Kalenti answered. "All is in readiness for our boys and girls. He located an Armenian friend on the outskirts of the city who will provide shelter for them before the attack. Kuban is hopeful the Armenian will protect our team afterward."

"I do not like the word *hopeful*," Zaquod interjected. "Remember the sign the German was able to send. Recall also our confidence in eliminating the American and the fate of our man who is still cooling on a slab in a Greek morgue."

"I'm not sure that any harm was done," Kalenti stated.

"It's the uncertainty of it all that bothers me," Zaquod insisted.

"Are you confusing risk with uncertainty?" It was Kalenti again.

"Maybe so."

"Are you satisfied with the team in America?" Kalenti asked of Zaquod.

"They are better than those who just kidnapped the ambassador. They will be fine. There is only one about whom I worry—the one who served in the American army. He has not lost anyone here in the fighting. Revenge and anger do not flow in his veins—only the excitement that accompanies killing."

Shamir and Kalenti nodded in agreement. The observation was something with which they should be concerned. But again, there was not sufficient time to find a replacement and the team was already too few. A knock at the door interrupted the deliberation.

"Come in. You're back so soon?" Kalenti looked up as Simone entered the room.

"Nothing happened." She paused. "Thank God, nothing happened. He is strange."

"What do you mean?" Shamir asked.

"He just looked at me and smiled. He must be queer," she said, more to protect her reputation than to explain the unanticipated experience of rejection.

"Did you find anything in the apartment?" Kalenti asked.

"Apartment? You mean two rooms and a portion of the balcony. No, there is nothing there to tell anything about him. Whatever he has with him, he carries. He is armed with a revolver. That is the only thing he was able to get out of his pants."

"Thank you, my kitten." Kalenti cut her off abruptly. "We are busy now." Simone left the room.

"Can we be certain that the Americans believe Hezbollah snatched the ambassador?" Shamir asked as the door closed.

Thirty years previously, Shamir had been responsible for

orchestrating the disturbances in the bazaars that prompted President Eisenhower to order the landing of the marines to quell the rebellion of radical Moslems. Ever since, the Christians turned to America to settle their disputes. Not so many years later the Christians did the same—protection from the anti-Christ invaders from the north. Reagan also sent in the marines, although they were withdrawn in the aftermath of the truck bomb that destroyed the marine barracks.

"Calm yourself." Kalenti sought to calm Shamir's anxiousness. "Our plan is not to see our friends come in for a short stay. That is why it is so important that the Americans suspect nothing."

"As you know, nothing is certain," Kalenti continued, "but let me say that the target we selected in America will force them to react. Killing the ambassador will only intensify the impact of the second stage. However, nothing is certain; we must do our part to encourage certainty to enter our homes."

"I had a reason for asking." Shamir placed his head into his hands and rubbed his eyes gently.

"Let's assume that everything goes well in the United States and all of our people retreat as planned. Leaving behind Hezbollah literature might not be sufficient. Wouldn't it be prudent if we could leave behind some additional evidence?"

"We will." Kalenti corrected himself, "They will. All of the weapons are of East European origin."

"Yes, I am aware of this, but so conventional." Shamir pursed his dry lips into a smile. "What if we also left behind at the scene a corpse with solid ties to leftist groups?"

"I am not following you." Kalenti looked puzzled.

"The young man who showed no interest in Simone. I did some checking with Choukasyan's family. In fact, his story about buying icons some four years ago is accurate. He is who he says he is—Jamie Casasnovas, born in Mallorca." Shamir waited before continuing. "More interesting is that we were also able to identify him as a field operative for the Red Army Faction. We also suspect that he has done work for the Popular Front for the Liberation of Palestine."

"What is your proof?"

"I received word from a trusted informant who was at the airport in Damascus three days ago. He observed special treatment accorded a ragged Westerner—who coincidentally fits the young man's physical description. The fellow had just arrived on a special flight from Tripoli."

"Very interesting," Zaquod observed.

"What's he doing here?" Kalenti sounded agitated.

"That I don't know, but let's assume that he is snooping around at the behest of some local Palestinian group. We've been quiet lately. They probably assume that we are planning some action." Shamir looked at his colleagues.

"Suppose we recruit the terrorist bastard, bring him to America, and at the appropriate time eliminate him to become our incontrovertible piece of evidence left at the scene of the crime?"

"Brilliant!" Kalenti said.

"But how do we keep him from the team?" Zaquod asked.

"That may be tricky. But we could recruit him to accompany you." Shamir looked to Kalenti. "He could be your personal bodyguard."

"The most dangerous time will be from the time you leave until you dispose of him in America. I would think that his sponsors would string him out as long as possible to learn what they can of our resources abroad." Shamir seemed satisfied with his analysis. He reached across for his cognac and sniffed the aroma before taking a sip. He rested his arm on the chair, still holding the glass, before continuing.

"Of course, we do not tell him that you are travelling to America to join Kuban and the team. He must remain ignorant about any hint of the operation planned there. As far as he is concerned, you are traveling to America on business and you are hiring him to be your protection." Shamir was planning as he spoke.

"We would route you through Athens, and Petrus would join the flight there and be your shadow until you arrive. In addition to covering you, he could assist in the last-minute preparations for the attack. I would think that you could use him to survey the target one last time. What do you think?"

"A bold idea," Kalenti said.

"The whole scheme is bold, but look what we get if successful—a free, independent, Christian nation, sequestered around Mount Lebanon, protected by Saint Maroon and the Americans." Shamir spoke with uncharacteristic enthusiasm accompanied with heavy raspy wheezing.

CHAPTER TWENTY-FOUR

Since Washington had turned down his request to travel to Beirut, Colin was as fractious as a race horse in the starting gate. He was physically tired and emotionally drained—more so than if he had flown to Beirut for the meeting. His frustration and irritation only increased when he learned that Frost had been robbed and subsequently missed the meeting. He did not realize how lucky Frost was to escape with his life, nor did he acknowledge that he could have been in the taxi and not Frost.

Colin had never been able to envision his own death, nor did he think anyone else could envision theirs. He was quick to say that Frost was responsible for the danger to which he was exposed. Conveniently, he dismissed any responsibility for his own close calls in Athens—the first when ICARUS came to his rescue and the second when Frost had the foresight to move him to a safe house.

"Just got this in from Beirut," Maura said as casually as she could, expecting Colin to explode when he read the message.

"Let me have it." Colin stood up as much to break off his thoughts about the hallway in Athens as to find out what was happening.

"He didn't make the meeting!" he declared. He scanned the

message and gave it to Kay, who had come into the office. She read it aloud.

1. *ICARUS did not show for scheduled—actually alternate meeting time and date. To this time he has not called to explain.*
2. *Also, wish to inform Headquarters that case officer paid unidentified elderly woman $1,000 in the now mistaken belief that rent was due on the safe house. A check with Beirut station administration indicates that rent was not in arrears. It seems that enterprising occupant of building was taking advantage of the situation.*

"Jesus Christ! Frost would not be qualified to deliver newspapers, and here we have him engaging in clandestine operations in of all places Beirut," Colin erupted. "Send him to Ouagadougou where he can spend his time learning how to spell it."

"Please, Colin, control yourself," Joan intervened. "The next time your life is threatened give some thought to the strain Frost is under."

Maura never thought she would hear Joan defending Frost. She suspected that Joan was baiting Colin for all the times that he remained calm before her stinging criticism of life, the world, or the circumstances surrounding her. If that was her intention, she succeeded.

"Joan, why don't you go back to your knitting?" Colin showed an uncharacteristic pettiness to cover up his embarrassment.

"What do you know about operations or for that matter making a meeting on time? In fact, what you do could be adequately performed by someone of Maura's intelligence."

"Mr. Gordon—that was not called for," Maura said, and she left for office without saying anything further.

A deathly silence settled on the office. It was the first time that Maura had ever shown her irritation to anyone. He looked over at

Joan. She had a "join-the-club" smile—or was it a grimace—on her face.

⁑*⁑

Once in the corridor, Maura decided to borrow a tin of coffee from a neighboring office—anything to escape the sharp exchanges. She understood why Colin was upset. Even so, he had no business to draw her into his exchange with Joan. In the past he was indifferent when Joan launched out on some tirade. Now he seemed to enjoy prodding her. Maura decided that she could handle Joan or Colin, but not both at the same time. Her heels clicked along into the beat of a popular hard-rock tune. Before she realized it, she had passed her intended destination and decided instead to go to the ladies room. After all, there was a new three-pound tin of coffee in the bottom of her desk drawer.

⁑*⁑

Colin sought to collect himself.

"Peace," he offered to Joan.

"Ump!" was all Joan could muster as she reached for her box of Black Russian cigarettes—only to discover that she had left it in her apartment. She would have to wait until lunch time to make a special trip home—such was her attachment, or was it addiction?

"Joan, let's see if we can get back to business."

"Good."

At least he was making progress. She was now uttering a word, even if it was monosyllabic. He returned to his desk and picked up the cable that he had received from Headquarters earlier.

> *Request Gordon provide his thoughts regarding the multiple passport delivery. Specifically, did he think that this report could in any way be linked to the reason for GANYMEDE's demise?*

Colin realized that Headquarters—that is, Kay, who was composing the messages—was seeking any indication that the two events were somehow linked. *Suppose there was some connection. What would it mean?* He jotted down the names of GANYMEDE, Horst, Frost, and ICARUS. He penciled in his own name. All could have inadvertently come into contact with the group planning an operation. But so what? From all indications the planning was still proceeding. However, the assumption was valid. What did it mean?

Under GANYMEDE's name he wrote:

He was killed to keep him from revealing information he uncovered related to a planned terrorist operation;
Specifically, he learned the target, timing, or sponsors;
The sign under the stamp was his attempt to reveal as much as he could—given his confinement.

For Horst, he wrote:

He was killed to minimize the dissemination of the clue that Hans was trying to convey;
The assassin or assassins were satisfied that the clue was sufficiently damaging to warrant Horst's execution

Under his name, he jotted down:

Only reason for sending the postcard was to confirm that meeting instructions provided by GANYMEDE were accurate, indicating that his interrogation occurred after he learned about the pending operation;
Those responsible for his murder were surprised to discover that GANYMEDE was associated with American intelligence and concerned about that association.

Colin underlined the latter phrase. *Why should that surprise* them? *A German businessman working with the Americans? That seemed natural enough. Why should that concern them enough to send the postcard? The two attempts on my life in Athens were meant to demonstrate this group's capabilities, or as a provocation—as a dare, or ...*

He was troubled by the last assertion. The group had nothing personal against him. If he had received the postcard—which they might have thought unlikely—they would have known that the information contained therein would have been transmitted promptly to Washington. As unlikely as it appeared, it seemed that the group wanted someone to know that they were out there. He then added to the last phrase.

> *... to deceive by throwing us off the track as to the allegiance of those responsible.*

He felt good about the last assertion, although he could not grasp its significance, if there was one. For Frost, he observed:

No connection to me established by group, else some attempt against Frost would have taken place, following unsuccessful attempt on my life;
Fact that no other American targeted indicates that group is well disciplined, intent, and almost surgical in its focus.

Regarding ICARUS, he could only assert:

> *Unlikely that he could be identified by group, even if he was observed prior to slaying of assassin in Athens hallway.*

Colin leaned back in his chair and noticed that Maura had placed a fresh cup of hot coffee in front of him. He had not heard her come and go five minutes earlier. At that instant, an AFN news flash penetrated the fog of his concentration. It was coming from Maura's radio in the next room. He got up from his desk to join Joan and Maura.

> *The US Ambassador to Lebanon, C. Jennings Hollingsworth, has been kidnapped and his security detail killed by a group claiming to be affiliated with Hezbollah. The US Sixth Fleet stationed in the Mediterranean has been put on alert.*

↕*↕*↕

"Well, so much for those Arabs being quiet," Kay said to Stacy as they both proceeded to the directorate of operations briefing room. The news of Hollingsworth's kidnapping and the murder of his guards had been reported minutes before Beirut's cable arrived by flash precedence. The Beirut cable contained no information that did not appear in the Associated Press report. On balance, the BBC radio broadcast was even more informative than either of the cables from Beirut.

"Stacy, I don't know whether it's worth both our time to attend this briefing," Kay stated, anxious to go back to her office. "All we are going to learn is that the US military forces in and around Lebanon have heightened their readiness posture. God knows what they think they can do when you think of other hostages who have been taken and released—no thanks to US ingenuity."

"I guess you're right." Stacy wanted to see some of the senior staff in person so she could associate exploits—even if apocryphal—with recognizable individuals.

They filed into the conference room, which was large enough to accommodate two hundred CIA operations people and analysts. After short introductory comments by the agency's press spokesman, a colonel from the National Military Command Center at the Pentagon began his briefing with a dazzling assortment of color transparencies. Kay characterized such briefings as wooden because the briefing officer never ventured from the script and remained in a rigid parade-rest stance and the delivery was usually in a dull monotone that discouraged attentiveness.

Kay looked over at Stacy with a forlorn see-I-told-you-so look minutes into the briefing. She regretted that government regulations no longer permitted her to light up a cigarette. Could she endure the pabulum that was being served? Next time—but she knew that as long as she remained in government there would always be a next time and a next briefing and a next resolution—she'd skip attendance.

"Time is simply not valued." Kay gritted her teeth.

"Well, it looks like we are taking this pretty seriously," Stacy ventured as they walked back to the office.

"That's what worries me. The military would like nothing better than to bloody someone's nose—anyone's."

"Don't you think Hezbollah is responsible?" Stacy asked.

"Of course, but I want our response to be considered, thought out—measured. Don't want us to hit the wrong target or to do anything that jeopardizes getting Hollingsworth back." Kay chewed the end of the newly lit cigarette. "Maybe it is not possible."

"What do you mean?"

"I don't know." Kay seemed perplexed.

"Do you think we'll invade?"

"If it were not for the ignominious retreat following the bombing of the marine barracks, we would be in there already. I think it will take more than a kidnapping," Kay added.

"What if they murder him?"

"It will get close then, but who knows? It depends on the politics."

"The politics?" It was Stacy again.

"Yes, the politics. The president can't afford another fiasco. He wants votes and Hollingsworth back—and in that order."

⁂

Jamie left his apartment before ten o'clock the next morning. He took the stairs down—not trusting the reliability of the elevator. On the ground floor, he saw that the door to the concierge's apartment was open. He looked in and saw him cleaning his weapon.

"Good day!" Jamie waved. The Palestinian looked up and immediately smiled a wide grin that revealed silver fillings far back in his mouth. At the same time, he motioned to Jamie, who waved to indicate he was busy; the Palestinian would not take no.

"I don't have time." Jamie kept his eyes on the front entrance.

"Ah, good, ah, good" was all the concierge could manage in English as he prepared two cups of Arabic coffee. Reluctantly, Jamie took a seat on the pillow—positioned so that he could spot Kalenti's Mercedes when it pulled up.

"You like sweet?" he asked, producing a brown bag of sugar.

"That's fine," Jamie replied.

"How you fine Beirut?" he asked as he poured the coffee in the small cups. Jamie was amazed at his expanding English vocabulary.

"Beautiful."

"And the women?"

"Very beautiful. Palestinian woman beautiful," Jamie complimented—deciding that this exchange by now would exhaust his host's English. Promptly at ten, Kalenti's Mercedes pulled up in front of the building.

Jamie got to his feet. He pointed to the car and using his hands indicated that he had to leave. The Palestinian, his breath reeking of garlic, hugged Jamie just before he dashed to the entrance.

The door was unlocked, and Jamie took his seat alone in the rear. A feeling of expectancy swept over him. Perhaps he had more to look forward to than viewing a collection of icons. The morning was clear and cool; the brilliant winter sun gleamed off the water, tousled slightly by the wind as clouds sailed high across the blue sky toward the city.

George was seated in the front passenger side. Jamie noticed that the ever-present duffel bag was at George's feet. It was zippered opened, and he assumed that the bag contained a compact Uzi submachine gun. The driver was expressionless. He was the same one who had dropped him off at the apartment yesterday. No matter what, Jamie decided, it would be a good day even if limited to examining the icons whose artistic expression captured the piety of the monks on the windswept islands of the Aegean Sea.

George grunted a greeting. The driver remained silent.

"Hello to you both," Jamie said, not to be deterred by their indifference. The car doors were locked before they pulled away from the curb with a squeal of tires.

"Simone not suit?" George asked, grinning at the driver. At first, Jamie did not know to whom the question was directed.

"Simone didn't suit?" George repeated.

"Oh, Simone—was that her name?" *Of course*, he thought, *they drove her to my place and must have remained in the vicinity to drive her back later.*

"I liked her. I'm just fast," Jamie answered. George looked around again with disgust. Jamie was certain that George thought he was gay. He was angry that he had not noticed their car staked out in the area when he returned from his meeting, and also that her visit was not prompted by an uncontrollable urge to copulate. He was thankful that he did not leave so much as an airline stub in the apartment for her to discover.

"How long you remain there?" It was George again—but this time seeking information that he had been directed to gather.

"Uncertain, depends upon Simone," he said, confusing George further. Perhaps George had not heard Jamie, or more likely did not understand. He turned to face Jamie again just as they started uphill along a narrow street.

"*Bavoom!*"

Jamie dove on reflex below the back of the front seat, pulling his revolver from his belt in one motion. The windshield in front of George had been shattered. George slumped onto the lap of the startled driver, who had hit his brakes to avoid a pickup truck that had crossed the road from an alleyway and was now blocking their path. Jamie looked at George. He seemed as if he was resting—except the right top and side of his head had been blown away.

Jamie caught the movement of a young Arab wearing a keffiyeh. He was at the left side, ready to finish off the driver with his automatic weapon. He squeezed two rounds though the shattered glass, hitting the attacker in the chest.

"Jesus, let's get going!" Jamie shouted, but the driver seemed frozen, as if didn't comprehend what was happening. He shouted again, reaching over and slapping the driver on the side of his face. Suddenly the driver came to life, pushed George off his lap, and started the stalled motor. The vehicle roared in reverse, knocking down two advancing Arabs, and drove over a third attacker as he wheeled the Mercedes into a tight arc toward the alley from which the truck had emerged.

Jamie fired two more rounds at another individual taking cover behind the pickup truck. The Mercedes bounced off another vehicle before speeding into the alley. He hoped that it would lead to a main road. He did not want to find himself in a blind alley with a heavily armed foe closing in from behind. The driver was in a state of panic, his hands frozen to the wheel. Jamie frowned at the odds—six rounds remaining. Then he remembered the duffel bag. He reached for it over George' body as the car lurched from side to side.

It was an Uzi, as he had guessed. A twenty-round clip was already in place. He took off the safety and fired a short burst through the rear window for effect.

"Let these chicken fuck-heads know that they may get hurt," he shouted with a mad gleam in his eyes. The driver for his part responded with a high-pitched scream, as if he were hurtling through space without a parachute. Jamie noticed that his eyes were closed tight as he careened through a wooden crate and a pile of garbage onto an open road. He paused momentarily before turning sharply to the right—accelerating the Mercedes to its full power.

Leaning against the rear seat for support, Jamie retrieved a second ammunition clip and placed it next to him. The driver's face was sweaty and pale. He glanced at Jamie for the first time in the rearview mirror. Jamie winked at him playfully. The driver looked away as they sped to the safety of the Christian sector of the city.

"So you think I'm queer too," Jamie said aloud even though the driver did not comprehend. "Are you repelled by the thought that you owe your survival to this Spanish homosexual?" he asked. The driver stopped screaming as he floored the accelerator. They reached an open road and continued on at great speed.

They drove to the French mission hospital with no further incident. George's body was removed from the blood-spattered front seat. Judging by his condition, a medical expert was not needed. George could just as easily have driven directly to the morgue. The driver, whom Jamie learned was Philippe, gave an excited explanation of what happened to the emergency room attendant. The information would then be registered with the authorities, a euphemism for the operations unit of the local Christian militia responsible for mounting a retaliatory action.

They returned to the car, where Jamie got back into the rear seat, and continued in silence to Kalenti's residence. The driver pulled up to the palatial stone three-story home, in front of which stood two guards. Off to the right Jamie noticed a stack of sandbags that could be hastily piled up in an emergency before the gallery-sized double windows.

Kalenti heard the stir created as Philippe exclaimed to the guards and a gathering crowd outside how the windshield had been shattered. He opened the door to greet Jamie and receive firsthand Philippe's account in excited Arabic. Kalenti frowned.

"Come with me." Kalenti invited Jamie inside, leading him

to the study. Shamir was sitting there in a deep high-back leather chair before an icon collection that was assembled in front of the floor-to-ceiling bookshelves. Before Shamir had a chance to exchange greetings, Kalenti spoke in a hushed whisper—again in Arabic—informing him of the ambush. Kalenti never asked Jamie for his account of the ambush.

"Monsieur Casasnovas, Philippe says that without you he would not have survived." Jamie nodded slightly but remained silent.

"It seems you are skilled with weapons," Shamir observed.

"In this city, I guess that's essential."

"How does it match your appreciation of icons?"

"I hope it's better than my way with your girl."

"My girl?"

"No, not *your* girl, but young girl," Jamie corrected.

"Oh, I understand," he said, annoyed that he was unable to penetrate Jamie's outward sense of serenity, or was it frivolity.

"Come, the icons." Shamir rose with effort to his feet.

CHAPTER TWENTY-FIVE

For the next two hours Shamir and Kalenti treated Jamie to a museum-quality icon collection. He examined examples of thirteenth- and fourteenth-century art—items that had recently been smuggled from the Soviet Union and had probably arrived aboard Soviet ships transiting between the Black Sea and the Mediterranean Sea.

"Your interest and appreciation are to be rewarded," Kalenti said as he produced for Jamie's viewing rare Romanian glass icons dating back to the sixteenth century.

"These too are available. However, any purchase would have to be most discreet. The Romanian government has informed insurance brokers that an official who defected to the West stole the collection from a state museum."

"Pity," Jamie managed.

"Please feel no pressure to decide," Shamir stated.

Jamie was relieved that his opinion of the collection was not solicited. He found it strange that no one asked about his clients, their tastes, or the price range they would be willing to pay.

"For a slightly higher figure per icon," Shamir added, "we could arrange delivery in Western Europe, or some other area free from civil strife."

"Yes, that could be attractive."

"Are you still working with the Red Army Faction?" Kalenti asked.

Jamie was caught off guard by the question.

"I see that I am known," Jamie said matter-of-factly. Kalenti's accusation was too specific to deny. He decided that they could not be that concerned since the guards were not in the room. He remained confident that he could strike some sort of an accord.

"We all must make a living," he said finally.

"Yes, indeed. Do not worry; we would deal with the devil for profit. But what are you doing in Beirut? Surely there are safer places to earn money?"

"I have severed my relationship with the RAF. Beirut is one of the few civilized, or perhaps once civilized, places to flee to and be reasonably assured that I won't be followed."

"What were you planning to do, steal an icon?" Shamir asked.

"Not a bad idea. I thought about it, but I don't like the odds against me in this town."

"Well, what were you planning to do then?" Kalenti probed.

"Offer my services," Jamie said, directing his gaze at Kalenti until the latter broke eye contact to look at Shamir.

"I decided as much," Kalenti said, pressing his lips thin like a French diplomat.

"Now that George has retired, I need someone with your skills and coolness for my personal protection."

"What is the pay?" Jaime was surprised at the abruptness of the offer, especially since his professional credentials had him at a minimum politically aligned with those considered adversaries. They had accepted his story too quickly. There was more involved, but he had no idea what.

"Something that you will not be able to turn down. I will reward you generously with an exquisite icon from time to time—depending of course upon your loyalty." Kalenti waited for Jamie to respond.

"I accept but insist on you demonstrating your generosity in advance. I want one of your treasures now—or else no deal."

Kalenti seemed to respect Jamie's boldness. He selected an icon that was probably painted in the late eighteenth century.

"Here, monsieur, for your contemplation and my safety. Your duties begin immediately. Please report to the housekeeper. She will show you your room. Philippe will arrange for you to select a weapon of your choice. You are free until four, when you will join us for a light repast. Andre will take you back to the apartment if there is anything you wish to retrieve."

"No thank you. I think I will do just fine in this sector of the city."

"Good, until four when we will discuss my, or should I say our, travel plans."

Jamie accepted his dismissal and the icon. His only thought at the moment was how he could send the icon to Brigid. Maybe it was time for him to try to contact the Americans again. At least his intuition was accurate on one count—the day had proved to be more exciting than simply inspecting an icon collection.

☩✻☩✻☩

"We have reached our cruising altitude. We expect to arrive in New York City in six hours and thirty-two minutes," advised the Sabena captain over the intercom.

Karina had boarded the flight in Brussels. An hour after the announcement, she unsnapped her seatbelt and stood in the aisle. She ran her hands down her snug-fitting knit dress to smooth the wrinkles before proceeding to the rear of the aircraft. The cabin lights had been extinguished, and she took note of the men reading as she walked slowly and deliberately. She stopped at the magazine rack. A stewardess approached from the galley.

"Where are you from?" she asked.

"From Beirut. I am on my way to visit family in New York."

"I've never made it to Beirut. I call San Diego my home.

Someday I'll visit Lebanon. But it will have to get a lot quieter," she said with a sad smile.

"Someday." Karina sounded optimistic. "May I have a cup of coffee?"

The stewardess poured a cup of freshly brewed coffee. They both sat in two vacant seats and continued their conversation until the stewardess excused herself to attend to a passenger. Karina decided to return to her seat.

Midway down the aisle, she stopped and leaned over the shoulder of one of the men, who showed more than moderate interest when she passed. He looked up in surprise.

"Care for some company?" she said, softly squeezing by him into the vacant window seat. "I can't sleep. I'm so excited."

He was in his late thirties and of slender frame, with a long white neck and a prominent goiter. He had the look of Ichabod Crane in the *Legend of Sleepy Hollow.*

"This is my first visit to America, and I simply can't wait until we arrive."

"Where will you be going?" he asked, leaning shyly away from her.

"New York, but I hope to do some traveling. Where do you live?"

"I live in New York—right in the city."

"Who do you have waiting for you?"

"I live alone—just a cat that a neighbor has been feeding in my absence."

"Never married?"

"Haven't found anyone yet." He seemed embarrassed.

"What do you do?" Karina continued.

"Advertising. I'm returning from a trip to our office in Paris." Every time she moved against him, she could feel him shudder.

"How exciting. I study architecture at American International University in Beirut." Her goal in engaging this lonesome traveler was not companionship but rather a place to stay in New York if Kuban failed to meet her when they landed.

"How about a drink?" he asked as the drink cart reached them.

"Oh, thank you. You are so kind." She leaned closer to him. "I am on my way to visit my grandfather and grandmother, and I can't wait to see them. It's been so long." Over dinner they shared a split of champagne—again his treat.

"I am hoping to find a position in the architectural field." She chatted on, happily and gaily—so animated and interesting.

"If I can be of help …" His words trailed off.

"Oh, thank you so much, but I think I'll be okay," she said demurely, but not before she accepted his business card with his office and home numbers and address.

The evening passed all too quickly for the lonely American. When the flight steward announced that they were beginning their descent, Karina returned to her seat.

After the aircraft touched down and taxied to the disembarkation point, he caught up with Karina and helped her with her carry-on luggage. They separated in the terminal—he to join the line for those with American passports and she the line for foreigners.

"I'll see you on the other side." He sounded eager. Karina waved in response.

"Look, Johnnie, I don't have all day." The border control officer jolted him awake. "Where's your passport?"

Focusing on producing his passport, he did not see that Karina had already passed through customs. She was walking arm in arm with Kuban toward the terminal exit. Not once did she look behind.

Later that evening Kuban would wake Kalenti with a telephone call announcing Karina's safe arrival. Kalenti encouraged Kuban by informing him that everything was going smoothly. For his part, Kuban said that there was no reason why everything would not be ready for the team's arrival later in the month.

⁌*⁌*⁌

"At the sign of the tone, please leave your message."

Jamie waited patiently for the signal. The connection to Athens was clearer than expected. He had spent the morning in the relative security of East Beirut, protected by the Christian militia of the Phalange. Only after he was satisfied that he was not being followed had he entered a small jewelry shop. He inspected the filigree gold chains that hung from a rusty nail hammered into a wooden beam.

After a sufficient time had passed in serious inspection of the jewelry, he asked, nodding toward the phone, "Can I make a brief long-distance call?"

"I'm not sure," the proprietor hesitated but immediately agreed when Jamie placed a fifty dollar bill on the counter and then distanced himself out of earshot. The tone sounded.

"Halo, you know who this is. I am leaving for New York via Athens. I am accompanying Kalenti as his bodyguard. Not sure if this is interesting. Tell your man to meet me tonight, or else I will call when I arrive there. Cheers."

The owner, who had already pocketed the bill, was relieved that the call was of short duration. Jamie bid him farewell.

He would have preferred to use a post office for his call but had decided that there was a chance that the call would be monitored, even though he had to admit that the chance was remote, given the lack of any central authority and the spiraling violence. It was clear that the shop owner had only the American currency in mind.

Fifteen minutes later, he used the same formula with the owner of a grocery store. This time he dialed a local number provided by Ben Yousef. The gentleman who answered had difficulty comprehending English. Jamie spoke slowly and clearly.

"This is a friend of Ben Yousef. I wish to report that I have made contact and will accompany someone of interest to New York on January 23. See no way for you to contact me here. When I arrive, I will call your office, or else I will call this number again.

I must speak with you. Please remember to make the deposit into my account."

Once outside, Jamie congratulated himself. It would do no harm to keep his ties with the Libyans. The Americans need not know. Brigid and he would find a use for the additional money. He just had to be careful. If the Americans discovered this arrangement, they might reduce his stipend—or worse.

Before returning to the room his hosts provided, he arranged with the freight department of MEA the shipment of some books he had purchased earlier. He addressed them to Brigid. Nestled securely between the two books was the icon that he had just received from Kalenti. He felt uncomfortable parting with the icon but decided that this unorthodox method of shipment was the only one open to him. He did not want to tempt his benefactors to renege on their generosity, nor did he intend to leave the icon behind in Beirut. He also rejected the idea of carrying the icon to America, where he could face customs problems.

☦ * ☦ * ☦

Frost regretted that he had not fled the safe house apartment when the first exchange of gunfire subsided. But he had not. When the second outburst sounded an hour later, he was terrified and chose to remain in the apartment. Now, hours later, his mind still echoed with the exchange of gunfire. He sat in the armchair that he had pulled up to the door and fell asleep.

When he woke it was still dark. He decided to leave while it was quiet. With the greatest of caution, he hugged the sides of the buildings and walked downhill toward the road leading to his hotel. That the streets were deserted at first he considered a blessing, but as he progressed further the eerie calm created phantom figures in every doorway that were intent on assaulting him. He looked over his shoulder constantly. When he reached the hotel he was out of breath. He had covered what normally was a twenty-minute walk in over an hour. The front door to the hotel was secured. He managed to attract the attention of the dozing night clerk and, as he had done on the night of his arrival, purchased a large paper cup of scotch to sooth his ragged nerves.

By early afternoon he had not stirred other than to allow the old crippled man into his room with a breakfast of bread, honey, and coffee. Never an elegant hotel, the Riviera had survived because of its location in the Druze-protected area. War did have its impact. The old man with his shirt opened at the collar and a green bar jacket cut for someone thinner constituted the entire hotel room service staff.

He finally summoned the energy to call the station to report that he was back at the hotel and that ICARUS had not shown for the meeting. He was sorry he had not obtained a still larger cup of scotch when he flipped on the radio and heard a BBC broadcast about the kidnapping of the American ambassador to Lebanon. A chill went through his bones that the Scotch did little to relieve.

He did his best to make himself comfortable and decided to rest his eyes. Two hours later, the ring shattered the silence of his room. He bolted upright on the couch where he had been reclining. He reached behind him for the telephone.

"Yes?"

"Frost, this is the office." Frost recognized the voice of his contact.

"Yes, I am listening."

"Your friend called. He wants to see you this afternoon. He will be traveling soon."

"What friend?" Frost sounded confused.

"The friend who calls Athens." His contact had hoped to keep the conversation as brief and as innocuous as possible.

"Where does he want to meet me?"

"Same place. But be careful. You heard about the kidnapping?"

"Yes, thanks." Frost hung up the phone, his hand beginning to shake visibly. He was suddenly overwhelmed by nausea. He rushed to the bathroom.

CHAPTER TWENTY-SIX

Kay walked through Brody's office door clearing her throat to announce her arrival. In her hand she held the cable that she had just received from Rome Station with information provided by the Italian intelligence service. Without a word of greeting, she gave it to him. He read the text aloud.

> *Source reports that terrorist operation is planned in the United States by group traveling from France.*
> *Timing of attack is thought to be in near future.*
> *Sponsorship for group, number of terrorists, or target(s) not known.*
> *Source is not, repeat not, expected to acquire additional information.*

"Well, thank you very much," Brody exclaimed, exasperated at the lack of detail.

"They don't tell you very much. This cable has been disseminated throughout the intelligence community and to selected government offices, even though it doesn't offer specifics. I don't have to tell you it will prompt bureaucrats to cover their butts by giving it even wider dissemination."

"Why is that?" Brody asked.

"Why is what?"

"We should approve any distribution—it is ops intelligence."

"David, the dissemination system has been in place for some time now. When are you going to grasp its dynamics and cease questioning its utility?"

"Umph! I just don't like machines making decisions."

"Better machines than no decisions."

"Are you suggesting …" He did not complete his thought.

"Only that this is not a bureaucratic control issue but a response to the demands of national security."

"So what should we do?" Brody returned to the cable.

"Let me tell you what the FBI did. They set up a response team that is scanning all flights originating in France bound for the United States. I have offered Stacy to join them in New York. We're waiting for their answer," Kay reported.

"Stacy who?"

"The young lady who works for me. She discerns patterns that even a computer program misses."

"Any fit with GANYMEDE case?" Brody was trying to reassert himself. He felt mildly annoyed that he could not place Stacy. If she had given a last name, he would have nodded recognition. "You're going to have to brief me more regularly on what's happening with Gordon and Frost. It seems to be getting out of control."

"To your question, I don't think there's any connection." She responded in a matter-of-fact manner. "We'll learn from Frost the reason for ICARUS's travel to the United States. They are due to meet within the next hour or so," she said, checking her watch and considering the six-hour time difference.

"My gut feeling is that ICARUS has gotten off track," Brody observed. "Anything more from the Israelis?"

"I just sent a message to Tel Aviv asking for an update," Kay answered.

"What about the ambassador?"

"Nothing since we rejected publicly the demand to pull out."

"Where is Gordon?" The question had just come to mind.

"He is still cooling his heels in Bonn. You know we turned down his request to travel to Beirut?"

"Yes, of course. Get him home. I want to see him." Brody reached abruptly for the stack of correspondence in the IN box on the right corner of the desk to close the discussion.

Brody wanted Colin home to get his views directly. He needed Colin for day-to-day liaison with the bureau in the event that the Italian report gained more credibility in the community. He also wanted Colin close so that he could take responsibility if anything went wrong. After all, it was Colin's agent that precipitated this crisis.

⁂

"At the sound of the tone ..." Jamie tightened the grip on the receiver. He wanted to hang up when the recording voice began to run but realized that they would not know who called. "B-e-e-p ..."

"Guess who this is. What the fuck is wrong? Can't you make a meeting? I haven't much time before I leave. Just make sure that you deposit my pay on time. I'll call again in New York. Yes, that's what I'll do."

He hung up and walked from the shoe repair shop. He realized that he had overreacted to the American's failure to show for the meeting. In fairness, he had not appeared for the first scheduled time. He had not had contact with the Americans since he left Beirut. He didn't know if they were trying to reach him. He dismissed the thought that they decided not to honor the commitments made in Sofia.

⁂

The cable from Athens station reporting ICARUS's call was

not received at Headquarters until that Monday, January 22. Kay scanned it quickly, noting that it contradicted an earlier message from Frost in which he claimed that he waited in vain for ICARUS to appear for alternate meeting time. Unbeknownst to Frost, the chief of station in Beirut had used a back channel to Headquarters suggesting that Frost return to Athens to await further developments. Kay had been in the business long enough to know that something was wrong with Frost to influence the station chief to make such a suggestion. Perhaps the pressure of the case and the abduction of Hollingsworth had gotten to him.

She reread the transcript of ICARUS's call and was inclined to believe that he had been left stranded at the meeting site. Frost was no longer reliable. He could only hurt himself and others if he remained engaged in the case. He must be removed and his association with the GANYMEDE operation severed.

She drafted a short cable for Brody's signature directing Frost to return to Athens. She then took this cable and others that required his signature and headed for his office. On the way, she saw a case officer assigned to the Greek desk.

"Frost is on his way back to Athens," she stated.

"Why is that? I thought his services were invaluable, or at least his cables suggested the same."

"No, it's time to have someone knowledgeable about the case coordinate the flow of traffic," Kay lied.

"Come on, Kay. For this case, Athens remains a backwater." Rather than debate the issue further, Kay continued to Brody's office. She was aware of a pinch in her left leg that caused it to drag slightly.

⁑∗⁑∗⁑

The Allenby Bridge crossed the Jordan River and connected the West and East Banks of what was controlled by the Kingdom of Jordan—that is, until the 1967 war. Since then the Israelis ruled the West Bank and scrutinized anyone entering Israeli territory from Jordan. Solid bunker-like huts lined the crossing point from which Israeli security and intelligence personnel observed the travelers discreetly.

"There he is," a short Italian-looking Israeli in his late forties exclaimed.

"You're right." His companion was younger and a graduate of the Mossad's intelligence school. He had recently been withdrawn from an assignment in Europe and placed at the crossing point to cool off operationally. He immediately picked up the drop line to the gate.

"Moishe, our man is approaching, dressed in green fatigues and a blue sweatshirt. Pull him and four others out of line and send our man to room seven—the rest to the other interrogation booths."

Five minutes later, the younger Israeli in room seven greeted the Arab, "Shalom."

"Shssh!" the Arab hissed.

"Please, it is important that we speak." In return for his cooperation, this Christian Arab, a resident of the West Bank, was allowed regular access to Israel proper, given preferential treatment in obtaining building materials for his business, and was able to establish a hard currency account—allowing transfer of funds to his extended family abroad.

"What do you want?"

"Do you have any more information on the passports for the Lebanese group?"

"I did not say Lebanese group." He pushed the unpainted wooden table sharply on the concrete floor. The Israeli controlled his reaction. He could have had the Arab thrown into prison and held without anyone being the wiser. However, he needed information.

"I'm sorry. I was not testing you."

"Good. Let me repeat that the passports were manufactured from scratch—the very best of paper and cachets used—price no object. Twelve were ordered, but it seems that the number needed was reduced and there's been some haggling over the price due—though money didn't seem to be a real issue."

"Who are the passports for?"

"I'm getting to that. Are you Israelis always in such a rush? When will you realize that you'd get more information and live longer if we conducted business as we Arabs do—with hospitality?"

"I don't think they are for Lebanese," he continued. "The usual way for Palestinians, Shiites, even Hezbollah, is not being followed."

"How is that?" the Israeli said trying to be patient. He also realized that he could not hold the Arab much longer without drawing attention to him.

"Number one, they don't have the money to use for anything but modified stolen passports; two, they don't order for groups; three, they want passports to cover Arabic-speaking or looking individuals. This requirement was for passports of Western countries. Finally, the passports seemed reserved for the second phase of the operation."

"Why do you say that?"

"They are only interested in travel within Europe and not entry onto the continent. What gives them such confidence that they can get into Europe in the first place?"

"You said not a Lebanese group—then who?"

"If I'd have to guess it would be an émigré European group. But I can't understand why they are turning to a Lebanese master to produce them." The Arab looked at his watch.

"Yes, we must finish," the Israeli said as he slipped his hand under his sweater and pulled out an envelope with dollar bills and a receipt.

"Here's for your trouble."

"Are you crazy? I leave here with that stack of bills and then claim that I was merely interrogated?" He pushed the envelope back across the table—but not before he counted them.

"Deposit it into my account. I must go."

"One last question. Who has the American ambassador?"

"What do you think I am—God? I don't know. I must go." The Arab rose from his chair.

The Israeli moved out of his way. He could already hear the men forming a line outside. The Arab put a convincing scowl on his face before exiting the room.

The Israeli stayed behind to draft his report to Tel Aviv. Once it had been sanitized to eliminate any identifying information on the source or place of acquisition, the Israelis would pass it to the Americans first and then to the other selected Western European intelligence services.

※ ※ ※

Air France 023 to New York was boarding at Charles de Gaulle Airport just outside of Paris. The regularly scheduled flight was chartered for Lebanese delegates journeying to the United States to attend a conference called by the International Red Cross. It was to be held in Washington, DC—concurrent with a UN session in New York that would be discussing the deteriorating situation in Lebanon. The theme of the conference was the plight of the women and children in war-ravaged Lebanon. The charter was full. A casual observer seeing passengers boarding the flight with armloads of duty-free purchases would be hard-pressed to believe that they were called to Washington to discuss the threat of starvation and poverty in Lebanon. Courtney, Jacques, Metro, Danny, and Michelle were in the crowd lining up to board the flight.

"Has any one seen Jon?" Michelle asked Danny.

"Nope," he said as they moved slowly toward the boarding gate. They would not learn until much later that he had gotten lost attempting to reach the airport by public transportation. He was caught in a horrendous traffic jam that would cause him to miss the flight.

The flight departed forty minutes behind schedule—time

that the pilot would make up across the Atlantic but lose later in a holding pattern over New York. The team members sat separately throughout the cabins of the DC10. With the exception of Michelle, each was immersed in a book or magazine.

"Where are you from, my dear?" a gray-haired lady asked. She was in her eighties. She had arching black eyebrows that seemed to curtain her dark eyes.

"Baalbek, but we have not lived there since Hezbollah moved in."

"Oh, I know, my dear. So much suffering."

"Where is your home, if I might ask?" Michelle seemed anxious to move the conversation to the old lady.

"Well, many years before your parents and perhaps even your grandparents, I was born in Beirut." She spoke with just a hint of a New England accent. "My family once had holdings throughout Lebanon and even maintained a family estate in Jerusalem and a residence in Venice. But that has past." She paused, a touch of nostalgia in her eyes. "That was when my father and uncle were in the import-export business."

"And now?" Michelle asked.

"Oh, for longer than I care to admit, I live in the city—that is, New York City."

"Are you participating in the convention?"

"Yes, of course. I am one of the organizers. Anything to help the women left widows and the children orphans. Are you participating in the event, young lady?"

"I regret no. I am off to visit my mother's family in Brooklyn. I was able to get a seat on this flight for a modest donation." To avoid more careful scrutiny, Michelle pulled out a book from her purse, smiled at her traveling companion, and began to read.

Upon landing, representatives from the ICRC greeted the passengers as they debarked and facilitated the entry procedures. Passport inspection was cursory as the group was advertised as participating in the one-week conference before returning to Lebanon.

Michelle and her four companions speculated that they would remain in New York where they suspected that their target was located. As they walked beyond the customs area into the flow of arriving passengers, Karina approached them.

"Hello, you weary travelers," she said, not making much of a display in her greeting. "Kuban is waiting outside in a van."

⁘⁕⁘⁕⁘

"If he could not make it to the airport on time," Zaquod said in a phone call later to Kuban when informed that Jon had missed the flight, "who is to say that he could negotiate the distance to and from the target?"

"Yes, it's an auspicious sign. We don't need ineptitude and confusion on the team." Kuban was secretly pleased that he would not have to depart for Beirut until the operation was completed. As Jon's replacement, he would drive for the team. He recalled years ago accompanying a Maronite delegation to Rome for an audience with the pope. While the purpose of the visit was not to redress past wrongs, he considered what was planned in America as serving his nation, which had been grievously harmed.

With the baggage stowed in the rear seat, Kuban started the engine for the drive that would take them to Mt. Kisco—a two-hour trip north beyond the city through Westchester County.

"Welcome to you all. I want to tell you that we will be staying with an old friend who left Lebanon some years ago. He knows nothing of our purpose. I have told him that you all have suffered during the fighting and you are here to recover from your experiences before returning home. Are there any questions?"

Kuban noticed through the rearview mirror that there were none. Karina, who was sitting in the front passenger seat, looked around at them.

"I want to inform you that I have secured eight AK-47s, four Colt forty-five caliber pistols, four thousand rounds of ammunition, and seventy-five pounds of C-4 explosive with primer cords and explosive caps." Her announcement was greeted by mild applause.

"We have sufficient ammunition to sight-in the weapons, though we all realize that firing at close range the process should be quite easy."

"I'm not sure I agree," Jacques interrupted. "Nothing is worse than assuming the weapons will not be fired any distance and …"

"Jacques, no one disagrees with you, but we simply don't have the time, nor do we want to do more," Kuban said to support Karina. "This is not Lebanon, you know. People are not accustomed to hearing weapons firing in the woods at targets. We can't take the chance of attracting any unnecessary attention."

They drove the rest of the way in silence with the visitors from Lebanon gazing at the fast-moving traffic and the high-rise apartment buildings giving way to sturdy single-family residences as they passed through the suburbs to the outer reaches of the county. On the outskirts of Mt. Kisco, they turned into a driveway leading to what was once a farmhouse. Kuban looked around at the team.

"How do you feel after your travel?"

"Ready to go and accomplish what we were sent for," Jacques said, and these words reflected the sentiment of each of the team members. They suspected that whatever they were asked to do was designed to gain the support of the powerful ally in whose nation they were now traveling.

Kuban pulled the van alongside a two-story wooden, single-family dwelling. He turned off the motor and got out to assist in pulling the luggage from the rear of the vehicle as Karekin came out to greet his visitors from Lebanon.

CHAPTER TWENTY-SEVEN

The old comrades came together on the eve of Kalenti's departure. It was a liturgical gathering of sorts. Reflection, community, and service dominated the simple mountain meal of lamb, peasant bread, and red wine from grapes grown north of Zahle. Their bond was as close as it had ever been. They toasted Kuban, whose company they missed and dedication they revered. Kalenti was the first to share his thoughts.

"Before we began we knew the path on which we were to embark was dangerous. Does anyone deny this?"

"I can only add," Shamir responded almost in a whisper, "that it is proving more dangerous than expected and no less significant for the future of Lebanon."

"I agree," Zaquod said. "Our motherland continues to slide toward oblivion as the Western giants—our allies—lick the thorns they endured for us. Thorns," he repeated, "while our life blood—our youth—is pierced with arrows loosed by the infidel."

"To the extent possible, we must remain objective. Nothing we have done to date need be uncovered; no plan we have put in place cannot be recalled." The circle was complete with Kalenti's comments. "Our protector, St. Marmoon, is working strenuously to make it so." He smiled and paused as he consumed a thin slice of lamb. The others nodded in agreement. Kalenti continued,

"The tall German's signal to his friends was not detected, though we might have been a bit too hasty in eliminating the mailbox in Bonn." Kalenti took a sip of wine.

"Our failure to kill the American does not seem to have caused us harm," Zaquod said. "In fact, it may have caused them to withdraw from the field of battle."

"The death of our man in Athens should have been avoided, but it now seems that it occurred before he could have revealed anything," Kalenti suggested.

"We have also succeeded in monitoring Israeli attempts to uncover information about the passports," Shamir added.

"And turn suspicion to Shiite groups," Kalenti stressed. "With the ambassador's abduction there is no turning back. Are we in agreement?" He looked around and received the agreement of each with a solemn nod.

"The ambassador must be killed, then," Kalenti continued, "at the proper time to heighten America's outrage. Our warriors are in place to administer the verdict. And then you will see that soon we will no longer endure the insults and taunts of our enemies."

"It is as serious a step as you depicted," Shamir spoke, dipping his napkin into a glass of Perrier water and applied to his burning eyes. "And, of course, there is no assumption that we will succeed. We can only assure each other that we will try and at the same time ensure that the Americans do not discover our responsibility." He paused and became reflective.

"Yes, the ambassador must be martyred—and soon." In a soft voice almost to himself, Shamir asked, "What will the Americans do if they discover our role and not that of Hezbollah in the killing? What will they do?" He emphasized the word *will* with his inflection accompanied by a thrust of his hand.

"I am not concerned about what they will not do," Kalenti replied.

"Will they abandon Christianity to Mohammed? I think not," Zaquod interjected.

"Will they deal with Hassad of Syria or Hussein of Iraq or an ayatollah from Iran?" Zaquod asked. "At worse, they will ignore the act by attributing it to the demented rage of some old men. At best, they will realize how desperate we are and intervene to bring order."

"As they have done before," Shamir interrupted. "Whatever happens, it is still worth the risk.

"In the final analysis," Shamir spoke again after all were silent, "you, Kalenti, are the decider. Because you must see to it that our second target is as effectively handled. Only you will be able to judge the impact firsthand." He looked into Kalenti's eyes.

"Yes," Kalenti said slowly, "we move forward to the killing of the ambassador. Let me assure you that the event in America will meet the criteria that we have set. It will shock, awake, galvanize, and provoke. It will create theater in its most dramatic and chilling enactment."

Silence again descended on those present as they fostered a collective feeling of a commitment to the retribution required to give each relief from the private agonies they and their nation had endured.

"We are agreed. We continue our death lunge," Kalenti was the first to speak.

"Why death lunge?" Zaquod asked, directing his gaze at Kalenti.

"Because once we act we cannot let go until our friends come to our aid and wrest control of Lebanon from the unwashed, pajama-clad Moslem illiterates."

"I am reminded of the black widow spider riding the back of the dog across the stream." Zaquod said. "In midstream it senselessly stings the dog and they both sink to their deaths. Is that the lunge?" Kalenti did not answer.

"We will miss you." Shamir stood to embrace Kalenti.

"I will call from America as to the timing of the ambassador's death," Kalenti announced.

"I will be waiting," Zaquod vowed.

❧*❧*❧

Colin threw his suitcase onto one of the two double beds in the hotel room. *Crystal City, Crystal City. Why here when there are hotels ten minutes from Headquarters?* Exasperated, he asked the walls of his room. He was tired and irritable.

The flight from Frankfurt was delayed by fog for eight hours at Heathrow Airport. That was bad enough, but so were about one hundred other flights. The international lounge was stacked with indistinguishable bundled bodies of South Asians and Africans stretched out on the couches, along with tidy, orderly, alert groups of Japanese, while clusters of tobacco-enriched Arabs sat around tables of stale beer.

Colin had finally found an empty corner and placed the issue of *The Economist* beneath him. He sat propped up in that position, pulling in the panoply of colors, sounds, and odors that filled the terminal until his flight had been called.

It was now almost four p.m.—nine p.m. European time. He would shower and shave before calling the office. He was not anxious to do anything other than relax this evening. Perhaps he would watch some American television. His years abroad had kept him from this addiction. However, at times like this the box held a certain allure for him. If past trips were any indication, it would take him a couple of days to realize the blessing of being free from the distraction.

I would rather perfect my lovemaking with Chris than be a blind follower of some network programming genius, he said aloud to the walls of the hotel room. He opened the zipper to the compact leather suitcase, a Christmas gift from Chris. A strange gift when he recalled how she detested his trips away from home. He pulled his stretcher and the accompanying neck brace from the top of his clothes. It was his traveling traction device prescribed by a doctor at George Washington University to relieve a pinched nerve that seemed to recur during long trips. He had not used the contraption for almost two years. The stress from the near fatal hallway wrestling match forced him to retrieve the device.

The shower refreshed him, as did the smooth feeling of his face after a shave. He dressed casually and helped himself to a scotch from the mini-bar. He looked at his watch—five fifteen. He picked up the phone and dialed Kay's number, hoping no one would answer.

"Where have you been?" There was no salutation, like "How was your trip?" or "What are your plans?" Only "Where have you been?"

"I was delayed ten hours in London," he exaggerated.

"Well, I went out to pick you up at eleven thirty. That was the time they said that you would be in."

"Sorry, nothing I could do about it." He felt guilty about the shower and the drink.

"We need you in right away. Where are you staying?"

"In Crystal City …"

"Where? What are you doing there?"

"Your office made the reservation."

Kay caught herself. Stacy lived in that area and probably considered it to be the center of town.

"Okay, Okay. Take a cab and be out here as soon as you can. We are scheduled to meet at five thirty. I'll hold off things. It's about an hour drive in rush hour. Too bad."

Colin asked for no clarification as to the urgency of the meeting. He knew that he would receive none from Kay on an open telephone line. He hung up and hurriedly changed back into a blue blazer and gray slacks—the case officer's uniform.

⁂

Brody was speaking as Colin followed Kay into the conference room. He looked up with annoyance in his eyes as they took the two unoccupied chairs in the rear next to Stacy. Once seated, Kay pointed out to Colin the representatives from the FBI, the

Department of State's Office to Combat Terrorism, the Customs Department, and the Department of Defense. Colin always felt uneasy with outsiders. He did not like to be in a position of meeting people as a CIA officer and later in the field under the guise of a Foreign Service officer.

"Intelligence from other sources indicates," Brody continued, "that we might be facing a serious threat inside the United States. We have received several reports from foreign liaisons that there is a possibility that a group is making its way here. If these reports prove to be accurate, we could be in for trouble." He paused and looked around the room.

"We are in trouble because to date not one—not one—of our unilateral sources has picked up anything that hints of this. As a result, we are completely dependent upon the sanitized reporting we have received, and hopefully will continue to receive, from our foreign friends."

Colin would have been more uncomfortable had he known that an overzealous officer working for Brody had invited the Israelis to attend. He wanted to show US appreciation for the reporting received to date. Brody, to his credit, squelched the invitation. He did not want the Israelis to be in a position to publicize their link to the American counterterrorism effort. Brody focused on forming a US interagency group to share the blame if the terrorists were successful.

Kay detected Colin's uneasiness. Unconsciously, he slid lower in the leather armchair, bringing his hands to his face. Cover had been his nemesis since he decided upon a career in the *Clandestine Service* twenty-five years ago. And yet, he knew his cover had always been unconvincing even to almost the casual observer. While bona fide Foreign Service officers exchanged erudite analyses on political and economic developments with counterparts in foreign ministries and embassies, Colin and his counterparts assessed those very same foreign officials to determine their access to intelligence and their vulnerability to recruitment to commit espionage. From his biased perspective, Colin judged that his Foreign Service colleagues were engaged in intellectual sophistry.

Everyone in the room suddenly turned to the back of the room, breaking Colin's travel-weary mind-drift. He looked in panic at Kay, who whispered that Brody had informed the audience of his presence and had asked if he wished to say anything. *Wonderful, great first impression,* he thought.

"No, not right now. I'm still on German time." He spoke up and immediately sank back into his chair.

He remembered once being similarly surprised and unprepared. Years previously, he attended a retirement luncheon for a high-level intelligence officer from a military unit. With no warning, he was called to the podium to present an award to the official. His only problem was that he had no award to present. As if it were yesterday, he recalled his embarrassment. He had been tempted to walk past the dais to the exit and disappear from the officers' club where the event was being staged. Instead, he spoke slowly into the microphone and announced to the four hundred officials in attendance how honored he was to be there and how he hoped that in retirement the individual would enjoy many years of good health. He concluded his comments by saying that any award present that day would have to be in secret writing. Without hesitating, he walked to the honored guest and shook his hand and returned to his seat.

Colin stifled a yawn as the customs official followed the immigration expert and explained a newly installed integrated computer system that was responsible for distributing the alert message of a possible impending terrorist incident in the United States. His presentation mirrored that of the previous presenters, and Colin concluded that each agency was working independently of the other, developing solutions that would not easily relate to another agency's communication systems. With all the dissemination of messages occurring, it would not have surprised him if the travel agents were receiving the sensitive information as well—so much for source protection. No wonder foreign liaison was reticent about sharing more detail in their reporting.

"Mr. Brody, is there a link between the kidnapping of the ambassador and the information about a possible action in Europe or the United States?" the immigration representative asked.

"Much too early to say, though I doubt any connection," he responded in a professorial tone.

"What's all the fuss?" Colin wrote on a slip of paper and passed it to Kay. She read it and turned her attention back to the proceedings. Colin felt rebuffed. He could not understand why he was called to Headquarters if it were not to introduce him to the world of intelligence as viewed by various government agencies and departments. *Was this a preview of his next assignment?* He mentally tabulated how long it would be before he was eligible for retirement.

It amazed him that everyone was taking the three or four intelligence reports received from liaison and somehow connecting them to the abduction of the ambassador. This was not the first time an American ambassador had been kidnapped. He grimaced in shame at his callousness, especially considering that he still mourned for the loss of his two agents. It was not long before he interjected himself into the debate about whether or not there was a connection to the ambassador's fate and the reporting received from liaison.

"With all due respect, I think that too much is being made of the intelligence and the ambassador's kidnapping." Colin spoke up as all those present turned in their seats to face him. "None of the information originated from CIA sources, but it came from unreliable and unspecific foreign intelligence reporting."

"What about the report concerning your agent's travel to the United States?" the FBI representative asked. Colin was shocked that he raised the matter since the other agencies in the room had not been cleared to receive the report.

"I think that report had limited distribution," Colin chastised him.

After a moment of silence and confusion on the part of the FBI representative, Brody spoke. "Gentlemen, we have covered what I had hoped in this meeting. I will keep you all advised of developments. Thanks for being patient while we waited for Mr. Gordon to arrive. That will be all." With that, Brody gathered his papers and left the room.

The meeting was over, and at that moment Colin's ears popped for the first time since he began his descent hours ago. He followed Kay and Stacy out of conference room.

"Where to?" Colin asked. Kay did not look up.

"To my office. We must get prepared to meet ICARUS when he calls."

"If he calls," Colin interjected.

"What am I doing here?" Colin asked once they entered Kay's office.

"Would you have preferred to remain in Bonn?"

"You bet! Anything is better than being with these liaison pukes."

"Come now. You exaggerate," Kay countered. "You don't think anything is going to happen, do you?"

"I don't know." He sounded less confident.

"I didn't ask whether you know; there's little we know in this business. It's your instincts—intuition—that we value. Let me ask again: what do you feel?"

"I feel ..." he said, emphasizing the word *feel*, "that this frenzied activity is misplaced. Those Arabs are no more ready to test their courage against us than they are prepared to invade Israel," he replied stubbornly and forcefully. He still feared that he was being set up for a tour of duty at Headquarters—a fate he feared as much as the Arabs trying to defeat Israel.

"If, for a moment, we were to link the intelligence reports with the murders of Horst and Hans, and the attempt on your life, and ..." Kay had to take another breath, "add the travel of ICARUS here and the kidnapping of Hollingsworth"—another breath— "what do we have?"

"A very fragile spider web."

"Oh, but how that fragile web nets such proud insects," Kay observed.

"Okay, Kay. I'll play your game. If, if, if, as you say, we have a deadly serious group headed our way—so well disciplined that we have not picked up even a hint of its intentions except through spotty reporting, what can we do?"

"We don't know its target, have not been able to penetrate the group or infiltrate its supporters, and have not the foggiest notion of what they hope to achieve." He paused. "I'd say we are in a pretty sorry state, and I don't have any bright ideas about how to counter the threat."

"Stacy just returned from New York, where she is working with the FBI task force. Right now they are sifting through the travel manifests of flights originating in France. Isn't that right, Stacy?" Stacy nodded.

"Why France?" Colin asked.

"Don't you remember what the Italians reported?" Kay responded.

"Oh, I forgot. Yeah, sure. Good idea. What are you looking for?" he directed his question to Stacy.

"For anything unusual." She colored in embarrassment. Colin sensed her awkwardness and did not pursue further.

"What else?" he turned back to Kay.

"Suppose you were right and the Arabs we are looking for are not Moslem fanatics but Christian fanatics?"

"Now wait just one moment. What are you saying?"

Kay had Colin's attention. "Well, I had this notion a couple of nights ago." Kay did not say that it came to her at four in the morning after she decided that she would waste no more time in bed trying to fall asleep. She didn't want to advertise that she was experiencing insomnia with greater frequency.

"Remember your trip to the Lebanese church the last time you were in Washington?" she asked. "Well, I've been thinking about your suggestion that maybe Hans was indeed outlining a Maronite cross as his signal to you."

Kay reached into her straight plaid skirt for a handkerchief to stifle a sneeze. The tip of her nose was red as an annual winter cold descended upon her.

"Assume for the moment that the plots to kill you, GANYMEDE, and Horst are all related, and let's include the current fear that there is something planned for the United States." Kay sneezed into her handkerchief. "Let's say that everything is related to the Israeli reporting about the passports …" Kay's voice trailed off as if she were following another thought simultaneously.

"So?" Colin sounded impatient.

"Well, what I did was to ask the Lebanese desk to draw up a list of prominent Christians within the Lebanese separatist movement who could be considered as more radical—let us say more militant—in their desire to partition Lebanon."

"And?"

Kay picked up three typewritten pages with two columns of names on each page. She smiled.

"Not much help, nearly 150 names," Kay said. "I then gave the list to Stacy. Before she rejoined the FBI task force, she created a profile on the group. Tell him what you were able to conclude."

"I first tried to determine," Stacy began haltingly, "something that was common to all of them. What I found out was that they were all members of the Maronite Church. As to age—they range from twenty-two to the oldest, who is seventy-seven. That is, if he is still living. In most cases our information was one to two years out of date." Her confidence was building.

"Despite the fact that many had close relatives who left Lebanon to reside abroad, these people seemed determined to remain in Lebanon. Though foreign travel was attractive and many had the opportunity to do so, we could establish the presence of only two of those on the list as being in the United States within the last six months. I have asked immigration to investigate whether either or both have departed."

"What are you trying to prove?" Colin directed his question to Kay.

"Give me time. From the beginning we have assumed that the Libyans or Hezbollah or the Palestinians were behind the killings and were planning to launch an attack or series of attacks on the United States. We have been frustrated that our agents who usually report on such groups have been quiet in a relative sense of the word until yesterday." Kay lit up a cigarette and inhaled deeply.

"And that's where I return to GANYMEDE's signal—the tree or the cross. Maybe the reason we have not picked up anything is that we have been looking in the wrong places."

"You're not suggesting that we ask the pope what's going on."

Kay frowned.

"Okay, Kay. I'll get serious. But why Christians?"

"Could it be that GANYMEDE was signaling a cross and not a tree?"

"Come now, Kay. So what—a cross. My question is why would Christians be involved in atrocities already committed and those about which we know nothing?"

"I'm coming to that. All I want you to consider is that perhaps GANYMEDE was saying, 'Hey, these Christian crazies are up to something and you'd better pay attention.'

"I think we all agree," Kay continued, "that GANYMEDE was taking a chance in sending the signal. He thought it was important enough, and one could argue that his murder was necessary to keep that information from us."

"If you are right," Colin said, resigned to think about the alternative, "what do we do differently; what do we do now?"

"Nothing, except expand our list of possible bad guys to include the ethnic Christians of Lebanon."

"Why do you say ethnic?"

"Ah hah. This is where I answer your second question about why would they be involved. I chose the word *ethnic* deliberately. There is nothing spiritual in their faith. You should know that acts of violence and revenge committed by Lebanese Christians rival and surpass anything perpetrated by Moslem fundamentalist groups. Are such actions representative of the Christ's message?

"Christian frustration with the chaos of Lebanon runs deep in the community, as with the Palestinians in their refugee camps." Kay reached into the ashtray and relit the butt of a cigarette. She drew deeply for the cold stale flavor and rested her case.

"Stacy, please buy me another pack down the hall. I'm over two packs today," she said, as if that was supposed to surprise anyone.

CHAPTER TWENTY-EIGHT

"Make yourself comfortable, Mr. Casasnovas." Kalenti took his seat in a plush blue armchair in the Olympic Airlines key club lounge in Athens.

"Thank you, I will." Jamie put down his carry-on bag and walked over to the service bar and helped himself to a sandwich, some peanuts, and a Coke. By the time he returned, Kalenti was writing in a thick ledger book that Jamie took to be a journal. He did not look up—making it clear that he was not encouraging conversation. After about a half an hour, he put his pen into the breast pocket of his blazer and the journal into his briefcase, which he then secured.

"I'll be right back." Kalenti walked to the men's room, and a few minutes later Jamie looked up to see him sitting in a phone cubicle. He too wanted to make a couple of calls, but he didn't want to raise Kalenti's suspicion. They would arrive in New York soon enough. When Kalenti rejoined him, Jamie was reading a paperback novel that had been left in the lounge.

"Well young man, it is time to board our flight," Kalenti said, rising to his feet. They walked together to the departure gate. Jamie looked at his boarding pass and realized that they were sitting apart during the flight.

"We'll meet beyond passport control in New York," Kalenti

said as he joined the first-class passengers lining up to board the aircraft.

Once in his seat in the economy section of the aircraft, Jamie secured his seat belt. He was next to the window in the last section of the 747 aircraft. The cabin doors closed with a muffled thud. Minutes later, the plane lurched as it was pulled from the loading platform. Once clear, the plane taxied to the end of a long runway and there stood motionless as prior aircraft were given the signal to take off.

He always became tense when the aircraft did not take off immediately. He attributed this feeling to the times when he crossed any international boundary with weapons hidden in his vehicle; and this tension translated to any time he was crossing a border—even if he was free of contraband. He was haunted by thoughts that the authorities had detected an abnormality in his passport and were about to board the flight. He glanced up at the steward walking up the aisle, making a last-minute check of the seat belts, but he detected nothing in the steward's demeanor to cause him alarm.

"Ladies and gentlemen, we have been cleared for takeoff," the pilot announced on the intercom.

The plane moved immediately into position at the end of the runway. Without a pause the engines roared to life. As they did, passengers disengaged from ongoing conversations to steal a glance through the cabin windows as the plane gathered speed. In less than three minutes, the plane was dipping over the crystal-blue Aegean as it sought the compass reading for the journey to New York. It continued to gain altitude, but by now most of the passengers had lost interest in the phenomenon of flying—returning to their glossy magazines, conversations, and thoughts.

This was Jamie's first visit to the United States. He hoped that the false passport provided by the Americans would pass the scrutiny of the authorities as it had when he was leaving Athens. His request for a visa from the embassy in Beirut was granted expeditiously. He wondered if his name had been entered on a watch list. By the time the seat belt signs were extinguished, the curtains separating the first-class section had been pulled back from the aisle.

From his seat in the back of the aircraft, he could not know that Kalenti—even before the curtains were pulled—had struck up a serious conversation with the passenger occupying the window seat alongside him. Jamie had not gotten a glimpse of the person outside the apartment building in Athens waiting for his companion to reappear. If he had, he would have recognized him as Petrus. Had Petrus gotten a glimpse of Jamie entering or exiting the apartment building that night—but he had not—he would have recognized him as the one who might have been responsible for his companion's murder.

⁂

The 747 touched down in New York's John F. Kennedy International Airport at 5:37 p.m., local time. Kalenti was waiting for Jamie to rejoin him at the end of the ramp leading to the terminal. Unbeknownst to Jamie, Kalenti's seatmate had walked on ahead.

"How was your flight?" Kalenti asked, more refreshed than Jamie felt.

"Oh, it was fine. I slept a bit." He felt sluggish as he walked behind Kalenti up the ramp; his rubber-soled shoes seemed to stick to the thick red carpet. To his relief, he cleared passport control without delay. He guessed that when his document was passed over a roll-top camera mounted into the base of the examiner's desk, the information was fed to a central data base. By the time he reached customs, he would know if his passport had been flagged.

In fact, the passport should have been flagged, but Frost had failed to forward the required data to Headquarters for inclusion on the watch list. That might have resulted in Jamie being pulled from the line. Instead the computer completed its search of the data in his passport in microseconds and he was cleared immediately.

"Here are my claim tickets. Both are large and dark blue in color. I'll meet you over there." Kalenti pointed to a column in the middle of the baggage area.

Jamie pulled both bags off the conveyor belt after watching a hundred bags pass. He had with him only a carry-on bag. He pulled the bags to Kalenti, and they both headed for the customs area.

"You can proceed directly. I will meet you once I have cleared the inspection." Kalenti pointed again where they would meet.

Jamie was waiting for Kalenti when he approached, pulling the bags with difficulty—though they had wheels.

"Here, let me take them." Jamie put his own bag on top and pulled both suitcases easily.

"Follow me," Kalenti said, striding confidently through the mayhem of the terminal.

Jamie felt like one of those Eastern European refugees who succeeded in reaching the West, trudging along following directions as the mass of humanity swirled around him. It was not the crowds that disoriented him but the realization that he had succeeded in reaching America finally. He pushed thoughts of Brigid from his mind.

"Once we get settled, you will have time to do some shopping," Kalenti said as he increased his pace. He welcomed the news, as he was anxious to get something for Brigid.

"Reminds me of Bombay," Jamie said.

"Bombay?" Kalenti did not slow his pace, nor did he look around.

"Yes, the stench." Kalenti tilted his head in disbelief at the observation.

"Only there, the stench was caused by the sweet smell from burning dung." Kalenti seemed to pinch his nostrils tight.

"Here it is stale tobacco, disinfectant, perfume, and cotton candy mingled to create the odor of a metropolis and over-used public toilets."

"Please, Mr. Jamie, can we change the subject?"

Jamie remained silent. Everything looked worn, including the people whose faces were ragged under the strain of life in the city. The women wore too much makeup and had a plastic, stiff look about them. New York was not what he expected, but he checked himself. After all, this was the airport at its peak travel time.

Outside in the dim artificial light, Jamie found no relief. The exhaust fumes from thousands of cars and buses that passed the terminal entrance each hour lingered in clouds, drifting among the arriving and departing passengers. The din of the police whistles, the squeal of brakes being applied suddenly, and the acceleration of cars and motorcycles proved deafening. Instinctively, he cupped his free hand to his ear. Fatigue coupled with the invasion of his senses by the sounds, smells, and sights contributed to a rising irritation he found difficult to control. He continued to follow Kalenti's lead. The latter had hardly spoken a word since they deplaned.

"St. Regis Hotel," Kalenti informed the dispatcher when it came their turn on the winding line at the taxi stand.

"After you," he gestured to Jamie, who slid across the rear seat of the taxi.

"Quite a nice hotel," Kalenti observed when they were both seated and the taxi moved slowly from the curb. "My wife and I stayed there during her first visit to New York after we married," he said with nostalgia.

"My first trip here," Jamie said, almost as if to excuse his childlike excitement as he took in all the sights.

Kalenti tried to give directions to the Ethiopian taxi driver, who feigned a loss of hearing and would not acknowledge the assistance offered. Jamie decided that Kalenti was either interested in demonstrating his superior knowledge of the area or wanted to put the driver on notice that he would not countenance any deviation from the direct route into the city for the purpose of running up the meter.

"It even reminds me of Beirut," Jamie mentioned. He was referring to the cars on the roadside, the filth that littered the roadway, the crude hand-painted signs that filled every available empty place on walls and fences, and the tattered, and sometimes abandoned, buildings.

"In fact, there are sections of Beirut that are in better condition despite the civil war."

"Don't be too hasty," Kalenti advised.

As they reached the east side of the city, Jamie became less anxious about his decision to seek asylum in America. Wealth and prosperity were evident in the stretch limousines, the multinational logos that adorned the entrances of the skyscrapers, and the enormous construction projects underway around the clock under floodlights.

As they pulled up in front of the hotel, a doorman dressed in an elegant, tailored, long coat opened Kalenti's door as he reached to pay the driver. A luggage man pulled a dolly to the taxi's trunk. Kalenti, followed by Jamie, entered the narrow revolving door into the lobby.

"I am Kalenti," he announced as if he were a visiting governor.

"Yes, Mr. Kalenti, your rooms are ready. Please fill out the check-in." Jamie lingered back. The sign-in completed, Kalenti reached around to give Jamie his key.

"Make note that I am staying in room 808. You are in 321."

"Yes, sir." Jamie found it odd that they were not on the same floor. What he didn't know was that Petrus was holding a reservation for the connecting room to Kalenti's and had just pulled up in a taxi from the airport.

"I will meet you in the lobby in two hours." Kalenti instructed, "Check your watch."

"Yes, sir." Jamie hoped that they would dine at that time.

Ganymede

While Kalenti probably fared better in first class, his meal had the taste of the plastic plates on which it was perched.

☥*☥*☥

Two hours later, Kalenti led the way to the restaurant just off the lobby.

"I am sure you will enjoy the cuisine," Kalenti said as they took their seats and were served menus. The conversation at the table was limited. Kalenti seemed distracted.

"Tomorrow I have some personal matters to attend and I will not be needing you. You are free to explore the city, since this is your first visit." Kalenti paused. "Be assured that you will be fully occupied later in our stay."

"That's fine." Jamie wondered why this sudden act of generosity. In Beirut, he was recruited to be a bodyguard and days later was granted the privileges and rewards of a good and faithful servant—privileges and rewards that he had not earned. Something was not right. Perhaps his luck was changing with an assist from a friendly god or a rewarding benefactor because he guided a vehicle through Beirut with a dead man riding in the front seat. He smiled as he thought about the icon that he had mailed to Brigid.

After dinner they bid each other good night and Jamie returned to his room. He turned on television. It held his attention for about an hour before the jet lag hit him like a heavy ache in his shoulders and neck. Though only ten o'clock, he realized that it was three in the morning Europe time. Tomorrow would be soon enough to call his American friends. He would also call the Libyans. They might even be more generous. He turned off the bed lamp and fell immediately into a sound sleep.

☥*☥*☥

Jamie woke with a start seven hours later. He was certain that he had overslept, but for what? Kalenti had given no hour to meet for breakfast, if they were to meet at all. He tossed his feet over the side of the bed onto the thick carpeted floor and padded his way to the window. His bare knee brushed against the hot radiator. He was in one of the last rooms that had yet to be renovated. He pulled aside the heavy drapes and gazed through the thick gauze into a gray hazy light that confirmed for him it was after dawn, but how long after he couldn't estimate. Not trusting his watch, he called the front desk and learned that it was 7:20. Relieved, he got back onto the bed and stretched flat on his back, gazing at the ceiling.

He wondered if his days of receiving funds from the Americans were coming to an end. He had not had contact with them since departing Athens, and that seemed ages ago. And here the best he could manage was to accompany a wealthy Lebanese businessman to the States. He expected that the Americans would not be much interested in the travels of an ally. If he were not careful, the Libyans might be similarly disinterested and might be even more frugal. He decided that he had to exaggerate Kalenti's importance with both parties.

He felt naked without a weapon. It was like reaching for a wallet in a crowd and discovering the bulge was missing. Now he had nothing but his wits to serve him in the presence of danger. When they met, he would raise the matter with Kalenti. But his first order of business was to contact the Americans. Right now he needed them more than they realized if Brigid and he were to realize their goal for resettlement in the States. He would have to refrain from revealing his growing dependence upon them.

CHAPTER TWENTY-NINE

"Here's an interesting flight." It was the same day in New York. An FBI computer analyst, a member of the task force established to track the arrival of passengers from Paris, was in the process of entering the flight manifests received from the French authorities. "The passengers are all Lebanese."

Stacy looked up from the stack of manifests that she was scanning after entry into the computer system. At the invitation of the task force leader, she had joined the group two days earlier.

"What are they doing here?" she asked.

"Attending an International Red Cross conference on war refugees in Washington from January 30 to 31." He read from a page in a black loose-leaf notebook at his side.

"Seems reasonable," Stacy uttered, still continuing to review the manifests.

"One of them missed the flight."

"What?" she questioned.

"It seems one of them missed the flight. The French flight manifest does not match our INS list at JFK."

"What's her name?"

"No, it's a him—Jon Boustani, traveling on Lebanese passport Z26789, issued January 1987 in Beirut."

"How old is he?"

"Don't have that information."

"Oh, well. He won't be the only one to miss a flight from Paris." Stacy returned to the stack of manifests. The work was tedious and required concentration. The reason was that the only guidance she received from Kay was "See if you can spot an anomaly"!

Fifteen minutes passed. Her FBI colleague had processed several other manifests in silence, while she scanned several with another word. It struck her that she could be here for days without more activity than moving her eyes down the faint print of the computer runoff or interrupting her boredom by walking down the hall to the canteen for another cup of coffee. Kay's words of advice returned to her.

"What is unusual?" she asked aloud, startling the analyst next to her. Kay could be as disconcerting. This time she wondered quietly about the chap missing the flight.

"Did Jon Boustani make it here on another flight?" she asked.

"Who?"

"Jon Boustani—the fellow who missed the flight."

"Oh, him. I guess so. Let's see." He entered the name into the terminal.

"Nope, it doesn't appear so. That was a charter flight, and he may not have had any other option than to buy another ticket," he said after checking alternate spellings through the central locator file.

⸸⁎⸸⁎⸸

"I want to show you something that Stacy has come up with," Kay said to Colin the next day. It was the information about the charter from Paris.

"See, a Jon Boustani misses the flight and apparently doesn't buy a ticket to continue his journey."

"Interesting, but not sure it's a big deal if one person doesn't make a charter," Colin said as he completed reading the two-page cable Stacy had sent from the FBI office in New York.

"Colin, it might not be the big deal we are looking for, but it could be a minor slipup."

Kay was losing her patience with him and was beginning to think that he should be one of those officers whose name she should forget. She reached for a cigarette, not for nicotine but to help her control a flash of frustration. She looked across at Colin and sensed that he regretted his flip comment.

"Read the report to the end. Stacy learned that this Jon Boustani did not have hotel reservations in Washington, nor had his name been submitted to attend the conference."

"What happened to him; where is he?"

"Don't know." She put down the cigarette and took up her granny-sized glasses and read aloud from Stacy's report.

> *Boustani's name does not appear on any ongoing flight to the United States or Canada as of this date.*

"What about elsewhere? Suppose he traveled within Europe somewhere. Say he missed the flight from Paris and elected to catch something out of Brussels. Has she tried that?" Colin asked.

"How would we do that? We are not sitting in Paris.'"

"What about an international reservation system—a few are US owned?"

"Great idea! Never thought of it. You're not as bad as I was beginning to think."

Kay picked up the phone and called Stacy in New York. While she was dialing, Colin wrote the name of the reservation system and passed the note to Kay.

"Hi, Stacy. Colin and I have been talking about your friend Boustani. Have you thought of tracking his travel through a reservation system?

"Well, Colin knows one called SABRE. He thinks it is owned

and operated by American Airlines. There may be others. It has a European operation as well.

"Yeah, SABRE. S-A-B-R-E.

"Exactly. Also, don't forget the European system. I don't know how you would get access." Kay saw that Colin wanted to speak. She gave the phone to him.

"Stacy, we once had an agent—he may still be registered—who helped us monitor the travel of Soviets using the European system. We'll try to track it from here." Kay took the phone back.

"Stacy, if the European system proves necessary, I'm sure there is someone up there who is a frustrated hacker. No one would be the wiser. Call us when you have something." Kay replaced the phone on the cradle.

"Smart girl. She catches on fast."

"Are you surprised?" Kay did not approve of the expression *smart girl*.

"You need somewhere to call home."

Kay led him to a small interior room that adjoined her office. The room had served as a vault for an ultrasensitive operation in which she was involved. The steel door was held open by a chair on which Kay had piled several files. The inside latch of the tumbler combination lock was visible.

"We ran a successful operation from here to spirit a Soviet and his family from Latvia before settling them on the West Coast. But like any good bureaucrat, I held onto this precious space."

"Colin, this isn't your retirement office—it's only temporary," she said with a mischievous smile.

"How unkind," he returned. "Who is expected to move the paper out, or should I leave it in place to smother the sound of my screams of frustration?" Kay had already left the room.

⟰*⟰*⟰

At seven a.m., Jamie left the hotel in the sweat suit and track shoes issued in Libya. Though he needed exercise, he also wanted to be sure to spot—in the unlikely event—anyone assigned to follow him. He rushed through the ornate lobby and disappeared through the revolving door and around the corner onto Fifth Avenue before Petrus, who was sitting in the lobby, was able to react.

Petrus was not overly concerned. Kalenti had assigned him to the lobby only as an afterthought, since he did not believe that his young Spaniard would wander too far afield—that is, if he expected to receive his salary.

Jamie ran steadily north on Fifth Avenue, staying close to the expansive windows of the luxury shops that lined both sides of the avenue. He was satisfied that he would notice someone in pursuit—especially if he were in street clothes. There were few pedestrians on the street. The sun had not yet risen high enough to be seen through the side street heading east. It took him only five minutes to reach Central Park. He selected the path on the right because it appeared brighter in the glow of dawn. He continued for almost a mile, passing a series of low buildings on his right. Satisfied that he was alone, he exited the park and found himself back on Fifth Avenue.

He ran cross-town until he reached Third Avenue. More people were on the street now. He turned south and slowed to a walk, winded. The saliva in his mouth was thick; he had not exercised since his training in Libya. He reached the massive foundation of a skyscraper—Grand Central Station—and decided to enter. He would make his phone calls from within. The flow of pedestrians disgorging from the station at this time was heavier still and reminded him of the main train stations in Europe. He relaxed his grip on two rolls of quarters he had been holding.

"Halo. Well, finally there is someone to talk to," he said. He had decided to call the Americans first.

"Yes, I am in New York. I am staying at the St. Regis Hotel. Room 321. Repeat 321.

"Yes, I am in my own room. I am accompanying a wealthy Lebanese who needs my assistance."

"I don't know when I'll be free. Good, call me after midnight."

As soon as he hung up he was sorry that he did not make more of this trip to the States. Unless he was more convincing, they might conclude that he was not worth the trouble or expense of seeing him. Worse, they might decide not to deposit the money they owed him. He must do his best to raise their expectations.

He walked around the interior of the station, looking for a telephone directory that had not been mutilated. When he found one, he searched and found the number for the Libyan delegation to the United Nations. He memorized the number. He wanted no incriminating evidence on him. He walked to the opposite side of the cavernous marble palace and selected a phone booth. He deposited a coin and dialed the number, covering the mouthpiece with his glove to alter his voice. *No sense making it easy for the telephone monitors.*

"Hello, this is Ben Yousef's friend. I cannot talk long, so please check with Tripoli. They know me. I will call again." He hung up, hoping that they had recorded the message—not trusting to the English competence of the duty officer. The brevity of the call would also thwart the police from tracing its origin. He was taking no chances.

Jamie had been correct. The FBI operated a real-time intercept capability at the local telephone exchange for calls to and from the Libyan establishment. Though the agent intercepting the call did not have sufficient time to identify the caller's location, he was able to record the message. Later, it would be analyzed to determine the caller's country of origin and whether the message, as brief as it was, matched the speech pattern of any previous caller. At a minimum, traces would be run on the name mentioned by the caller.

Jamie strolled out of the building and walked north for a block before he resumed a steady pace alongside the curb—dodging the tidal wave of people rushing in all directions. *They wear angry glances created*, he thought, *by the brick, steel, and cement that surrounds them*. Though looking lost, he observed them making good time, but to where? He returned to the hotel, passing Petrus, who was slouched in one of the only chairs in the lobby. As Jamie disappeared into the elevator, Petrus looked at his watch and noted the time in a notebook.

⁘

The FBI Command Center in New York equaled the premier facility maintained at FBI Headquarters in Washington and far exceeded the CIA and Department of State's facilities in state-of-the-art technology. At the time, it was an expensive investment for the FBI. The modernization program was the brainchild of an FBI veteran who was known for the blue-sky technology visions he entertained. Usually he succeeded in being transferred before he could be held accountable. However, this time the program—surprisingly—was a great success.

Stacy was accepted as a full member of the twenty-person task force and was assigned to a cubicle where she had access to the full range of communications and databases available. With the exception of an occasional appearance of a Department of State representative from the UN delegation, Stacy was the only non-FBI official with full access privileges. She adjusted to the systems available and soon was manipulating the archival retrieval system easily.

The Special Agent in Charge (SAIC) in the FBI's Tulsa office established contact with the American Airlines official responsible for overseeing the SABRE reservation system, and he established a link that Stacy was able to access. On the premise that Jon Boustani had continued his journey under the same name, Stacy entered into the system all possible variations of *Boustani*. She had no luck. This confirmed her suspicion that charter flights have no use for SABRE. Only when a bloc of seats on a charter becomes available does SABRE enter pertinent reservation information.

Stacy was not to be discouraged. She then approached the problem of finding Boustani by entering every city in Europe that offered flights to the United States. Again, no name close to *Boustani* arose. She expanded her search now to cities in Canada, Mexico, and the Caribbean—still nothing. Entering variations into the system, she looked like a chess player competing against the clock. *If Boustani did not have another travel document, what would he have done?* she pondered. If he missed the flight—in mid-thought, she concluded the SABRE would not help her locate Boustani. She needed access to another system. She would not give up.

"I need some help here," she said to the senior watch-stander. "Do you have someone who can work this system to locate this fellow on a European flight?"

"I believe we do. I'll see if we can get him down here."

Thirty minutes later, a medium-sized, dark-haired, youthful-looking individual, with reading glasses balanced carefully above his forehead, took a seat at a neighboring terminal. With one hand he pulled the glasses onto the bridge of his nose.

"I hear you do not believe that the SABRE system will provide the information you need." He logged onto the terminal.

"That's right." Stacy looked at the identification badge that he had clipped to the lapel of his tweed sports coat. He was not a government official but a contractor and had a slight accent of undetermined origin. Stacy noted he was granted full access to the most sensitive areas within the FBI Headquarters building.

The gentleman said nothing more to her but made a few telephone calls between periods of intense study. After an hour he let out a laugh. On the screen before him was the European equivalent to SABRE. Stacy learned from a task-force team member that he was a computer genius who was supporting the FBI's technological revolution.

"Let's see what we have," he said, inviting Stacy to sit next to him. "J-O-N Boustani," he typed. Immediately on the screen appeared a list of from ten to fifteen names. One of them was Jon Boustani. From the information on the screen they learned that Boustani had returned to Beirut the next day on MEA flight 691 from Paris.

"So here we have someone scheduled to fly to the States on a cut-rate charter flight, misses the flight, and returns to Beirut on a full-fare ticket," Stacy observed.

The man, who had not introduced himself, rose from the chair, flipped his glasses back onto his head, and departed without a word. Stacy decided that he sought and solved technical challenges and was not interested in currying favor or in engaging in light conversation.

⁌*⁌*⁌

The computer genius was David Haddad. It was only with enormous effort that Kuban's son was able to control the cold steel fear that gripped him as he searched for Jon Boustani in the international airline reservation system. Working in the command center he became aware of the reported terrorist threat. He had not given it much thought—not the first time that a terrorist threat emanated from the Middle East. He was struck speechless when a Lebanese Christian became the subject of interest to the task force monitoring the threat.

What if...? He could not finish the question. His best efforts at locating his father in one of the New York hotels had not succeeded. From Beirut he learned that his father had not returned from his trip. The FBI was trying to locate a Christian Lebanese in connection with a possible terrorist action reported by the French. Without Stacy's knowledge, he had also ran traces on his father and had to conclude that his father had not left the States. His gloomy disposition reflected a genuine apprehension that somehow his father was involved. He was at a loss to say what he could do for his father—if he was involved—for himself, or for his family. Instead he closed the door to the command center and returned to the computer laboratory he maintained.

⚜ ⚜

"Kay, Boustani returned to Beirut the next day on an MEA flight," Stacy reported over a secure line.

"Yes, I thought so," Stacy agreed. "Yes, it was a full-fare one-way ticket, paid from Beirut."

"No, there is no way to check that. He simply reported to the MEA counter and they issued the prepaid ticket." Stacy's voice sounded the excitement she was feeling.

"Also, could you send a cable to the station in Paris and ask them to contact the French for Boustani's photo. It should be available from the French passport control office at De Gaulle.

"Thanks, Kay, for your encouragement. I'll be here if you need me." Stacy hung up just as the shift supervisor was walking by.

"Hi, just want to let you know I got the agency to send a cable to the station in Paris, requesting Boustani's photo."

He rolled his eyes. "I've already sent a message to our Legal Attaché in Paris for the same."

"Oh, I'm sorry. Let the French decide what to do." Stacy was beginning to experience the bureaucratic turf battles that often clouded issues and interfered with operational needs.

CHAPTER THIRTY

Later that day, Kay fingered the photograph that they had just received from Paris. She was amazed at the service; it had been transmitted electronically. Not so many years ago, she would have waited a week to receive a pouch from abroad. She gazed at Boustani's photo—fat round face, eyes looking off to the side, high forehead, light brown hair cut short, parted on the right side, and a close-trimmed beard.

Strange that someone would make all the arrangements to travel to the States, miss the flight, and then return immediately home. Maybe he got sick. But you'd think that if he was sick enough to cancel the trip, he would wait until he recovered before returning.

She paused and wondered with whom he was traveling. Her eyes brightened as she reached for the phone to call Stacy.

"Stacy, it's Kay. I have the photograph.

"Good, glad they sent a photo to each of us.

"Can you arrange to have your cell mates run a quick check with the organizers of the conference to see if anyone recognizes Boustani?

"Good. Also, why not ask that they review the flight manifest to see if there are others on the charter not registered to attend?

"Those that don't check out, we might want to ask the French for photos. Also, I am not sending a message, so make sure your guys know it is up to them to draft the message to Paris. That's all I have. Stay busy." Kay laughed at Stacy's reply.

An hour later the phone rang on Kay's desk. "Hello?" She covered the phone and informed Colin that it was Stacy again. Kay was silent for most of the brief call.

"Stacy is good. She decided on her own that if a terrorist operation was planned for here it might involve a high level government official to increase its impact." Colin nodded agreement.

"So she voiced her concern. It generated sufficient enthusiasm among her listeners. A check was initiated of the calendars of the president, vice president, and cabinet officials."

"What time frame did they use?"

"She credits an FBI analyst with suggesting the time immediately before and after the Red Cross conference—since the charter was booked for return passage to Europe."

"Good thinking."

"For the next two weeks the schedule is light for New York. The president is supposed to give a speech at the Press Club on January 29, and the secretary of state is scheduled to be at the Harvard Club on the thirtieth."

"What's the secretary doing there?"

"It's the five-year gathering of an alumni group that was founded by the Harvard class of 1927 to commemorate some obscure event." Kay read from some notes she had jotted down. "They use the occasion to take stock of their successes. You may recall that the secretary, as he prefers to be called, graduated from Harvard and has been one of the club's active supporters since graduation. He hasn't missed the event—ever; so says Stacy."

"Wonderful. Who says we don't have an aristocracy here?" Colin asked.

"I didn't." Kay graduated from what was then American International College, an agricultural college in Amherst, Massachusetts. She knew about aristocracies.

"I presume we can get both to offer regrets," Colin said.

Kay laughed. "Silly boy! It won't be so easy with these politicians. Mark my word. Such innocence." She smiled at Colin. "And let me add that Brody would unlikely be willing to raise the cancellations with his National Security counterpart," she offered. "He is politically astute enough to know that the president's conservative political advisors don't like to interfere with schedules as they plan the next election."

☩*☩*☩

It was past midnight. Jamie had still not adjusted to Eastern Standard Time. He sat before the television, waiting for a phone call from the Americans. He feared that they had decided to sever contact with him, and with that fear, a momentary chill and flash of anger rushed up the back of his neck. The chill lingered, but the anger dissipated into a feeling of frustration and despair.

How can I get Brigid to the United States? What could I do for a livelihood? He felt helpless without the Americans. The television flickered on—his eyes glazed in self-pity as he recalled how he saved the American in Athens. *Don't those bastards realize what I've been doing?*

The telephone rang at that moment. It startled him, and for a moment he did not realize where he was—so deep had he slipped within the web of his anxieties. He picked up the phone.

"Halo." His voice sounded louder in the hum of silence that engulfed him. He pressed the instrument to his ear. Colin was on the other end of the line.

"Yes, I recognize your voice. Where are you?"

"Here? What are you doing here?"

"As I've been looking for you," Jamie countered. "I'm accompanying the Lebanese fellow I mentioned. He's staying on another floor."

He hoped that he could convince the Americans to honor their commitment even if his present duties were far afield of the Libyan target.

"Let me write it down—outside I walk to the right, turn right after a couple of blocks and left after a couple of blocks more?"

"When will I see you?"

"When I'm clean?"

"Yes, when you know no one is following me. Good, I am anxious to meet. I'll be downstairs in five minutes."

"Okay, fifteen minutes. Till then," Jamie repeated.

Thirty minutes later at the corner of Fifty-Ninth Street and Park Avenue, Colin approached Jamie and they shook hands.

"It's been a long time, my friend." Colin was the first to speak. "Tell me what you have been doing since we last met."

Jamie recounted his trip to the Libyan consulate in Milan, his success in getting a visa, his flight to Tripoli and being escorted upon arrival to the training camp, and his meeting with Ben Yousef.

"Tell me more about Ben Yousef," Colin asked. Jamie spoke uninterrupted for fifteen minutes as they walked the streets. Jamie provided a physical description and general impressions that matched what Colin knew about him. He described what Ben Yousef wanted him to do in Beirut.

"Basically, he wanted me to uncover any indications that the Christians in East Beirut were planning some sort of action to embarrass Qadafi—something that Qadafi feared."

"Who did they want you to meet and where?"

"He told me about a hangout—the Bacchus Restaurant—and the fact that one of them, Kalenti, was an icon expert."

"A what?" Colin was more familiar with the term weapons expert than icon expert.

"Icons—you know drawings of saints on wood?"

"Oh, yes, I understand."

"Well, you are fortunate that I know something about icons. I found the place, met this guy Kalenti, and before I knew it was being offered the assignment to protect Kalenti on his business trip to America."

He did not mention the ambush from which they escaped,

nor did he mention the veiled warning he received from Ben Yousef about a friend who was sent on a similar mission and had disappeared.

"So what are you doing here?"

"I only just arrived." Jamie sounded defensive. "I'm sure you'll be satisfied, but I don't know anything yet. I only just arrived," he repeated.

"That's okay. All is well." Colin reached into his pocket and produced an index card.

"Here are in telephone contact numbers. Before you get back to the hotel, commit them to memory and destroy the card."

"Next, I want you to see this." Colin walked beneath a streetlight and opened a bankbook and allowed him to examine it. It was assigned to Jamie Casasnovas and confirmed the agreed-upon deposit as recorded in the account dating back to their meeting in Athens, plus a fifteen thousand dollar deposit for his first interviews in Sofia.

"I am thankful," he said, not able to suppress a smile. He returned the book to Colin.

"Well, my friend, it is time for you to return to the hotel. I will see you soon."

They parted at Thirty-Eighth Street. Jamie reversed his directions to the hotel. His pace quickened with the relief he felt renewing contact with the Americans. He was also satisfied that he described his association with Kalenti as being more important than he judged it to be. The American seemed to accept it. He was surprised that the American was not more inquisitive. When he reached the lobby of the hotel, it was two thirty in the morning.

I*I*I

As Kay had expected, David Brody was not convinced. When Kay and Colin met with him late in the afternoon, a day after reestablishing contact with ICARUS, he resisted taking any action on their newly formulated hypothesis—namely, that a group of Lebanese Christians was behind the current scare. Brody came close to ordering them from his office when they suggested that the Christians might be involved in the abduction of the ambassador.

"What are you two smoking?" He was incredulous.

"Why do you judge that only the bad guys, like the Palestinians, are allowed to be desperate? Why can't the Lebanese Christians be just as desperate?" Kay reasoned.

"If we'd appreciate what has happened in Lebanon in ten years of civil war, I think we would all agree that they have sufficient reason to strike out." Kay pressed her argument.

"Did you know," Kay continued, undaunted, "that in 1975 the Lebanese pound was valued at three to one US dollar? Now you need four hundred to buy one US dollar. Some change, huh?"

Brody was trying to ignore her by scanning papers on his desk.

"How would you feel? What would you do if you saw your savings or pension evaporate overnight and with no sign that things would improve?"

Brody was intransigent.

"And that's just the economics of the tragedy. What about the internecine killing? What about the two hundred thousand armed Palestinians within Lebanon's borders, or the ten thousand Syrians soldiers? And have you considered the Qadafi supporters?"

Kay was relentless. Almost without a breath she continued. "And of course there are the Hezbollah loyalists. Did you know there are even mercenaries from Bangladesh of all places to join the fight?"

Brody was beginning to become restless. He could not continue to shuffle or stare at the papers indefinitely.

"And what about the war-weary Lebanese? The war-weary Lebanese," she repeated, "who if every man and woman able to wield a weapon, they could not meet the threat posed? What about the moral breakdown where former tomato growers are turning to the cultivation of crops from which drugs are derived and later smuggled into Europe? Does nothing touch you?" Kay sounded exasperated.

"Kay ..." Brody looked up, but Kay continued.

"Instead of questioning whether the Christians could be responsible, you should ask what took them so long."

Brody was unable to look directly at Kay. She seemed determined to remain in place. Colin fidgeted uncomfortably in his chair. Just then Stacy entered with an envelope.

"I thought you'd like to see this," she said as she gave the envelope to Kay, who opened it and scanned its contents and passed it to Colin. It was the passenger manifest for the charter flight from Paris. Alongside the names of eleven individuals appeared an X.

"Those marked are not scheduled to attend the conference," Stacy explained.

"It seems that to make ends meet, or to earn money on the side, the organizers of the flight sold off the vacant seats to individuals not associated with the relief initiative."

"Are they scheduled to return on the same flight?" Colin asked as he passed the document to Brody.

"Three of them are," Stacy replied.

"Can we get photos for all of them?" Kay asked.

"At my suggestion, the FBI has already requested the same from the French. We should receive them by tomorrow."

"Okay, okay," Brody broke in. "I will see the director this afternoon and explain your concerns." He emphasized *your* as he looked directly at Kay.

"With his blessing, I will go over to the White House." He meant the Old Executive Office Building where his National Security Council contact—an army major on detail—had his office. "And see if I can influence a change in the president's schedule."

"Don't forget the secretary of state," Kay added.

"Yes, yes. Let me get back to work. There are other demands calling for my attention."

Brody did not mask his irritation at being pushed into taking some action. Colin and Stacy, followed by Kay, walked out of the office.

⚓*⚓*⚓

A lone figure was braced at the bow of the cutter as it plied through the rolling seas ten miles off the Lebanese coast under a gray late-afternoon sky. He felt the penetrating chill when the spray glanced across his face. The drone of the powerful engines created in him a mood of introspection. His eyes scanned the bleak horizon—broken at times by a solitary seagull intent on reaching its destination before dark.

The Israeli patrol boat was returning to its port of Haifa at half-throttle. Aided by a sophisticated sensor and radar technology, the cutter played a role in an elaborate electronic screen that protected the Israeli coast. And yet even this was not enough to prevent the infiltration by a determined Palestinian demonstrating the same ingenuity that others displayed fleeing from East to West Berlin.

Off to the right a low-flying crane caught the lookout's attention. In the fading light, it seemed to be making no progress. The swollen seas obscured the bird from view.

"Sol, what would a crane be doing here, and in January, no less?"

He talked through cold-stiff lips into the handheld communication set to the bridge—pointing at the same time in the direction of an unidentified object. The cutter wheeled about in a large arc at three-quarters speed and then full throttle. The young Israeli held onto the bow and gripped tightly the lanyard as well, regretting that he had sounded the alert before he made his way back to the cabin.

In seconds the vessel had closed the distance and determined that before them was a motor launch adrift. The Israeli would take no chances that there were a few Palestinians pressed to the floor of the launch waiting for the Israelis to get within range. By now six Israelis armed with assault rifles and wearing body armor were in position on the deck of the cutter—their weapons leveled on the launch. Several high-speed passes around the launch in ever tighter concentric circles created such turbulence that the launch nearly flipped over, but in the process of the maneuver it was clear to all that no one was on the launch. The Israeli captain down throttled. A line was fastened to the launch before the cutter resumed its journey to Haifa—arriving before dark and before a second larger cutter moved out to take its station off Lebanon's coast.

⁂

That afternoon another immediate cable arrived at Headquarters. It was from the Station in Tel Aviv.

1. *Israeli Coastal Defense Forces discovered an unmanned motor launch several miles off the coast of Lebanon. The launch had been abandoned and was found drifting southward toward Israel when it was intercepted. There was no sign of any other boats in the area.*
2. *Israelis speculate that those who occupied the launch were somehow connected to the kidnapping of US ambassador. The same Hezbollah literature found at the scene of abduction was strewn in the boat.*
3. *Israeli forensics team was unable to discover any additional clues.*
4. *We believe that the launch was used to transport ambassador to a larger vessel waiting outside Lebanon's territorial waters. This might explain how ambassador was taken in area controlled by Christians and then spirited out to sea.*

"A bold plan," Kay said after reading the message. "There is just no way to tell where they are holding him." Her lips tightened. "Maybe I shouldn't have pushed Brody so hard to do something on the theory that Christians are involved. It looks like Hezbollah was involved. Oh well, who said intelligence analysis is supposed to be an exact science or free from error?" Colin and Stacy said nothing.

CHAPTER THIRTY-ONE

FBI investigators had fanned out among the conference delegates in Washington with photographs of the eleven individuals who were on the charter flight but were not scheduled to attend the conference. Information gathered on five of the eleven cleared them from suspicion. However, the bureau was only able to gather minimal information on the remaining six. One of the six, Jon Boustani, had not made the flight, and no one interviewed could identify him.

One of the FBI interviewers arranged to meet with Mrs. Salwa Adib, a resident of Greenwich Village section of lower Manhattan in New York City. Her thick gray eyebrows framed deep penetrating eyes and reached almost up to her short gray hair. She was in her eighties yet was still active in philanthropic events. If it had not been for the sudden death of her husband of sixty years while they were visiting family in Paris, she would have made a presentation at the conference.

"My condolences on the death of your husband," the special agent said as soon as he was seated in the large living room filled with museum-quality artifacts from some forgotten age. Persian rugs overlapped on the hardwood floor of the apartment in a building constructed almost a century earlier.

"Thank you, young man. What can I do for you?" Mrs. Adib was all business.

"You were on the charter flight, Mrs. Adib, out of Paris?"

She nodded.

"Can I show you some photographs of those we are trying to identify?"

"Of course." She took the offered photos and studied each one carefully.

"Here, I know this young lady. She sat next to me during the flight. Her name is Michelle, and we talked endlessly— charming young lady."

"Anything more you can add?"

"Well, I didn't trust her."

"Mrs. Adib?"

"Yes, I didn't trust her. According to her account, she had been selected in Beirut months ago to attend the conference and had received her seating at that time. I didn't challenge her, even though I knew she was lying."

"Lying, Mrs. Adib?"

"Yes, lying. You see, young man, the sudden death of my husband forced me to cancel his seat just a week ago. His seat was to be alongside me. So I believed little of what she said, including that she would call when she was traveling through New York back to Beirut."

"Why do you say that?" he asked looking up from his note pad.

"Because all her questions were about New York. How one gets around—where do the Lebanese live—questions like that."

"That doesn't seem unusual to me; after all, you live in New York, not Washington."

"Young man," her eyebrows arched and touched her hairline, "if she was so interested in New York because I live here, why didn't she ask me where I lived?" Her voice croaked with age.

"Here a destitute Lebanese girl meets a not-so-destitute widow ..." she paused, twisting her antique silver wedding ring in the lamplight. The agent looked around the room and noticed for the first time that it seemed that it was a storehouse of oil paintings and objects d'art. She did not have to finish the sentence. Her point had been made. He closed his notebook.

⁂

"Well, here we go again," Kay said as she appeared abruptly at Colin's desk in the vault. "Read this from the FBI in New York." It was the report from the interview with Mrs. Adib.

"What do you think?" Colin asked after reading the one-page memorandum slowly.

"The question is whether we have enough here to speculate that the Lebanese missing from the charter could be involved in planning an incident in the United States and, if so, could the venue be New York?" Kay wondered.

"And how does this track with what the Israelis reported about the launch and speculation about its purpose?" Colin added. "Or is it possible that the abduction and whatever else we are picking up on are not connected?"

"I think we must keep the two separate and focus for the moment on whether something is planned for New York."

"Agreed. So what do we do?" Colin leaned back in his chair and looked up into the steel ceiling of the vault.

"Have we received traces on the six travelers from Beirut and Larnaca, Cyprus?"

"We just got something in from Larnaca—basically the information that appeared on their visa applications. Stacy is checking the information with our files.

"Nothing from Beirut. I don't expect much there. Two embassy bombings, several evacuations of personnel, and resumption of street fighting have reduced the station to caretaker status."

"Have any of them traveled to the States previously?" Colin asked.

"Yes, I forgot to mention, Stacy is also running traces with INS to see if they have something. We discovered that Boustani—the chap who missed the flight—lived in New York three years ago. I think he was here for six months while he was attending Columbia University's School of Journalism." Kay lit up a cigarette before continuing. "And if it wasn't getting chaotic enough for you, the FBI intercepted a call from an unidentified male to the Libyan UN mission in New York. The caller did not give his name but described himself as a friend of Ben Yousef."

"What is Ben Yousef doing here?" Colin blurted out.

"No one said he was here. The caller just said that he was a friend of his," Kay corrected.

"What's the bureau going to do?"

"They all geared up to try to locate the caller when he checks in again. They have people at the telephone exchange and will remain there ready to pounce if he comes within reach. Stacy is heading back there this morning.

"They assure us that after checking Arab diplomats arriving within the last two weeks, Ben Yousef does not appear. I told Stacy to double check."

"How about asking Stacy to energize the bureau to get what they can on Boustani from the registrar at Columbia and from the landlord where he stayed?"

"My, you are alert. Should I attribute it to a caffeine high?"

"I'm afraid not. I'm just concerned that we're running out of time and haven't seen the government able to ramp up to meet the speed of events."

A louder-than-normal voice-over could be heard from a neighboring office. It announced that a US flotilla had anchored off the Lebanese coast, indicating that troop landing was not to be dismissed and might occur before Ambassador Hollingsworth's fate was determined.

"I don't like this, Kay, especially when there is a possibility of Christian involvement in the abduction."

"I'm not so sure the Christians are involved," Kay wondered aloud. The phone rang. It was Brody.

"Yes, David," Kay answered and listened.

"Great job. What about the secretary of state?' She listened.

"You're not serious?" she asked. "Okay, thanks." She hung up.

"Brody succeeded in convincing the White House to cancel the president's appearance at the Press Club, but the secretary was adamant about attending his Harvard event.

"I wouldn't be surprised if Brody did nothing to convince the president to cancel his attendance but rather learned that the event had already been rescheduled," Kay added.

"And why would he do that?"

"This man wants to look good to those around him."

"He could become dangerous," Colin suggested.

"Oh, you think so?"

"What about the secretary?"

"We see him tomorrow."

"We?"

"You and me."

⁂

Jamie was taking no chances. Though everything went well in reconnecting with the Americans, he felt a need to keep his contact active with the Libyans. Rather than call, he decided to walk directly to the Libyan mission. If, as he expected, his first call was intercepted, he wanted to avoid a second call. The consulate was located on the east side of New York. A New York City policeman stood off to the side of the entrance. Jamie, a stocking cap pulled around his ears and his rain jacket zippered high over his thick woolen sweater, opened the large brass door and entered.

As soon as he showed his passport to the receptionist, without a word he was ushered into an interior room—far from the common reception area. They were expecting him. He was left alone to thumb through an Arabic-language newspaper. He could not decipher where or when it was published. In less than five minutes Ben Yousef entered. He looked distinguished in his European-tailored suit—like someone about to present his credentials.

"My dear, Mr. Jamie." Ben Yousef took his hands and kissed him on both cheeks. "So very special to see you again."

"Ben Yousef, I didn't expect you'd be here." Jamie was flattered by the attention and pleased with his decision to keep in touch with the Libyans. Clearly, they valued him.

Ben Yousef walked him further into the inner recesses of the building—into a comfortable library setting. There they would not be disturbed.

"Tell me how you got into the employ of the Christians."

For the next hour Jamie described his introduction to the Christians. Just yesterday he was doing the same for the American. He told about the ambush and their escape and how this resulted in him being offered a position to protect Kalenti. Where possible he exaggerated his responsibilities to impress Ben Yousef. He needed money more than trust.

"Tell me more about Kalenti. Why has he traveled here? Who is he going to meet? How long will he stay? Does he plan to travel elsewhere in America?"

Rapid-fire questions for which he did not have satisfactory answers, but with each word he uttered Ben Yousef took detailed notes. Jamie had not noticed this intensity previously. When he had literally been drained of information, including answers that kindly one would describe as exaggerations, if not lies, Ben Yousef instructed him to call a special number—not assigned to the consulate—at any time if he had additional information to report.

"You must know that anyone entering this building is photographed by the Americans. Therefore, for your safe departure, we will take special precautions." He rose and led Jamie along a hallway to the pantry.

"Put this on." It was a long coat that fit over his jacket. He was

Ganymede

given a dark female wig—almost black—to wear over his blond hair. "Abdul will drive you. Follow his directions. He knows what to do. He has been trained."

"Good-bye my friend." Ben Yousef embraced him as he did upon entry.

Jamie followed the driver to the basement and as directed sat next to a woman in the rear of the diplomatic-plated vehicle. The driver drove out of the underground garage slowly. The FBI agent in the observation post at a second-story window across the street did not consider anything unusual to see two of the diplomatic wives leaving on a shopping trip together. He should have—the Libyans rarely allowed their wives to wander anywhere in the city without one of the male members of the mission accompanying. When the driver was satisfied that he was not being followed, he directed Jamie to shed his disguise and in the middle of the next block stopped the vehicle for him to exit.

By noon of that day, a lone Libyan national student, a resident in the United States for three years, entered the lobby of the St. Regis Hotel. Outside was his companion in a vehicle double-parked down the block. His objective was to identify Kalenti from the description they had received and follow him where he went—recognizing that the primary goal was not to be detected. This meant that he was to risk losing Kalenti if it appeared that he had become surveillance-conscious.

The deployment of this special surveillance capability was unusual at a time when the Libyans were facing increasing scrutiny from the US authorities. The fact that the surveillants themselves were Libyan nationals who might have attracted hostile interest in their activities made this assignment even bolder.

☾∗☾∗☾

Ben Yousef complimented himself on his good fortune. Kalenti, a sworn enemy of Libya, was in his target sights after so many years. And he owed all this to the young Spaniard who could not think past his next dollar. He hoped that he had not betrayed the importance of the Spaniard's information on Kalenti. He did not want to alert him, lest the Spaniard spend the next session renegotiating salary and benefits.

As Ben Yousef leaned back in his desk chair and closed his eyes, Kalenti was getting off the elevator in the lobby of the hotel. He strode confidently outside and entered a battered Volkswagen van parked twenty yards from the entrance. Twenty-five minutes later, the van was proceeding at moderate speed north on the Westside Highway to the Major Deegan Expressway and then continued north on its way to Mt. Kisco. Three car lengths back the two Libyans were maneuvering through the cross-town traffic—always keeping the cumbersome van in sight.

I*I*I

"Mr. Secretary," Colin was speaking, "I appreciate your determination to attend the celebration in New York—"

"Young man," the secretary interrupted, "it is not a celebration, but a quiet gathering of the clan. Private, confidential—call it *secret*, if it will make you more comfortable. Invitations have been issued, and I intend to be there."

Kay and Colin had not made any headway though they had tried for over thirty minutes to convince the secretary that he should stay close to home for the next two weeks. It was clear to both of them, however, that the secretary was not a supporter of the intelligence mission. Brody surely knew this, and that was probably why he decided to send Kay and Colin to meet with the secretary. Brody wanted to distance himself from any association with a mission-impossible scenario.

"Look," the secretary continued, "you are trying to tell me that I might be the target of a terrorist attack. What's new? That's why I have a protective detail that follows me everywhere except to the head and to bed with my wife." His voice had the pitch of authority.

"I'll tell you what's new," he continued, feeling recharged. "You are telling me not to worry about the Palestinians and Hezbollah fanatics but to turn my attention to the danger posed by our friends, the Lebanese, the Christians. Why don't you tell me to worry about the British, the French, and the Germans?"

Without drawing a breath, the secretary candidly revealed why he had such a dismal appreciation of intelligence—as a product, a process, or even a profession.

"In my younger days assigned to the Middle East, I accepted the assurances of that amorphous so-called intelligence community of competing baronies that there would be no Israeli-Egyptian conflict." He paused.

"That was in 1973, just before Yom Kippur and the carefully executed and coordinated surprise attacks of the Egyptians and Syrians upon the Israelis." He continued his lecture.

"To make matters worse, when the conflict brought the United States into a direct face-off with the Soviets, that same arrogant intelligence fiefdom had the chutzpah to claim that it had predicted the outbreak of the war—that is was the fault of senior policy makers who had not acted promptly on the intelligence."

"Balderdash!" the secretary proclaimed.

"Therefore, my dear people, I am not going to change my plans to accommodate these fanciful illusions of a Christian threat to my safety. Didn't you read the report from the Israelis that should have erased any doubts about who was responsible for Ambassador Hollingsworth's kidnapping? On board the craft was the same literature found at the scene of the abduction. What more do you need?" He did not want an answer, and none was offered.

"Look, I'm busy. The best I will do is to allow you or someone from the agency to be with my detail in New York. I also support the FBI's efforts to monitor the movement of any radical group into New York. But they would do that anyway. I wish to repeat, I am going to the reception as planned by my Harvard classmates. Good day, Miss Grady, Mr. Gordon."

He did not salute, but Kay and Colin were dismissed

as effectively. They walked silently down the corridor on the seventh floor of the State Department. It was not until they were outside—awaiting the arrival of the agency sedan for the ride back to Langley—that Colin spoke.

"Well, I guess I'll go to New York."

CHAPTER THIRTY-TWO

When Jamie returned to the hotel after his visit to the Libyan consulate, there was a message on his phone from Kalenti.

My young man, pack your bag and be ready to check out when I return later. In the meantime, arrange with the concierge for the rental of a four-door sedan on a weekly basis. The concierge has on file my credit card information and international driving license. I will return in the early evening. In the meantime, enjoy yourself.

Jamie accomplished what Kalenti directed and then spent the rest of the day in his hotel room relaxing. At five thirty in the afternoon, the room phone rang.

"Halo.

"You're back, Mr. Kalenti.

"Yes, the car is arranged." Kalenti was all business.

"Yes, I will be down in a minute."

Jamie hung up the phone. He gathered up his bag and the magazine he was reading and turned off the television. He looked around once before leaving the room.

In the lobby, Kalenti was paying for the rooms, and as he passed the concierge he took the keys to the rental car.

"We are moving into a small apartment on the East Side, a few blocks away," Kalenti mentioned as they walked together to the revolving door.

"Here are the keys."

A white sedan was double-parked on the street. Once the bags were packed in the trunk, Jamie went to the driver's side.

"Head straight ahead and make a right at First Avenue," Kalenti directed. "When we reach Forty-Third Street, turn right again. You are looking for East Forty-Third.

"You will like these accommodations. We are in view of the UN headquarters with the East River just beyond."

He did not say anything in return. He was concentrating on his drive in the city's evening rush-hour traffic. He had no idea how long they would be staying in New York, and he thought it best not to ask. At least he felt productive with his chauffeur duties, though he could not let go of the feeling that he was a pawn in a larger game.

Once Kalenti's two suitcases and his bag were unloaded, the doorman at the building directed Jamie to an open parking space.

"What do you think?" Kalenti asked as they entered the one-bedroom studio apartment.

"Sort of small," he responded.

"Don't worry. It will be fine for you. I will be staying close by." Kalenti's voice sounded paternal.

"I must run off. Let me have the car keys. Make yourself at home. Here's something for you to spend on a nice dinner. Make note of the phone number if you should be out and I will leave a message." And with that, Jamie found himself on his own again.

⁑*⁑*⁑

Early the next day, after a restless night, Jamie was out on the balcony looking over the city. From his vantage point he could only catch a glimpse of the south side of the UN building, but his view of the East River was spectacular on this clear winter morning. Barges plied their way in both directions, loaded with building material and refuse heading to destinations along the river and beyond. The phone rang. He was glad that he had left the balcony door ajar.

"I have arranged for the delivery and installation of new kitchen appliances, so remain in the apartment," Kalenti instructed.

Jamie could not understand what was wrong with the appliances in the apartment, but he did not question Kalenti.

"I'll be here." He remained in the apartment in vain waiting for a delivery that never materialized. He thought about going out to place a call to the American but decided against it.

When Kalenti returned by six in the evening he was more alive than Jamie had seen him, even when compared to the time he returned with the body of his guard slumped in the front seat of the car—like a racehorse approaching the gate.

"We will be taking a late-night supper, but first I must attend a business function to which I want you to drive me." He went into the bedroom area, showered, and changed into a business suit. By seven fifteen they were on the elevator down to retrieve the car.

On the street, Kalenti tossed Jamie the ignition key to the rental car. It was parked illegally on the street, but under the watchful eye of the stooped Irish doorman, it had not been ticketed. Kalenti got into the passenger side.

"Make a left at the corner and a right on Forty-Fifth Street," Kalenti directed. His directions were crisp, even military-like. Jamie suspected that there was more going on than driving around New York in the rush hour. For the fifteen-minute drive, Kalenti was silent.

Jamie noticed a set of tension lines around his eyes, plunging to his mouth. He found it strange that again he would not accompany Kalenti to what he guessed was a meeting of some significance. At the corner of Forty-Fourth Street and Fifth Avenue, Kalenti motioned for him to stop. The traffic light turned red just as he pulled over on the west side of Fifth Avenue.

"I'll get out here," Kalenti said in the whisper of someone in church.

"What do I do now?"

"Circle the block and park somewhere midway between First and Sixth Avenues on Forty-Fourth Street. Don't leave the car. I will find you."

"How long will you be?"

"Two hours or so." He exited the car and walked swiftly up the north side of Forty-Fourth Street.

He's a strange one, thought Jamie. The light turned green, and he started slowly trying to merge to the left to avoid a bus broken down ahead of him. However, no one in New York— especially the taxicabs—was interested in accommodating this native of Mallorca. He glanced to his right. Kalenti was no longer visible. He had probably entered one of the brownstones that lined the street. There was an opening in traffic. He gunned the engine, and with a squeal of tires and the resounding horns of speeding cars, he was in the lane he wanted.

⁌*⁌*⁌

Kalenti had walked the six steps up into the lobby of the Harvard Club. The receptionist released the lock on the glass door, and Kalenti walked up the additional two steps. He presented his membership card to the receptionist, a young Puerto Rican, who checked it carefully.

"Welcome back, Mr. Kalenti. Can I help you with anything?"

"No, thank you."

Kalenti walked hurriedly straight ahead through the double glass panel doors to the dimly lit but spacious reading room. He took off his coat, slung it over a wooden chair, and sat in the one opposite, drawn up to a chess table. The evening newspaper had been left on the chess table. He checked his watch—seven thirty. *The young people must be ready in ten minutes.* With a couple of minutes to spare, he picked up the discarded newspaper. In bold headlines, it proclaimed:

> United States Contemplates Retaliation in Lebanon
>   Following the discovery of Ambassador C. Jennings Hollingsworth's body, senior administration officials said today that they had not dismissed the possibility that the United States would retaliate against those responsible ...

He read no further. A tight smile formed, breaking around his lips. He looked at his watch: 8:01. He rose and left his coat on the chair. He returned to the lobby and took the wide staircase on the right down to the basement and the men's room. As he reached the last step, he walked thirty paces, passing the barbershop. A man leaving the men's room leaned back to flick off the light switch.

"Good evening," he said as he passed. Kalenti did not return the salutation. It was now quiet except for the receding footsteps and his own steps as he approached the men's room entrance.

He entered, turned on the light, and pulled the door shut behind him. He looked to see if there was anyone else there, checking the stalls on either of the two walls. Satisfied that he was alone, he went to the frosted glass window on the opposite wall and unlocked it. He had difficulty lifting it but suddenly felt the weight disappear as the window rose effortlessly behind the strength of Jacques.

Kalenti moved aside as Jacques, dressed in a dark blue jump suit, eased himself without a word over the window ledge and into the room. Metro followed, similarly dressed. He passed three duffel bags to Jacques, who placed them directly in the stall furthest from the entrance. In so doing, he slapped a metallic "Out of Order" sign on the entry door. Courtney, Danny, and

Michelle followed closely behind with a loosely packed third bag that contained the automatic weapons.

Courtney was the first out of his jump suit, followed by Metro. They were both dressed in tweed sports jackets and slacks. Courtney ran his hands through his hair and lifted what appeared to be a bag for a squash racket from the duffel bag and handed a second to Metro. Inside were fully loaded Uzis with four additional ammunition clips and propaganda literature from Hezbollah. The material was the same distributed at the site of the ambassador's abduction and in the abandoned launch and most recently with the recovered body of the slain ambassador. In this most recent tract, a more ominous, but undefined, threat was made—namely that if the United States did not pull its interests from Lebanon, Hezbollah would extract an increasingly severe penalty from the occupiers.

As they had rehearsed, Kalenti led Metro and Courtney in silence from the restroom. Upon reaching the lobby, Kalenti returned to his seat in the reading room, but not before he approached the young Puerto Rican.

"My good man, can you get me some sheets of stationary? I have a few notes to write."

"Yes, sir, immediately," the young man said and disappeared down the corridor.

With more people milling about in the lobby and the absence of the concierge responding to Kalenti's request, Metro and Courtney walked through the lobby and continued up the staircase to the library on the second floor.

Michelle and Danny remained in their jumpsuits, emblazoned with *EMPIRE PLUMBING* on the back. Michelle wore a blue knit cap that lent her a masculine profile. As planned, she simulated work on a fixture in the event that someone ignored the sign and entered. She laid out several wrenches on the floor next to the duffel bag that contained the explosive device that would be armed and concealed next to a key support pillar to cover the team's retreat and at the same time cause extensive damage to the building.

Jacques's role was to remain behind as a rear guard. He placed a shaving brush and razor on the shelf below one of the mirrors to disguise his true intentions. Dressed in a dark evening suit, he appeared to be a club member preparing for drinks or a late-night dinner in town. His Uzi was inside a black cashmere overcoat that was hanging on the wall alongside the stall nearest to him. Once the bombers had completed their task, they would depart through the same window. Jacques would remain behind until Kalenti signaled him on his pager that the secretary had entered the Biddle Room—the location of the event that he was scheduled to attend. The Biddle Room was also located on the second floor, close to the library, where Jacques would join Courtney and Metro. Everything was proceeding as the team had planned and rehearsed.

⁂

Colin regretted that he still had not been able to contact Jamie.

"When did they check out?" Colin had asked when he called the hotel.

"Yesterday evening, sir."

"Did they leave a forwarding address?" he asked, exasperated.

"Sorry, sir, no forwarding address." Colin hung up the phone. For all he knew, they were on their way back to Beirut. *So much for ICARUS's value. Good riddance! I didn't trust him anyway,* Colin said to himself glumly.

Before he got too critical he recalled that it was ICARUS who came to his rescue. The struggle in the hallway was still a vivid memory along with the fear that accompanied the incident as he began to lose consciousness under the grip of the assassin. *Come payday, he'll show up,* Colin thought.

Connecting with the secretary's security detail was smooth.

He was directed to be at the northwest corner of Park Avenue and Sixtieth Street at seven forty-five. At the appointed time, an armored Lincoln Town Car pulled up. The passenger side window rolled down.

"Are you the spy in search of some action?"

"I am," Colin answered.

"I'm John Latimore. Hope in. This is Phil Graham." As soon as he was seated in the rear, the driver got back into the flow of traffic heading south. They made a right turn and drove to the Essex House on Central Park South. There, Latimore got out and walked inside. Colin and Graham were left alone in the backseat.

"So tell me where you traveled." Graham said as he watched the entrance to the Essex House.

"Oh, I have spent most of my years in Europe and the Middle East," Colin answered.

"Were you always a spy?"

"I guess you could say that—though I masqueraded as a diplomat."

"What can you say about your duties?" Graham asked, clearly wanting to have full advantage of their time alone.

"You won't believe me when I tell you that the average CIA spy would do anything to trade places with me right now." Graham looked at him, uncomprehending. He was certain that Colin was underplaying his experience.

"Well, for my part I wasn't always protecting State Department officials," Graham volunteered, as if to get Colin to open up. "When I was younger I was a Fairfax policeman."

"When you were younger? You jest. I could be your father."

"You jest; I'm not as young as I look."

"Have you been abroad on any of the details?" Colin asked, changing Graham's line of inquiry.

"Yeah, we accompanied the secretary on his recent trip to India. John was the lead, and he took me along. He thought I needed some experience. Long trip. Glad I didn't drink anything that wasn't bottled. More than one was felled by a severe case of Delhi Belly." He laughed.

At that moment, Graham's eyes widened and without a word he jumped from the car. Colin looked up to see the secretary led by Latimore come through the revolving door. The secretary walked fast, with long, confident strides. He was still buttoning his dark overcoat by the time he reached the passenger-side door of the limousine held open by Graham, who eyed those passing on the sidewalk, his jacket open for easy access to his Glock sidearm. The secretary insisted on riding in the front seat, and no amount of talk from Latimore changed his decision.

"All aboard?" the secretary asked as he turned around to Colin.

"Welcome, my young friend." Colin was moving to the center seat as Latimore pushed in behind the secretary.

"Thank you, Mr. Secretary, for allowing me to accompany you."

"It is my pleasure." The secretary was in an expansive mood. He turned to Latimore. "This chap also argued that I shouldn't attend this gathering." Then he turned back to Colin. "I am confident that you will enjoy the evening." The vehicle started up and was on its way to the Harvard Club.

"I'm sure that you made the correct decision, sir." Colin felt dishonest saying this. If nothing happened, the secretary would be confirmed in his beliefs.

⁕⁕⁕

Kuban and Karina were waiting in the Volkswagen van that Kuban had double-parked on Forty-Fifth Street. They had hoped that by arriving at six fifteen in the evening, they would locate a parking spot of their choice on this block.

"Goddamn it," Kuban uttered when he pulled up. To their consternation, the spaces were in a no-parking area that was not lifted until seven o'clock.

Kuban felt cold and damp, though the temperature was an unseasonably warm at thirty-eight degrees. The weather report predicted a cooling trend—even a slight possibility of snow. Instead the air outside had a close, almost a fog-like quality. He turned off the motor. The hazard lights were flashing. As the windows fogged, Kuban used his dirty handkerchief to keep the front and side windows clear.

It was Karina's responsibility to monitor the signal from Kalenti and Jacques inside the club. When Jacques indicated that he was on his way with Courtney and Metro to the Biddle Room, Karina would detonate the car bomb concealed in the Peugeot that Kalenti had leased for Jamie. In addition to the explosive device, inflammatory Hezbollah literature was stored—some of which would survive the blast and point to Hezbollah as responsible for the outrage about to be perpetrated within the Harvard Club.

"Remember. Wait to detonate the bomb in the basement until Courtney, Jacques, and Metro emerge from the alley on Forty-Fifth Street." Kuban was perspiring and continued to run his handkerchief over the car windows to keep them clear. "I hope Michelle and Danny have no problem returning on their own to our rally point."

"Don't worry about them. Danny once served under me, and I trust him to fulfill the mission," Kuban said between wipes.

Suddenly, a flashlight shone into the van, startling them both. Kuban reached for his revolver, but with her left hand Karina stilled him. With her right hand she rolled down the window.

"Yes, officer?" she asked.

"No parking here. Move on," the New York City policewoman ordered with more force in her voice than the situation seemed to require.

"We're waiting for our crew to finish some emergency plumbing repairs inside. We'll be just a minute more," Karina offered politely and with a smile.

"I said no parking; move on."

Karina noticed in the side mirror that a patrol car was parked to the rear, and from the dome light she saw that the officer's male partner sat waiting.

"Okay," Karina said, still gripping Kuban's hand, "I guess we will just have to circle the block." Under her breath she whispered to Kuban, "Her backup is behind us."

Kuban started the motor and put the van into first gear and proceeded up the block. Slapping the wheel in frustration, he increased his speed to Sixth Avenue where he made a right and another right onto Forty-Seventh Street. The light turned red as they reached Fifth Avenue.

"When is it going to change?" he asked, his voice rising in pitch. The light changed, and they proceeded south again on Fifth Avenue.

"What are you doing?" Karina asked as he pulled up in the bus stop at the corner of Forty-Fifth Street.

"We can see the alley from here. Hopefully, we won't be bothered again."

CHAPTER THIRTY-THREE

Inside the club, it took all of Kalenti's restraint to remain in the reading room. He checked his watch—8:40, the designated time. He rose stiffly, trying to control the trembling and excitement in his limbs. He slung his coat over his arm and proceeded to the coat-check room located around the corner to the left—down a short corridor away from the elevators. He stood motionless, distracted before the African American woman attendant. She looked at him kindly.

"Yes, suh?"

"Oh, my coat." He put the coat on the counter, embarrassed at his fumbling. She gave him a claim check—423. *It will be my lucky number*, he thought. He retraced his way to the elevator, where the door opened as if it were waiting for his touch. He was so startled that he dropped his coat check. One of three young businessmen exiting the elevator bent down and retrieved the check for Kalenti. The three resumed their animated conversation toward the door. He had not acknowledged the young man.

He took the elevator to the second floor. When the door slid open, he turned to the right and found himself before the Weld Room, which he recalled was adorned with several paintings of bull elephants. He could not remember if there was an elephant-head trophy affixed to the wall, even though he had been in the room on countless occasions. Perhaps he was confusing the trophy with the one prominently displayed on the ground floor over the war memorial that Teddy Roosevelt donated. He could not say with certainty. His mind was reeling. He touched his forehead and decided that he might be getting a fever; he felt clammy and his tongue was thick with cotton balls of phlegm. At that moment, he realized that he should have turned left off the elevator, and he reversed his steps quickly.

There before him was the Biddle Room, and further down the dimly lit corridor was the North Room. He turned the knob and pushed opened the well-polished wooden door. He remembered the mirror panel on the inside. His eyes squinted in the bright light of the reception already in progress. He seemed disoriented as he gazed into the room.

"Monsieur Kalenti, or would you prefer *Moose*?" Tucker Davis asked—a classmate and the organizer of the event—as he grabbed Kalenti's hand in greeting.

"Tucker," Kalenti managed.

"Come; let me get you a drink," he said as he guided Kalenti to the open bar.

"This gentleman needs a large glass of Johnnie Walker Black Label on the rocks." He turned to Kalenti. "See, I remembered."

"So good to see you," Kalenti managed after a sip of his drink that made his eyes tear. Tucker was looking over Kalenti's shoulder and noticed a new arrival.

"See you in a bit; the secretary should be here in ten minutes." Tucker was off to greet another guest.

There were over forty persons gathered in the room, milling about, exchanging stories, laughing comfortably with their old classmates. No longer did they exchange business cards—they had already achieved their lifelong ambitions. At this time in their lives they sought to enjoy the success they earned. They were, however, no less intense, especially when the conversation turned to national-level politics and foreign-policy issues. This was the attraction of remaining in touch with a global-oriented fraternity.

The evening had special meaning—one of their own had achieved the august rank of secretary of state. To a man—there were no women present—they anticipated with unusual eagerness the arrival of the secretary.

Kalenti smiled nervously at those around him but he was like someone who was viewing the scene from behind a one-way glass window. He checked the pager in his trouser pocket. He would trigger it when the secretary entered the room. He had rehearsed the procedure so often that he could do it blindfolded. He hoped he remembered everything—he didn't want to make a mistake. It was time for him to stop questioning his preparations. The self-doubt reflected the natural nervous jitters he was experiencing as the hour of reckoning neared.

"Mr. Kalenti, Tom Ridges," a classmate said as he extended his hand.

"Yes, Tom, it has been so long," Kalenti responded, his eyes tearing from a second, deeper swallow of the scotch.

"Have you come from Lebanon?"

"Yes. I arrived a couple of days ago."

"How is the situation?"

"Quite gloomy, and my forecast—not better." As Kalenti spoke others in the vicinity moved around him to hear his response.

"There is no law and order on the streets. Neighborhoods are pitted against neighborhoods. Moslems are fighting Moslems and then turning on Christians." He took another sip of his drink and decided he had to hold off. He felt lightheaded.

"Only the Christians stand united in the mountain redoubt we have occupied for centuries. We will continue to repulse all invaders."

"Will you be victorious?" another classmate asked.

"Yes, but we still need our allies—the Americans and the French must come to our assistance."

"Didn't we try before and—"

"Please, would you retreat in the face of determined heathens?"

Kalenti felt belligerence toward the questioner. Another joined the circle.

"I support sending in the marines again; only this time let them go in prepared."

"Thank you for your voice," Kalenti said as if he were signing up volunteers. The tension he had experienced seemed to be lifting as he considered victory within his grasp.

Kalenti was beginning to feel like a celebrity, almost as if the gathering had been called to honor him. Just then he looked up as the secretary entered, accompanied by what appeared to be his four-man security detail. One of them—the one with gray hair—reminded him of someone from Lebanon. Of average height, his clothes and look gave him away as an American. The individual seemed to be fifty or so—not as athletic or compact in appearance as were his companions. He just could not place where they had met. Kalenti was relieved that none of them seemed to be carrying anything more lethal that a sidearm.

Someone had fixed the secretary a drink, and he moved through the group slowly, responding personally to each by name. Although he was less than six feet tall, his frame was solid. His open smile and steady gaze held this gathering of overachievers in awe. Kalenti did not seek the encounter, but before he realized it he was reaching out to shake the secretary's hand.

"Moose, so good to see you," he said before Kalenti was able to say a word.

"I guess if you could make the reunion there was no reason for me to miss it." The secretary glanced back at Colin.

"Mr. Secretary, my pleasure. I would not have missed this evening for the world."

"I should have paid more attention to you forty years ago. Maybe I would not be having the problems with your side of the world that I am now." There was a note of true sincerity in his voice. "Will you be traveling to Washington during your stay?"

"I have no plans, but if it is your pleasure, I could."

"Please, I would welcome some unofficial advice." He turned to the young security officer at his side.

"Graham, give Mr. Kalenti my private number." He turned back to Kalenti.

"Good to see you." He moved on.

A momentary twinge of regret and guilt flooded over Kalenti. He did his best to regain his composure by thinking about all the loved ones and friends killed or crippled under the onslaught of the infidels while America stood idle. His face tightened as he thought about the poverty and starvation that now hounded the streets of the once-prosperous cities and villages of Lebanon. In moments, he succeeded in turning the pity he felt for the secretary to anger. The secretary represented the failure of friends to support Lebanon in its hour of need. The secretary also represented the path to salvation. In his death, the West would awaken and Lebanon would be freed from the scourge from the East.

Someone nudged Kalenti from his stupor. Everyone was moving through the open large mahogany doors into the connecting room where chairs had been set up for the evening's informal address by the secretary. There was no podium; the secretary was among equals, friends, or at a minimum former classmates, and he planned to sit with them. Kalenti took his seat near the rear. The door from this room was behind him. The secretary's place was directly in front, while the double doors connecting both rooms were on Kalenti's left. He placed his glass on the floor between his feet. He reached for his pager. He would wait until everyone was seated and the secretary opened the meeting before giving the signal for which his team was waiting. The transmitter felt cold to his touch. He had handled it so often there was no need for him to pull it from his pocket.

At the other end of the room Colin watched as Latimore followed the secretary to his seat. Graham and the third member of the team remained behind while the waiters gathered the glasses and left the room. They would be summoned back at the close of the session to serve a light buffet and nightcap. In the meantime, those with the secretary would not be disturbed by the clinking of glassware.

It had been Latimore's decision to hold the speaking engagement in the room adjoining the Biddle. Training and experience influenced him to make last-minute, seemingly unnoticeable changes in schedules and agendas as a way to trip up or expose an adversary's execution of a well-rehearsed plan. The secretary did not give the move into the other room a second thought; in fact, he was even unaware that they were no longer in the Biddle Room.

Colin pulled up a folding chair and sat down with his young companions near the moveable bar that had been rolled against the far wall before the reception. As they were accustomed, both checked their weapons and returned them to their shoulder holsters. Graham took a seat next to Colin.

"Do you carry a weapon in your line of work?" he asked in a whisper. Colin suppressed a laugh.

"Not usually." Colin did not want to destroy his image of the CIA. In fact, Colin had not fired a weapon in close to thirty years, when he was in training.

In the next room, the North Room, Tucker stood before the chair alongside the secretary. He waited until those present had ceased shuffling and the friendly conversations became whispers before silence reigned, interrupted by the cough of someone sitting close by.

"Mr. Secretary, we know the demands that are made upon your time—especially now. We feel doubly honored that you could find the time to join us this evening."

With no further introduction, Tucker gestured toward the secretary, who had remained in his seat. The room filled with quiet applause.

"I hope you do not mind if I remain sitting," the secretary began. "This is the first opportunity I have had in weeks to relax among friends."

"You're just trying to make yourself a smaller target," a

successful Wall Street lawyer offered in a stage whisper that drew smiles and laughter from those present.

Kalenti was not certain that he heard the comment correctly, but he looked around nervously— half expecting someone to point a finger at him and say, "It is Kalenti. He's the guilty one."

"You cannot hide those two hundred pounds plus that easily." It was a responding comment from someone sitting in the middle of the audience. General laughter followed.

"I want to thank my friend for underestimating my weight by twenty pounds," the secretary interjected as he reached into his pocket and pulled out some oversized index cards on which he had scribbled some notes.

"I would like to lead a discussion tonight on where I think the Middle East is heading politically, economically, and culturally within the next fifteen to twenty years," he began.

"I am serious about leading a discussion. I need your input. I am here to learn through the exchange of ideas. Who knows, I may come up with something here that will help me deal with the ten or so crises per week that arise in that region."

He paused to review his first index card. He was not a man uncomfortable with silence. In fact, he preferred silence to the feeble attempts of some to fill such voids with meaningless chatter. He looked up again.

"I should have brought a map. The region I am talking about—the Middle East—consists of Lebanon, Jordan, Israel, Saudi Arabia, the Gulf Sheikdoms, Syria, Iraq, Egypt, Iran, Libya, and," he paused and then continued, "Turkey and Greece.

"Though Lebanon has been in the headlines repeatedly, and it is Lebanon that seems to be disintegrating from the Lebanon of just few years ago, I don't want to dwell on it."

The secretary was trying to spot Kalenti in the audience and finally noticed him slumping in the back of the room.

"For me, Lebanon is a player in a much larger drama that is unfolding."

Kalenti flinched when he heard these words, which he

interpreted as meaning that Lebanon was no longer central to resolving the crisis in the area. In fact, it seemed to Kalenti that the secretary had relegated Lebanon to be only a minor influence in the region where Lebanese banking and financial institutions and culture had once dominated the region. A flush of anger colored his face.

"Gentlemen, I thought I'd begin with a brief outline," he paused, reviewing his notes, "of what I perceive to be US objectives over the next twenty years. I would like to follow this with my assessment of the Soviet Union's interests in the region. Finally, I will attempt to demonstrate the dynamics in US-Soviet relations during this period." He spoke in measured tones. His wide girth enriched the resonance of his voice.

Kalenti fingered the pager. He had heard enough. It was time to remind the world that the destiny of Christian Lebanon was more than an aside during a discussion of superpower interests. He wondered if Jacques and the others were ready—if Kuban was in place, if Michelle and Danny had positioned the bomb. He listened to the words from the secretary and turned his gaze to someone on the left.

"Moose, if your view is obstructed, I'll move over a seat," his neighbor asked.

Kalenti could not comprehend the words nor recognize the identity of the questioner. His hand began to shake in his jacket pocket where he had placed the pager. The once-familiar feel of the device—no larger than a pack of cigarettes, whose outline he had traced countless times in preparation for this moment—suddenly seemed alien to him.

All heads in the audience were turned to the dialogue that was taking place between one of those in attendance and the secretary. In defiance, Kalenti turned to the right and looked through the curtains at a building he could just make out across Forty-Fifth Street. At that moment, he pushed in the preset signal three times, and as he did so he turned back to the exchange taking place before him. He felt a surge of relief, as if a safety net had been placed below him and released his grip. But at the same time his tongue felt like it was coated in cotton, and he was beginning to feel nauseous. He shifted his weight in the chair.

I must be ready to fall to the floor at the instant my team enters the room, he thought. *Enters the room ... enters the room,* he whispered over and over aloud until someone in front of him turned around with an annoyed expression on his face. Kalenti glanced at the closed double doors through which he and everyone else had entered their cocktails.

"Oh, my God," he gasped. "We are no longer in the Biddle Room." In that instant he remembered why he had recognized one member of the secretary's security detail. He had viewed a surveillance photo taken in Athens by his man who was later found dead in Piraeus. The photograph was taken of an American leaving the embassy there. He could never forget that face and that youthful haircut. He drained of color.

Kalenti pulled the pager from his pocket, brought it up to his eyes, and began to press up and down on the signaling button. His neighbor on his left was too polite to look directly at him. In fact, he turned away to minimize the distraction and to allow the distraught classmate to sort out his problem on his own. Kalenti was oblivious to the scene he was creating and the confusion of those who received this unplanned jumble of transmissions.

CHAPTER THIRTY-FOUR

"What is happening? What does he mean?" Karina said suddenly, looking down at the pager. They were still parked in the bus stop.

"What are you talking about?" Kuban slipped his glasses on to inspect the signaling device.

"The secretary must have left the room." Her voice reflected her confusion. She looked at Kuban. "What do you think?"

"Karina, maybe. Suppose they've been tipped off?"

"It's bad enough for him to have left for a moment. Tipped off? My God! How am I supposed to trigger the explosives in the Spaniard's trunk? All hell would result, and the secretary could escape."

✞*✞*✞

"What is the old man doing?" Courtney hissed. He was on his way to the Biddle Room with Jacques and Metro.

"The impatient old bastard." Courtney pushed ahead of Jacques and led the way down the corridor to the Biddle Room. Weapons pulled free of their cases, he turned the knob. It was locked. Each of their weapons was fitted with a silencer. He stood back and spat four rounds into the lock, making noise only on contact with the metal.

At the sound, the young security officer shoved Colin to the floor behind the bar while Graham extinguished the lights. Colin was momentarily blinded while his eyes adjusted to the darkness. Suddenly, the door swung open on what appeared to be an empty room to the intruders. The faint glow from the wall lamp in the corridor outlined the three figures in the doorway.

"Where is he?" hissed Courtney, moving into the room followed by Jacques with their weapons raised. Metro remained at the door. They heard a stir and could make out the outline of a door about forty feet to the right.

"Maybe there," Courtney whispered as he and Jacques moved toward the double doors.

"Freeze! Police! Hands …" Graham called.

Both Jacques and Courtney hit the deck immediately and fired several rounds in the direction of the voice. Metro was still at the door. He did not understand *Freeze*, though *Police* seemed to translate in any language. He pulled back immediately, but not before receiving a round in his left arm. At that moment, he heard the door down the corridor open and a man came rushing at him, arms gesturing frantically. It was Kalenti, but in the dim light and the confusion that engulfed the scene, Metro did not recognize him, nor did he comprehend the words he spoke.

"The American is here in …" Kalenti did not finish the sentence as Metro knelt mechanically into position and fired six rounds into his chest. Kalenti was dead by the time his face hit the carpet thirty feet from Metro. The rounds from the police weapons resounded in the room. Another exchange and a shout from a stranger convinced Metro that Jacques or Courtney had hit his mark. With the butt of the Uzi, Metro knocked out the bulb in the wall fixture. It signaled the swift retreat of Jacques and Courtney.

"Let's get out of here," Jacques shouted, leading the way down the stairs to the second and then the first floor. A commotion had erupted in the lobby at the exchange of gunfire. Club patrons rushed out onto the street. As they had exercised before the operation, the three of them, one clutching his right hand over his wound, discarded their weapons on the staircase and joined the pandemonium in the lobby. They did not follow the crowd but took the stairs to the basement. They returned to the men's room from which they entered the club. Hurriedly, Jacques opened the window. He jumped through and waited for Courtney to lift Metro into a position from which Jacques could ease him to the ground. Courtney closed the window behind him as they rushed together down the alley onto to Forty-Fifth Street.

As they exited the alley, they could hear the wail of sirens as the New York police responded to the emergency with dozens of police cars and vans. The threesome rushed across the street, looking in vain for the van.

"Where the fuck are they?" Courtney shouted. They had started to run down the street toward Sixth Avenue when the van pulled alongside.

"Hurry," Karina said as she slid the rear door open.

"What happened?" Kuban asked, looking over his shoulder and back in the direction where he was steering.

"It was a trap," Courtney managed between gasps as he sucked air violently into his lungs. "No one was in the room except the police."

"Did you blow the car?" Jacques asked.

"Aiyee! No, I didn't," Karina screamed. "Kalenti confused me with his signaling."

"Jesus! Do it now!" Jacques commanded.

"Are we too far away?" Kuban asked.

"Do it now! We're not going back!" Jacques raised his voice louder. Karina pushed the plunger on the detonation box.

"Do it again!"

"I don't hear anything." Kuban had opened the window and cocked his ear. He had just turned north on Sixth Avenue.

"God be vigilant. Have you detonated the bomb in the basement?" Jacques's words were spoken in rapid fire.

"No."

333

"Do it!" A muffled explosion could be heard from behind them seconds later.

"Who knows? Press each one again." Jacques turned to Metro. "How's your shoulder?"

"I still don't hear anything," Kuban interrupted as he wiped his forehead with the same handkerchief that he had used on the windshield.

"I'll be okay," Metro moaned.

"I am satisfied that one of the bombs went off," Jacques said more calmly.

"Right now, I'd settle for just one. Nothing we can do anyway. Maybe both of them went off. We can't hear anything with all these buildings."

"Just concentrate on getting us back to the house," Jacques said to Kuban. "We'll regroup there."

⁌*⁌*⁌

When the lights came on Colin looked to his left. The young security officer was administering to Graham, who had received two rounds—one glanced off the floor and grazed the side of his face while the other shattered his right wrist. The shock of the firefight had created an eerie silence. The wood paneling seemed to reverberate from the exchange. It smelled to Colin like an indoor firing range. He sneezed involuntarily from the thick plaster released from the holes ripped into the walls and creating dust clouds in the air

The young security officer's adrenaline was still pumping furiously as if he were pursued. He turned his head from the door to the side and behind, training his weapon to cover the particular field of fire. A muffled explosion sounded in the depths of the building as if placed behind a barrier of mattresses. The movement and earnest whispers in the next room quieted, fearing the return of the attackers. Silence descended once again, though shouts could be heard on the floor below.

The first units of the police antiterrorist force arrived at the scene and immediately rushed to the second floor where the secretary was located. They had not been informed that occupants of the Biddle and North Rooms had yet to be told that an all clear had been declared. A deadly accident was avoided when Graham's security team held their fire as the first police officers appeared in the open door.

"Identify yourselves," Graham shouted from his prone position.

"Police," the entry man called, holding his badge above him to catch the light in the hallway.

"It took you long enough," Graham could not resist calling as he was helped to his feet.

"Latimore, our relief is here," he shouted behind him to the door that separated the two rooms. Latimore opened the door, weapon in hand.

"Let's move the secretary and guests out," Latimore commanded.

"Hold on a minute," the tactical chief of the police unit called out. A police lieutenant appeared and assigned eight of his most hardened veterans to provide personal protection to the secretary as they prepared to leave the building by the staircase.

"We'll take your statements as soon as we get you to a safe area," the lieutenant informed Latimore. "We will bus everyone from the club to the armory on Sixty-First Street."

"Lieutenant, I want Colin Gordon to remain with you," Latimore said, pointing to Colin. "He's from the agency and assigned to my team."

"No prob," the lieutenant reached across to shake Colin's hand.

"I'll contact you later," Latimore said to Colin as he headed off with the secretary.

The police inside the club were conducting a room-by-room search of the building, while the tactical units outside the building were in the process of establishing a perimeter around the Club.

Forty-Fourth and Forty-Fifth Streets were closed to vehicular and pedestrian traffic, causing a major backup that stretched north and south and east and west to the rivers. In the immediate vicinity of the club, the sound of honking horns and the sirens from the arriving and departing emergency vehicles was overwhelming.

Medical units arrived and assumed responsibility for Graham. As they were placing a sheet over the body in the hallway, Tucker Davis approached a policeman standing by.

"That's Moose Kalenti," he said, holding his hands together as a priest would, approaching a family member.

"And who are you?" the police officer asked in a thick Brooklyn accent.

"I'm Tucker Davis, the organizer of the event for the secretary." The police officer took notes.

"It's hard to believe with all this firing there were only two casualties," Colin observed as he walked with the lieutenant to the command post.

"The security guy said he hit one of the attackers," the lieutenant replied. "See, there's his blood," he said, indicating the area in front of the door to the Biddle Room.

"He must have panicked when the firing broke out," Colin suggested, looking on the sheet covering Kalenti, "and instead of following the command to lie flat on the floor, he tried to escape."

"Do you know, I was in the room when Latimore shouted, and I could swear someone rushed from the door seconds earlier," Tucker interjected.

"Okay, gentlemen, could you step back?" A second policeman was stringing crime scene tap to seal off the hallways and rooms. "The forensic team is on site."

Tucker and Colin withdrew down the staircase to the lobby.

"Look what we have here," one police officer was calling to a second. "It looks like three Uzis. Get the forensics boys up here."

As he was speaking, two police officers in brown fatigues

rushed up the stairs with their bomb-sniffing dogs. When they reached the landing they proceeded down the corridor to see if the dogs alerted on anything beyond the closed door. Each of them held a master key to allow entry to all rooms.

"Come with me." A police inspector motioned to Colin. "You're the guy Latimore left behind?"

"Yes, Colin Gordon, that's me."

"I want to show you the damage in the basement." He led Colin toward the stairs to the basement.

"Here, wear this." He handed Colin a mask with a bottle of oxygen attached and put on a similar device. They descended down the stairs; plumes of smoke were still rising. Colin began to cough as the mask fogged up.

"You've got to turn it on," the inspector said as he twisted a screw for Colin. In a rush of air, he was breathing normally.

"Look here." They were in the basement men's room. "This is where the explosives were placed; I estimate about twenty pounds."

Colin moved closer to view the shattered interior of a closet and to see the exposed iron supporting beams.

"Had they more time and dug out a crevasse for the package, we wouldn't be seeing this but a pile of rubble from the street. This side of the building would have collapsed."

Engineers in white hard hats were scouring the area for any sign of structural damage beyond the immediate area.

"The bomb seems to have been used to cover the retreat of the attackers—we think three," the inspector continued.

"It did its job and probably destroyed any evidence as well."

Colin followed him as they retraced their steps and went out onto the street from the lobby.

"We've set up a mobile command center," the inspector said as they moved to a brown bus parked just down the street. Inside, police intelligence analysts were sitting at terminals, logging in evidence.

"We have direct access to our central database and yours as well."

"Mine?" Colin asked.

"Yes, you're FBI, aren't you?"

"Oh, yes," Colin lied, thinking it too complicated now to explain why the inspector was catering to him.

"We also have a line to the armory where the interviews of those inside the club are underway as we speak."

"What about the people on the street?"

"Look over there," the inspector said as he pointed to a building about fifty yards distant.

"That's where pedestrians and the like are being interviewed. Once they have been screened, they are free to leave the area."

⁌*⁌*⁌

Jamie was one of those individuals led to the building lobby to be interviewed. He had been sitting in his vehicle double-parked for almost an hour when he heard what he thought was the backfire of a truck in the area. Then the approaching wail of sirens broke over the cacophony of sound to which New Yorkers become accustomed. His first impulse was to drive out of the area, but he realized too late that his exit onto Fifth Avenue was, or soon would be, blocked by the emergency vehicles already entering the area.

While he could not be certain, the emergency workers seemed to be entering the building into which Kalenti had disappeared almost two hours earlier. The coincidence—and he did not believe in coincidences—was too great not to conclude that Kalenti was somehow involved in the scene unfolding fifty yards from where he was parked.

Thirty minutes later, the same policewoman who ordered Kuban to drive on approached Jamie's car. "Let me see some identification," she asked, her hand resting on her holster. She left with his license and passport and returned with two burly companions.

"Sir, you will have to come with us," one of the two said as the policewoman continued up the line of cars, asking for identification.

Jamie was not being given a choice. He regretted that he had not bolted from his car after the policewoman first approached him.

"Yes, officers!" He left the key in the ignition and followed them down the block.

As they passed the building where all the action was occurring, an armed escort, guns drawn, led an elderly man in a dark pin-striped suit from the building into a limousine parked between several police vehicles with their emergency lights flashing. Before he ducked into the rear seat, Jamie got a look of his flushed face. He seemed to be out of breath, his complexion gray. He had seen that look before on the streets of Beirut.

"Well, hello! Some coincidence?" Colin was just returning with the inspector from the interview center.

"What are you doing here?" Jamie asked casually, controlling as best he could his surprise to see the American. His mind was racing, trying to fit all the pieces of the puzzle together, though several pieces were missing.

"He can come with us," Colin told the police escort. The inspector nodded agreement, and Jamie moved toward Colin.

"What were you doing in the area? Where the hell have you been? Why didn't you call in?" Colin asked in rapid fire.

"I'm sorry. I was going to call after I finished driving my guy around." Jamie was fighting for time so he could sort out the events of the last twenty-four hours.

"Who? The Lebanese?" Colin persisted.

"Yes, I dropped him off at the corner a couple of hours ago. He told me to wait."

"Where did he go?"

"I'm not sure. He entered a building in this block."

"Was it this building?" Colin asked glancing over his shoulder.

"Where is he?" Jamie sensed something was wrong.

"Upstairs. He's dead—killed by some Arab terrorists."

"Are you sure?" Jamie's face was impassive.

"Afraid so. The bad guys were after the secretary of state, and your guy simply got in the way."

"How do you know they were Arab terrorists?"

"We collected the same propaganda they have been distributing at other crime scenes."

At that moment, the stretcher bearing Kalenti's body was being carried out to a waiting ambulance. Colin and the inspector approached.

"I have someone who can also identify the fellow." The attendants paused and Colin pulled back the sheet.

"Yes, that's him," Jamie said with no emotion visible; though he was in turmoil, he felt no remorse. He had seen many people die and had even caused the death of a few. Should he have felt guilty about failing to defend Kalenti, since he had been hired to be his protector? His inability to break out of the silence of his soul disturbed him more than the evident pain Kalenti suffered as evidenced by the scowl on his face.

CHAPTER THIRTY-FIVE

The ride out of the city went smoothly for Kuban and the team. They reached the Henry Hudson Bridge, where Kuban paid the toll, and continued north into Westchester County on their way to the Mt. Kisco retreat. No one had spoken since Jacques's last words as they turned onto Sixth Avenue. Each was immersed in his or her thoughts.

"What about Danny and Michelle?" Courtney asked.

"We did not see them exit the alley, but I assume everything is okay," Karina replied.

"Why didn't you see them?" Jacques questioned.

"A cop made us move," Kuban replied, looking into the review mirror at Jacques.

"Jeeeeesus! I have never seen something so screwed up," Courtney exclaimed.

"How's your arm?" Jacques said and turned to Metro.

"Not so good. I've lost movement in it."

"You'll be fine when we stop."

"What a failure." Courtney sounded distressed.

"Quite the contrary," Jacques countered. "As far as the Americans are concerned, Hezbollah tried a daring operation to whack the secretary of state. They failed, but in failure they have thrown down the gauntlet."

"I'll wager," Jacques went on, "that the secretary is on the phone right now reporting to the president. I would not be surprised if the Pentagon is already dusting off one of its contingency plans to occupy Lebanon. Maybe it's their only plan. If so, we won."

Jacques had almost convinced himself. Kuban looked back at him in the mirror to see if his expression betrayed whether or not he believed what he was saying. For the remainder of the ride the only sound in the van was the straining Volkswagen engine as it negotiated the winding road and steep hills.

⁑⁑

After Petrus had concealed the explosives in the trunk of the rental car Jamie was driving, he drove on to Mt. Kisco to await the rest of the team. He did not hear the hooded figures—a Libyan special operations team—enter the house, so engrossed was he in watching a basketball match on the small-screen television, even though he did not understand the rules. He was overpowered by three husky Libyans and forced to sit at the heavy wooden table, his body tied tightly to the chair.

"When do your friends return?" he was asked in a flat voice by a sullen Arab. Petrus spit on the floor in disgust. The Arab grabbed his hand and laid it flat on the table. With one swift stroke, the Arab cut Petrus's right thumb from his hand with an axe he had suddenly produced. Petrus howled in pain.

"Well, let's try again. When do your friends return?" Petrus only moaned. Another swift stroke removed his left thumb. Petrus head fell to the table in pain as the blood spurted over him. The Arab wrenched his head up by the hair and administered a third stroke, which severed the index finger on his right hand.

"Stop, stop," Petrus screamed. "They return as soon as they finish in the city. I only know them as Michelle and Danny—they'll be here within the hour. Kuban, Metro, Karina, Courtney, and Jacques follow."

With a nod to his companion, a second Arab still in his ski

mask fired a bullet to Petrus's head, ending his suffering, and hauled him into a bedroom.

⁂

True to Petrus's word, Michelle and Danny arrived and entered the house, unsuspecting what awaited them. They were overpowered at once. They, too, were bound, and the first Arab stepped forward.

"Where is Monsieur Kalenti?" Both Michelle and Danny sat expressionless and silent. Impatient, the Arab pulled his weapon and executed Danny before Michelle.

"Well, do you still choose not to cooperate?" he asked Michelle. She said nothing.

He placed the barrel of the gun directly before one of her gray-blue eyes. He was forced to respect the female's courage as she continued to glare at him, eyes wide open. She did not flinch when his grip tightened on the trigger. She died with the same tight glare.

⁂

The Libyans waited in their assigned positions in the woods. Their patience and discipline were rewarded when they heard the approach of a vehicle, the grind of gears as the driver negotiated the hill leading up the long driveway. Then they saw the sweep of the headlights. The van jolted to a stop. The lights were on in the house. Michelle and Danny's rental car was parked in the driveway alongside the house, and they could see Petrus's vehicle behind it. Kuban exhaled loudly as he pulled up behind. He turned off the motor and set the hand brake. He was relieved that they had reached the house safely.

"You know, Jacques," Kuban said as he prepared to leave the van, "I tend to agree with you. We have been successful. At least we didn't have to leave anyone behind. Help Metro out. We must treat his wound." He turned to Karina. "Why don't you find the medical kit?"

"Do you think the Spaniard survived?" Karina asked.

"Can't worry about that now. Let's get into the house." He turned off the headlights and reached for the door handle as Jacques leaned across Metro to slide the rear door open.

Neither was able to complete the action. A devastating volley of automatic fire erupted from the trees that lined the driveway—fifteen feet distant. The weapons had been fitted with silencers. Along with the muffled pop of breaking glass, the hollow thuds of the jacketed shells penetrated the lightweight aluminum body of the van, sounding like a child throwing gravel against a screen door.

The surprise was complete. Karina was the first to die, followed by Metro and Kuban, who had not succeeded in swinging the door open. In the flash of death, only Jacques had a millisecond to reflect on life—sufficient to visualize the joy his wife and children had given him when they were alive. The rest died as the warriors they were. Courtney moaned softly before his breathing ceased. The attack was over in less than thirty seconds.

One of the attackers made a quick survey of the van's occupants. The others remained in place, covering his progress as he went from one body to the other, confirming what they had suspected, that all of the occupants—there had been five—were dead in their seats.

With equal precision, another of the hooded figures rose in place and lit an incendiary device and tossed it through the shattered windshield of the van. It immediately erupted into flames. A third intruder, holding a similar device, dashed to the house and disappeared inside. Seconds later he emerged as flames engulfed the interior. Their work completed—without a word—the five of them reached the black Mercedes parked in the cover of the trees. The car started down the driveway before the last door had closed.

❦

Someone driving by had heard and later spied the brilliant red flames breaking through the darkness of the night. He reported the fire to the Mt. Kisco volunteer fire department. By the time he reached the perimeter of the property the wood-frame house was gutted and the vehicles alongside smoldering ruins. Almost twenty nearby residents came rushing to the scene to help but realized almost immediately that it was too late to help anyone who might have been caught inside the dwelling.

"Can't figure out how the vehicles caught fire as well," one of them commented to a neighbor as they felt the heat on their faces.

"Maybe the fire started in that van and spread to the house," another speculated.

"Yeah, a spark reaching a dry shingle on the roof," a third opined.

A bucket brigade was formed to haul water from the well located on the fringe of the property. It was a valiant but unsuccessful effort to prevent the flames from spreading to the surrounding woods. Twenty minutes later the first fire engine from Mr. Kisco arrived with shouts of welcome. In minutes, the volunteers responded under the direction of the senior firefighter at the scene. In less than ten minutes, the fire marshal arrived in his yellow van, the red strobe lights revolving on top.

"If we don't get reinforcements, the fire will be out of control," the senior fireman reported to the fire marshal.

"I hope the police are on the way," the marshal said. "This smells like arson."

"Arson?"

"Yes, arson. I was in Vietnam. There is no way to disguise the smell of burning flesh." The marshal gagged as he tried to suppress a wave of nausea that swept over him. "I was a young infantryman; we entered a desolate flat expanse the size of three football stadiums," he continued. "Hours before a rich, moist dense jungle forest stood there along with a Viet Cong battalion." He turned gray and sweaty as he recounted, "Napalm had been dropped, and what we found was only a rich, greasy smell of burning flesh. Just like this."

❦

The announcer broke in on the scheduled performance of Eugene Onegin, Kay's favorite opera. She was listening from the laundry room sound system in her apartment building in Arlington, Virginia.

An attempt was made this evening upon the life of the secretary of state. He was attending a reunion of his Harvard University classmates at the Harvard Club when at least three attackers were repulsed by the secretary's security detail.

"I knew something would happen. We were right," she said aloud. No one was in the vicinity. Without listening further she left her wash spinning in the machine and walked quickly to the elevator. Once in her apartment, she called the CIA Operations Center.

"This is Kay Grady. Please contact Stacy at the FBI Command Center in New York and have her call me immediately." She paused listening. A frown crossed her forehead as her call was transferred.

"Hello, this is Kay Grady. Yes, my number is N-53-21-7." Finally the connection was made.

"I am trying to reach my assistant Stacy at the FBI Command Center in New York. Could you please have her call me immediately?" Kay's face flushed. In her excitement, she could not recall Stacy's last name.

"I would call her myself, but I don't have the phone number at home. Oh, okay," she said as she wrote down the telephone number. After she hung up, she put the phone down and said, "Smartass!" Still embarrassed, she dialed the number given to her.

"Hi, I am trying to locate my assistant. This is Kay Grady."

After a few minutes that seemed like an eternity, Stacy came on the phone. "Hi, Kay," she said.

"What we know is that an attempt was made on the secretary's life. He has been escorted safely to La Guardia Airport and is already on his way to Washington. One of his security detail was injured—not life threatening—and was taken to the hospital. One of the attackers is believed to have been hit in the exchange of gunfire. A prominent Lebanese, Pierre Kalenti, a classmate of the secretary, was killed in the hallway outside the meeting room." Stacy paused. "Hold on, Kay, this just came in. A meeting of the National Security Council, chaired by the president, has been called for later this evening."

"The way it looks here," Stacy continued, "they won't convene before midnight."

"Sounds like there will be a lot of pressure on the administration to retaliate against Hezbollah. What's the sense there?"

"Kay, these guys are cops. They want to catch the bad guys," Stacy observed. "No one here can spell Hezbollah."

"You're right," Kay corrected herself. "Well, Kay Grady says—not for attribution—we are on the brink of sending troops back into Lebanon. We are no wiser than we were when all those marines died in the bombing."

"Let me know if you hear anything about the director attending the meeting," Kay added, "I should probably go in to see if Brody needs any help preparing something."

"I'd better go. Stacy, call me with anything."

Kay next contacted Brody's home and learned that he had just left for the office. Kay decided to do likewise.

⁑*⁑

A police officer was making his way down the line of double-parked cars on Forty-Fourth Street, just down the block from the Harvard Club. He was checking the interior of each vehicle and stood by as the driver opened the trunk for inspection. When he approached the car Jamie had occupied, he was more alert, since the driver was not to be seen. As he approached the rear of the vehicle, he detected a wire hanging loose from what appeared to be a tiny makeshift antenna. It reminded him of a technique that he had been told recently was used to detonate car bombs remotely. He decided to call in some assistance.

"You were right on, officer," the team leader of the EOD unit said, confirming his suspicions. "We'll need a wide perimeter, just in case there's a problem."

Police reinforcements cleared the street—almost fifty yards in either direction, evacuating the buildings closest to the possible impact area. It was only when these precautions were taken did one of the EOD experts approach the trunk in what looked like a space suit, though armored suit would have been more accurate. His two-way radio in place, he moved to the rear of the vehicle.

"Okay. Do you read me?" he asked. "I am at the rear of the vehicle and am working to release the booby trap attached to trunk." Silence prevailed as the officer worked gingerly to free the lock from the trip wire for the explosives.

"I have freed the wire and am opening the trunk.

"It's open. You guys can approach. All clear." The armored truck with EOD painted in bold yellow letters started up and parked close to the vehicle.

"Oh, that's nice," one of the newcomers commented. "How much do you think?"

"At least a hundred pounds of C-4 molded above the gas tank and throughout the interior of the trunk. I'm surprised the smell didn't overwhelm the driver—forget about any explosion."

"If that wire had not slipped from the antenna connector, the pulse would have been received and the vehicle and driver would be history," one of the new arrivals commented.

"And what about the buildings in the area?" An officer looked around. "We would have had a piece of Beirut in New York." He shivered at the thought of the devastation.

ⵣ

"Mr. Gordon, your buddy was driving a white Peugeot, wasn't he?" the police inspector asked. They had returned to the second floor of the club. Jamie nodded affirmatively.

"Well, my guys tell me," he turned to Jamie, "that you would have been sitting on the rooftop in pieces had the bomb in the trunk detonated."

"The what?" Colin asked. Jamie wasn't sure he understood, yet he still turned ashen.

"Yes, your friend was driving a car bomb about."

"You're going to need some protection," Colin said as he turned to Jamie, who didn't seem to have any reaction to the discovery. "It seems that bomb was meant for you," he said with a gesture to Jamie, "and they just might return to finish the job."

"If it had gone off, at least it wouldn't have given me time to do much reflecting," Jamie said, not revealing that he no longer felt safe with the Americans. The bomb was meant for him—of this he was certain. *Time to move on*, he thought.

"Personally, I think the bomb was meant for Kalenti," Colin suggested. "You were incidental collateral damage." Jamie remained expressionless.

"The fact that Kalenti had already been eliminated saved your ass." But his reasoning was flawed, and he knew it. The operation was designed to kill the secretary of state—that is what the inflammatory literature proclaimed. Something did not make sense.

"Stay here. I'll be right back." Colin headed off to call Kay.

A police officer escorted Colin to an office where he could make the call in privacy. He passed the Mahogany Room.

"Classy, huh?" he commented. The officer nodded.

"Kay, how's it going?" Colin said as he made himself comfortable in the leather chair at the rolltop desk. "Oh, we're fine here, at least for now. The police are going about their work.

Should be here for a while collecting evidence. In fact, they'll be here for some time. You know how that goes.

"The reason I'm calling is I have some doubts.

"So what took me so long? I should have listened more carefully to you." He laughed for the first time in some time and he felt an instant, if temporary, release from the tension.

"Thanks, Kay, I needed that." He paused. "It's the murder of Kalenti that puzzles me. He couldn't have been the target—the secretary was. The thought even came to me that maybe his murder was a mistake.

"Remember our discussion of GANYMEDE's death—the Lebanese cross on the stamp, the theory that perhaps Lebanese Christians were responsible for all the deaths and even the attempt on my life." He could hear Kay's affirmative reply.

"Well, suppose Kalenti was one of the prime movers in this plot and he stumbled outside in the corridor at the wrong time and was shot without being recognized.

"It is not farfetched, Kay. Let me explain. The secretary was to address his classmates in the Biddle Room. We were in the North Room when the action broke out. Kalenti was rushing down the corridor toward the attackers and the Biddle Room. Doesn't that strike you as an odd coincidence?

"Oh, I've caught your interest, have I? Well, it took a while.

"Yes, I can get down to you as soon as I take care of Jamie. I'll call when I know the flight I'll be on. Cheers." He hung up the phone and went in search of the Spaniard.

When he returned to where he left him, Jamie was not to be found.

"He said he was joining you," the officer in the area said as he continued to inventory the evidence in the area.

☨*☨*☨

Colin would have done anything to get back to Headquarters immediately. But there was no way that he could have caught the last shuttle at nine thirty that evening in the thick of the New York traffic, even if he were the president with a Secret Service escort. He had to settle for the six thirty shuttle the next morning. He wasn't disappointed. He now had more time to think about the unfolding drama and ICARUS's disappearance. He called Kay with his new travel plans.

"Yes, I'll take a taxi directly to Headquarters as soon as I get in—should be before eight.

"I am not particularly worried about ICARUS. I'm sure we'll hear from him. He won't do anything to jeopardize the monthly retainer. And without Kalenti, he'll need money even more. And you know we have his passport. See you tomorrow first thing."

CHAPTER THIRTY-SIX

By the time the taxi reached Headquarters in Langley, it was almost eleven. Before security cleared him, fifteen more minutes passed.

"I am sorry I'm so late. You know security equals inconvenience," he observed to Kay, "and the more inconvenience, the better the security."

"Well, you're here," Kay said as they entered her office.

"I feel like I traveled across the country and not two hundred miles from New York." He took his seat. Kay remained standing. She reminded him of one of his nuns in grade school.

"The international situation is getting worse as we speak," she began. "We are days from invading Lebanon—maybe less—and launching a retaliatory strike against the suspected perpetrators."

"So?"

"So you say. We are not even sure who the enemy is. That's so." Kay was impatient. "Further, just before you arrived, our police liaison office called to tell me of a mass murder that took place at a home in Mt. Kisco. By the police account, two maybe three individuals meet a grisly death in the house, and another five were found in a burned-out vehicle alongside the house. There is no doubt that arson and multiple murders were committed. Shell casings littered the area."

"I'm still not following you," Colin said.

Kay seemed exasperated with Colin's responses. "One of the cars was rented by a Lebanese national who arrived on that charter flight from Paris." Before Colin could ask the question, Kay continued, "Yes, he was one of the five unaccounted for at the Red Cross conference.

"Have you located ICARUS?" she asked—seeming to change the subject.

"He'll turn up," Colin responded.

"We need him down here." There was urgency in Kay's voice. "We have to find out if Kalenti's death and the murders in Mt. Kisco are linked. If they are, there's a chance that the Christians are not the sponsors of this grand conspiracy as we've speculated."

"What would ICARUS be able to tell us?" Colin didn't seem to follow Kay's rationale.

"Well, for starters, what did he know about the Mt. Kisco safe house? Also, what were the explosives doing in his car? Who put them there?"

"I agree, Kay, that he might be able to help. Let me call New York and see if he's turned up."

When he hung up the phone, his face was gloom.

"Nothing. No one has seen him."

☩ ∗ ☩ ∗ ☩

After he left the club, Jamie walked for hours to clear his mind—first going west to the Hudson River and then following the path south to Battery Park at the tip of Manhattan. He stood by the railing and observed the lights of the ships anchored outside the shipping channel. In that time he came to realize for certain that he—and not Kalenti—was the target of the explosives in the car. He was to be the evidence left behind to deflect attention from these Christian crazies who were responsible for murdering the American ambassador and who planned to take down the secretary as well.

Now it made sense to him. He was the sacrificial lamb to be left at the crime scene. That's the reason they hired him and why he had so much free time with no assigned duties to perform. He was to be eliminated so the police would confirm his terrorist connection. And if there was any doubt the same Hezbollah material was to be discovered among his remains.

Why me? he asked. But no answer was necessary. He now he understood why Kalenti directed him to rent the vehicle and why he only gave him back the ignition key when he directed him to drive him to the club. How ironic that Kalenti, who must have been a key planner, should be killed in the execution of his operation.

He started walking with determination north, reaching the pathway that skirted the East River. This was no time to be under the protection of those unable to believe that fellow Christians were running around New York plotting the murder of a prominent statesman. He had to protect what he had in the Swiss account the Americans set up. He found an all-night drugstore and purchased stationery. At the coffee counter he wrote a letter to Brigid, directing her to close the account. He affixed more than sufficient postage and placed the letter in a receptacle on the street and continued walking.

It was almost six in the morning. It was time to call the Libyans. He needed their help to get out of the United States. They also owed him money—his salary—for two months. He winced at the thought of depending upon the Libyans for his escape from the Lebanese and the Americans—both of whom were supposed to be allies. He decided to revert to his mantra—it is better not to trust anyone.

☩*☩*☩

Three days later, ICARUS had still not surfaced.

"You never know with him," Colin said, trying to sound confident.

"We never could discover where Brigid was in Greece, or if in fact that is where she actually is."

"Who knows? Maybe she never left Bulgaria." Kay reasoned.

"What do you make of these? Stacy just forwarded them." She passed Colin copies of three diplomatic messages that had been intercepted, deciphered, and translated by the National Security Agency. The first was from the Libyan People's Bureau in McLean, Virginia, and had been sent to Tripoli two days ago:

All went well. The surprise of Allah was complete. The Berbers return separately across the sands.

"The second originated in Tripoli and was received by the Libyan UN mission in New York the same day."

Your success in not complete until the Moor is delivered to Allah.

"Here's the third, sent yesterday,"

In the service of Allah, Ben Yousef.

"Puzzling—worrying," Colin answered. "The dates seem to coincide with the turkey roast in Mt. Kisco." He regretted the analogy as soon as it left his lips.

He looked up at Kay. She had ignored him and was in the process of adding bright rouge to her gray skin and dry cheeks. He had forgotten how old Kay looked to him. During these last weeks, she was ageless as his intellectual and professional companion.

"I think it is more appropriate to say that 'the success' in the second message refers to Mt. Kisco," she corrected.

"Do you believe it's the same Ben Yousef?" Colin sought to change the focus of the exchange.

"Yes and it seems that he is here in the States. Not good, Mr. Gordon."

Colin reread the message.

"Goddamn it! Then the Moor is ICARUS!" he concluded.

"That's what I fear," Kay agreed.

"If we're correct, the Libyans under Ben Yousef were responsible for the killings at Mt. Kisco. To cover their tracks, Ben Yousef is under orders to eliminate ICARUS."

"But why?"

"Obviously, ICARUS was somehow involved in tipping off the Libyans as to where Kalenti and his followers would assemble." She paused. "Which means that he was less than candid with you."

"It looks that way. He probably only fessed up to what he thought I wanted to hear. What do we do now?"

"Wait patiently. An ad in the lost persons' column wouldn't help."

⁌*⁌*⁌

"Halo," Jamie was calling the private number that Ben Yousef had issued to him from a phone booth near Grand Central Station.

"You know who this is. Have my friend call me in an hour at this number." He hung up and returned in an hour just as the phone was ringing.

"Hello, my friend." It was Ben Yousef.

"I need money and travel documents," Jamie said.

"I will take care of you. Go to the southwest corner of the Fifth Avenue entrance to Saint Patrick's Cathedral at exactly five forty-five today. I will be there." Jamie hung up, a smile on his face.

⁌*⁌*⁌

Ganymede

It was already dark at five thirty in the afternoon. The weather was still unseasonably warm. Jamie wore a long-sleeved polo shirt as he walked to St. Patrick's Cathedral. It seemed like months and not days ago that he had driven Kalenti past the cathedral on his way to the Harvard Club. He remembered how intense Kalenti had been—not nervous, just intense. After all, Kalenti was going into battle.

In retrospect, he marveled at Kalenti's composure at the time. He must have been quite a leader in his day. Off he went into battle without more than a nod. Emotion and attachment had not clouded his judgment. He had dismissed Jamie as if they would meet in a couple of hours—and here he knew that a bomb was riding silently in the locked trunk.

Why had he not suspected something when Kalenti returned to him only the ignition key? *Yes,* he thought, *there are many things I should have questioned, going back to the first visit to the Bacchus restaurant.* He now understood why Ben Yousef directed him to the Bacchus. His mind seemed to rewind a reel of the past. What must the Libyans have thought when he first showed up at their embassy in Athens? Or, for that matter, the Americans when he and Brigid entered their embassy in Sofia?

There seemed no end to the questions, or to the reel rewinding in his mind. Yet he knew somehow that it was all tied to his destiny, his path, his journey in this life. Nothing ever made sense to him looking forward—ahead. He took consolation in being able to look behind for the path that was unfolding. Even with these recent experiences, he could not project any further than his upcoming meeting.

He sensed that his luck was turning. He had almost thirty thousand dollars in his Swiss account that Brigid would soon be able to withdraw. She might already have received the icon that he sent from Beirut. Soon he would have in hand another twenty thousand dollars. Fifty thousand dollars plus the money from the sale of the icon—it was more money than he ever had in his life. He would employ his negotiating skills if the Libyans tried to deduct something for his false passport. He doubted that they would ask for anything. The speed with which Ben Yousef agreed to meet him suggested that his bona fides were established. He was important in Libyan eyes.

The streets were thick with pedestrians hurrying in all directions for transportation out of the city. Jamie was relieved not to be driving here. The evening with Kalenti and the discovery of the explosives had satisfied his interest in driving for a long while. He still wondered why he simply did not leave the area when he heard the sirens. It was certainly not because of any loyalty to Kalenti—*God rest his soul, the bastard!* Had he remained in the car because he couldn't decide, or because he was tired of running?

If what he heard about people who are under constant strain was true, he questioned whether the thrill of the game was wearing thin. Was his subconscious finally saying *enough?* Disturbing thoughts for someone about to put himself in the hands of an Arab, who was traveling in the United States on a false passport. What a paradox. Here he was arranging to flee his protectors with a passport manufactured by the Libyans—a recognized terrorist center, a country that had given rise to the concept of state-sponsored terrorism.

Jamie's mind drifted back to the last time he had been with Brigid. He did his best to keep her from distracting him during the day, but he had to admit that he missed her. It was an increasingly new feeling for him. He wished that he had been able to express his concern for her when they were last together, but he was just not good at it. His ability to survive in the unfriendly world in which he operated was founded on distrust—distrust of anything and anybody. Brigid complicated his philosophy, but he knew that he had not changed too much when he remembered the ease with which he was able to sever the ever-deepening relationship with the American. It was time for the Americans to fight their own battles. He would no longer be there to seize assailants in hallways or provide information to lead them to the real threat they faced from friends.

☦*☦*☦

Inside the cathedral's gift shop, located at the rear beyond the pews and holy water founts and closest to the exit beyond which Jamie was waiting, a thickset, dark-complexioned man looked intensely at the items—rosaries, manger scenes, sympathy cards, key chains—for sale on a wall shelf. The sales clerk, a young college student who worked there part-time, approached and asked him if he needed assistance. He remained stationary, except that he turned his head toward her. He uttered not a word in response when she repeated her offer of assistance but simply allowed his eyes to look over her body without expression. His look frightened her, and she quickly retreated to her post behind the counter.

The evening religious service was just concluding. With a furtive glance, she noticed that the man had now moved to a position near the exit door through which the people had begun to leave. She saw him reach into his overcoat pocket and pull out what looked to be a short shiny chrome stick. He seemed to be making an adjustment to the gadget, even though he kept his eyes on the door. *A strange man,* she thought, *dressed in an overcoat and wearing gloves on this spring-like evening.* After checking his watch, he straightened his already erect frame and moved into the stream of visitors leaving the church. Before he disappeared through the heavy brass door, he shifted whatever he had pulled from his pocket into his right hand.

☦*☦*☦

Jamie had climbed the steps to the cathedral and was now looking across Fifth Avenue. He was unaware that fifteen feet away the dark stranger who had lingered in the gift shop was making his way toward him within the swarm of people heading for the steps. He looked at his watch—5:40. *This is not a good place to wait,* he thought, *with the surge of people buffeting me, a swirl of humanity flooding over the bottom steps.* He started to move to the shelter of the stone folds of the edifice. Just then a tall man paused momentarily alongside Jamie before continuing on with the crowd.

Just as he passed, Jamie felt a sharp pain in his arm. He looked quickly to his left but no one turned to apologize. *Must be a muscle twinge*, he thought. He rubbed his arm. There was a slight numbness, but the pain seemed to ease. He continued to follow the backs of the departing churchgoers as they became lost in a sparkle of lights created by the rush-hour traffic and the glitter from the shops—a dazzle of reds, whites, greens, and blues that converged and then separated.

His hands and feet felt suddenly cold. He regretted that he had not decided to wear a sweater. He shuffled in place to increase the circulation but became aware of the effort each movement required. He experienced a shortness of breath and consciously tried to regulate and slow the rhythm. He turned his attention to the pedestrians around him but found himself creating in his mind a concentric circle that formed the path around which the people moved. Instead of following the rush of one or even groups of individuals, he found himself trying to program their movement along the paths he set for them in his mind. A rising sense of frustration seized him as they varied their paths or interrupted their pace.

He felt an ache in his jaw muscles as he clenched his teeth in a rapidly increasing motion. He wiped the perspiration that had formed on his now marble-cold brow. His whole body felt wet and clammy. *Oh, how refreshing,* he thought, *to be under a cleansing spray of warm water.* With excruciating effort he was able to return his attention to the people approaching the church—but only for a few seconds. He lost his hold again as his mind wandered off to a gypsy circus he attended as a youth. He remembered holding a rifle poised, trying to anticipate where and when the metal target in the silhouette of a rabbit would pop up.

Focus! Focus! he repeated slowly to himself as the outline of those around him blurred into double vision. He wanted to be the first to spot Ben Yousef. With great physical and mental effort he commanded, urged, and pleaded his eyes and attention back from the colorful gypsy scene.

What is happening? he asked himself as a reflex reaction to his loss of control. His grip on himself and his surroundings loosened further. Without intention, his mind wandered off again, this time to his next plane ride home. He fantasized about being with Brigid in bed as he had the last time he was with her. One more time he pulled himself back to New York and the steps of the cathedral. He tried to convince himself that it was a pleasant evening in January, but the shudder that ran through his body and the nausea building in his stomach smothered the hint of spring in his mind. He raised his watch close to his face as if someone had extinguished all light. It was already 6:12, or was it 6:21? His eyes began to burn.

Then, in a flash of searing white heat at the base of his skull, he realized what was happening to him. In that same moment the significance of the sharp pain in his arm moments earlier and the cause reached his consciousness. He reached his right arm to touch the spot where he remembered the initial pain, but he could not seem to bring his hand in close to touch the area. It was as if he were bundled in layer upon layer of foam rubber. Instead his arm searched vainly in a wide arc and brushed the backs of startled pedestrians, wary of unprovoked violence in the city.

He moved down the steps, counting aloud a random number, as he brought his feet together on each step before proceeding to the next. He imagined that he was playing a childhood game, or was he creating one? He must remember the rules, he decided. His legs felt swollen and thick, as if they had fallen asleep. Each step caused a thunderous sound in his ears and head. Finally, he reached the sidewalk. He looked up at the crossing point, but it was like gazing through the opposite end of clouded binoculars. He had to look down at his feet to avoid a dizziness that would swing him to his knees. He moved through the crowd toward the traffic light about fifteen feet distant. He was intent on crossing the avenue. Far back in the recesses of his brain, he sensed that his unknown assailant had crossed the street before him. He must find him.

His eyes fixed on the shoes, purses, and briefcases of those in front of him. Suddenly, in unison, the crowd moved across the street. Jamie followed, but not before he was pushed by those behind him. He felt that he was running, but in fact his movements were ponderously slow and awkward. He lurched from side to side and then forward in pursuit of those before him. He appeared to be intoxicated. The harsh looks of the pedestrians confirmed the diagnosis. The crowd approaching him opened its ranks wide to allow him to pass. No one wanted to touch him—to be defiled. With brisk clarity he concluded that Ben Yousef would not be coming to meet him. He reached the far side of the street but became confused as to where he was or what he should do. His mouth was thick with phlegm.

"I ... must ... call." He could not control the tears that began to flow from his eyes. He tried to reach into his pocket for change, but his hands were balled up in fists and he could not release them. He turned in a sweeping motion and came face to face with a short, squat street vendor manning a pushcart on which chestnuts were roasting. The sweet, rich aroma reminded him of incense and enveloped the vendor who had been observing Jamie intently. Unlike the mass of people moving swiftly past, he alone sensed Jamie's pain and suffering. He reached out his rough dark hands and pulled him gently toward him.

"Mi amigo," he whispered as Jamie slumped to his knees, losing consciousness and his life in the arms of this Central American refugee.

Observing the scene unfolding from the shadows of the darkened entrance to a travel office was another man. Of medium height, with dark skin and a distinctive black shiny moustache, he was dressed in a fashionable dark topcoat. He wore rich leather shoes. He had witnessed Makhmoud's strike, to which Jamie had at first not reacted. But it had transpired just as Makhmoud had promised.

Ben Yousef had not been convinced. Assurances aside, beads of perspiration had formed on his forehead as they had on Jamie's, but the cause of Ben Yousef's was anxiety mixed with fear. His face had become taut when Jamie began his dash from the steps of the cathedral across the street in his general direction. Frozen in time, he thought at first that Jamie had spotted his observation post. His hand had clutched tightly the revolver in his coat pocket. His face relaxed visibly when Jamie stumbled into the arms of the peasant in the black stocking cap and oversized raincoat.

"It is consummated," Ben Yousef said under his breath as he left his position and walked slowly out of the area. He kept close to the building line to avoid the pace of those plowing a central path along the street.

CHAPTER THIRTY-SEVEN

The blinds allowed just slivers of gray light into the otherwise darkened office. Feet up on the desk, Colin sat alone in silence gazing at the vertical shadows created by the stick-like trees outside. He got up and walked to the window and pulled up the blinds. Before him was a swirl of paper-dry maples leaves, grown grass, and tire tracks in the frozen red clay. He could feel the cold wind against the window and noticed the ridges of scattered soil on the outside ledge of the window.

In his thoughts he had drifted to the colors of purple, orange, and gold of a New England autumn years ago. He had been called back from Europe to cover the opening of a UN General Assembly session in New York. Chris and the children had remained in Europe. During a lull in the proceedings, he had rented a car and driven alone through the New England countryside. It was late afternoon. The windows were open despite the chill in the air. He wanted to catch the smell of the leaves burning. He remembered stopping by the side of the road to gaze at some Arabian horses feeding on a hillcrest.

Fifty yards distant he watched a young boy, about the age of his son at the time, raking leaves into a high mound. The boy applied himself with the concentration of someone who had other plans once the task was completed. At that moment a feeling of melancholy engulfed him. Maybe he identified with the boy, who sacrificed the beauty of the now for the promise of the future. The same melancholy had reached into Colin's heart this moment. A knock on the door brought Colin back to Langley, Virginia, and the Headquarters building of CIA.

"Yes?"

"Hello, Colin." Kay entered. "I'm truly sorry about ICARUS."

"Thanks. What did they say?"

"The bureau reports that he was struck in the arm with a syringe-type needle that pumped a deadly poison into him." She paused. "The medical examiner estimated that death followed within fifteen minutes."

"Anything else?"

"Only that the assassination technique is the same perfected by the Bulgarian intelligence service as an effective response to the protests led by artists."

"We don't think they were responsible?" The fact that ICARUS had first sought American assistance in Sofia did not escape him.

"No, doesn't have to be, but I guess we could say that anyone who sends people to the Soviet Union for training could be."

"Like the Libyans? Like Ben Yousef?"

"Or someone under his direction," Kay speculated.

"What do we do now?"

"What do you mean?" Kay asked.

"It seems like it's time for me to go back to Germany. The terrorist plot was thwarted, the terrorists are dead, and just about every agent I was involved with in this case is dead."

"Don't be melodramatic," Kay counseled. "There's still a problem."

"What's that?"

"Well, our leaders appear determined to proceed with plans to deploy an invasion force, or should we call it an occupation force—to Lebanon."

"What are you talking about? Isn't it clear that the Christian radicals murdered Ambassador Hollingsworth and planned the same fate for the secretary of state—to have us do just that?"

"It's clear to me, and maybe even the leadership here, but no one is willing to accept the terrorist threat we faced was from a friendly nation—Christian Lebanon. Instead," Kay continued, "at a classified briefing they are linking the killing of an American agent to a radical Moslem group friendly to the Soviet Union." She drew a deep breath.

"At least, that's what they announced at the White House briefing. By implication, they are tying ICARUS's murder to the attempt upon the secretary's life. The planning for an invasion is moving forward. An advance force has already landed in East Beirut to coordinate the reentry of US forces—if and when the decision is made."

"That's mad. The Christians have achieved their objective even though the operation failed."

"You're so right, Colin."

"Have you talked to Brody?"

"I have …" She hesitated to go further.

"What is it?"

"I learned this morning that he never raised with the director our early suspicions that the Christians could be responsible."

"He did what?" Colin interrupted.

"It isn't what he did but rather what he didn't do. He did nothing about our assessment that the Christians might be responsible."

"I can't believe it. What was his reasoning?" Colin asked.

"He told me that it would be politically unpopular with this administration to argue that the Christians were guilty of anything—you know the Christian Majority voting bloc." She dragged on her cigarette to keep it lit. "After all, the Arabs are the evil ones—at least that is the view held by most American voters. In short, he did nothing with our information."

"But we've proved it now."

"Yes, indeed, he'll admit that, but he is even less inclined to go forward now. 'It would be bad for the agency.'"

"That arrogant son-of-a-bitch. He's more concerned about the damage to the Harvard Club."

"Say," she said, trying to introduce lightness to the exchange, "did you know that the club netted a brand new men's room?"

"Get serious, Kay."

"I'll be serious. Did you know how they were able to hush up the cause of the damage?"

"No. How?"

"At the secretary's suggestion, the board of governors for the club withdrew their appeal to a city order to removed asbestos from the walls and ceilings of the structure. A major reconstruction project is underway first and foremost to repair the bomb damage, but under the cover of complying with the environmental directive," Kay stated. "Clever, huh?"

But Colin was not to be distracted or soothed. "So we are going to trundle in a marine expeditionary force into Lebanon—and lose some marines in the process—to support the creation of a Christian enclave at the behest of Christians who killed our ambassador, and attempted to kill our secretary of state, to say nothing about the killings or attempted killings that took place in support of this provocation!" Colin was becoming heated. "We are just going to ignore what these madmen engineered." His voice was rising with every word.

"What's the timing of the landing?"

"I haven't the faintest idea, and I'd bet Brody doesn't know either. But it could happen in the next few weeks." Kay detected that Colin was struggling in vain to control his anger and frustration. He got up and headed toward the door.

"Where are you going?"

"To see Brody."

"I'll come."

She followed him down the corridor, seeing the distance between them increase as his steps lengthened and quickened while hers shortened and slowed. Her leg was no better. Colin was already in Brody's office, and could hear his voice behind the closed door as she entered the receptionist area. She walked to the closed door, opened it, and saw Colin standing directly in front of the large wooden desk. Brody was slumped down in the high-back chair, a feigned casual, almost smug look on his face. Brody would do anything to remain in control. If Colin became any more unhinged, Brody was assured of victory.

"My good man," Brody interjected in a condescending voice, "I am responsible for understanding the big picture—the agency's future is in the balance. For you, this Lebanese affair is the most important case you've been involved. For me, it is and will be one of many that frame our role and responsibilities for the future."

"Stop the bullshit! You didn't have the balls to present our assessment to those above you, because with all the respect years in intelligence has gained, you remain an insecure son-of-a-bitch who is still looking for your next promotion."

Colin remained before Brody. His agitation caused him to lean slightly forward. Brody did not seem to change his calm expression, except that there was now a hint of a smile reaching around his lips and eyes. Brody, the master of manipulation, sought to regain control, but Colin would not be swayed.

"I am going to say this only once, so remember it," Brody said quietly. "You have no sense of the geopolitical issues that engulf the Middle East. You are equally naïve regarding the domestic political scene in the United States, and, finally, your outburst tells me you have no loyalty to the organization—to the agency." He drew a breath, and his smile widened. "I suggest that you calm down and reflect on what I have said; return as soon as possible to Germany. I am prepared to forget—" He did not get a chance to finish the sentence.

"Fuck you!" Colin turned on his heels and walked through the open door alongside which Kay was standing. She observed that he was no more or less upset than when he arrived. The length and pace of his stride were about the same.

"Impetuous bastard," Brody allowed in as subdued a manner that he could muster. His smile was obvious now—he had controlled the encounter. Kay was his witness.

Kay said nothing. She felt suddenly empty. She turned silently and left without closing the door. When she reached Colin, she found him making a credit card call to Chris in Germany. While the connection was being made, he looked up and winked at her. If Colin had not emerged victorious in this encounter with Brody, he did not know it, and Kay was not going to inform him otherwise.

"Don't worry, Kay, everything is going to be just fine."

"Hi, Chris," he began almost cheerfully. "Nothing's wrong. Just thought I'd call and tell you I'm horny."

Kay did not know whether she should leave the room. His total attention was on enjoying the presence of his wife three thousand miles distant. *He's marvelous*, Kay thought. *It's as if they're dating and she is just down the block.*

"Look, Chris, I've got something to do and I want to know if it's okay with you," he asked. His voice was serious now.

"Yes, it's important." There was a pause.

"I'm going to resign from the agency." A longer pause followed.

"Yes, I am going to resign from the agency." Another even longer pause followed.

"I know it's a quick decision, but trust me, it's a good one, almost as sound as my proposal to you a week after we met." He laughed.

"No, that's not all, but it's too complicated to explain right now. Trust me, though when I do explain, you'll understand." A shorter pause followed.

"Thanks, I love you more." He hung up the phone.

"What are you going to do?" Kay asked. He had forgotten she was in the room.

"You heard me." He pulled a sheet of paper from the desk draw and fitted it into the typewriter. With no hesitation, he typed letter-perfect the text of his letter of resignation to the office of personnel.

Effective this date, I submit my resignation.

I have enjoyed and prospered from my association with the agency and the extraordinarily talented colleagues with whom I have labored.

The time has come, however, for me to move on to new challenges. I only hope that I will discover in the future the same satisfaction that I experienced in protecting the national security interests of this great nation.

I will make myself available at your convenience to complete the necessary administrative procedures.

Unless advised to the contrary, I am returning this date to Bonn to assist my wife in closing down our residence there.

Most Sincerely,

Colin Gramley Gordon

He pulled the paper from the typewriter and gave it to Kay to read. She remained silent and felt her stomach tighten. *A pity*, she thought. She smiled when she came to the phrase *unless advised to the contrary*. He would press the system to finance one last airline trip. *Gramley*—she wondered the origin of the name. It was the first time that she recalled seeing it. She was about to ask him about the name but decided against it.

"Are you sure this is necessary? Don't you think you should reconsider?" He only laughed in response.

"Kay, will you see that this gets to personnel? Give a copy to Brody."

She nodded, and he checked his briefcase to ensure that his passport and return airline ticket were there. He made one short call to the airline office to change his reservations. He rose and extended his hand to Kay.

"Don't worry. Everything will be just fine," he comforted her as if he were a doctor on a house call. Then he was gone.

⁜∗⁜∗⁜

Days later, Brody received a thick packet in the pouch from Bonn. It was addressed to him and marked *Eyes Only*. It was from Colin. Brody expected Colin to withdraw his precipitous resignation. He tore open the envelope. The word vindication was on his lips. He reached for his glasses and began to read the covering letter aloud.

> *Dear David:*
> *I trust this letter finds you in good health. I apologize for any anxiety that I might have caused you during our last meeting …*

Brody paused and smiled confidently. Colin always did have a habit of being wordy. His eyes returned to the text.
or that I may cause you now.

Brody felt a warning indicator in his consciousness turn on.

> *I am sorry that I did not attain the same degree of geopolitical sophistication in which you pride yourself. I suspect that I have spent too many years abroad in operations. As a result, perhaps I was not smitten by the Washington political scene.*
> *In my defense, however, I believe that I retained a firm conviction about the value of intelligence—its collection, analysis, and dissemination—and how the value can be compromised if the political objectives, regardless of motives, influence the process.*

The smile and confidence had waned from Brody's face, and he was becoming uncomfortable as he continued reading.

> *I think that I have explained sufficiently my conviction that it was indeed a fringe group of Lebanese Christians who were responsible for the recent terrorist actions directed against*

the United States. I believe that the intelligence supports this contention as well as establishes that they were motivated by a sincere, albeit misguided, attempt to provoke the United States into returning to Lebanon to protect Christian interests there.

As much as I sympathize with these people, I will not allow the United States to embark upon a dangerous course of action that is based upon a faulty, to put it kindly, interpretation of the facts.

You will read in the accompanying attachment a copy of the full account of my involvement in the GANYMEDE operation—from the time when we first learned that my agent had succeeded in renewing his contact with Ben Yousef to the finish of our final discussion in your office.

I said "copy" because there are six other copies of this document in existence, all awaiting delivery within days if you do not succeed in convincing our senior decision makers that radical Palestinians, the Shiites, or Hezbollah were not responsible for the recent provocations but rather a desperate Christian faction. You may discover that in sensitizing our national leadership to the Christian community's sense of betrayal and increasing isolation from the United States, a more constructive and conciliatory foreign policy might be developed and implemented.

So much for the geopolitical essay. Be assured that I will read with interest and expectation an announcement that indicates that the United States is no longer contemplating a return of its forces to Lebanon.

Oh, I nearly forgot. Those scheduled to receive my opus are:

The New York Times
The Washington Post
The Los Angeles Times
The Christian Science Monitor
The Chicago Tribune

Cable Network News

*Warm Regards,
Colin Gramley Gordon*

CHAPTER THIRTY-EIGHT

Three months had passed since Kalenti and the others had lost their lives. Shamir and Zaquod occupied a corner table in the Bacchus Restaurant where the plot had first been hatched. They sat reflective, in a loneliness that old men experience when they outlive compatriots, family, and friends.

After several moments of silence, Shamir raised his glass. "To the memory of my dear friends, Kalenti and Kuban, and to our brave young ones." He returned the glass to the scuffed table and stared at his hands, which he had gathered before him as if in meditation or prayer.

"You know, Shamir, all was not lost in New York." Zaquod's voice was hushed. Shamir looked up, questioning his meaning.

"Nothing has appeared in the press or elsewhere hinting of our involvement in the debacle. No one has sought to investigate further who was responsible for abducting the ambassador, nor even who had invaded the precincts of New York, and to what purpose," Zaquod continued. He would not have talked louder if he were making his last confession to his priest.

"The Americans have landed a team of advisors to administer to our medical and recovery needs; their announced purpose—to reverse the abject poverty of Lebanon. A military assistance program has been revived, and the first batch of Lebanese officers is on their way to the States. And I hear that sophisticated communication systems are now in our military's inventory, thanks to Western generosity.

"No invasion, but weigh the situation. America is once again a friendly mediator at the crossroads of the Middle East."

Shamir considered his friend's words and raised his almost empty or half-filled glass.

"To the memory of Kalenti and Kuban and our brave young fighters," he said with emotion.

✣✣✣

That same day, Ben Yousef met with his advisors in Tripoli to discuss their success in eliminating a threat posed by the Christian infidels in Lebanon.

"We must remain vigilant," Ben Yousef stated as the meeting opened. "Was it a pyrrhic victory in New York? Instead of discovering the intentions of the Christians, the Americans have only increased economic and political support to them.

"Surely by now they know that we dispatched to the grave those responsible for heinous provocations." Ben Yousef delivered the words from lips that were drawn tight. "And we learn once again how spineless are our capitalist enemies. They are simply unwilling, or unable, to accuse the guilty as they refuse to condemn the Israelis and the atrocities committed against the Palestinians."

"And what of the Spaniard?" one of Ben Yousef's closest advisors asked.

"An expendable foot soldier whose death confirmed the daring mission in the United States."

Delivering his view of ICARUS's contribution to the endgame of this deadly match caused Ben Yousef to smile with pride in the flawless execution of this counter operation.

"With his death, the Libyan hand was concealed," he

concluded. "Now we are gathered to consider our next operation against the Christian infidels and their supporters."

☦ * ☦ * ☦

Weeks later, Brigid returned from Athens to the small village where she had been residing. She had just finished transferring Jamie's Swiss account to a German bank. Propped against the door of her room was a battered package addressed to her in his handwriting.

"Finally," she said aloud as she rushed to the package, dropping the plastic bag filled with groceries. "At last some word." Her elation was quashed when she read the date of the Lebanese postmark. It had been sent over three months ago.

She opened the package carefully, reverently. With a certain foreboding, she sensed that this was to be his last communication. She was not surprised that there was no note. It was not easy for him to express emotions openly. Between two books she discovered an antique icon. It appeared in excellent condition. She wondered where he had acquired it. A single tear formed in the corner of her eye. She missed his optimism and confidence as they had planned their new life in America.

☦ * ☦ * ☦

At the same time that Shamir and Zaquod were toasting their fallen comrades and Ben Yousef met with his advisors and Brigid received her last message from Jamie, Colin was to receive the Intelligence Star, the agency's highest award, for his contribution to the GANYMEDE operation.

Since before dawn, he had been sitting on the deck of his townhouse. To ward off the unseasonable frost, he was bundled in an old ski jacket and wore a khaki-colored woolen helmet liner that he had found forty years earlier during his rowing days. During their years of traveling around the globe, he had always seen to it that liner was included in the bag reserved for carry-on luggage. He insisted upon this despite Chris's gentle taunting that he had begun to display his eccentricity by the special affection he held for this inanimate object.

Colin had gotten up twice from the low wicker chair and its brilliant red cushions—once to refill the two-handled ceramic mug that he had purchased on a visit with Chris to a Trappist monastery gift shop nestled along the Shenandoah River in Virginia and the second time to wake Chris after he had fixed a tray of juice, Danish, and coffee for the two of them. He returned to his perch, and Chris joined him wrapped tightly in a thick white terrycloth robe and sheepskin slippers. She would have preferred to remain indoors, but she understood his need that morning to be in the silence of the early-morning chill.

"Well, what are your thoughts?" she asked as she sipped the steaming coffee.

"Not sure I should have listened to you," he responded after a time.

"Oh, please, stop being so dramatic." She said this gently and with deep understanding of his feelings. "All is well. You've done good, and the agency wants to tell you that."

On the ride they were silent. Chris respected his need to allow the memories to pass through his mind and heart. Try as he might, he could not overcome the loss—the emptiness he felt. It was not the building, or even the work, though he missed it sorely. No, it was the people—the talented, creative, energetic people who populated the institution—even those colleagues whom he did not particularly appreciate.

"Can you believe that Brody will be honored at the same ceremony?" he said in a tone sharper than he expected. "Do you know he's been appointed to the number-three position in the agency?"

"Colin, when are you just going to be comfortable with yourself? Don't be dragged back into past concerns," she gently responded.

"Do you know why I love you so much? You can't be overwhelmed by my superior logic."

"Is that what it is?" she laughed.

They exited the George Washington Parkway where it intersected Dolley Madison Highway and headed west to the main entrance of the CIA Headquarters complex. Colin gulped deeply when he turned right and headed toward the security gate.

"This is not going to be an enjoyable morning."

"How could it not be otherwise?" Chris remained ever positive.

"Maybe I am accepting the award because I felt I was still part of the organization—if somewhat alienated—or because I owe it to GANYMEDE and ICARUS, or I didn't want Brody to occupy the stage alone, or …"

"You're here because I insisted," Chris said firmly.

"Identification please," the young female guard asked. Colin provided his driver's license. She returned with a pass and directed him to the VIP parking in the front of the main building. They drove on and were met by a young lady from the director's office.

"Mr. Gordon, your parking space is there," she said, "next to the flagpole."

"Well, my dear, you made it," Chris said, taking her purse as he opened her door.

In his working days he remembered rushing through the entrance and inserting his badge into the reader, poking in his identification code and rushing on to the elevators. Now he was among the unwashed and had to wait for an escort to lead them to the director's elevator located off the alcove to the left.

Within seconds, it seemed, as if in a trance or dream, Colin entered the director's conference room followed by Chris. About thirty guests were already present—faces from the past that he had placed on the invitation list, and others who were on Brody's list. The first to approach—she had taken up her position near the door—was Kay. She reached out her hand to shake. There would be no hugs from Kay.

"I'm sorry I have not called," he said. Her grip was firm as she looked into his eyes, holding her emotions in check. Since she had not walked over to him, Colin could not tell how her leg was healing.

"I miss you not having to try to keep up with me as we dashed between meetings."

"Is that all you miss?" Kay smiled.

Stacy stepped forward. "Hi, stranger. Hi, Chris; he talks of you all the time," she said, forgetting for an instant that she should have used the past tense. Others followed who just wanted to shake Colin's hand, meet Chris, and inquire about his plans.

Colin looked over their heads. Brody had not yet arrived. He caught sight of Frost lingering in the back of the room. Frost looked away as Colin broke off from his guest and walked toward him.

"Hi, Frost. I didn't know you were back." Colin extended his hand.

"Good to see you, Colin," Frost said in clipped fashion—his eyes glancing past Colin. "Asher and I are here on home leave and consultation."

"Great. Where are they sending you?"

"Rome. I'll be deputy there. Pretty important job, you know."

"Yes, indeed," Colin said, smiling for the first time. *Doesn't this pompous shit know that I'm supposed to compliment him on the importance of the assignment?* Yet, in a perverse way, he had to admit that he missed even Frost.

At precisely eleven o'clock, a stir arose behind Colin. He turned to see the director enter from the door of his office, followed by David Brody, who appeared almost in lock-step with the director. A broad expansive smile covered Brody's face as he introduced the director to the outside guests—drawn for the most part from senior-level government officials, individuals with whom Brody had to deal in his new position and who would be most flattered by a personal introduction.

"Ladies and Gentlemen, may I ask you all to assemble before the podium so we can begin the ceremony?" the executive assistant to the director announced. Colin moved to the front of the conference room while Chris stood alongside Kay in the back.

"Mr. Director, pleased to meet you. I am Colin Gordon."

"No need to be so formal. I know who you are." They shook hands.

Colin took his place alongside Brody, facing the audience. Brody's wide smile—frozen in place—did not change.

"Good to see you," Brody whispered. Colin did not reply.

The director moved to the podium. "We are here today to honor two courageous Americans who played a vital role in uncovering a terrorist conspiracy that was responsible for the murder of our ambassador in Beirut and, if it had not been foiled, the assassination of our secretary of state."

The director continued reading without emotion from the text prepared for him. Nothing was said about who were the perpetrators of the terrorist actions, nor was the loss of Horst, GANYMEDE, or ICARUS mentioned. Instead, the director repeated the usual disclaimer at such events where outsiders were present: "You will appreciate that we cannot go into more detail because of the sensitivity of the operation."

Colin looked at the nods of agreement of those facing him. Their natural curiosity and professional interest were suppressed in the interests of national—or was it political—security. *After all,* Colin thought, *it was the Lebanese Christians who were involved, not the Libyans or Hezbollah.* When the director concluded his comments, he turned to the recipients. The executive assistant handed the director an open, flat box in which was displayed the Intelligence Star. The executive assistant read the citation.

For selfless courage displayed in conducting a most complex and demanding counterterrorist operation that resulted in thwarting a serious threat upon a senior decision maker at the national level of government, the Intelligence Star is awarded to Colin Gramley Gordon on this date.

The director stepped forward to pin the medal on Colin and shook his hand. Colin stepped back and listened to the same citation read for David Brody. The official photographer took photographs of both recipients. Chris joined Colin for his photograph. Two waiters then moved through the assemblage with trays of champagne.

Fifteen minutes later, Colin and Chris retraced their steps behind the protocol officer to the main entrance. Once out of the building, they walked quietly to their car. Colin felt lighter, as if he left a burden behind at the reception.

"You know, it wasn't as bad as I anticipated," he said as they were driving off.

"How about stopping for lunch in town?" Chris smiled, accepting the thanks in his remark.

AFTERWORD

A rope line of cormorants flying low seemed to pause to observe the solitary figure sitting on the sand facing out to sea. Satisfied regarding his intentions, they continued north into a breeze that had been building since Colin's arrival hours earlier. Their movement stirred him from his revelry. He stood up and brushed off the sand from his jeans and retraced his steps home.

Life is good, he thought, *with all the twists and turns on the journey.* He felt at peace, in harmony, and looked forward to his first cup of coffee for the day. This morning, he had traveled as if in a time capsule to a past replete with characters—both good and bad—he had been blessed to encounter and who had contributed to the person he had become. He almost regretted that there was not one more role for him to play, to feel that rush of adrenaline when one encounters surprise—even danger.

But he checked himself and returned to the present moment. He felt his steps squeeze the sand, paused again to view the thread of cormorants disappearing into the brisk breeze, smelled the fragrance of the salt air, and heard the silence that surrounds as he anticipated his first cup of coffee. Yes, life is good, he repeated.

Ingram Content Group UK Ltd.
Milton Keynes UK
UKHW011837100723
424887UK00012B/225/J